GONE

THE MARK OF IISILÉE

DRAGON

BOOK II

of the Gone Dragon series

T.P. SHEEHAN

QUERENCIA
BOOKS

Published by Querencia Books

ISBN: 978-0-6480928-2-7 (paperback)
First edition print - 2019

Querencia Books
info@querenciabooks.com
Querenciabooks.com

Follow the Gone Dragon series: GoneDragon.com

For Max and Georgia. I love you more than all the stars.

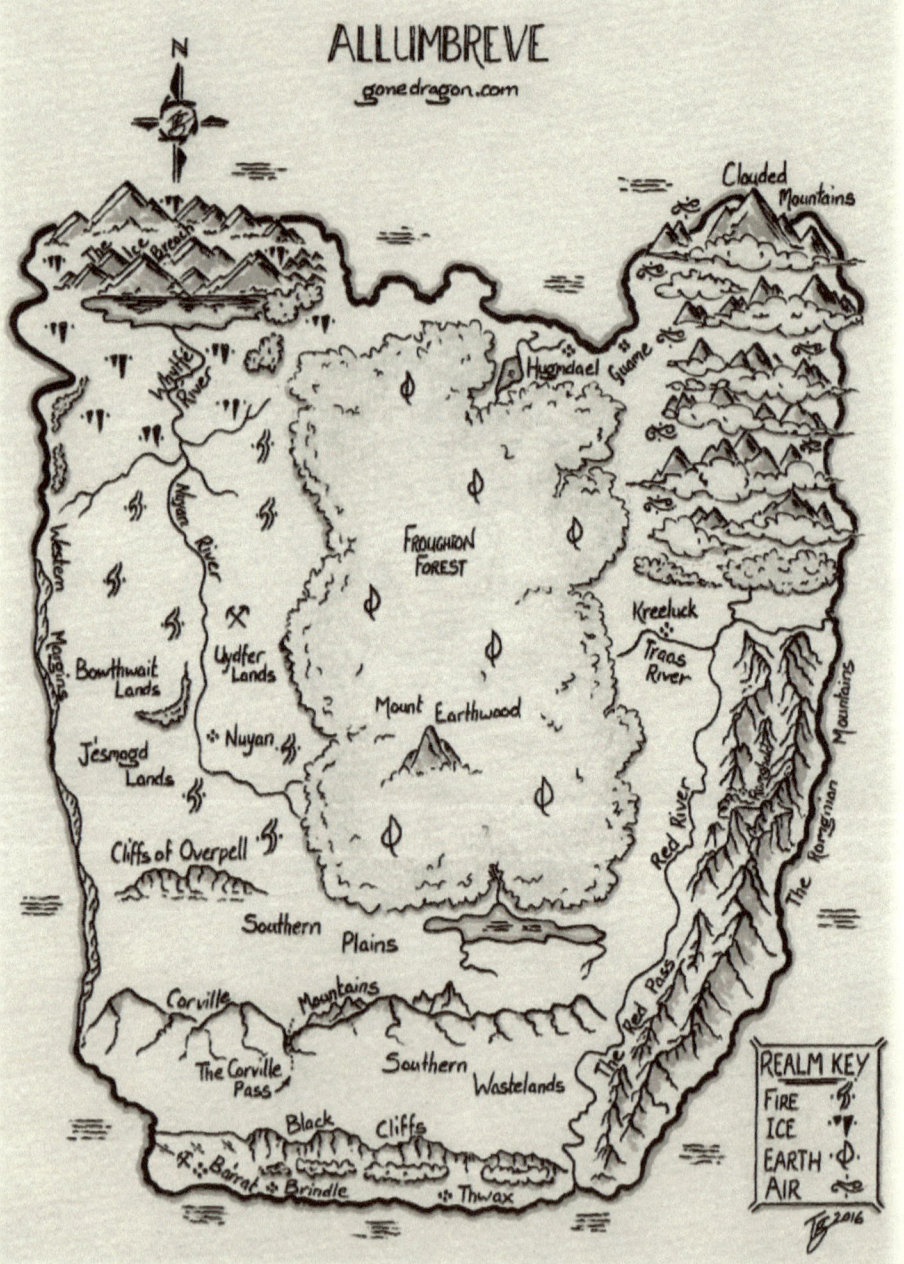

PROLOGUE

"A friend as a brother has fallen to darkness."

"You speak of Lucas."

"There is but a single chance to reconcile, else fate be challenged."

"Are we not always challenging fate?"

"Challenges are a part of life. To survive them and meet your inevitable fate is irony."

"How then do you see a second chance to reconcile with Lucas to be challenging fate?"

"Because to do so will be beyond the will of the gods."

THE MORNING AFTER

The white tip of Lucas's fleu-steel sword pointed at Magnus.

'No holding back, Magnus. Show us what you've learned.'

'What I've learned, Ganister?' I've learned how to kill...

Behind the white of the sword and the blue of Lucas's eyes, a grey mist appeared, spreading from one side of Ganister's training hall to the other. The mist became opaque, folding over itself and mutating into the shape of men—a hundred of them.

The hundred ghosts of Ba'rrat's arena...

Dead at my hand...

Come to testify to what I have learned.

The ghosts drew toward Lucas, morphing together until as one with him. Lucas shuddered and bowed his head. Magnus shook in fear.

"No!"

Lucas slowly raised his head. His eyes—now steel-grey—held the souls of the hundred. *'You have indeed learned to kill.'*

Lucas's words scratched at the raw wounds of Magnus's conscience.

"NO!"

Magnus woke from the nightmare, scrambling for his sword—*Lucas's* sword. He spun about in circles, pointing the sword in every direction. There was the river, the trees, the Black Cliffs and the wrens singing their morning song, but he was alone. Magnus sighed in relief, remembering Catanya told him to rest while she bathed at the river. He lay again beneath the beech tree, closed his eyes and let the wrens' song sooth him.

Still... Magnus contemplated. *Something is not right...*

The figure appeared as a shimmering phantom disturbing the spears of morning light through the water. Catanya strained at the end of her breath. Chasing bubbles to the surface, she willed the Quagman to look away. Knife in clenched fist, she breached the surface of the river and silently let her breath go. The cool water cascaded down her long, black hair and over her naked back. She hesitantly opened her eyes—they met his.

He has seen me...

"Of all the rivers beyond all the Realms of Allumbreve, looky-here what I've found..." Removing his spiked, black helm, the Quagman's deep-set eyes groped Catanya's body. He hunched, reached for Catanya's hair and pulled her toward him.

Perfect...

Catanya drove her arm up, sinking her knife into the Quagman's throat. His black eyes widened inside their bony sockets then dulled as his life drained away. He fell forward toward the river. Catanya took the weight of his body in case a splash drew unwanted attention.

"That's for the arrow in my back yesterday."

Catanya slid her knife back into the thigh of her Ferustir armour. She pushed the corpse beneath the river's surface and fed it into the strong current. There were more of them—she was certain of it. The previous evening, as Catanya fled from Ba'rrat with Magnus, a Quagman wounded her. He then fled when he recognised Magnus for who he is—for *what* he is...

The *Electus.*

Catanya was sure the Quagman had returned and tracked them up river and was equally sure he wouldn't have come alone.

She heard them first. Moments later she saw them. Three Quagmen were approaching on the opposite side of the river. *They've found where we crossed.*

Catanya peered across the river to the embankment at the foot of the Black Cliffs where Magnus lay sleeping beneath a beech tree. *"Wake up, Magnus..."* Catanya strained her thoughts, willing him to hear her. *"WAKE UP!"* She knew it was in vain—it took years of training for an Irucantî to master telepathy. Even then, most priests needed a dragon present. *We could do with a dragon about now.*

Taking a breath, Catanya dove deep and swam across the river, stroking diagonally to offset the current. Surfacing at the northern riverbank, she cupped her mouth with a hand and coughed. Looking at her palm, it was spattered red with blood. Her nose wrinkled at the sight of it.

The voices were getting closer.

The rest of Catanya's armour lay on the riverbank. She refitted her torso armour, wincing from the pain in her back. She fitted her vambraces and tightened their buckles, took hold of her Ferustir's lance and counted her knives—*two, four, six, seven.*

"Shh."

"What is it?"

"Where's Maddrock?"

"On the south bank."

The Quagmen fell silent for a moment.

"He's supposed to be within sight!"

"He can manage himself."

"Wyvern crap! He fled as soon as he spotted the Electus."

"What would you have done, Elmot?"

All three appeared at the river's edge. Catanya sunk into the water, ducking her head beneath a thick beech root that arched from the bank into the river.

"THERE!"

The dead Quagman had surfaced and was floating right by them.

"They must be over the other side!"

All three Quagmen leapt into the river and waded across. Catanya watched on, knowing if any of them turned they would see her. Then they would come after her or worse—*one carries a loaded bow*. With a twenty-foot embankment climb to get to Magnus, she would be an easy target for the archer.

The river's current was strong and the Quagmen moved sluggishly thanks to their heavy armour. Catanya had another idea. She could swim with the current and intersect them mid-river. Underwater, she could slay the archer and perhaps another before the third knew she was there. It was risky. If her timing was wrong or they spotted her too soon, she would be dead. *And perhaps Magnus would be too...*

The Quagmen reached mid-river. If she was going after them, it was now or never. Catanya drew another breath and sunk beneath the waterline, sheathing her lance. She pushed off the bank toward the middle of the river, dove deep, and speared through the water. The current carried her downstream to the Quagmen even faster than she anticipated. Less than twenty feet from the archer, Catanya redrew her lance. Ten feet away, the current was driving her straight at him. Ignited and pointed, her lance was aimed at the archer's belly and then, just a foot from her foe, something heavy smashed through the water overhead and drove her body to the riverbed.

Held fast against the bedrock, Catanya managed to keep a grip on her lance. She wrenched her head about and saw the Quagman beside her, one foot and a huge arm pinning her down. Another came, reinforcing the hold with an extra boot. She thrashed about, but her sword arm was soon pinned with a third boot.

Catanya exhausted all air in her lungs as she struggled desperately to break the Quagmen's relentless hold. Her right arm was still free. She reached across her back. The pain of her wound sent spasms through her body making her gasp, drawing water. Coughing, she retracted her arm and forced it beneath her abdomen, reaching out the other side for a weapon. Her fingertips scraped over one of the throwing knives in her thigh armour but she could not get a grip.

The boots suddenly lifted and large hands pulled Catanya from the water. The Quagmen bellowed deep war cries at her. She went to scream a warning to Magnus—"Ma..." all that came was a lungful of water.

The Quagmen drove Catanya's body into the water again, holding her beneath the surface. Her left arm had lost her lance but was free. She swept it across her thigh, pulled a knife and sunk it hard into the nearest of the warriors. From beneath the water she heard a muffled roar.

Catanya was pulled from the water again. Her waterlogged senses heard cursing and yelling. Her arms were wrenched behind her back and she gasped for breath, blinking her eyes into focus. A Quagman held her while the archer had an arrow aimed point-blank at her forehead. The third was stumbling about—curses foaming from his mouth—with Catanya's knife buried behind his right kneecap. Even in her predicament, Catanya was helpless to prevent a smirk from crossing her face.

The whirling sound of a fast approaching object drew the archer's attention. He turned to his right just as a fleu-steel sword drove through his neck. He fell into the water. Catanya was wrenched about by the Quagman holding her and faced the assailant. In mid air, with rings of flame dancing about his body, Magnus flew toward her and the remaining two Quagmen.

Catanya also spotted her lance resting by her feet at the riverbed...

"WAKE UP!"

"Catanya?"

Magnus woke again and leapt to his feet—Catanya's voice ringing through his head. Was it a dream? *No. Something's definitely not right...*

From beneath the cover of beech trees, Magnus climbed the embankment and gazed over the river. His heart seized at the sight before him—on the far side of the river Catanya was defending herself against three Quagmen.

Casting his robe aside, Magnus took a running leap from the embankment, out over the river. Lucas's fleu-steel sword ignited in a ring of ochre flames even before Magnus had drawn it entirely free of its scabbard. The sword left his hand just as quickly, hurtling toward Catanya's greatest threat—a Quag archer with an arrow pointed right at her head. The sword buried itself deep in the archer's neck. Magnus's dragon blood burned fury through his heart, lungs, body and limbs. Before his feet broke the river's surface, he cupped his hands forming a fireball that he threw at the body of another Quagman who was wrestling with a knife buried in his knee. The ball hit him square in the chest, engulfing him in flames and freeing him from the burden of his wounded leg. He dropped into the river—a charred, bloody mess.

"Catanya!"

The remaining Quagman held Catanya fast to his chest. In a swift-footed manner, Catanya's legs rose from the water, bringing her lance with them. She swung her legs up over her head and drove the sharp pommel of her lance into the warrior's forehead. He loosened his grip enough for her to pull an arm free, catch the lance, ignite it, and end the warrior's life.

Magnus pushed through the water toward Catanya. Her eyes were wild and her lance splayed red light from its Fireisgh engravings between her white-gripped knuckles.

"You okay, Catanya?" He placed a tentative hand on her shoulder.

"I'm okay." Catanya blinked herself free of her frenzy and extinguished her lance. "I was hoping their war cries would wake you."

"It was *you* that woke me," Magnus affirmed. "I heard you calling me in my thoughts. You were telling me to 'wake up'."

"You heard that?" Catanya spat blood into the river. "That's good… I suppose."

Magnus saw blood on Catanya's lower lip.

"You're hurt."

Catanya shook her head. "I think this lot are the follow up." Magnus was not sure what she meant. "To yesterday's attack. There's another downstream." She wiped her lip with a finger, frowned at the sight and licked her lips.

Magnus traced a finger across a bruise forming on Catanya's cheek. "I'm sorry I fell asleep."

"No, I'm sorry I wasn't watching over you like you were watching me all night."

"I hoped we were clear of all this." Magnus considered the dead Quagmen. "What do you think… have we seen the last of it?"

"From what they were saying, I think that's all of them." Catanya did not sound any more convinced than Magnus felt. "We should get moving?"

"Definitely," Magnus agreed.

Catanya retrieved her knife from the Quagman's smoking carcass. "He never saw that coming."

"The knife or the fireball?"

"Both!"

They chuckled as they pulled all three of the warriors to the southern bank.

"With their bodies to the south, travelling north of the river may throw any followers off track," Magnus suggested. They swam across the river and started running upstream.

HANNAH - ONE

Hannah sat on Catanya's bed in silence, chewing indifferently on a handful of pine nuts. In her lap sat her sister's diary that she kept in her dresser draw for safekeeping. Her mother and father were arguing again—something that only started when Catanya left with their uncle to join the Irucantî. When they argued, Hannah came to her big sister's room seeking solace.

Hannah opened the diary to its centre page where a single pressed iris hid. She admired the flat purple petals and the long green stem, remembering when Catanya first showed it to her.

'Do you want to see my most precious thing, Hannah? Except for you of course,' Catanya whispered to her when she was five years old.

'Yes! I do,' Hannah had replied.

Catanya had taken her diary from her dresser draw and sat beside Hannah on her bed. She opened the diary, revealing the pressed iris in its pages. *'This was from the first flowers Magnus picked for me, years ago. I knew they would wither in time and so I took just one, placing it here for safe keeping.'*

Hannah had felt the flower with the tip of a finger. *'It's really pretty. Why do you keep it?'*

'Because I'm a hopeless romantic. But it's our secret. Everyone knows I'm hopelessly in love with Magnus. They don't need to know I'm a hopeless romantic as well,' Catanya had said, winking at Hannah.

'Does it remind you that you love Magnus?'

'I don't need anything to remind me of that, Hannah.'

Hannah would listen to Catanya's stories while she braided her hair. They would nibble on pine nuts or blackberries and drink lemon water. Catanya's favourite stories were of Magnus and their adventures together. Hannah thought Magnus was wonderful—tall and handsome. It was not fair that Catanya could not marry him. Perhaps then, when Hannah was older, *she* would marry Magnus. *Kind of the way mother married father after Austagia joined the priesthood.*

Alessandra had loved Austagia dearly, but he left. Hannah had only learned of this in recent weeks from eavesdropping on her parents' conversations. It was hard to grasp the full story, but her father was angry about everything lately, and her mother was sad.

Hannah reached for Catanya's pillow. It still smelled of the jasmine oil she used to rub into her hair. Catanya said it gave it 'lustre'. Hannah wondered if her sister was able to use jasmine oil in the Romghold but knew her hair would still be beautiful, regardless.

Her legs hung over the end of the bed. She played with the three remaining pine nuts in the palm of her hand and listened—the shouting voices were still audible from the kitchen, even though her mother had shut the kitchen door.

Hannah popped the nuts in her mouth and finished them off, then closed Catanya's diary and replaced it in the dresser draw. She jumped back onto Catanya's bed and bent backward into a backbend before springing her feet up into a handstand. She held this pose. The sound of the kitchen door opening preceded her father's heavy footsteps into the bedroom.

"Hannah," he asserted.

"Aye." Hannah could feel her face flush red as she held the handstand.

"Your bed is for sleeping. The ground is for handstands."

"It's not my bed."

There was a moment's silence, then the sound of Xavier leaving the room with heavy footsteps again and out the back door of the house. Hannah fell to her stomach, rested her chin on folded arms and closed her eyes.

Some time later, Hannah woke. Voices were coming from the kitchen as before only this time the door was open. It was her mother's voice and another she recognised—"Aunt Csilla." Hannah sprung to her feet and tiptoed out of Catanya's bedroom toward the kitchen, avoiding the squeaky floorboard second from the door. She listened from around the corner.

"Does Hannah know?" It was Csilla asking.

"No," Alessandra answered.

Hannah spun around the corner. "What don't I know?" The adults looked at her. Alessandra then turned away, wiping tears from her eyes. Csilla stood and came to Hannah.

"You don't need to get in the middle of this, Hannah." Csilla smiled. "All this feuding over love and war… It's not for you to worry about." Csilla took Hannah's hand and smiled, then addressed Alessandra—"I'm going to organise safe passage for the two of you through Froughton Forest. You'll be safe there with the ⊖hUid folk until this war is over."

Alessandra kept silent.

Csilla and Hannah left the house together and walked through the garden that had not been tended to in months. It was something Catanya used to do with their mother. They would sing as they gardened and laugh at one another's stories. Since Catanya left, Hannah would see her mother wander about the garden but she would rarely so much as pull a weed.

Csilla sat on the wooden bench that captured the late morning sun, stretching out and crossing one ankle over the other. She laid her sheathed sword on the ground beside the bench. "Come," she said, frowning at Hannah. "I'm sure the god of fire wants to shine his greatest creation on your pretty little face before this summer is over."

"I come out into the sun sometimes, Csilla." Hannah squinted in the blinding sun as she sat beside her aunt.

"It's not as pretty as it used to be." Csilla pointed to an arrangement of weeds that were strangling blossoms of thin lavender stems.

"Not since Catanya left." Hannah could feel Csilla's eyes on her. She returned her gaze.

"You should help your mother in the garden."

"I hate gardening. I'd rather eat greens!" Hannah frowned.

Csilla laughed. "You sound so funny since you lost that front tooth. *'I'd rather eat greenth,'* you said!"

"Very funny. I don't mind the vegetable patch around the side. At least I can eat while I tend to it. So long as it's nothing green."

Csilla wrapped an arm around Hannah and gave her a hug. "I'm just teasing. But hey, happy birthday for last week."

"Thanks," Hannah said twice, trying to avoid snagging her tongue where her front tooth used to be.

"I cannot believe that my youngest niece is six."

"I'm seven now! And you know that I am." Hannah punched Csilla in the ribs, making her laugh. "Anyway, how old are you?"

Csilla stopped short and stared at Hannah. "That's no question for a lady."

"You told me you were no lady. You are a 'warrior'."

"That's right. I stand corrected. I am a warrior just like your father. And, I am the same age as your father."

Hannah's jaw dropped. "You're not that old."

"I am—and your father and I are not old. We schooled together. We trained the sword together." Csilla leant in close to Hannah and whispered, "I was always better than him."

Hannah studied Csilla to see if she was serious. "You did not become a knight?"

"Neither your father nor I wanted to be knights. When your uncle was drafted into the priesthood, your father changed." Csilla feigned a smile.

"Father misses Austagia?"

"Yes."

'I thought it was mother who misses Austagia.'

Csilla tried to hide a smile. "You don't miss a thing, do you?"

Hannah nodded. "Yes. I miss Catanya."

"I know you do, Hannah. I know you do." Csilla put her hand to the sun and splayed her fingers, letting the rays shine through. Hannah studied the scars on her aunt's face and arms. She had a few new ones from the battle with the Quag, which her father said was 'dragging on too long' and 'we need the dragons to end it.'

Csilla sighed. "Austagia wanted to be a knight. Your father wanted to work in the quarries, or be a farmer."

"Truly?" Hannah tried to picture her father as a farmer. "Catanya wanted to be a farmer." Hannah said.

Csilla frowned again. "She did?"

"Yes—with Magnus. In the J'esmagdlands."

Csilla nodded. "Of course." *Magnus...*

WEIR

With the broadening river to their right and the sheer Black Cliffs to their left, Magnus and Catanya covered ground quickly. They were a good ten miles clear of Brindle and, they hoped, any more Quagmen.

By midday, they came upon a stone weir with a bridge allowing them to cross the broad river. From the bridge, Magnus observed how the walls of the Black Cliffs no longer had the smooth, mined surface they had nearer Ba'rrat but a rough, natural texture that comforted him—*the further from Ba'rrat the better.*

Magnus turned his attention to Catanya. She was leaning over the bridge parapet, watching the water flow downstream over the weir's stone wall. Like him, she was covered in sweat from running. She stood with one leg cocked behind the well-toned calf muscles of the other. Her arms were folded inward, accentuating the equally toned muscles at the back of her arms that twitched and flexed as she strummed her fingers across the parapet. Magnus was mesmerised by her. He always had been, but this was different. Before him now, the girl he grew up with was a strong and confident woman. Magnus felt his heart beat awkwardly, but there was no charge of dragon blood to rectify the awkwardness—no escaping his own emotions. He released a breath that came off his lips as a whistle.

"I see you looking at me," Catanya said in a smooth voice, still looking at the river.

"You've eyes in the back of your head!" Magnus laughed, trying to shake his awkwardness.

"If I did, I wouldn't have let that Quagman score me with his arrow yesterday." Catanya shifted her weight to the opposite leg.

Magnus stood right behind Catanya, placing his hands ever so gently on her shoulders and drew on the scent of her hair. "Jasmine."

"And sweat. And dirt." Catanya turned about. "Probably blood as well." She stood on her toes and gave Magnus a slow kiss on the lips. Magnus placed his hands on Catanya's hips as she dropped slowly to her heels.

"I think the swim washed some of it off. I can't even begin to imagine how I smell," Magnus chuckled.

"Pretty much all of that, plus saliva from the wyvern that tried to take your head off in the arena."

"I think it's time to rectify it." Magnus dropping his sheathed sword and overcoat at Catanya's feet then leapt onto the parapet. He stood, arms spread wide, wearing nothing but the burnt remnants of his leather pants and a pair of black leather boots he procured from a deceased Quag guard as he left Ba'rrat.

"Oh, and there's the chargrilled smell from when Brue tried to burn you to death."

"There is that, too." Magnus recalled his altercation with the fire dragon. Brue had most certainly tried to kill him, only to flee with a sword wound to the nose.

Magnus dove off the parapet, over the weir wall and plunged into the depths of the river. All at once he was consumed by the beautiful cool of the water. He closed his eyes and let it cleanse the grime from his body and the disquiet of six months a slave from his mind. He was free again. He was with Catanya again.

The silence of being submerged in the river was broken by another splash. An explosion of bubbles rushed to the surface. When they subsided, Magnus's eyes fell upon Catanya's. They drew closer, doing little more than gently feel one another's lips. Magnus could taste the sweetness in hers—even beneath the water.

Waist deep on the southern side of the river, Catanya scrubbed Magnus's back clean, feeling for knots in his muscular back and working them free with aggressive thumbs. Magnus winced at the pain but fell under the spell of her touch. Every once in a while she would stop and explore the creases between his muscles with her fingers, find another knot and dig a thumb in once again.

When she was done, Magnus wanted to check the wound in Catanya's back. She reached over her head to peel off the wet torso armour but grimaced from the pain. Standing behind her, Magnus lifted the armour free of her midsection until she was able to take a grip behind her shoulders and pull it over her head. Catanya held the suit to her chest and glanced at Magnus. He could see she was blushing a little but was certain he was blushing more as he looked at the naked, fair skin of Catanya's back that contrasted with the olive complexion of her arms and the thin strip about her midriff.

Magnus refocused. He studied the wound close to Catanya's spine where an arrow had pierced the day before. Neither of them had seen the Quag horseman approach. They had been running from the confusion and violence of the battle in Ba'rrat but the battle itself made little sense. The Irucantî had come to Ba'rrat to find the 'Electus'—the prophesised inheritor of the blood of fire dragons. Magnus had inadvertently received this 'bond of fire' six months earlier thanks to a dragon youngling named Thioci, unaware it would lead to such things. He was unaware the dragon blood would give him the strength to survive a hundred fights in Ba'rrat's arena. He was most certainly unaware the priests wanted him dead. It took six months but they found him and when they did, they brought dragons with them.

As fate would have it, Catanya found Magnus first thanks to her uncle—Austagia. An Irucantî himself, he encouraged Catanya to flee the order of priests and find Magnus. Once the order arrived in Ba'rrat, an old feud ignited between the Irucantî and the Quag, and between dragons and the Corville Mountain wyverns. The Battle of Ba'rrat had begun. *But where would it end?* Magnus pondered. *What of Delvion who fled the Black Capitol? What of Lucas who killed his own father in the arena?*

"Magnus?"

Magnus snapped himself out of his convoluted thoughts.

"Magnus... are you okay?" Catanya enquired.

I am fine... Magnus tried to speak yet his breath offered only a sigh. Catanya's head turned to the side. Magnus observed her profile. She knew his thoughts—he was sure of it. She could not read them, but somehow knew him intimately. She reached behind with a hand and held one of his, squeezing it firmly—an affirmation of understanding.

"All will be well, soon enough," Magnus said.

Catanya's wound had sealed over, thanks to his Electus powers that heated the barbed arrow tip until red-hot. He then reshaped it, allowing him to pull the arrow free, cauterising the wound as it went. It would scar in time and he thought it unlikely to reopen, nor invite infection.

"I think the arrow may have nicked a lung. That's why you're coughing blood."

"Else it cracked a rib which nicked a lung," Catanya said. "Either way, I'll be fine."

"Does it hurt to breathe?"

"I'll be fine... really."

Magnus gently rubbed and cleaned Catanya's back as she had done to him. "You're very tense," Magnus said, knowing full well he was as much the cause of it as anything else. Catanya let her shoulders drop a little and Magnus felt her tension ease.

"It's been a long time." Catanya's voice was distant.

"A long time?" Magnus wanted to hear more.

"Since we've shared affection." Catanya sighed. "At least in the Romghold I had company. I was being mentored. But you… I can't imagine what kept you going all those months in Ba'rrat."

Magnus's thoughts wandered again. Catanya had seen the dungeons beneath Ba'rrat where he had been kept a slave for half a year. He did not need to say how terrible it was. Worse still, that he became accustomed to living in Cage number '6', as though it were his lot in life. That feeling, at least, was only there near the end, when he thought all was surely lost. Except for that brief darkness, there was always hope.

"I had to fight. Each and every day, I had to fight for my life and for Sarah's life. I wanted to find my parents as well and I swore… I swore every day I would fight until I was with you again."

Catanya's arms lowered and she threw her Ferustir armour to the riverside. She turned about, looking at Magnus with soft eyes.

"I can't believe you found me in that place." Magnus almost choked on his words. Catanya wrapped her arms around him and squeezed his back firmly making several of his vertebrae pop. "That feels better," Magnus chuckled again, feeling a little lighter of heart. Catanya laughed into his chest then placed a hand in its place and caught his eyes with hers. Magnus found her expression so alluring he was speechless. He looked down at her body for the briefest of moments. Catanya raised an eyebrow then turned her back to him again. She tied her hair back on itself in a wrap-around ponytail leaving her Irucantí markings visible over the left side of her head. She then retrieved her armour.

Once cleaned and dressed, Catanya re-sheathed her Ferustir's lance while Magnus reclaimed his robe and slung the scabbard of Lucas's sword over his shoulder. He joined Catanya at the riverbank just as a flight of swallows burst out from between two beech trees, startling them both. The birds dove close to the surface of the river, back and forth, plucking insects from the water's surface. One of the swallows stood out from the rest. It flew higher and zigzagged its own flight path. As it drew closer, Magnus saw it *was* different. Unlike the other brown barn swallows, this one had a *'white belly, yellow flash, blue wings…'* Magnus recalled Eamon's description of a 'messenger' swallow.

The little bird spotted Magnus on the south bank. It flew straight, landing beside him and let out a series of chirps as if announcing its presence.

"Who's your little friend?" Catanya squatted to touch the bird's beak. It bit her finger. "Ouch!" She laughed. "That's an 'Ahrona' swallow."

"You know of these?" Magnus said, spotting a small note tied to the swallow's leg with string.

"Aye. The old priest, Trax, uses them in the Romghold. They hail from the Air Realm city of Ahrona in the Clouded Mountains. Trax sends messages to Irucantî posted all over Allumbreve. They have a knack for always finding the person they seek. I have no idea how they do it."

Magnus gently slid the note free from the bird's leg and unfurled it as Catanya picked the bird up and held it with soft hands. Magnus read the message on the note aloud—

"Magnus, Catanya,

I trust this message finds you safe and well. I have remained with Austagia in an advisory capacity. He works to restore order among the Irucantî and seek out a Quag stronghold believed to be in the Corville Mountains. Joffren heals slowly. To what extent and purpose, time will tell. Jael has been a good help in that matter. Brue has not been seen since your altercation with him in Ba'rrat, Magnus. I assume you're intentions have not changed. I suggest you seek out Marsala. She is a mystic living in the abandoned town of Thwax, east of Brindle. She will help you find the best path. I will be sending Joffren to her for healing once Färgd can spare time for the journey.

Travel safe, dear friends.

Eamon."

Magnus re-read the words and scratched his chin. "Should we find this 'Marsala' then?"

"It seems a little out of our way, when we are trying to get north of here."

Magnus looked upward at the sheer cliffs just a hundred feet to the north. "I cannot see a way of getting up there. Not without a dragon."

"If we head to Thwax, we could wait for Färgd to arrive with Joffren. Perhaps Färgd could help us get north?"

"And visit the mystic while we wait," Magnus said. "Perhaps she'll have a better idea."

"To Thwax it is, then."

Magnus thought of responding to Eamon's letter, looked about for something to use as a pen, but the swallow wriggled free of Catanya's hands and was gone.

"He wasn't waiting for a response," Catanya said, staring over the river.

Magnus following her line of sight, watching the Ahrona swallow fly northward and up the black granite cliff face before banking westward toward Ba'rrat again. Something else about the cliff caught his eye. There was something climbing *down* the mountainside.

"Do you…" Catanya began to ask, pointing at the cliff.

"I see it," Magnus said. It was a dark creature about the size of a deer. Its muscular legs rolled from one deliberate foothold to the next and its claws scratched across the granite as the creature descended.

"I think we should leave, Magnus."

The creature stopped, lifted its head and stared with ghostly, white eyes across the hundred-foot distance separating it from Magnus. He knew those eyes. They belonged to the same creatures that stalked him months ago in Froughton Forest. The staring creature opened its jaws revealing two pairs of long, white fangs. It let out a ghastly cry—something half howl, half screech. Two more of the creatures appeared elsewhere on the cliff face.

"Magnus!" Catanya was pointing at the weir bridge. Another of the creatures was peering over the parapet. It leapt on top of it and locked eyes on Magnus then Catanya. It too cried its ghastly screech.

Magnus and Catanya turned and fled south of the river, through the trees, over a wooden fence and into an open wheat field beyond the looming shadow of the cliffs and into the summer sunshine. They pushed on as fast as they could, daring not turn to see if the creatures had followed. Half a mile from the river, Magnus and Catanya pulled up and stood back to back in silence. Catanya drew her lance and Magnus his sword.

The tall stems of wheat moved in the midday breeze like a golden sheet rolling seamlessly across the undulating field. Magnus felt the sun bathe his face with its warmth. The smell of the wheat funnelled old memories.

"It smells like the barley fields north of the Quarry back home," Catanya whispered, as though the words were stolen from Magnus's mouth. They turned about, keeping their backs to one another, but saw no sign of the black creatures in the wheat field. "What were those things?" Catanya asked.

"I saw them in Froughton Forest."

"Did they attack you?"

"No. They stalked me."

Still at his back, Magnus felt Catanya shudder. "That's even worse."

"But they were alone. These ones look like a hunting pack." Unease churned in Magnus's stomach.

They continued in an easterly direction toward Thwax with their weapons drawn, always looking for stalking eyes. Magnus glanced at Catanya's lance, curious about it.

"Here," Catanya said. "Take a look." She handed the bronze, cylindrical weapon to Magnus. He held it by its ends, intrigued by the red light prowling beneath the glyphic carvings in the lance's frame. "So, you squeeze the grip and it ignites?" Magnus asked.

"Aye."

"And it will only do so for you?"

"So they say. They became common use after Steyne's fire-sword killed Balgur, so that never again could a priest's weapon be used against him... or a dragon."

"It's like there's a creature pacing back and forth within, waiting to be unleashed." Magnus considered testing the lance to see if it would ignite for him, but thought it disrespectful.

"You do not wish to try it, Magnus? See if your powers can wield a lance made for another?"

Magnus shook his head. "No. It would not be right even if I could do so."

Magnus went to give the lance back to Catanya when out of the corner of his eye he spotted a black shadow moving through the field. It was brief and silent and Magnus could have dismissed it for a trick of shadows but for the cloudless skies that cast none.

"Catanya!" Magnus warned with a stern whisper. He handed her the lance and she ignited it as Magnus reinforced the grip on his sword. Back to back, they crouched among the tall stems of wheat.

SARAH

Sarah sat atop the rise half a mile away from the abandoned chancel. Catanya was right to tell her this would provide a good vantage point, not only to look over the chancel but also westward toward Ba'rrat. If the nightmare of the previous six months were to follow her to Brindle, she wanted to be the first to know.

To an extent, it had. Sarah's memories had come with her. Months of projecting thoughts to where freedom may take her never once hinted that she would take the nightmare with her. "*Flo ena*, Sarah," she whispered to herself in the Old-Words once again. "*Flo ena unna gwatter flemabee*—move on and let the past be as it be." Lamenting the past was not the gypsy way but it was raw in her mind and tragedy could still be born of it. "It is not yet in the past."

People were arriving in Brindle at a steady pace. Sarah looked about for a familiar face. *Magnus, Catanya, Bonstaph or Ganister...* As the day grew old the numbers increased. Some of the Brindle townsfolk became hostile toward travellers. Sarah was not at all surprised, as some travellers were guards from Ba'rrat, no doubt fleeing the Black Capitol and the siege that was taking place. Altercations were erratic until one man in particular arrived. He was a bearded man with long, scruffy hair, dressed in rags. He organised people into groups. He had them make fortifications at the city's western border with armed men and women barring the way. His methods were impeccable and he seemed to command the respect of the townsfolk, even with his ramshackle appearance. Sarah rubbed her eyes and stared harder, wondering whom the man could be. "Curse my ageing eyesight."

As the sun set on her first day of freedom, something familiar came into view. It was a horse—a Wardemeer—with a Quag warrior astride his back. He shared the company of several more Quag warriors approaching the fortifications with trepidation. The warriors were of no concern to Sarah, but the horse was.

Sarah began to sprint down the hill face toward them, never taking her eyes off the Wardemeer. "Tameror!" It was her husband's warhorse, still being ridden by the warrior named 'Daxton' who told her Ganister had died at his feet.

"Get ready to fight." The young boy from Brindle handed Bonstaph a flask of water. He nodded in thanks, downed three good gulps then coughed to clear his throat. "Stand your ground and be ready to fight."

"Yes, Commander." The people of Brindle seemed most appreciative to have Bonstaph take the lead. He did not think much of being called 'Commander' after all the years of distancing himself from the Authoritarium, but it seemed to motivate them.

As soon as Bonstaph had ridden into Brindle on a horse—requisitioned from a Quagman—he could see trouble escalating. With Ba'rrat emptying of its townsfolk and guards, a good portion were heading eastward to Brindle. The town was an obvious target. Just twenty miles from the Black Capitol, the townsfolk were a mixture of gypsies, fisherman and assorted others who had long suffered under the dictatorship of the ruling Quag. With the Quag now desperate, Bonstaph knew Brindle's townsfolk would feel the brunt of their desperation. It was a simple, tactical reality to the retired Knight Commander—*Without an organised defensive unit prepared to counterattack, they will perish.*

Without review or consultation, Bonstaph took the initiative to organise the town of Brindle. Within an hour, fortifications were underway from the poplar-strewn northern river to the Neverseas. With swordsmen and archers at the ready, Bonstaph made it clear—"None cross this line unless a friend to Brindle."

Then Bonstaph saw Tameror.

With a white-knuckled, left-handed grip on the Quag blade he had acquired in Ba'rrat's arena the previous day, Bonstaph climbed over the hull of a fishing boat that formed part of the fortifications and walked toward Ganister's warhorse.

"Commander!" a voice shouted in warning. Bonstaph was not listening. Ganister had lost his life only the day before and the very Quagman who stole his best friend's Wardemeer was within sight. The Quagman led three of his own kinsmen. *No doubt to assess the patency of Brindle's defences.*

Bonstaph shouted over his shoulder—"We are now an 'offensive'. The leader is mine. Archers, sight his companions. They don't dismount and they don't advance within fifty feet of our fortifications." He heard the smooth sliding of arrows being drawn from their quivers and the sinewy stretch of bowstrings. As a young Knight of the Realms, these two sounds were disconcerting when heard from behind, but years of battle changed that—they gave him reassurance.

Just as Bonstaph suspected, the Quagmen drew to a quick halt fifty feet short of the fortifications. An age of warring with the Quag had taught both sides not to breach the fifty-foot line until sure they were ready to fight. Bonstaph was breaching all etiquette, still walking with intent thirty feet from the Quagmen. They grew skittish except for Tameror and his rider. Bonstaph expected nothing less from Tameror, knowing he would choose to fight long before flight. He was unsure what to expect from his Quag rider, but then, he did not give a damn.

With Bonstaph twenty feet out, Tameror's rider alighted and drew his two black blades. It was what Bonstaph expected. Bonstaph threw his own blade to the side, continuing his assertive advance with no weapon in hand. The Quagmen's knuckles began to roll nervously about the pommels of his blades—a sign of apprehension Bonstaph also expected.

Ten feet out, Bonstaph broke into a run. The Quagman hesitated before raising his blades—the third thing Bonstaph expected. He knew the hesitation was born of unease, giving him the advantage he needed. The Quagmen's blades were raised a moment too late. Bonstaph tucked his head low, parried to his right, then back to his left, bringing his right shoulder into the Quagman's chest. The Quagman had pushed a heel back and braced well for the impact. With Bonstaph too close for a blade attack, the Quagman sunk a heavy elbow into Bonstaph's back, losing the patency of his grounding in the process. Bonstaph swept his right arm up between the Quagman's legs and lifted him, throwing him over and onto the ground. Bonstaph fell with him, quick to place the Quagman into the vice-grip of a headlock. Reinforcing the grip with his spare arm, Bonstaph used his legs to fend off the enemy's flailing blades. The Quagman tensed his thick neck muscles, making a clean snap of the spine difficult for Bonstaph.

Out of nowhere, a flash of purple swept across Bonstaph's grimacing face accompanied with a harrowing yell. The brute-strength of the Quagman waned and so Bonstaph rolled away from the chaos, springing to his feet to face the confusion.

The purple flash was Sarah. Dressed in a torn, weathered dress, her billowy blonde hair twirled about in a murderous dance with the red blood of the Quagman whom she was stabbing repeatedly with the blade Bonstaph had discarded moments ago.

Offside, Bonstaph saw the remaining Quagmen dismount horses and draw blades. Bonstaph shouted, but not to Sarah—"Release!"

Back at the fortifications, a volley of arrows was released. There was a moment's silence then dull thuds as three arrows apiece struck each of the remaining Quagmen, killing them.

Bonstaph came to Sarah, who was still stabbing the Quagman. He was dead at least three times over. From behind, Bonstaph wrapped his arms around her, drawing her close. "It's over, Sarah. He is finished," he spoke gently.

Heaving for breath, covered in the Quagman's blood, Sarah let the blade slip from her reddened hand. Her body continued to shake as she fell back into Bonstaph's chest, Bonstaph letting them drop to the ground together.

"It's over," Bonstaph repeated twice more.

Sarah tempered her breathing. Bonstaph released his embrace and stood, helping Sarah to her feet. She turned, wiping a smear of blood from beneath her nose with the back of her thumb, eyes fixed on Bonstaph. She reached for Tameror's reins, drawing the Wardemeer closer, her gaze still fixed. Bonstaph looked to her—he had too much respect for the wife of his best friend to do anything else. Eventually, after a good long moment had passed, words escaped Sarah's mouth—

"He is dead, isn't he?"

BLACKSMITHS

Silence...

Magnus curbed his breathing and scanned the field at waist height. Catanya did the same. The wind blew steadily across the heads of wheat making them rustle in a rhythmic manner. But there was something else—something not at all rhythmic. "To my left."

"I hear it," Catanya said. The black creatures were on the move and they were doing so with purpose. "We are being hunted," she murmured, confirming Magnus's suspicions.

Magnus released a long breath through flared nostrils. To his left, the black shadow moved again and then another to his right, and then another. "I count three so far," Magnus said. He thought back to the creatures in Froughton Forest. The first was encountered when he entered the forest. Its ghost-eyes had stared out at him in the darkness. The second was in the Valley of Shadows. The stalker had followed him until the dragon youngling—Thioci—killed it, tossing its tasteless carcass aside. Magnus was haunted by these memories and here they were again.

The first creature to attack bowled through the stems of wheat with an open jaw targeting Magnus's face. With a horrible screech it was thrown off its path and fell to the ground. The creature to the right came next—it too was thrown off course, screeching just the same. Both creatures lay mortally wounded at Magnus's feet with long, steel bolts protruding from their necks.

Magnus and Catanya danced about one another in a state of confusion. Three more came out of nowhere—two at Catanya and one at Magnus. Magnus's sword tore through the underbelly of one while Catanya's lance stabbed at the head of another. She raised a forearm to the third black beast. Its scissor-like fangs—two upper and two lower—locked around her vambrace. Catanya pulled her head clear of the fangs that tried to chew through her arm to get to her, yet the armour held strong.

Magnus was over the creature, driving his sword through the sinuous muscles between its front shoulder blades. The creature's thick neck muscles tensed as it reinforced its bite. Catanya grunted through gritted teeth. Magnus drew his sword back so he could thrust it again but before he had a chance, the beast fell dead to a crossbow bolt to the head. Catanya pulled her arm free of the creature's slack jaw. She and Magnus spun about, looking for anything that may attack. Then Magnus heard voices.

"There!" Catanya said, pointing her lance. Magnus stood beside her, poised. Two men pushed through the tall stems, each armed with an oversized crossbow.

"You're okay then? Nobody hurt?" The elder of the two men asked, looking from Catanya to Magnus. Magnus eyed them both. The second looked to be the elder man's son—dressed in a similar brown tunic that flowed to the knees with simple leather boots suited to farming more than fighting. Both wore oversized hats that dropped lazily at the neck. Magnus imagined he and his father used to look much like this, farming the Western Margins. The elder man looked closely at Catanya.

"Young Miss Semsü. Fancy seeing you in these parts."

Magnus looked to Catanya who was frowning in thought.

"I remember you," Catanya looked to the younger of the men. "Dale and..." she looked back to the elder man. "I'm sorry, I don't recall your name."

"Willem is my name," the man replied. "I don't recall ever telling you my name back in the Romghold, Semsü. But I'm sure Dale is most pleased you remember his!" The younger man rolled his eyes and shook his head as if embarrassed.

Magnus studied both men and equally as much their weapons. They were both loaded with bolts ready to use again and so he remained wary, particularly since they were clearly adept at using them.

"This is Magnus." Catanya extinguished her lance and turned to Magnus. "These gentlemen forged my weapons back in the Romghold."

"Much obliged," Willem said, taking a step closer and offering a hand to Magnus. Magnus shook it then looked to the younger one named Dale who stepped forward and did the same.

"This is your handiwork?" Magnus looked to the dead creatures lying beside him.

"Aye," Willem answered. "Worgriels... More often now, they venture into these lands."

"Five in one day though, father?" Dale remarked. "There's never been that many scouting at once."

"It is vexing, Dale." Willem frowned.

Catanya sheathed her weapon and so Magnus did the same. Relaxing a little, Magnus spoke freely. "Worgriels… I saw these in Froughton Forest." Willem was listening intently to Magnus, but Dale seemed distracted by Catanya. He withdrew his gaze once he caught Magnus looking at him.

"Froughton Forest, you say?" Willem asked.

"Aye. One to the west and one again in the Valley to the north."

"They venture south, they venture north… What draws these creatures from the darkness of the Caves of Cuvee and into the summer sun?" Willem rubbed a wrinkled nose.

"The Caves of Cuvee?" Magnus repeated. "They are beneath the Corville Mountains, are they not?" He looked to Willem for an explanation, for between the Corville Mountains and the Black Cliffs were the Southern Wastelands. *An arduous journey for anyone—let alone a creature that shies from the sun.*

"They are," Willem replied. "And such caves are countless and connect with a labyrinthine network of tunnels that time has pushed a long way south." He pointed his crossbow northward to the Black Cliffs themselves, spanning from west to east. "There are three known exits along the face of the Black Cliffs. One at Ba'rrat, one north of Brindle and one north of Thwax. It would seem they perhaps exit into Froughton as well."

"These tunnels were not carved by nature," Dale added. "The worgriels carved them with tooth and claw." Magnus looked at the granite cliff face once again—another reason to despise it.

"How far deep does the granite run?" Catanya asked.

"All the length of the Southern Wastelands," Willem said. Magnus and Catanya looked at him. Dread shuddered through Magnus.

"Back home in the Uydferlands we mine sandstone and have done for generations," Catanya said. "It's toilsome work. Are you saying these creatures carved tunnels through granite all the length of the Wastelands with tooth and claw?" A look of revulsion washed over her face.

"Over the three ages of Allumbreve—yes. A creature of such resilience leaves one pondering what else they are capable of." Willem handed his crossbow to Dale then knelt down to retrieve the bolts from the Worgriels bodies. Magnus reached for the one beside him with the bolt through its head. He looked closer at the creature. Even dead, its large pearlescent eyes held a haunting stare. Magnus put a foot to the creature's head and pulled the bolt free. The crimson blood smeared across the bolt turned black before drifting into the skies as a pungent black mist.

Black blood, black blades, black magic... Magnus was reminded of the black substance the healers drew from Lucas's wound back in the Uydferlands after the wyvern attack. He thought of the waiter at the Hugmdael Inn and how Crugion's right-hand-man—*Briet*—had killed him with his dagger, but not before torturing him slowly with the infected blade. His arm turned black and a mist oozed from his wounded neck. He thought of Lucas again and the black mist he used to defend Delvion, to quench flames and Catanya's throwing knife. There was black magic at play here—Magnus was sure of it. *But what is its source?*

Magnus handed the bolt to Willem who paused, appearing to examine the expression on Magnus's face. "I'm guessing you two have been through worse than this of late," Willem asked directly.

"We have," Catanya answered. "Far worse. What of you, Willem? Do you live around these parts?"

"No. And quite frankly, we'll be glad to get back north to the realms," Willem confessed. "We're too close to Ba'rrat for my liking. Alas, we go where our skills are needed."

"You're making weapons in Brindle?"

"We've spent the past month in the farmlands here, building new tillage ploughs and, well, putting components of the old ploughs to good use." Willem pointed to the crossbows. "These are Dale's design."

Magnus looked to Dale and his deadly weapons. "You made this from an old plough?"

"Aye," Dale smiled sheepishly.

"I grew up on a farm, but never gave thought to creating something like this from our plough." Magnus found the idea amusing. "I daren't think what you could do with a horse cart!" He and Dale laughed.

"A catapult, perhaps," Dale said, raising the laughter further.

Willem recovered the remaining crossbow bolts, stored them in a heavy quiver and slung them over his shoulder. "We will continue to scout the field back to the river for any more of these vermin, then retire to our camp in the afternoon. If you've time to spare, you are most welcome to join us for an evening meal."

Magnus looked to Catanya. She nodded affirmatively to Willem. "Aye. Thank you. We would appreciate that."

The western field as far as the river proved free of any more Worgriels. It was easy, though, to find their tracks leading back to the weir and the Black Cliffs. Willem pointed out a cave entrance half way up the cliff face.

It was mid afternoon when Magnus and Catanya followed Willem and Dale across the fields to a farm homestead. Here, Magnus shared Catanya's delight in seeing that Willem and Dale were two of many artisans that had set up camp in a garden area a short distance from the homestead.

"This is exactly how they set up in the Romghold," Catanya smiled.

Within the garden, there was a large white tent and many smaller tents surrounding it. The central tent was a communal area. There were two long tables, each with benches either side for sitting. Several people were busy laying out spreads of breads, salads and fresh fruit down the length of the tables, others were cooking at portable ovens and, outside in the summer sunshine, two pigs roasted on spits. The smell of the roasts made Magnus weak at the knees.

"Wow," Magnus whispered to Catanya. She took his hand and gripped it excitedly.

"Wow, indeed."

"Everybody," Willem announced in a loud voice. "We have company!"

Every face in the artisans' camp turned toward Magnus and Catanya. Eyebrows raised as several of the artisans seemed to recognise Catanya. One among them was a woman of about fifty. She came to them, wiping her hands clean over her white apron.

"Oh my! I did not expect such company for this supper," the woman said. "Semsü." The woman bowed to Catanya.

"Ivy," Catanya replied. The woman's eyes widened.

"You've a good memory." Ivy smiled.

"She remembered our son's name, too." Willem raised his eyebrows twice. He and Ivy both looked at Dale, who shook his head and walked off toward the roasting pigs. Magnus was beginning to get the picture—*they seem to see Catanya as a suitor to Dale.*

"Please, call me Catanya." Silence immediately fell over the camp of artisans. All turned to Catanya and looked at her. Apparently, Magnus realised, this was not the thing for a priest to say. As if to divert from the awkwardness, Catanya was quick to add—"And this is Magnus." Ivy shook Magnus's hand. "Ivy made my Ferustir suit," Catanya explained to Magnus.

"One of three seamstresses and one of many artisans, Semsü." Ivy bowed again. She stood beside Magnus, looking him over. For the first time, Magnus felt awkward at his appearance. He was still wrapped in Eamon's large cloak that thankfully covered most of his scorched pants but not the torn boots he scavenged from the dead Quag guard. Ivy then looked Catanya over. "Your suit has seen a few battles, I see."

"Aye," Catanya said. "It has fared far better than Magnus's attire." She looked at Magnus and winked. Magnus refrained from a cheeky retort.

"Your sword holds up well," Willem said. "I saw you wielding it against the worgriels. If I'm not mistaken, that be made of Icerealmish steel, am I correct?"

Magnus pulled the dark red leather scabbard from across his shoulder and pulled the pommel a few inches out from it, handing it to Willem. He thought the blacksmith would appreciate taking a closer look at Lucas's sword. "Aye, it is. Although, not forged in the Ice Realm."

Willem drew the sword free of its scabbard. "What a delight." He looked Lucas's sword over, drinking in every detail. "A fire-bronze pommel and cross guard... interesting." Willem went to say more but stopped himself as he examined the engravings, looking at Magnus then back to the sword. "But if I may say, this sword was not made for you."

Magnus looked at Catanya but she was preoccupied with Ivy who was examining her damaged vambrace. Catanya seemed comfortable in their presence, so Magnus entertained Willem's enquiries. "It is one of two swords forged together. There are differences. The other is mine. This belongs to... a friend. A brother of sorts."

Willem nodded. Dale returned, sinking teeth into a large chunk of roasted pork. He looked over the sword. "Fleu-steel?" he mumbled through a mouthful of food. "And bronze. Made in the Fire Realm?" Magnus was distracted by the delightful smell of the food. He began to salivate.

"Manners, Dale!" Ivy scorned at her son. "Where are your manners?"

Dale's mouth snapped shut and his eyes widened. He looked at Magnus, then Catanya. Magnus smiled. He was warming to Dale for he was very much like a younger version of himself. "It is," Magnus said. Dale looked to him again. "It *is* made in the Fire Realm. A good friend of my father's made it."

Willem rested the sword just above the cross guard on his forefinger, shifting the sword until it balanced on his finger. "The bronze runs deep through the blade—deeper still than a conventional Fire Realm blade. Needed, no doubt, to counterbalance the lighter fleu-steel. Interesting. To what purpose were these blades forged, may I ask?"

Magnus looked at the sword balancing on the artisan's finger. He knew full well the purpose of the swords construction. The contrast between it and his own told a tale as Sarah had explained—*The differences represent your maternal origins, the similarities show your link to the Fire Realm… the realm of your fathers.'*

"Like I said, they were built as a symbol of brotherhood," Magnus reiterated, his mood dampening a little.

Willem handed Magnus the sword and scabbard and spoke gently as he did—"I think you could do well with a hearty meal and cup or two of ale. What do you say?" He said nothing more on the matter of the swords.

Magnus appreciated Willem dropping the subject. He sheathed the sword, swung its scabbard over his shoulder and looked at Willem. "If it suits Catanya to do so, then yes, thank you."

In the large central tent, Magnus and Catanya sat at one of the long tables in the company of fifteen artisans and nearly as many farm hands. They worked their way through the most glorious meal either had eaten in half a year. The roast pork was just the beginning. Grilled river trout, steamed opal beans and Kreeluck carrots, stewed rhubarb smothered in thick, honey-sweetened cream and the best ale either of them had ever tasted.

A good hour passed. Magnus looked at Catanya. A contented smile came to her own face and she took Magnus's between her hands. "I could sit at this table forever," she smiled, her eyes glazed with tiredness. "But I'd just as soon go to sleep." She seemed about to kiss him when the table fell silent. Magnus gathered Catanya's intimacy was a further display of un-priestly behaviour. He and Catanya turned away from each other.

Willem broke the silence. "Where does your journey take you from here?"

Magnus looked at the blacksmith. He seemed like a nice enough man, but there was something about his interest in Lucas's sword that made him wary. It was not so much the sword, but Willem's ability to deduce so much from it and so quickly. To say he was travelling to Thwax could give more away than he was willing. Given that this man knew these lands of the south coast better than he did, Magnus thought it best they keep Thwax to themselves.

"We're headed east," Magnus said, keeping things general.

"We've a scheduled meeting tomorrow," Catanya added. Willem looked at Catanya, perhaps hopeful he could garner a little more information. She seemed to sense it. "As Magnus said—to the east." Willem nodded, still staring at Catanya.

"What of you?" Magnus redirected to Willem. "Are you and your companions here for the rest of the summer?"

Willem looked back to Magnus. "That was the plan. We have some work to do in Brindle, a day's journey west from here. We will remain camped here and commute, as we need to. Brindle is that little bit closer to Ba'rrat. The Quag have a hold over Brindle which is not to our liking."

Magnus realised the artisans and travellers were likely unaware that Ba'rrat had fallen. Telling them the news would garner a lot more questions. Willem excused himself and moved away. Catanya shifted closer to Magnus, turning to face him.

"You were right to not speak of our intentions."

Magnus rubbed his mottled beard and mumbled through his fingers. "I see no advantage in them knowing who I am."

"It's likely more Quagmen will stray this way. Perhaps we should warn them of that."

"If they think we bring trouble, it may be easier for them to turn us over to the Quag."

Catanya looked about again. "Anyone here could be a spy for Delvion. But then, I'm confident we're among friends."

Magnus agreed. "They all seem to know each other quite well. A stranger here would stand out as much as us."

Catanya's eyes started to look heavy and soon she closed them. Magnus looked at her, observing the scar on her left ear. Forgetting the company they were in, he stroked her earlobe between his thumb and forefinger. With reflexes faster than a scalded cat, Catanya had Magnus's wrist in a vice grip. Her eyes were wide and wild. Magnus had never seen reflexes—nor instincts—anywhere near this in all his one hundred battles in the arena. He looked to Catanya's hand, muscles flexing as her grip reasserted itself.

"That's what comes of disrespecting a Ferustir, young man."

Magnus turned to the source. It was a man of about forty. Dressed in white linen clothing as many of the other artisans were, he was exceptionally neat with the most deliberately manicured dark hair and beard he had even seen. His eyes shifted repeatedly between Magnus and Catanya.

Catanya loosened her grip and stood. "Delik?"

The man bowed politely. "Semsü."

Catanya looked to Magnus for moment. "Magnus, I'm sorry."

"Don't be." Magnus smiled.

Catanya turned back to Delik who appeared intrigued with their interactions.

"I apologise. I've interrupted you," Delik said.

"Not at all," Catanya replied.

Delik smiled. "I just arrived and was immediately informed you were here. It is wonderful to see you again."

"It's good to see you, too," Catanya said. "Magnus, this is Delik." Her eyes flashed a sharp warning at Magnus.

Magnus stood and shook Delik's outstretched hand. Delik's eyes widened as they touched. Magnus was intrigued by the softness of his hand. He had a deliberate, firm grip, but not one of strength. He looked Magnus over then shifted his gaze back to Catanya. "I see your Ferustir armour has held you in good stead."

"For the most part." Catanya said. "Until this afternoon." She held her left arm up. Her vambrace was missing—Magnus had not noticed. "Ivy has taken my vambrace for Willem to repair."

"That must have been quite an altercation," Delik smiled.

"Well, it wasn't me, I swear," Magnus humoured. Delik laughed and the remark made Catanya smile and relax a little.

"Will you be staying with us a while?" Delik questioned. "I would be curious to hear of your quests since last we met."

Catanya stiffened once again. "We've just arrived. I guess we'll play it by ear."

Catanya was being diplomatic, nothing more. Magnus was ready to leave, but as if on cue, Ivy arrived. "You two need beds and rest. Semsü, Dale is working on your armour right now. You can try it on in the morning," Ivy said. She came to Magnus and handed him a fresh set of folded clothes and a newly made pair of leather boots. "You look as though you need a tidy up and you've come to the right place. Everything was made by us." She grinned and winked.

"Thank you," Magnus said. For a moment, Ivy's kindness reminded him of Sarah. He looked at the clothes. His gratitude turned to grief. Wherever Sarah was, it was only a matter of time before she would learn the truth about Lucas killing Ganister... *her son killing his father... her husband...*

"There's a bunk for you in the men's quarters and one for you, Semsü, in the women's. Sleep well. Both of you." Ivy turned away before Magnus had a chance to snap out of his thoughts and thank her again. She broke into conversation with Delik.

Magnus and Catanya were quick to move out of the large tent. The heat of the summer day had given over to a balmy coastal breeze and the sky was sprinkled with evening stars. Magnus studied Catanya's strained expression. "Are you okay?"

Catanya released a pent up breath. "It's strange. I thought I had the measure of that man." She studied Delik who was moving briskly away from the tent without having eaten. "Just now though, he seems so different to me. I guess I've changed a lot since I first met him."

Catanya explained how Delik led the group of artisans who made her Ferustir suit and how meticulous he was. Catanya had respected him for his professionalism at the time. Six months and many deceptions later, it seemed, had made Catanya wary of almost everyone. "Maybe I just need to rest," Catanya yawned.

"Don't discredit your intuition, Catanya. If you think you can smell a rat, then perhaps you do."

"What do you think, Magnus… Should we spend the night? Start fresh in the morning?"

Magnus thought about things. He was holding the folded clothes and boots, feeling the fine fabric of the shirt. "I'd like to move on but sleep in a soft bed, perhaps followed by breakfast, sounds inviting." Magnus smiled, certain he was getting ahead of himself.

"I've just had a thought," Catanya said. The strain in her face eased into a coy smile. "The last time we were ready to hightail it, my father intervened and it was the last time I saw you until a few days ago. Now we wish to flee again and Ivy would have us sleeping in separate quarters. I'm not sure I want to let you out of my sight." She pinched Magnus in the ribs.

"Perhaps you can sneak me into the women's quarters." Magnus could not resist the joke.

"In your dreams," Catanya said, rubbing her eyes with the palms of her hands.

"I think we should sleep, Catanya. Even if just for a few hours."

Magnus led Catanya around the encampment and into a field to the north. In the darkness and away from the lamps outside the tents, the moonlight seemed to shine brighter. A few hundred feet away to the east was a rise in the field.

"Catanya. Do you think you can wake an hour before sunrise?"

"Yes. I've most certainly learned to sleep lightly in recent times."

"Then we'll meet over there, on the other side of that rise, and take our leave." Sure no one was looking, he stole a kiss from Catanya.

"I'll see you in the morning," Catanya said.

HANNAH - TWO

"Is this necessary?"

"I can no longer tolerate these distractions."

"Distractions?" Alessandra leant back in her chair, crossing her arms over her chest. Hannah looked from her mother to her father—the three of them were seated at the square kitchen table. A fourth chair was empty, as it had been for many months since Catanya left.

"What I'm saying is, I will feel all the better knowing you are both safe. Trying to defend our lands, all the while knowing what will happen to you if we are overrun, is a *distraction.*"

"It was Csilla's idea," Hannah contributed. She liked to contribute to her parents 'adult' conversation where she could. It reminded them she was there and seemed to soften their mood.

"You're right, Hannah." Alessandra pulled a half-hearted smile as she reached across the table and squeezed her daughter's hand. "It was Csilla's idea and it was thoughtful of her to do so. However, travelling through Froughton Forest? To *The Core?*"

Hannah waited for her father's response. She was quite excited to be going on a journey. The last time she had travelled anywhere further than the Nuyan River or the Quarries was before the war began. *Before Catanya left.*

Xavier chewed slowly on his steak and pointed his fork at Alessandra. "Your sister is right suggesting you take refuge with the ӨhUid folk. A month ago I'd have suggested you travel to Guame."

"I like the markets in Guame," Hannah smiled. Xavier smiled back.

"Guame, it is rumoured, is under siege. My next choice would be the Ice Realm. However…" Xavier paused to wipe his mouth with a handkerchief. "And this does not leave this table." He looked from Hannah to Alessandra. "Rumour also suggests the Rhydermere of the Ice Realm are responsible for the siege of Guame."

Alessandra paused for thought before responding— "Perhaps there is no other choice, then."

"Without the time nor resources to send knights to verify these rumours, the only clansfolk who hold fast and share our interests are the ӨhUid."

Xavier gave an affirmative nod and lifted his glass of red wine. Hannah imitated him, nodding with a frown. Xavier winked over the top of his glass at her, making her smile.

"Csilla knows someone who can guide us?"

"To guide and protect you, yes. His name is Creighton. What Csilla does to protect our borders, he has long done to protect his people's interests at Mount Earthwood. Csilla has liaised with him for years. He has been consulting with us for the past three days and leaves for home in the morning."

"That soon," Alessandra said.

"And perhaps…" Xavier hesitated. "Perhaps the time apart will allow us to get our heads around the matters that vex us of late."

Alessandra stood from the table. Hannah saw the uncomfortable expression on her face. "Come, Hannah. We need to pack."

"Pack light, my wife," Xavier said. His wife turned to him. "I'm sure regret and shame weigh heavily enough on you."

Hannah was too excited to sleep. She wished for night to pass quickly so they could begin their journey. Even more exciting, Hannah knew Froughton Forest was to the east. *So are the Romgnian Mountains.* The thought of having even the slightest chance of finding Catanya would be a dream come true.

Hannah packed her leather travel bag.

"Hannah, your spare summer dress."

"I have it, mother."

"Hannah, your winter dress. And your long boots."

"I have them both."

"Your brush."

Hannah scrunched her nose. She hid her brush under her bed, happy to forgo the torture of having knots in her hair brushed out by her mother. "I have my brush, Mother."

What Hannah did not tell her mother were the extra things she packed for Catanya. Her favourite bottle-green scarf, a few sticks of salty liquorice root, and the half bottle of jasmine oil from Catanya's dresser draw. It was well into the night when Hannah finally fell asleep in Catanya's bed.

"Hannah."

Hannah was in the thickest part of sleep, where dragging yourself into the real world is like dragging yourself out of quicksand—impossible without a nagging adult on the other side pulling you out of it.

"Hannah, wake up."

A hand touched her forehead and stroked her hair. Hannah moaned in protest, forcing one eye open. The east-facing window was black. "It's not morning yet."

"It will be soon enough," Alessandra said. "We need to be well clear of here by then. Come. Get up. Get dressed."

Hannah did as told and stood at the side of the bed. "I *am* dressed." Hannah was ready to go, wearing her favourite pomegranate-red dress and Catanya's old, brown suede jacket to match her travel bag.

"So you are," Alessandra said, hanging an oil lamp from a hook in the wall above the bed.

"That was quick." Csilla entered the bedroom. Hannah looked her aunt over. She was dressed in her usual copper and blue Uydfer armour, carrying her crimson gown over her arm. Her bronze-silver longsword was sheathed and strapped to her right side, with three long knives sheathed to the left in her plaited belt. "I have something for you." Csilla knelt in front of Hannah and showed her a belt similar to her own with a single knife sheathed in it. "This will protect you. It's a special blade, just like mine. Here, let me show you a spell." Csilla drew the knife and whispered— *'Fara gin parshin-ar!'* A ring of flame danced along the shaft of the knife, then disappeared.

"Oh!" Hannah thought it was marvellous. "Perhaps I will become an Irucantî!"

"Perhaps not." Csilla's face turned serious and she flashed a look to Alessandra. "But it will serve you well when you need it." Csilla tucked the knife into the belt and fastened its buckle about Hannah's waist. "A perfect fit!"

Hannah looked at the plait pattern of the belt. Just like Csilla's, it was a 'pousse-plait'—her mother's characteristic pattern of plaiting consisting of a three strand plait with a fourth threading lengthways through the middle. The fourth strand was imbued with a mix of enchantments to keep the plait true.

"Drink this, beautiful fire-girl." Alessandra handed Hannah a cup of green tea. She gulped it down then picked up her travel bag, hanging it across her back. "I'm ready!"

The three of them left the house. Alessandra lingered at the door, looking back for a moment. Csilla placed a hand on her shoulder. "You'll be back some day, sister."

Alessandra reached for her daughter's hand. Hannah felt her familiar grip. "With Catanya gone and everything I love by my side, I have this feeling, Csilla, this is goodbye."

"Catanya is not gone forever," Csilla assured her sister.

Alessandra looked resignedly at Csilla. "You once said that about Austagia."

Hannah could not see the point of her mother's pessimism. As sure as the sun rising in the east, she was certain travelling that way was the start of her journey to find her sister. She was going to say as much, but her jaw dropped at the sight of two approaching riders. Leading was her father riding his silver Wardemeer—Trillium. The second was a stranger. He was a solid man with red hair and a big, red beard. What he was riding left her speechless.

"Mother... Csilla... What is *that*?"

"That is a 'Dwyer' bull," Csilla explained.

Hannah gawped at the enormous creature. Easily twice the size of Trillium, the red-haired bull drew up beside the warhorse, dwarfing it in comparison. The creature's thick, white horns curved forward at the sharp ends and were about five feet across.

"Is he fast?" Hannah asked.

"Not as fast as Trillium. But nothing can stop him once he's moving," Csilla said.

Hannah saw the bull was all muscle. Its red hair was short except for a hairy patch that seemed to hang over its face.

"Can he see where he's going?" Hannah asked.

"Auroch found his way to you, young lady." It was the big, bearded man. Unexpectedly, a young girl jumped off the back of the bull and strode over to Hannah. Even in the dim moonlight Hannah could see she had long, curly red hair.

Csilla held a lamp so the two young girls could see one another. "Hannah, this is Nëven. Nëven, this is Hannah."

The two girls looked at one another. Nëven extended a hand. "Pleased to meet you, Hannah." Hannah shook her hand. Under Csilla's lamp, Hannah studied the young girl. She could not have been more different to her—curly red hair, pale skin, and freckles over her nose and cheeks.

"Right, now that the girls have met and know what each other looks like, best you extinguish that light, Csilla," Xavier said. He looked around as though scouting for something.

"I like your dress," Nëven said to Hannah.

"Thank you." Hannah looked down at her dress then smiled. "Are you travelling to the forest with us?"

"Aye. We're taking you to our home. There are lots of exciting things to see along the way. I think you'll like it!" Nëven smiled. Hannah was even more excited about their journey.

Alessandra's horse was packed and they were ready to leave.

"Up you get, Hannah," Xavier said.

"Wait!" Hannah remembered something. It was the most important of things and she had almost forgotten to pack it. She ran back into the house. In Catanya's bedroom, she opened the dresser draw and took out Catanya's diary. Hannah opened it and looked again at the pressed iris. She carefully prised the flower from the diary, leaving an indent in the pages the shape of the flower. Replacing the diary in the drawer, she ran back out of the house, kissed her father and climbed to the front of her mother's saddle, still holding the flower.

"What is that for?" Alessandra asked.

"In case we pass the Romghold along the way," Hannah explained, tucking the flower into an inside pocket of her jacket. "I can give it to Catanya to remind her of her love for Magnus... In case she has forgotten, the way uncle must have forgotten for you."

A look of shock crossed her mother's face but she soon softened and as they rode away from their home and Xavier, Alessandra put her mouth to Hannah's ear and whispered—"He has never forgotten, Hannah."

WARNING

Catanya struggled to sleep at all. She lay staring at the white canvas ceiling. The summer breeze blew gently against it making it balloon into the room, then outwards again, like the rolling lungs of a sleeping dragon. The breeze blew through the entrance flap of the women's sleeping quarters and over her body, making her tingle with alertness. It should have nursed her into a restful sleep, but it didn't. Something about this place did not seem right. Catanya tried repeatedly to dismiss it as folly of the mind but the warning in her heart proposed otherwise.

Was it the worgriel attack? That was ferocious, relentless, but no more so than the wyverns when flying with Färgd around the coast south of the Dormiul Path. No more than Demi's attack in Brindle in the middle of the night, or the Quag attack at the river that morning. *No…* The worgriel attack was about the most normal thing she had experienced all day.

Things seemed off from the moment she met Willem and Dale in the field. It just seemed out of place. When last she saw them, in the Romghold, they were part of an elite team of artisans employed to make the best Ferustir armour and weapons for her—the new Irucanti recruit. And here they were, a day away from Brindle, two days from Ba'rrat, making farming tools. It just did not seem right. Ivy seemed polite enough, as did the other artisans, but none of the sorcerers who helped forge her suit were here. Catanya sat up. *The sorcerers who took samples of my blood and scanned my mind…* Her heart beat its warning again.

That was when I was most vulnerable…

My blood sample was used to forge my lance—with the sorcerer's spells…

My mind was examined for spells—with Joffren overseeing the process. Joffren… who sent Demi to kill me…

Then Delik arrived. His politeness this time seemed contrived. He either did not want them there or… *knew others were looking for us.*

The cool breeze stopped. It had tried to lull Catanya to sleep, but failed. Catanya stood, unsheathed her lance and prised a throwing knife from its pouch. *What was the time?*

Swiftly and silently, Catanya walked to the tent's entrance, peered out and looked to the stars to gauge the time. It was several hours until she would meet Magnus. *Damn...* She was not prepared to wait. If they were not safe here, they had to leave immediately. This meant getting to Magnus in the men's sleeping quarters. Catanya scanned the sleeping bunks in the women's tent. In the dusky grey of night, every one of the nine women appeared asleep. Catanya slipped away.

The night lamps were extinguished except for one in the dining pavilion, but that was fifty yards to the west. The men's quarters were twenty yards to the south. Catanya rounded the tent she had just left and saw a dim light glowing inside another tent twenty feet to the east. Curious to get a clearer picture of the goings on, she moved swiftly toward this tent.

Just outside, Catanya could hear a rhythmic tapping. She found the entrance flap folded back on itself. Peering in, she saw Dale seated at a workbench. He had her vambrace in a vice and was tinkering away, working his tools, mending the broken armour.

"Call it a night, Dale." Willem's voice came from the back of the tent. Catanya shifted until her eyes found him. "You can finish it in the morning. Delik may see things differently, but it's good to keep your hand in at the craft you love."

Dale did not respond, but his tinkering continued. Willem moved about, sorting through tools and pieces of armour for the next few minutes. Willem then bid Dale goodnight. "Try to get some sleep, son." He tapped Dale on the shoulder and headed for the entrance. Catanya sheathed her weapons and scampered silently into the long grass nearby. Willem headed to the men's quarters and Catanya returned to the tent entrance.

Dale was now standing at a small forge. He placed something inside, closed the door and returned to his seat at the workbench. With a pair of pliers and a small sanding file, he started to shape a small silver buckle. Catanya looked at her other vambrace. The three buckles were a match, but bronze in colour. She turned away, crouched, and looked at her right forearm with the missing armour. The vambrace may not have saved her life, but it spared her arm. Catanya dearly wanted to get it back. She looked into the tent again. Dale was returning to the forge. He removed Catanya's vambrace, took it to his workbench and fitted two new silver buckles. He laid the finished work on a strip of cloth and leant back with his hands behind his head.

He's finished...

Dale jumped to his feet.

"Sorry," Catanya said softly. "I didn't mean to startle you."

Dale rubbed his hands on his overalls and looked about, nervously. "That's okay."

"You're working late," Catanya smiled.

"I like the peace and quiet, and… I wanted to get your armour finished. I…" Dale's awkwardness was making Catanya feel awkward, too. "I wanted it done right, but compromises had to be made."

Dale picked up the mended vambrace and came to Catanya. "You see— the fibres of the armour could be repaired." Dale ran his fingers over the burgundy fibre patterns in the black armour plating. "However, the buckles were made of fire-bronze, like your lance. There are no dragons around here to fire the bronze, so…" Dale turned the vambrace over. "The two new buckles are made of hardened steel."

Catanya looked at Dale's handiwork, hardly believing he had done such fine craftsmanship in such a short amount of time. She could see where the repairs were made, but to her, it gave the armour character. The centre bronze buckle remained whilst the other two were now silver. Catanya looked at Dale. His eyes were fixed on her the way they had been when they first met in the Romghold.

The unease in Catanya's heart softened a little. Her motives, however, were hard fixed. She knew it was in her interest to leave, but looking into Dale's green eyes, she somehow could not believe he would do anything to harm her. *Whatever is going on here, Dale either does not know about it, or has no choice in the matter.* This seemed to fit with Willem's words moments ago. He told Dale he could finish his work but— *'Delik may see things differently…'*

"Does Delik mind you working on this for me?" Catanya asked. Dale drew a sharp breath. "I wouldn't want to get you into trouble, Dale." Catanya tried to soften her obviously blunt question. "I can see you have a lot of other important work to do here."

"It's not like that. Delik is happy with my work." Dale hesitated. "Things are different now."

Catanya kept looking Dale in the eyes, knowing it kept him focusing on her, but it was more than that. He had the most honest eyes she had ever seen. She doubted they could hide a lie if they tried. Magnus's eyes always told of his love for her, but Dale's were eyes of innocence. The fact that the first thing he ever told her was how beautiful she was, with no regard for etiquette, was more than a quality she admired—she adored it.

Catanya wanted to push Dale for more information about Delik, but dreaded the thought of those green eyes clouding over when he recognised her agenda. No, she was not going to play games with Dale. Instead, there was an awkward silence between them. Dale took the initiative and broke it. He took a step forward and kissed Catanya—briefly and for just a second—on the lips.

"Here." Dale handed Catanya her vambrace. "It's best you leave now, Semsü." Catanya opened her mouth to reply—with what she was not sure—but Dale cut her short. "I don't mean leave the tent, I mean leave this place. It's not safe for you." Dale looked nervously at the tent entrance.

Catanya had questions, but her heart was thumping a firm warning to leave immediately. "Are *you* safe?" It was the most pressing thing on her mind.

"Semsü?"

"Don't call me that." Catanya kissed Dale back. It was a more passionate kiss but quick, nevertheless. She pulled back, placing a hand on his chest. "Are you safe staying here?"

"For now, yes." The second kiss seemed to snap Dale out of any hesitation. "When the time comes, my parents and I will make our way north again. Where will you go?"

Catanya shook her head. "We've a long journey ahead of us. Many wrongs need to be righted, Dale. But if you need sanctuary, you'll find it in the Uydferlands… in the Fire Realm."

Dale nodded. "Is it true—your companion? Is he who they say he is?"

Catanya was floored. *How in all of Allumbreve would he know?* Catanya turned to see if any eavesdroppers were at the tent's entrance. She was quick to consider all manner of ways these people knew Magnus was the Electus. She was sure now that Delik knew when we they spoke earlier. The question now was—*What would Delik do with the knowledge that the Electus was here in the artisans' camp?*

Magnus!

Catanya looked one last time at Dale. His eyes were a mixture of confusion and desire. "Best I don't answer that question." Catanya walked to the entrance of the tent, fitting her vambrace as she went. "Goodbye, Dale."

Walking into the night, Catanya fended off a flood of emotions. She somehow felt responsible for Dale's safety. She felt responsible for Willem and Ivy's safety. Magnus, though, was in danger—of that there was no doubt. Catanya looked about but only for a split second. She had made a fatal error.

She had put her emotions before evaluating her immediate situation. It was basic Irucantî training that had become second nature to her and saved her life on more than one occasion. Now though, she slipped. She did not notice figures in the dark. They struck from behind. Blinding pain tore through her head and her vision blacked out.

Catanya fell, but was dragged to her feet. She fought from losing consciousness. Her arms were bound behind her back and several people were manhandling her, dragging her somewhere. Her vision started to return and she tried to scream as a warning to Magnus but her mouth was smothered with a gag tied around her neck. Then a sack was shoved over her head.

Catanya had been captured.

FURY

"By the gods, she's a feisty one!"

"This man is of no concern to me, but I protest your assault on an Irucantî."

The first voice was unfamiliar to Magnus. The second was Delik's. Both voices washed through Magnus as a hazy dream. It was mixed with convoluted memories and nausea. The nausea was different to what he had experienced since becoming the Electus. That was 'Anunya'—the sickness that came as a side effect of his body learning to adapt to the dragon blood that now coursed through his veins. With the nausea Magnus was experiencing now, there was no sweating or rigors. He felt as though his body was fighting some kind of sickness.

"Was the nightshade meant to kill him?" It was Delik again.

"That, or knock him out for a few hours. It looks like he'll pull through, but not for some time," said the unfamiliar voice.

Nightshade? They poisoned me... His muscles and heart burned—Thioci's blood was working its magic and the poison's effectiveness was dwindling faster than his assaulters were anticipating. Magnus's consciousness was returning. He opened his eyes to a blurry squint. There was an altercation in the far corner of the dimly lit tent. A body was thrashing about and several others were trying to hold the victim still. Muffled yells pulled Magnus out of his daze. The thrashing body was Catanya.

Magnus blinked, clearing his vision enough to assess the situation. To his right were three Quagmen with Catanya and to his left was Delik. Lucas's sword and scabbard were resting on a chair midway between him and Delik. His hands were shackled behind his back and chained to an iron stake driven deep into the ground. He kept as still as a statue and closed his eyes again, not wanting to compromise the element of surprise. He concentrated on the shackles, trying to bring heat to them. Heat built in his torso and thrust through his limbs making him jolt. Magnus squinted his eyes open again. The Quag warriors were too busy settling a thrashing Catanya to notice. Delik, however, was looking right at him. The heat in Magnus's arms mounted, yet had little effect on the iron shackles. *Curse them.* Frustrated, Magnus wrenched his head about. It was as if the shackles, chains and stake were of a *dead* metal. They would not respond to heat.

"MEN!" Delik shouted a warning.

One of the Quagman turned and looked to Delik, then to Magnus. "Get this wench under control!" the Quagmen demanded of his accomplices. Magnus directed his strength into pulling on his shackles in order to tear the stake from the ground.

"It's pointless, *Balgur,*" the Quagman grunted, clearly recognising Magnus from his time in Ba'rrat's arena where he used the pseudonym 'Balgur' as a tribute to the great dragon slayed by Delvion. "That steel is 'black-steel'. More spells on that than any dragon can unfurl—least of all you. But, by all means, fight it! The more exhausted you are, the easier it'll be for Delvion to deal with you."

Catanya was forced to the ground beside Magnus. Her shackled arms were chained to the same stake he was. The gag from her mouth was pulled free. Catanya spat on the ground next to her and glared at Delik—her eyes wild with anger.

"Catanya!" Magnus slurred his words. Catanya stared at him, blinked, shook her head and stared again.

"Magnus?" Catanya was groggy and her eyes were out of focus.

"You've been concussed."

"How did they catch you?"

"Poison. Somehow... the ale perhaps."

The three Quagmen left the tent in discussion. Magnus looked at Delik who was pacing nervously. Whatever his agenda was, Magnus sensed it was not going entirely to plan. Catanya shimmied over to Magnus, resting her body on his. Magnus looked at the back of her head where she'd been struck. Blood was matted into her hair and over her neck. He looked at Delik again.

"I assume you know what you're doing, Delik?" Magnus asked. Delik drew himself tall. "Delvion and the Quag have fallen in Ba'rrat. You've a thunder of dragons at your doorstep and you hold us captive?"

Magnus's words seemed to agitate Delik even more. His pacing quickened and he started to blink erratically. Magnus continued to stare at Delik but his mind was wandering—no doubt an effect of the nightshade. Flashbacks of the violence in Ba'rrat's arena burst bloodily into sight. *A hundred fights. Then Briet, then father killed Crugion, Lucas killing Ganister and Delvion escaping...*

"Magnus," Catanya said.

Magnus blinked and shook his mind free of the past.

"They know you're the Electus," she whispered.

"I gathered as much." Magnus looked Catanya in the face. Her eyes widened and blinked. She was still suffering the effects of concussion. Magnus was furious. It was the fury he'd become accustomed to and knew he'd inherited from Thioci. Thioci had died, but he went down fighting with fury in his eyes. Whether today or another day, he wondered if he would go the same way.

"So it is true then," Delik stopped his pacing. "You are the Electus." Magnus stared at him. His manner had done a complete about face. He was calm and snake-like, taking everything in. "When did it happen? When did you receive the blood of a dragon?"

Magnus found Delik's erratic change of manner confusing. Was he being serious? Was he allowing his curiosity to override the apprehension he felt moments ago?

There was a cracking sound and Catanya moved restlessly. Another cracking sound made Catanya moan. She pushed her head into Magnus's shoulder and whispered something. Magnus leaned over such that her mouth was at his ear. "I'm free," Catanya whispered again. Magnus looked into her eyes and saw she was actually awake and focused.

Without looking at her further, and to avoid suspicion, Magnus returned his attention to Delik who was still considering him and Catanya, but kept his distance. Magnus gathered the well-groomed artisan was not sure of what to make of them. "What makes you think there was a dragon involved?" He asked Delik in response to his own question. It was a stupid, cryptic question, but he sensed it would intrigue the inquisitive man. Sure enough, a smirk came to Delik's face.

"So, you've found another means of achieving such powers. I suspected this was the case, seeing that the Fire Dragons are still alive. That's not the usual custom—"

"And you think no other Realms possess living dragons, do you?" Magnus interrupted Delik, continuing his folly. Delik was silenced. "You've spent too long away from the realms. Too long in bad company craving what they crave and can't have."

Delik retorted—"A wise man once said to me, 'all virtuous men come to desire power—'"

"'But not all are destined for it.' I've heard it myself," Magnus finished the words Delvion had spoken to him back in Ba'rrat. They gave verification that

Delik had been consorting with Delvion. Delik was silenced. "You see Delvion as a wise man? Wise enough to manipulate you, perhaps."

Suddenly, Catanya was on bended knee with an arm outstretched. Magnus looked at her then back to Delik. He had a knife in his throat. The man staggered while Catanya ignited her lance and used it to split the shackles on Magnus's wrist. Whatever spell kept him from manipulating the steel of the shackles had little defence against her fire-bronze weapon. Magnus got to his feet and caught Delik before he hit the floor. He lowered the man to the ground in silence and retrieved Lucas's sword.

Catanya extinguished her lance and sheathed it, then looked at her hands. Both her thumbs were dislocated. *To free herself of the shackles,* Magnus realised. She snapped her thumbs back into position then felt the back of her head, wincing. "Ouch…" Catanya scrunched her nose.

The three Quagmen re-entered the tent. Magnus stood between them and Catanya. The Quagmen drew their black blades. Magnus drew Lucas's sword and pointed it at the first Quagman.

A GYPSY'S OATH

The fire was hardly necessary. It was a balmy summer evening with a temperate breeze blowing in from the Neverseas to the south. Still, Bonstaph was glad to have it. The fire seemed to give Sarah something to focus on and perhaps even clear her head.

In all the years he had known Sarah—since Ganister has managed to win her gypsy heart—Bonstaph had never seen her like this. *Nor have I needed to tell her such horrific news...* The day after he saw his best friend slain, Bonstaph told Sarah he was killed by Delvion's sorcerer. Amidst the dust and confusion of the violent and political skirmish, Ganister was slain in the flash of an eye. *Six months imprisoned and Ganister never tasted freedom.* Bonstaph believed some justice was paid forward in having slayed Delvion's son that same day. *Twenty years after slaying his eldest son. At least I put an end to his lineage...*

Sarah had listened in silence as Bonstaph explained her husband's death. Not once did she take her eyes off him as he told her everything that had passed. That was two days ago. Sarah had been silent ever since. She stared into the fire for hours, occasionally reaching out with her hands, feeling the flames lick her palms, then drawing back into herself. Bonstaph knew it was more than just mourning she was going through—Sarah's mind was at work.

During the intervening two days, Bonstaph had busied himself forging Brindle into a stronghold of defence. The fortifications to Brindle's west were holding strong, but Bonstaph knew they needed more. He formed a committee with members of the Brindle townsfolk together with refugees who were fleeing captivity in Ba'rrat.

"You need to rid Brindle of its former Quag dictatorship and defend it from invasion. There is no time for lamenting what is lost, nor claiming rights to ownership," Bonstaph explained to the committee. He was taking the role of Commander, but reiterated the need for the committee to be autonomous. He yearned to move on and had a myriad of reasons for wanting to, but he pushed them aside to focus on the task at hand.

By order of the committee, Brindle's regime had to be strict. As each person arrived at the western border seeking refuge, they were vetted. Those too weak to work were provided food and medicine. Everyone else was put to task. Cooks, builders, blacksmiths and swordsmiths were utilised for their skills, others became cleaners, scouts, messengers, or joined the fighting regime. The people were split into working shifts around the clock. Local fisherman and farmers would source food to be cooked in homes then taken to the town square for distribution. Everyone met at the town square for two meals each day. Only those forming the wall of defence were fed at their posts.

Two days in, Brindle was finally running with the precision Bonstaph demanded. One of the young refugees quickly won Bonstaph's confidence and became his right-hand man. He was a tall, wiry lad with curly black hair. Bonstaph guessed he was about Magnus's age. His name was 'Walt'. Walt was a healer, but after months as a slave with shackles on his ankles, being forced to heal wounded Quagmen, all he wanted to do was run. Bonstaph soon learned he was good at it. Walt established a network of runners, mostly made of young boys and girls too slight to build fortifications or wield a sword, and too restless to clean or tend to the sick. Yet, they were fast enough to form a network of communication between Bonstaph, committee members, the fortifications that were extending around the entire perimeter of Brindle, and scouts who monitored the lands as far north as the Black Cliffs.

Bonstaph learned that Walt knew Magnus and was taken into custody at the same time as him. During his time in Ba'rrat, Walt had been able to garner information about the battle in the Uydferlands. Bonstaph learned that the defences of Nuyan were holding strong along the banks of the Nuyan River, and the Quag had abandoned their assault to the north along the Quarry border. But this was not all. Walt also explained Lucas's story in detail, from his altercation with the wyvern until he fled from Csilla's command in the Uydferlands.

For much of the two days in Brindle, Bonstaph grieved for Lucas, for Ganister, and for the truth that Sarah would someday have to learn. However, no matter how he tried to broach the subject, Bonstaph could not bring himself to do so, for he was sure Sarah did not have the strength at this time to cope with such knowledge.

During the day, Sarah had taken on a remedial role in Brindle serving meals in the town square. Bonstaph could see her role allowed her to avoid conversation and intuitive inclinations—both qualities that Sarah used to thrive on. For three nights in a row, Bonstaph had found Sarah resting atop the hill overlooking an abandoned chancel. It was a peaceful spot and gave

Bonstaph an effective vantage spot to survey the township and the fortifications beyond. Bonstaph had lit a fire each night and the two of them would stare at it without conversation.

"Tell me about this sorcerer," Sarah asked on the third night, finally breaking her silence. "What of him now?" Sarah was pushing. Bonstaph knew she would not relent.

"He fled with Delvion. As I could tell, northward over the Black Cliffs toward the Corville Mountains."

"You saw it with your own eyes? You saw the sorcerer flee?"

"Aye. Riding a large mountain wyvern. The largest I've ever seen."

Sarah drew a long stick from the fire and prodded, making wood and embers tumble and flare angrily. "And what did you think, when you saw my husband's killer take his leave?"

Bonstaph was being tested. He should have killed the sorcerer—that is what Sarah wanted to hear him say. "At the time, I cursed after him, swearing I would kill both the sorcerer and Delvion." It was the truth. Bonstaph recalled shouting words to this effect. *Just moments later, Magnus handed me Lucas's sword.*

Sarah threw the stick into the fire and contemplated things a moment longer. "In my lifetime, I will see this sorcerer dead," Sarah finally declared. "As sure as I will find my son and hold him in my arms again." Sarah looked at Bonstaph. "As I have held Magnus these past months. I held him dear to me as a son, Bonstaph."

Bonstaph was without words. Sarah reached beneath her tunic and drew a blade. Wrapping a fist around it, she pulled the blade free, slicing through the flesh of her palm. Blood ran between her fingers and she reached the hand out over the fire. The fire sizzled as her blood dripped over the glowing embers. "A gypsy's oath…"

"Sarah, don't." Bonstaph moved to pull her hand free of the fire but she warned him off with the other hand that still held the blade. Sarah held her bloody hand over the flames that licked at her wound, scorching it. She did not flinch.

"Born of blood and bond of fire. This sorcerer I will see dead in this life."

Sarah's gypsy oath was sealed.

MARSALA

"It's a ghost town. That's all Thwax is." Catanya rubbed her thumbs.

"You'll have aching bones when you're old if you keep dislocating joints like that," Magnus said, smiling. He could not help himself. Catanya frowned and shouldered his arm.

The parched wooden sign marked 'Thwax' lay covered in dust and dead leaves on the overgrown roadside. True as Catanya said, the town seemed to be abandoned. Arriving at night did little to make the place seem inviting. A southerly wind blew misty, salted air from the ocean, cloaking the moonlit coastal town in a blue fog. "So, this is where Eamon says we will find Marsala." Magnus had his doubts. But then… *Nothing is ever straightforward with Eamon.*

It had been two days since they left the artisans' camp east of Brindle. They could have made the journey in one and were inclined to, having slain the three Quagman and Delik. However, Magnus recalled and regretted telling Willem they were headed east. By staggering their progress to Thwax and doubling back a way every few hours, they were certain no one had tracked them.

Magnus felt uneasy with the way he dealt with the three Quagmen back at the camp. He used none of his powers as he did to defeat Briet in the arena, or the Quagman at the river. *'Why was that?'* Catanya had asked him. He could not think to explain to himself, no more to Catanya, why he took them on with sword only. It was a conscious decision that came with risk. But here now in Thwax, cloaked in the blue fog, it seemed to come to a clearer mind.

"It *was* Briet," Magnus lamented. Catanya had been scouting Thwax for any signs of life. She stopped to give her attention to Magnus. "I was always afraid of confronting him again. I'd always run from him. In the arena, I had to face him but I hesitated." Magnus recalled how he wounded Briet, cutting him deep in the thigh. "It was right then, I stood back and hesitated. It was as though I had done what I feared I couldn't do, but then couldn't believe I had done it."

"You hesitated but you overcame him again. He only cut you with his sword after you halted the fight with the blow of the Quag horn." Catanya's voice grew stern. "He broke the rules of the fight and you improvised."

"Aye…" Magnus's thoughts wandered. "I dropped my guard."

"And this is why you fought these Quagmen as you did?" Catanya said. "To reassure yourself that you can beat Delvion's warriors as Magnus-the-swordsman, without the assistance of Magnus-the-Electus?"

"I guess so, yes." Magnus stroked his beard, feeling the sea mist moisture in it.

"Then tell me now, are you reassured? If it comes to it, are you going to take on Delvion with your bare hands for further assurance?"

Magnus was unsure how much Catanya spoke in jest, but she made her point. "I am reassured, Catanya. And I'd rather not face Delvion for any reason."

Catanya stroked Magnus's beard herself. "I think that's a healthy attitude to have."

Magnus and Catanya walked through every building ruin and down every overgrown street of Thwax searching for any sign of Marsala. In time, the ocean breeze abated. Stillness overtook the town. Each step Magnus took crunched over broken rubble—sufficient to give away their whereabouts to any onlooker who may be watching.

"Are you thinking we're being watched?" Catanya asked.

"Aye. By the dead or the living?" Magnus said. Catanya stopped. She reached for her lance. "Catanya. I was making a joke—"

"Over by the jetty. Beneath the lamp." Catanya pointed. A little over fifty yards away, a jetty jutted out over the ocean and into the night. At the very start of the jetty, a lamp was dimly lit. Beneath it was the dark silhouette of a person sitting on a chair.

"That lamp was not lit before." Magnus was sure of it.

"I walked down that jetty earlier, while you were over there." Catanya pointed off to her left.

"What?" Magnus whispered. "We've not left one another's side. Not once the fog blew in."

Magnus and Catanya locked eyes. They looked back to the stranger, unmoving and dark beneath the lamp. Slowly, they walked toward the jetty. Catanya held her sleeping lance. Magnus was ready to draw his sword. Twenty yards short of the jetty lamp, the stranger lifted their head and looked to them. It was a woman. She had the palest of skin and the wildest of hair in every colour imaginable. Some hair sat tall, some hung in matted lengths down her body. Her cheeks each had a small tattoo and her eyelids were painted as dark as her lips. She sat cross-legged on her chair in silence. Having considered Magnus and Catanya, her head lowered. She was knitting what appeared to be a shawl. Without lifting her eyes from her knitting, she spoke.

"You move with less discretion than the priestess." She looked again at Magnus and then Catanya. "Then again, that is what she's trained for." Magnus and Catanya did not move. "Come. I've been waiting for you." The woman stood and placed her chair against the jetty railing then folded her knitting and placed it on top of the chair. "Come!" she said again and walked away toward the centre of the abandoned town.

"Should we follow her?" Magnus whispered to Catanya.

The strange woman shouted back—"Aye, you should! That is why you came. Come!"

Magnus assumed this was in fact Marsala and so he took Catanya's hand and they followed after her.

After a brisk walk along back roads and down a narrow alley Magnus realised they had missed in their search, they stopped at a home. From the outside, it looked no more habitable than any other house in Thwax. The woman extended an arm, inviting them inside a small doorway covered with overgrown vine. The doorway was no more than four foot high in the middle of a cylindrical stone building with a cone-shaped roof that was all but obscured by overgrown lantana. Magnus and Catanya did as she asked and entered.

Inside, candlelight and glowing embers from a fireplace dimly lit the single room dwelling. Magnus found the warmth inviting, but little else was appealing about the room. Everywhere he looked there was mounted and preserved remains of dead animals, or parts thereof. An owl, many cats, an eagle, various species of beetles and bugs and even a deer head with its large antlers protruded into the one-roomed home. Many—in particular the cats— were not mounted at all but stood on the ground as if frozen in time. Between the macabre collections of animals, the walls were stacked high with books, piles of parchments and scrolls of papers. The room had a pungent smell of sage mixed with the sweet, milky scent of burning sandalwood. Magnus found the combination a little overwhelming and Catanya covered her nose discretely as she looked around the room.

"You are Marsala?" Magnus asked the woman.

"That is true. And you are the Electus," Marsala said as a statement rather than a question.

"How do you know Eamon?" Magnus asked, more for his own curiosity than any real need to know. Marsala shook her head and frowned.

"Eamon… He's been around for a long time—a very long time. Certainly a lot longer than you and the pretty-priestess here." Marsala looked at Catanya as though waiting for a reaction. Magnus knew Catanya was not so easily embarrassed. She stared blankly at the mystic woman. "Tell me something." Marsala kept her gaze on Catanya. "The dead priestess you left at the back of the chancel in Brindle. She came to kill you, didn't she?" Catanya reached for her lance, slowly drew it and held it tentatively at her side. Marsala was not deterred and carried on as though Catanya had not reacted at all—"I warned her—I warned that priestess woman. 'Demi' was her name. A year ago now, she were here. I told her there'd be one she'd try to kill who was going to kill her first. I said to her—*'your comeuppance is coming and it'll be from one younger and better than yourself.'*" Marsala shook her head. "No, no, no. She did not like that one bit."

Catanya turned to Magnus. "No wonder Demi didn't like me. From the moment we first met, she must have known it would be me."

"So you *do* speak, then?" Marsala jested. "What may your name be, pretty-priestess?"

"I thought you'd be able to tell me that, witch-lady," Catanya retorted. Magnus placed a hand on Catanya's shoulder to settle her. "I am Catanya," she said. The words looked to be bitter in her mouth.

"You know we are here at Eamon's suggestion?" Magnus produced the letter Eamon sent him and handed it to her.

Marsala waved the letter away. "I have plenty of letters myself." Marsala opened a draw beneath a low table at the centre of the room. She removed a stack of small letters bound and tied off with a piece of string. "Eamon writes to me often. Of late, it's mostly about you." She pointed at Magnus. "The last letter he sent said this…" Marsala licked a finger, prised the top letter from the pile, then read it—

"If Magnus arrives half-naked as he was when he departed my company, and if it suits him so, give him my old Ferustir suit and shape-shift it to him."

Marsala looked Magnus over. "You seem to have found some clothes. All the same, I've spent the last two days removing the artisans' wards that bound

Eamon's suit. Would you like it?" Marsala retrieved the Ferustir armour from a stool.

Magnus looked it over. "But, I'm no Ferustir."

"It's beautiful armour, Magnus," Catanya said, admiring the suit.

"Come, come… I've had little sleep in days stripping the wards from this thing. Would you like it or not?"

"Aye, thank you."

"Then put it on while I prepare supper and tea."

Marsala went to the back of her room and left via discreetly hung curtains leading to another area Magnus had failed to notice before. Footsteps could be heard and it sounded like Marsala was headed down a staircase—perhaps to a basement. In her absence, a small black cat pushed through the curtains just far enough to take a look at the strange guests. It stared at Magnus for a good minute before doing the same to Catanya, then turned and left the room.

Magnus looked at the suit. "Shall I put it on?" He was not certain it was the right thing to do.

"The witch-lady will be annoyed if you don't," Catanya mumbled.

Magnus was quick to strip and Catanya helped him into the Ferustir armour. She buckled the lightweight components, observing where it was similar to hers. It extended to cover his chest, back and abdomen with a plackart ending in a 'v' shape at the waist. Like Catanya's, Magnus saw it was forged of a hard black material. Unlike hers, the material's burgundy weaves threaded into glimmering fire-bronze pieces of armour along the vambraces and greaves that were exquisitely engraved.

"Wow. This *is* beautiful," Catanya remarked as she made final adjustments.

"It's a little loose." Magnus shifted his body about.

"That's where spells come in to play," Marsala said, returning with a tray of food that she placed on the table. The black cat followed and jumped across several piles of books before settling atop the tallest stack in the room, giving it a good vantage point to watch the goings on.

Marsala stood in front of Magnus. "Right then." She placed a hand on the armour covering Magnus's chest. "As Eamon said, it will require a shape-shift to make it fit right." She closed her eyes, took three very deep breaths and mumbled what Magnus assumed was her shape-shift spell. Magnus felt the armour warming over his body. She continued her mumbling spell and the armour's heat continued to build until Magnus began to sweat. He was about to say something when Marsala stopped, stood back and opened her eyes.

"Well?" she asked.

As soon as she asked the question, the suit shape-shifted until each piece was sculptured over Magnus's body as though it was tailored to fit. It felt great. Magnus moved his arms and twisted his body about, hardly believing how nimble he felt. "It's wonderful! Thankyou, Marsala." Magnus looked at Catanya. "Does your suit feel this good?"

"Aye, it does," Catanya smiled. "Until you've been wearing it for weeks on end."

"I've reinforced it with new wards stronger than a Dwyer bull," Marsala explained, opening a wooden chest and removing a pair of long, fire-bronze daggers. She came to Magnus and knelt, sheathing the daggers in holsters either side of the greaves. "And it'll take a Dwyer bull to break the fibres of this armour." She pointed at two chairs. "Now, sit!"

Magnus and Catanya settled into the green leather chairs, each draped in exotic silks and knitted shawls much like the one Marsala had been knitting by the jetty. Magnus felt as if his body was sinking into a billowy white cloud. Catanya sighed a long, moaning sigh and closed her eyes, smiling.

Magnus looked around. The small abode was so different to anything he had seen before, yet it reminded him of Sarah's home back in the western margins, only far more eccentric.

"Eat while it's hot," Marsala said. "It is a stew of sorts, though some would call it soup." The bread is sourdough—fresh this morning. Eat. Then we will talk." Magnus and Catanya thanked her and needed no further enticement, delving into their bowls of stew-soup. The taste was immediately familiar to Magnus. It was just like the food Eamon had cooked back in Froughton Forest long ago. *Too long...* He savoured every drop and could see Catanya did the same.

"Thankyou," Catanya said.

"Yes, thankyou. This tastes a lot like a meal Eamon cooked for me long ago." Magnus said.

"That was not so long ago. And so it should. It is his recipe." Sitting cross-legged in her own chair, Marsala leaned forward, took the teapot sitting on the serving tray and poured three small cups of steaming herbal tea, handing one each to Magnus and Catanya before leaning back and taking sips from her own. "You are at a juncture in your lives." She paused as if waiting for clarification.

"We have been told you could advise us on the best way to get north, perhaps into Froughton Forest," Magnus explained.

"You wish to find your way home?" Marsala asked.

"Perhaps." Magnus was wary about sharing their intentions to travel to the Romghold.

"And what of you, priestess? Do you yearn to return to your home?"

Catanya sipped from her teacup. Her posture stiffened and Magnus could see she was not happy being called 'priestess'. "Yes, I want to go home and find my family. Please though, my name is Catanya. I am no longer a part of the priesthood."

Marsala pointed an accusing finger at Catanya. "Your role as priest is far from over. We are in the dying days of the third age and all players will be brought to the table to make their contribution. You swore an oath to the priesthood. Such oaths are not easily broken."

Catanya nodded as if she understood. Magnus was surprised she would accept Marsala's words, but then she did seem to be getting to something. "Look at Eamon. Long ago he left the priesthood yet here he is, still playing his part at the turn of the tide."

"You know of his history as a priest, then?" Magnus asked.

"I met him soon after he left the priesthood."

"You knew him as 'Steyne'?" Catanya asked.

Marsala paused for reflection. "I will tell you more so that you understand how much you mean to Eamon." She looked into Magnus's eyes. "Do you understand?"

"Aye, I do."

Marsala nodded. "He was lost in life after he left the Irucantî. After all, he had served with them for more than thirty years. Having lost faith in their ways, he travelled aimlessly for a long time, searching for answers. We found sanctuary in one another's company." Marsala smiled. "In time, he transitioned away from 'Steyne' the priest and during this time, I prophesied he would meet the one who would become the Fire Realm Electus. He would guide this Electus, protect them, and offer them wisdom. And so I offered him a new name—'Eamon'—the Paragon word for *protector*. It was many years and a lifetime of travels, but fate brought you together. And here you are now."

The black cat climbed its way down the stack of books and jumped onto Marsala's lap where it settled itself in comfortably, still observing Magnus and Catanya. Marsala stroked the cat as she continued.

"The gods call all of us to a role. Eamon's was to find you."

Magnus was enamoured with Marsala's story. "How did you know all this would come to pass?"

"Look around," Marsala said. "Books, scrolls, journals, maps... Have a gypsy stay in one place long enough, her mind does the journeying for her. I have spent my journey observing patterns, prophecy, evolution, timing... Life seems at once a game of chance, but it is anything but."

"I wonder if Eamon knew I would be the Electus when we first met?"

"I believe his vocation made him aware of the needs of others." Marsala nursed her teacup in the palm of her hand. "He helped you get where you needed to go. The rest was as the gods intended."

"What do you know of Balgur's death? Eamon harbours a lot of guilt over losing his sword to Delvion," Magnus asked. "Delvion, meanwhile, flaunts Balgur's death as a symbol of his greatness."

"You must learn Balgur's side of the story," Marsala said. "Beyond Eamon's sorrow and Delvion's ego, with Balgur you'll find the truth."

THE MARK OF IISILÉE

"Can you see what's in store for us, Marsala?" Magnus asked.

"Show me something dear to yourself, other than pretty-priestess, and I will see what I can see."

Magnus lifted Lucas's sword off the ground beside him. It was the only thing he had, yet, he was unsure he could say it was dear to him. Nevertheless, Magnus handed the sword to Marsala who slowly unsheathed it. She held it as Willem had done a few days before, studying the pommel, the leatherwork and the blade. She finally laid it on the table between them. She grabbed the teapot and trickled some of the herbal tea down the length of the blade and watched the tealeaves float along the metal work.

"A friend as a brother has fallen to darkness."

Magnus was alarmed at how quickly she scried the sword. "You speak of Lucas."

Marsala continued—"This brings pain, death, and but a single chance to reconcile, else fate be challenged."

"Are we not always challenging fate?" Catanya asked.

"Fate is written." Marsala passed a glance at Catanya. "Challenges are a part of life. To survive them and meet your inevitable fate is irony."

"How then, do you see a second chance to reconcile with Lucas to be challenging fate?" Magnus asked.

"Because to do so will be beyond the will of the gods."

"Can you tell me what the gods have planned for Lucas?" Magnus did not want to hear the answer to his own question, but if the answer was forthcoming he had to know. He could feel Catanya looking sympathetically at him.

"I can tell you that this sword is not complete," Marsala explained slowly. "There is another."

"Aye. My own sword—"

"Reconcile them," Marsala interrupted Magnus. "Sooner, rather than later." Her words came off as a warning. "Your friend Lucas will make a veiled appeal for clemency. This will be his single chance." She returned the sword to Magnus, who was more than happy to sheath it again.

Marsala sat cross-legged in her chair again. "As for you two... You will benefit from mutual support. In time, you will garner support from others, but the next part of your journey requires anonymity. You had best find your own way north and not seek help in getting there," Marsala said, ruling out Catanya's idea of asking Färgd for a ride.

"Give me your hands—your left hands." Marsala closed her eyes and reached out, twiddling her fingers. "Come!" Magnus and Catanya both extended their left hand. Marsala took hold of them. Her posture became rigid and her breathing deepened. A minute passed and she shook Magnus's hand away. "*Left* hand, I said." Her eyes were still closed. Magnus and Catanya exchanged puzzled looks. "Come!" Marsala clicked her fingers. "You are left-handed, yes? As you all are from the Fire Realm... Come!"

"That *was* his left hand," Catanya said.

Marsala opened her eyes. Magnus still had his left hand extended. Marsala blinked once and held it again, closed her eyes and resumed her deep breathing, this time twisting her brows in concentration. Moments later she stared at them both. "Pretty-priestess—your parents are of the Fire Realm?"

Catanya rolled her eyes. "Yes."

"And yours?" Marsala considered Magnus.

"My father is. My mother is of the Ice Realm."

"But with your Electus blood, that should be of little consequence. Give me your other hand... quick!"

Magnus did as told and Marsala gripped Magnus's right hand with both of hers.

"Nothing!" Marsala placed the cat on the floor next to her. It scurried back up to its previous position atop a pile of books. Marsala opened another draw beneath the table and removed a well-worn wooden box. She cleared the table of soup bowls and teacups then placed the box at its centre. From inside, she pulled out numerous cloth bags tied with string at their tops. She arranged them in a row, mumbling as she went. "Oak is to the Fire Realm as pine is to the Earth Realm, blossom is to the Air Realm and... the birch tree is to the Ice Realm."

Birch tree... Magnus thought. "My mother planted many birch trees around our lands. They reminded her of home."

"Yes, birch tree it is." Marsala selected the bag labelled 'birch'. She placed it before Magnus. "Open it."

Magnus loosened the string and upturned the bag. A dozen thin sticks of birch wood slid out into the palm of his hand. Each had a unique symbol carved into it. The symbols were foreign to him.

"Rune sticks," Catanya remarked.

"Aye. Now hold them firmly in your hands." Marsala leant forward and held Magnus's hands, clasping them gently around the sticks, all the while careful not to touch them herself. She sat back with her arms wide and watched.

Magnus took a deep breath and closed his eyes. A vision of his mother came to mind as clear as a dream—as clear as the dream he had of her the day he left Ba'rrat. They were standing in a field of pure white snow. The sky was a cloudless blue so bright it was almost blinding. Alavia was right there, wearing the same azure robe Magnus had seen in his previous dream. She had a serious expression on her face. Behind her, in the distance and waiting in silence, was a legion of hundreds of horse-mounted warriors. *Rhydermere...* The Rhydermere were all on white Astermeers or silver Wardemeers whose hides reflected the snow. Magnus looked to his mother. Her expression had softened, but her sapphire eyes burned as brilliant as blue flames.

"Magnus..." Alavia's voice blew over as a whisper... a warning. The sky, the snow and Alavia's eyes began to burn white, blinding Magnus for a moment. When his vision returned, Magnus was standing alone in the snowfield, now a forest of birch trees stripped of their leaves and iced over in winter frost.

Magnus's heart ached and he choked on his emotions. *I miss her...*

"Magnus, are you okay?"

Magnus opened his eyes and blinked away tears. He saw the concern on Catanya's face.

"Yes, yes," enthused Marsala. "Now cast the sticks across the table. Let us see."

Magnus did so, sending the twelve sticks scuttling across the top of the table. The sticks rolled and spun over one another before coming to a stop.

"Now..." Marsala studied the arrangement of fortune-telling rune sticks. Her eyes carefully moved from one stick to another and back again. She spent quite some time examining the arrangement and then cast her hands over the sticks and whispered a spell—a spell Magnus thought was in gypsy tongue. However, midway through the spell, her voice faltered and a shocked expression washed over her face. Magnus looked from her to the sticks, wondering what the problem was. The sticks were changing. They were starting to form ice on them and soon they were frozen over, just like the birch trees in his daydream. Marsala's face turned even paler than normal. Magnus watched on, unsure what to do or say.

"Marsala!" Catanya shouted.

Marsala blinked herself back to attention. Then, in one violent swoop, she wiped the table clean of the frozen rune sticks. The black cat arched its back and hissed. Marsala jumped up on her chair, distancing herself from the sticks that were scattered across the floor. Magnus and Catanya looked on in disbelief as the sticks turned luminous white then shattered like glass into a million pieces. Magnus felt a pang of cold shoot through his entire body making him jolt forward from his chair.

"What just happened?" Catanya asked.

"A future kept untold to keep a veiled truth!" Marsala raised her arms, splaying her fingers. Her eyes were as wide as the cats. "But the spell itself is revealed." She looked to the cat, which hissed again. Marsala nodded and hissed in reply.

"What are you saying?" Magnus asked, shivering from the persistent chill.

"You've a spell on you!"

"To keep a *veiled truth*? There's no truth to me the whole of Allumbreve will not soon know."

"What we saw just now was not a spell of fire." Marsala jumped to her feet and paced about the room, her eyes still wild with wonder. "Frozen, shattered rune sticks," she mumbled. "That was a spell of the Ice Realm! What truths are hidden, even from you?" Marsala's accusing finger pointed at Magnus this time.

"I have always been of mixed-blood," Magnus said.

"Until your blood was replaced," Catanya added. "Your blood is Thioci's blood now."

"Perhaps..." Marsala mumbled.

Magnus felt himself begin to succumb to a familiar sickness—that of 'Anunya'. He grunted and looked at Catanya who sighed and gave a nod, for she knew what he was going through. Magnus's vision began to fade. The strange, shooting cold he felt before was quickly washed away by more familiar flushes of heat and nausea, dizziness and perspiration. Through the delirity of Anunya he heard Catanya appeal to Marsala for assistance.

Before long, Marsala was pushing a cup to Magnus's lips, which he drank from greedily, hoping that whatever she was giving him would work as well as the elixir Eamon had given him back in Ba'rrat. It did, and his faculties returned quickly. Magnus rose from the ground, surprised to see Marsala kneeling in front of him. She lifted his chin and stared deep into his eyes. Magnus did the same, examining the mystic's bright green eyes—eyes that reminded him of the 'Meliae'—the seductive creature of the trees back in Froughton Forest.

"Rhuderburry," she said. "That's done the trick?" Magnus nodded. "You have been getting sick like this ever since receiving the bond?" Marsala had a serious tone in her voice.

"Aye."

"That is not right… even for the Electus." Marsala continued to stare. "Your body should have adapted long ago." Marsala scratched one of her coloured, matted locks of tangled hair. She turned quickly to Catanya. "Pretty-priestess, when did Anunya subside for you?"

"My fever broke on the fifth day," Catanya said.

"And you—six months or longer?" Magnus nodded again. It felt like an eternity to him. "Too long… even for the Electus."

"Then why does it persist?" Catanya questioned. Magnus felt like a child being examined by a healer with a concerned mother asking after him.

"There is a fight within you." Marsala jabbed a finger toward Magnus. "The blood of the dragon should have taken control by now but something fights back—Something that stakes a claim over you."

Marsala got up and ran around the room, checking the spines of her books. She searched feverishly, mumbling as she went. Eventually she returned to the table with a large, thickly set book and placed it on the table. Its leather cover was pale blue and embossed with silver glyphs Magnus recognised as 'Iceralma'—the realmish language of the Ice realm. Magnus knelt by the low set table and studied the book closer as Marsala opened it and leafed through the pages feverishly, licking her index finger every third or fourth page.

"This is a copy of the 'Iceralem'. It is the almanac of the Ice realm. It was gifted to me from a cousin of mine. Tell me, what do you know of your mother's ancestors? Which clan was she of—Imnf? Weíra? Rhyder?"

Magnus was most curious as to the relevance of her line of questioning. "She is of the Rhyder clan. None other survived the wars of the north. Her father was an elder. 'Hasledom' was his name. He was one of the Rhydermere, as were his sons."

"And his father before him? Do you know his name?" Marsala seemed to be growing impatient, flicking quickly through the pages toward the end of the book.

"I do not know," Magnus said. He had no recollection of his mother talking about her grandfather.

"Think!" Marsala insisted.

"I do not know his name, Marsala—I swear to you." However, he did remember Sarah's 'history' lesson back in the dungeons in Ba'rrat. Sarah said his great grandfather was... "He was the youngest of four sons." Magnus said.

Marsala pushed a finger firmly into a page of the book. She began to read from it—

"Iisilée, Female Ertwe Ice dragon of the third age.
"Bonded to Hasdereq, the youngest of four sons of the Rhyder clan. Iisilée deceased.
"Hasdereq had one son of his own named Hasledom.
"Hasledom had three sons of his own and one daughter.

"Hasledom's sons are not named..." Marsala looked at Magnus who realised now what she was alluding to. "Neither is his *daughter.*"

"You are thinking my great grandfather was Hasdereq? The daughter... is my mother?"

"Indeed—and inheritor of the bond of Ice from *Iisilée*. Which means you, Magnus, have *two* powers struggling within you."

ALAVIA

"Stop."

The Rhydermere cavalry drew to a halt in perfect formation along the cliffs of the Western Margins. One hundred fifty Astermeers, thrice as many Wardemeers together with their Rhyders, formed a mile long entourage. From beyond the cliff tops the sea winds blew, tugging and furling their dark blue robes and long blonde hair. Calmly, they waited.

Leading the cavalry, Alavia alighted from Isêr—her newly sworn Astermeer. She glanced over the cliffs to the impenetrable storm-grey waves of the Neverseas. The waves slammed against the vertical cliffs with an explosive roar of foam. Alavia drew on the ocean's salty scent and felt it's formidable strength permeate her body. It was different to the Ice Seas of the north. It was more temperate, more… *forgiving*. Even so, she welcomed the ocean's strength and manipulated it to suit her body's needs, allowing a curt chill to course through her body.

Alavia turned eastward to look across the J'esmagdlands. Holding dark thoughts at bay, she addressed her first in command—"Remain here." Her intense, sapphire-blue eyes conveyed her conviction. Such conviction made all but the most steadfast of the Rhydermere take a step back. It was the steadfast among them Alavia chose as her 'Rhydermaël'—her commanding Rhyders.

Isêr ran.

The Astermeer moved as a white spectre. She carried her foresworn toward the homestead ruins. Isêr possessed flighty energy. Her youth gave her agility. Alavia knew over time such traits would mature into the fortitude Breona had. They arrived at the gravel-strewn courtyard before the burnt carcass of her former home. Beside the still-intact stone well, Alavia alighted once again.

Isêr trod tentatively. Alavia sensed the mare had found Breona's scent as she sniffed about, paying particular attention to the soot-tainted horse trough. Alavia drew a pale of water from the well and placed it before Isêr to drink.

"Thank you…" Isêr shared her thoughts.

Alavia was hardly listening, but Isêr's thoughts served to remind her once again of Breona. Alavia learned months ago that an Astermeer had died and was found in the Valley of Shadows. She knew it was Breona. She had experienced an overbearing sense of loss some time before this, when her connection with Breona, which was distant and remote since they had parted ways, had come to a sudden end.

Alavia's eyes were intense again, staring at the well. Her long fingers reached for a folded towel that still rested on the well's stone wall. After all these months the towel still held her son's scent. Her heart skipped a beat. She drew her shoulders back, gripped the pommel of *Iisfael*—her Icerealmic sword—and drew a terse breath. This was not the first time Alavia had visited here since escaping the Quag prison carriage months before.

Many months before, in a Quag prison carriage headed to Ba'rrat...

'I beg of you, Alavia,' Bonstaph had insisted. *'We have stood together. We do not need to die together. Find our son.'*

The prison carriage was in the middle of the Southern Wastelands, beyond the Corville Mountains. Ganister had explained how he rescued Magnus from their burning homestead. She was relieved, until he explained further how he had put Magnus to task—sending him to Guame to get help. As night fell, the merciless Wasteland winds gave over to the cold, northern ice winds.

The night was cold. Conditions were perfect...

To escape, Alavia would need to draw on powers long hidden. Bonstaph knew this and knew what it meant for Alavia to draw on a power she swore long ago to never reveal. But Alavia agreed. She withdrew into a corner of the carriage and began the process of creating a 'negating' spell. It was a spell to undo a spell and it was complicated. Alavia had crafted the masking spell many years before when Magnus was only two years old and had just started to exhibit traits of her power. She had been thorough with its execution. No stone was left unturned in creating an untraceable spell to mask her past and Magnus's inheritance of it. Alavia's negating spell would lift the mask for her but keep it in place for Magnus. After hours of manipulation, she wielded the spell. It took but a moment to take effect.

Alavia then braced herself for what was to come. A searing chill coursed through her, plummeting her body's temperature as low as an Ertwe Ice dragon's. She held firm to a steel bar of the prison carriage and it iced over, cracking the steel through. With a twist of the wrist the bar snapped clean.

She had her way out. Alavia gave Bonstaph a final embrace. The cold of her body had shocked him.

"Do what ever you have to do," Bonstaph said.

"I will do far more than that…" Alavia promised.

Bonstaph and Ganister created a distraction. They targeted one of the Quag warriors, ridiculing him to the point of eliciting fury. Other Quagmen moved in to diffuse the situation. Alavia then lowered her body temperature ever further and created a ward to mask her scent. In the dark chill of night, she was untraceable to the patrolling wyverns.

She slipped away.

Alavia had then headed directly west to the coast and followed the goat tracks along the cliff faces of the Western Margins. Cloaked in darkness and cold as ice, Alavia encountered several wyverns patrolling the coast. They were unable to feel her heat, unable to draw her scent. Once Alavia was safely north of the Corville Mountains, the wyverns no longer patrolled and she was able to lift her ward and breathe heat back into her body. She then walked overland to the J'esmagd homelands. The lands had been abandoned by the Quag—their job done and the fighting shifted to the Uydferlands.

Alavia had sat on one of the collapsed hardwood beams that lay brittle on the foundation of her destroyed home. She reflected on the fact that this was the second time her family had been destroyed. Alavia screamed long and hard, way beyond the point of pain, stopping only when her breath was depleted. She coughed blood. An ice chill rose from her chest and washed over her throat making her shudder as it healed the wound. Alavia swallowed hard, pushing the chilled blood down her throat and in its place she embraced an icy demeanour.

Sweeping debris aside with her boots, Alavia knelt to the stone foundations, beneath which her path was hidden. It had always whispered over the years like a ghost of the past, waiting for such an occasion. Even so and even now she refused to see it as inevitable. *Nothing writes the fate of the Rhydermere. Nor even the fate of their Electi.* Alavia's gaze focused on a specific stone in the ground. It was the very stone from which she had averted her attention for eighteen years. She gave no pause for reflection on what it meant and what she was about to do. Instead, Alavia recalled the gypsy enchantment Sarah had shown her to keep her past hidden beneath the earth—*"Líf letta."*

The stone rose an inch. Alavia drew the stone out with fingertips, revealing the hidden chamber beneath. She fed an arm into the chamber and removed three packages wrapped in suede and bound tight with fine, silver rope. A second spell was Icerealmic—*"Sho-ve-aal."* The silver ropes flashed a white light, releasing their hold on the packages. Unwrapping them, Alavia was immediately confronted with her Icerealmic past. The first package contained her tailored Rhyder outfit in storm-grey with pointed grey knee-high boots. The second contained her long, azure robe. The remaining package she had kept wrapped.

Alavia had then carried her belongings to the stone well. She drew a pail of water and removed her clothes, washing herself clean, paying special care to her long, blonde hair. She dried with a folded towel that still rested beside the well—it smelt of Magnus... *He must have used it to wash when last he was here...*

Alavia had then dressed in her Rhyder outfit, her boots and her robe. She wrung her long, straight hair free of water and brushed it out, leaving it to hang over her robe where it fell to her waist. She then reached for the third package, hesitated, and cast her eyes once again at her destroyed family home. This had been her second chance at life. It was a new beginning with a fate unwritten. *It was a beautiful life.*

Alavia threw back the wraps from the long object and stared at it—a five-foot sword carved from the purest of fleu-steel. Its name was 'Iisfael'. It was an Icerealmish longsword that belonged to her father. The sword was named after an ice dragon as all Icerealmic swords were, and Iisfael was Iisilée's mother. Alavia had inherited it as the sole survivor after her father's murder and the subsequent murder of her siblings and grandfather. And now, perhaps, her son would not survive to inherit it, or the powers of his forbearers. In her ice-cold mind she had assumed the worst. History was being repeated and hiding from it would no longer suffice.

Alavia wrapped fingers about the grip of Iisfael's pommel, felt the texture of the white leather, and drew it from its matching scabbard. A flash of pale blue light had danced about the hilt of the sword and across Alavia's hand—as if familiarising itself with her—before spiralling down its blade and dissipating. "Not good enough," Alavia whispered. She gripped harder. This time the blue light built, at first from the pores in the back of her hand then creeping along her fingers and down the length of the sword. The Icerealmish steel of the blade revealed Icerealmic glyphs that blazed a bright ice blue. She had then walked to the horse trough and thrust the blade deep into the water. With an eerie crackling sound, the water froze over. Alavia drew Iisfael from the ice and sighed a long, deep breath until the blade had calmed, mellowing back to its resting state of white.

Alavia had then heard movement behind her. She spun the sword about and pointed it toward a pair of dark eyes that were staring at her from behind. It was 'Staeda'—Bonstaph's brown Wardemeer horse. Staeda stood, waiting for her response. Alavia sheathed her sword. *"Come."* Staeda came as told, walking out from the half-burned stables, still wearing a saddle across his back. Alavia gathered the wraps from her parcels and rest them over the well's wall. She folded the towel again and drew one more time on Magnus's scent, placing it where she found it. She then climbed into Staeda's saddle and charged northward to the Ice Realm and the lands of the Rhydermere beyond the Ice Breach.

At the homestead in the J'esmagdlands again, a full winter, spring and half a summer later, Alavia replaced the towel for the last time on the stone well. It would indeed be the last time she would stand here—that she was certain of. The sound of horses galloping from the west drew Alavia from her reverie.

"I said to remain where you were," Alavia said as the approaching Rhydermaël and two flanking Rhyders drew their steeds to a stop.

"A messenger brings word, Ma'am—from the south," the Rhydermaël spoke.

"How far south?"

"Ba'rrat." The Rhydermaël alighted and came to Alavia with a scroll.

Clenching her jaw, Alavia stared a moment into her subordinates eyes. She took the scroll from the man. It was sealed with dark blue wax imprinted with the Ice Realm symbol of two icicles. Breaking the seal, Alavia unfurled it. The message was addressed to her, written first hand by one of her scouts. Positioned in Ba'rrat, he had witnessed the destruction of the Black Capitol at the hands of the Couldradt Fire dragons and the Irucantî. And there was more.

Alavia looked to her men and dismissed them. With silent bows, they turned and rode westward to the cavalry. Alavia reread the latter part of the scout's message—

"… Furthermore, I have news of both your husband and your son…"

Alavia walked to the well, tore up the scroll and threw the scraps down the long, dark shaft. She then walked to the rise in the field, north of the homestead. Here, she sat cross-legged facing southward—toward Ba'rrat.

After some contemplation, Alavia formulated her second negating spell. This time, it would lift the masking spell from Magnus.

Alavia knew full well Magnus would no longer be hidden from his Icerealmic past, nor keep his powers in hibernation. She prayed though, to the god of Ice, that the mark of Iisilée would save his life.

SPELLS

"How could I never have known my mother was an Electi of the Ice Realm?" Magnus searched for memories that would hint at the truth. The process was futile.

"The first thing you need to get your head around is this, Magnus," Marsala was emphatic. "Your mother was protecting you, not lying to you—know the difference."

Magnus was sure Marsala was right and told her how Alavia's family was killed by the Quag.

"The rune sticks shattered as part of the spell's process—to veil the truth. Anything revealing your connection to Hasdereq or Iisilée places you in danger. Your mother knows the Quag would never cease trying to kill you."

"With the strength of the Electus, I could have protected myself." Magnus tried to counter Marsala's reasoning.

"Her family was slaughtered. They were all Electi and well-trained Rhydermere. You were a child."

"I think your mother was very clever," Catanya contributed.

"I can see that," Magnus conceded. "It's just... difficult knowing my mother hid from something so powerful for so long." Magnus had a thought and shared it with Marsala. "If my mother's spell hides Iisilée's blood in me, why then does Thioci's blood not finish its process?"

"Your mother has not taken her strength from you, she has masked it. I doubt anything can take it from you, not even Thioci's blood." Marsala put a finger to her lips as she pondered. "Thioci was intent on protecting you. Is there any way Thioci could have known you carried Iisilée's blood?"

Magnus immediately thought of Breona. She was the reason he faced Crugion, Briet and the other two Quagmen in the clearing in Froughton Forest. It was Breona who charged forth to protect the dragon youngling. "I was just following Breona," Magnus half mumbled to himself. He shook his head, piecing things together as Marsala was suggesting. "Breona... my mother's Astermeer. She would have known for certain. She spoke with Thioci before she died." Magnus knew Breona had made a connection with Thioci. His mind was permanently etched with a vision of the two of them looking at one another. "Breona told me that I had my mother's heart—that I was the 'chosen one'. Thioci then said Breona had 'shown' him… that I was the Electus."

"And you were badly wounded. For some reason, Iisilée's blood did not heal you. Thioci acknowledged the Electus power within you thanks to Breona and decided you should live."

"And in doing so, made Magnus a *double* Electus," Catanya concluded.

"Precisely."

Catanya stared at Magnus as if waiting for him to comment on their collective deduction. Magnus stood and paced about the small room. This was far too much to comprehend.

"It seems you owe your life to two mystical creatures… *three* actually, if you count Iisilée." Marsala grinned.

After Magnus's overwhelming revelations, Marsala suggested he get some fresh air and asked Catanya if she could spend some time with her alone. Magnus agreed and went for a walk. Marsala turned her attention to Catanya.

"Pretty-priestess, the whole time you've been here you've had a strong scent of jasmine oil to you."

"Everyone is telling me that," Catanya said.

"You should use a little less. It gives notice of your presence where you may wish to remain anonymous." Marsala nodded at her own advice.

"I've not used jasmine oil since leaving Nuyan," Catanya retorted, wondering why it was such an issue.

'That is interesting." Marsala directed Catanya to sit again and stood behind her. "If you don't mind, I'd like to check for any impediments placed upon you."

"Impediments?" Catanya said. "I believe my Semsdi did this in the Romghold." Even as she said it, Catanya's heart jolted a stern warning just as it had in the artisans' camp. Once again she remembered back to when her Ferustir suit was being made. Joffren supervised as Delik's sorcerers checked her mind for spells and curses that may have been placed upon her. A feeling of dread ran through her as before in the form of an unwelcome chill. *Joffren… Delik… the sorcerers…*

Marsala placed her hands on Catanya's head, splaying her fingers over Catanya's temples. Almost immediately Catanya felt the mystic's presence in her mind.

"I'll share thoughts with you as I go so you know where I am and what I'm doing," Marsala explained, telepathically.

"Very well," Catanya reluctantly agreed.

"Your thoughts are your own, I'm just looking for any sign of—"

"Any sign of what?" Marsala was silent. *"Marsala? What are you looking for signs of?"*

"This!"

Catanya's thoughts flushed with a vision of her mother—

Alessandra was young—no older than Catanya was in that moment. She nursed a baby in her lap and was singing to her. Her mother had a vial of fluid. She was dabbing it on her fingers and smearing it across the baby's forehead, cheeks and chin, singing a Fireisgh enchantment as she went. She said her name repeatedly—'Catanya… Catanya…' The fragrance of jasmine crossed Catanya's nose. Then the vision changed. Her mother was gone and her baby self was gone. They were replaced with a shadowed, overbearing presence like an all-seeing eye watching over her. The fragrance of jasmine became overbearing. It was as though she were drowning in it. Then, all of a sudden, it was gone.

Catanya opened her eyes and spun her head about. "What did you do to me?"

Marsala stood back. "Did you see him? Did you see your Semsdi in your thoughts?"

"No," Catanya replied. "I saw my mother with me as a baby. She was placing enchantments on me, just as Joffren and the sorcerers observed back in the Romghold."

"He has done more than observe you, pretty-priestess. Your Semsdi placed a spell on you. Your mother's protective enchantments were made with jasmine oil—a rhythmic essence that is powerful at night when you are most vulnerable, and wanes during the day. He knew this. His spell piggybacked off these enchantments, enhancing the scent, allowing you to be tracked. All a tracker had to do is utter the words of your mother's enchantment and they would be drawn to you."

Catanya was shocked. "Can you remove the spell?"

"I just have."

Catanya breathed a sign of relief. "You're sure it was him? I sensed a shadow but could not see its source."

"Aye. He covered his tracks, but I saw him in the spell, just as you saw your mother. Catanya, your Semsdi obviously wanted to keep a close eye on you. He did not trust you."

"Joffren…" It was then Catanya realised—"Joffren told the spell to Demi who used it to track me to the old chancel in Brindle. At least I can rest knowing the line of deception ended there."

"And I'm betting she tracked you at night, when the scent was strongest?"

"Aye," Catanya said.

"To meet her inevitable fate," Marsala concluded. "Like I said—that is irony."

Catanya considered a further irony—Eamon was to send Joffren to Marsala for healing. "Marsala, have you received notice from Eamon about Joffren?"

"Aye. He should be here soon enough. I've handled characters more difficult than him before. We'll see where his fate takes him soon enough, pretty-priestess."

Time alone gave Magnus the chance to settle his mind while walking the silent, crumbling streets of Thwax. The rising sun drew away straggling remnants of ocean mist. Magnus walked toward the jetty where the fog still clung and tried to make sense of Marsala's revelations. *Why does fate see us finding sanctuary in the house of a mystic who makes riddles of our lives?* He knew the answer to his own question—"Eamon." Magnus had learned not to doubt his friend, but he was starting to have doubts about himself. He was only beginning to understand what it meant to be the Fire Realm Electus and now… *Now I'm being told I've always been the Electus, but of a realm I know nothing about.*

Fire made sense to Magnus. He was drawn to it. He craved its comfort and reassurance. Thioci's blood warmed him during the lonely nights in Ba'rrat and healed him when he was wounded. He knew how to manipulate fire. He could create it and he respected it. But not ice. Ice was cold and chilling. It seemed heartless, merciless and unyielding. He thought of his mother and saw none of these traits in her. *Then again, what do I really know of my mother?*

Magnus drifted the length of the jetty. He was still acclimatising to the uncanny fit of Eamon's Ferustir armour. It felt so nice against his body and thinking about it took his mind off his mother, Iisilée and the Ice Realm. An involuntary smile came to his face. He caught its reflection as he passed a small steel cabinet mounted on a jetty lamp pole. He doubled back to look again and this time, the reflection stole his smile. A chill ran through his body at what he was seeing. His eyes were luminescent blue—just like his mother's in the dream. He did not recognise himself for this one difference. Reeling away, he stumbled to the other side of the jetty and held himself against the old railing. He peeked back at his reflection. Through fog, all Magnus could make out were those eyes. Looking away again, Magnus loped to the end of the jetty.

The end railing was half missing. He sat and leaned against what remained of it. Here at the end of the jetty, over the petrol blue sea, it was cold. *He* was cold. Magnus folded his arms across his chest. He had not felt cold since before he met Thioci.

It was Catanya's turn to pace about Marsala's living room. She glared at the black cat that was eying her as she circled. "It seems whenever I wade through the depths of deceit among the priests, there's a deeper, more insidious layer to be negotiated." Catanya cursed and looked at Marsala. She felt a fool for carrying on. "I'm sorry, Marsala. It's not my place to speak this way in your home."

"Catanya," Marsala interjected. Catanya studied her. It was the first time the mystic had used her name. "You're a strong woman and entirely entitled to speak your mind."

Catanya blinked away shock. Of all Marsala's riddles and revelations, she did not expect this.

"You're a good person and a warrior. And I can see you're brilliant at both."

"Thank you." Catanya felt awkward, but was grateful for the compliments.

"As for you and your lover out there," Marsala whispered firmly. "Your fates are tied. In fact, your fate is tied to all of this, pretty-priestess." Catanya smiled, now more appreciative of the nickname. "Yes… you are most certainly meant to be lovers. Any path you choose where you are parted ends in tragedy."

Catanya let the mystic's words settle then reached for clarification. "Do you mean 'parting company', or 'a parting of the minds'?"

"At times, you'll find yourselves at loggerheads. Perhaps even at opposite ends of this world. So long as you remain true to each other, it will serve you both well."

As long as we are 'true to each other?' Catanya felt a pang of guilt for having kissed Dale back at the artisans' camp, even though it was to serve a purpose.

"There will be temptations and interests for both of you." Catanya was glad Marsala turned away as she spoke. "There is one who would gain much to have you as a suitor. And not just him—his kinsmen would gain much as well."

Catanya was intrigued. "But it would lead to tragedy, you say."

Thinking, Marsala put a finger to her lips again. "It would certainly make things interesting, yes. In fact, others have ambitions of their own that will make the Electus a desirable suitor, too."

Catanya turned away, feeling awkward at Marsala's prophecies.

"I think I'll find Magnus, if you don't mind."

"Come see me before you go," Marsala insisted.

Magnus had been leaning over the railing at the end of the jetty. He was looking into the blue water as it splashed rhythmically over the rotting pylons that sunk deep to the ground below. He wondered at the men who built it. Was it in times before the Quag arrived in Allumbreve? Were they part of a bustling town, thriving with its fishing trade, their children running and leaping from the jetty in summer, spending winters at warm fires in the white-stone cottages that now lay in ruins? He thought of his own home, most certainly in ruins. In another time, in another age, would a young man like him walk through the ruins and wonder who lived there?

"How are you doing with all this, Magnus?"

Magnus gritted his teeth, turned to Catanya and waited for her reaction to what he had seen in his reflection. Instead, she wrapped her arms around him and look fondly into his eyes.

"Our fates are tied," Catanya smiled. "We are meant to be lovers, according to Marsala." She raised a cheeky eyebrow. Magnus tried to share her humour, but was feeling more than a little out of sorts. Catanya's smile slipped away. "Your eyes…"

"You see that?"

"They're so blue." Catanya stared so close their noses almost touched. Magnus blinked. Catanya leapt back. "Magnus!"

"You see it?" Magnus was desperate to know. "What do you see?"

"You're eyes just…" Catanya shook her head slowly. "For a moment there, it was like…"

"Like staring at my mother."

"Exactly!"

Magnus sighed. He crossed his arms again, shivering.

"Are you cold? I didn't think you got cold."

"Not since Thioci gave me his blood," Magnus said. "I'm thinking what Marsala said has some truth to it."

"Magnus, your eyes have been different since I found you in Ba'rrat. They change with your mood. Perhaps... perhaps this is just another mood." Catanya feigned a smile. Magnus could tell she no more believed what she was saying than he did.

"Something is not right. I've been living with this for six months, but just now, something has changed, Catanya." Magnus looked at the palms of his hands then turned them over. There were a few scars, but none were earned after he met Thioci, courtesy of the healing powers of dragon blood.

Magnus scrunched his hands into fists and squeezed them tight, waiting for Thioci's fire dragon blood to course its way through his body and build in his fists. Catanya watched closely.

"What do you feel?"

At first there was nothing, but Magnus's entire body soon started to warm over. The warmth turned to heat and the heat spread through his body, as he was accustomed to. The relief made him sigh—he was glad for the familiar feeling. Magnus relaxed his hands. "I feel better."

Catanya hugged him again, staring into his eyes. "There you are—the Magnus I know. Your normal *new* eyes... Blue with a kind of amber ring pulsing about them."

"True?" Magnus was beginning to think he should look at his reflection more often. "You never mentioned this before."

"I was so glad to have you back. I knew you were the Electus. I guess I expected something to have changed, other than the obvious." Magnus looked at Catanya to see if she was being serious. "Well, look..." Catanya explained, "I've been living with dragons for the past six months. It kind of changes your view on what's normal."

"I imagine it does." Magnus held Catanya's face in his hands and kissed her. Her familiar touch was like a blissful remedy to the changing world around him. "I kind of like what's normal."

"So do I."

They kissed again then started to walk back to Marsala's home.

Marsala was waiting in the street. She had packed provisions into a pair of duffle bags that she gave to Magnus and Catanya. She also handed each of them a dark coat. "Here, you look conspicuous marching about in Ferustir suits. Also, I've a horse you can take. Come."

Marsala led them back into the house, through the curtains at the back of the room and down a flight of stairs. At the bottom of the stairs, Magnus saw a kitchen through an archway to the right. Marsala continued ahead to a door at the back of the house leading to a garden covered with trained vines over a large pergola. Grazing in the back of the garden was a horse.

"This is Tilly. She's no Astermeer, but she'll get you where you need to go. You be patient with her, she'll be patient with you."

"A little like Mr Overstreet?" Magnus smiled, remembering Eamon's old donkey.

"Yes! She's a lot like Mr Overstreet!" Marsala chuckled. Her smile reminded Magnus of Sarah once again. "When you get to where you need to go, send Tilly on her way. She'll follow her nose to Kreeluck on the Traas River where my mother lives. I'll fetch her before winter."

Magnus and Catanya thanked the mystic for her hospitality and packed their gifted belongings onto Tilly's saddle. Then Marsala handed something to Magnus. It was a Juniper stone.

"I'm sure Eamon has shared the benefits of these?"

"Indeed," Magnus said, thinking of the numerous times a Juniper stone had come in handy during his travels.

"Good. You've a small breast pocket in your suit. Keep it handy."

Magnus tucked the stone away as Marsala instructed.

"Farewell, Magnus. Farewell, Catanya."

"Farewell, Marsala."

Magnus and Catanya set course for the Red River.

FIRST WAVE

"Commander!"

Bonstaph stuck his chin out and itched his dirty beard, turning away from the voice. He spat blood on the ground. It had been a rough night. After leaving Sarah to dwell on her 'gypsy oath' that effectively condemned her son to death, Bonstaph threw himself into an altercation with two Quagmen who insisted on testing the patency of the newly assembled fortifications to the north. It was a bloody scuffle, but served as a valuable lesson to the greener swordsman of Brindle—Quag warriors are brutal in battle. *Move to attack. Don't stand and defend. Fight hard and fight once,'* Bonstaph has instructed.

Now there was Walt, who insisted more than most on addressing him as 'Commander.'

"Commander!"

"For the love of the Gods, Walt…"

"Sorry, sire." Walt bowed awkwardly, breathless from his run. "It's just that… I grew up with stories of your achievements during your time with the Knights of the Realms."

"It was before you were born, Walt. Move on."

Walt was not the only one digging up the past, but Bonstaph knew he was the catalyst for an awful lot of it. As chief runner, Walt was effective at getting information from one end of Brindle to the other faster than Bonstaph could ever have hoped for. Frustratingly, Walt usually delivered this information as instructions from 'the Knight Commander'.

"What have you got for me?" Bonstaph asked.

"The census is done. Everyone is accounted for."

Bonstaph had put the runners to task the previous afternoon to do a census of every person in Brindle. The town's population before Ba'rrat fell was just over three hundred and thirty. "Break it down for me, Walt."

"There is five short of nine hundred souls in Brindle," Walt said, bouncing on his feet. Walt gave him the numbers of men, woman, children and wounded. Bonstaph turned the figures over in his head. When he was done, he gave Walt another task.

"Call a committee meeting in one hour in the town square. I want every member there."

The calculations verified a hard truth—there were not enough resources to sustainably feed the swelling population in Brindle. Not for long, anyway.

Bonstaph paced the northern defence line, turning numbers over in his head. It was important to keep ahead of the game. Even without Ba'rrat strip-mining Brindle of its fish, meat and crops, the townsfolk would soon realise they cannot support such a large influx of people. *That could lead to disorder,* Bonstaph knew. *Nothing will weaken the town's defences more effectively.*

The paradox was that many of the extra people were essential to man the defence at Brindle's borders. Bonstaph needed a plan to solve issues of supply and defence. Fortunately, the solution came in the form of a third need. Many of the recent arrivals were keen to move on to their homes and of these, most were from the Four Realms north of the Corville Mountains. For them, Bonstaph knew it would be a perilous journey home. They needed an effective strategy of departure and protection.

An hour later, the forty men and women of Brindle's committee were gathered in the town square. Walt placed a wooden stool at the square's centre for Bonstaph to stand on to give his announcement. To his right, Bonstaph saw Sarah collecting plates and cleaning up after the first communal meal for the day. Bonstaph turned his attention to the committee.

"Before the fall of Ba'rrat, Brindle's population was a little over three hundred. We are now pushing *eight* hundred." Bonstaph paused briefly to allow the chatter to subside. "If we keep fishing, if we keep farming, and without Ba'rrat stripping supplies, we can comfortably sustain a population of five hundred." The chatter rose louder this time. Now that Bonstaph had lit the fuse of truth, he needed to diffuse it.

"Forty eight hours from now, the population will be four hundred fifty." The committee were silenced and all eyes stared at Bonstaph, including Sarah's.

"We cannot force people to leave," a man spoke out. Bonstaph recognised him as a Brindle townsman, which he saw as a good sign. *Hopefully there will be no pre-emptive tension between people.* "They will go to their deaths if they leave our guarded borders."

"No one is leaving here unprotected. It will be a calculated undertaking." Bonstaph was aware he spoke in his stern, Commander's voice. The townsman gave a nod. "These are the numbers you need to know. All Brindle folk will remain—that is a given. In addition, twenty wounded who are not from Brindle, and not capable of travelling, will remain."

"What of our defences?" a voice called from the rear of the gathering. Bonstaph could not place the source of the voice, but he knew it spoke for many of the quicker-thinking Committee members.

"Half of Brindle's population is capable of bearing arms. Half of the refugees, such as myself, are also capable. A share of those refugees will remain to support the defences."

"How many is that share?"

"An extra one hundred."

The committee members talked amongst themselves with varying opinions and perspectives falling on Bonstaph's ears. An elderly townswoman was first to speak out. "That's not enough. There is no point in sending away good fighting men. If we can sustain five hundred, we must fill that number with such men."

Bonstaph was not accommodating a vote on the matter, let alone the incompatible priorities of the various committee members. He was quick to reinforce his decision. "These numbers are fixed. Brindle will be left with two hundred sixty capable fighters—nearly the equivalent of your entire population."

"What of the wounded? All but three are not Brindle folk. Who shall tend to them?" the woman pushed.

"Who tended to your fortifications and built a defence system around this town?"

"We all did," a voice shouted.

"And with a sustainable population of four hundred fifty, you will continue to work together." Bonstaph looked to each of the committee members in turn. "Work together, keep what systems we have put in place going, and the Quag will withdraw in time."

"How can you be sure?"

"The Quag will only continue to challenge Brindle if one of two conditions are met. Either they're making progress or they're learning our weaknesses. We will not allow the first and we have no weaknesses.

"The Quag numbers are few. Significant portions of their resources supply the battle that continues in the Fire Realm. What remains is scattered," Bonstaph continued. "With any luck, they will soon board their ships, sail through the Southern Gap and beyond the Neversea, never to be seen again.

If not, keep fighting strong and never, under any circumstance, find cause to quarrel among yourselves. Nothing will compromise your defences faster."

"Three hundred ninety five men, women and children…"

With the committee meeting over, Bonstaph turned his attention to those leaving Brindle. Paramount to a clean departure was *discretion*. Three hundred ninety five refugees marching out of Brindle would give the Quag reason to attack either the travellers or the fortified town—both now appearing vulnerable. The solution was to have people leave in small groups at regular intervals. There was also the matter of the *extra one hundred* people Bonstaph had not publicly accounted for.

Bonstaph gave Walt orders to distribute amongst his runners. Each knew what they had to do with their information. "Groups of thirty three will leave Brindle every four hours, beginning half an hour after sundown. Twelve groups in total. Each group will have ten capable fighters and an equal number of men, women and children. It does not matter where they want to go, all groups will take the same route in the beginning. Safety in numbers until we're well clear of Brindle.

"We shall travel East toward Thwax and regroup there, three days from now. Once our numbers are consolidated, we travel the eastern reach of the Black Cliffs, then north along the Red Pass. Once clear of the Corville Mountains, we can regroup at the Plains Lake—a broad lake at the southern border of Froughton Forest. The lake will provide a good source of nourishment before we go our separate ways."

Once Walt had given the command to his young runners, he returned to Bonstaph with the obvious question—"Sire, I told you there were nearly *nine* hundred folk in Brindle, not eight hundred."

"Is that so?" Bonstaph winked slyly and took Walt aside, ensuring they were out of earshot.

"Walt, there are spies here in Brindle in the employ of the Quag."

"Are you certain? Who?" Walt glanced about as though he may see who the rogue persons were by looking.

"I cannot name them, nor point them out," Bonstaph explained. "But in a population as large and diverse as this, where most are strangers to one another, the primary honour is self preservation. There are guaranteed to be a number of spies. Trust me on this."

Walt nodded quietly in agreement. He looked nervous, but Bonstaph knew he was a smart man and was quick to learn. "What do we do?"

"Everything goes as planned," Bonstaph said under his breath. "The first group leave half an hour after sunset. The second leave four hours after that. This will establish a pattern. The pattern will more than likely be relayed via spies to Quag scouts who will take what they know to their superiors. They will not attack right away because their intelligence has revealed Brindle's evacuation is a forty-eight hour ordeal. The more that leave, the better for them."

"And the third group leave four hours after midnight?" Walt anticipated.

"This is where things change. The remaining groups leave every *half hour* after midnight. The ten remaining groups will be out of Brindle by sunrise."

"Very good," Walt remarked. A slight smirk came to his face.

"Now... for the *one hundred* extra people only you and I know about," Bonstaph whispered. Walt was wide eyed. "These will be the hundred most capable warriors we have who are not Brindle folk. Many of these warriors are our own people from the Fire Realm. Fifty of them shall form a one-mile guard line east of Brindle, shepherding the travellers. The other fifty shall remain to reinforce the eastern fortifications. This is the most likely point of attack."

"Very good, sire," Walt enthused. "So then, how many in total shall be leaving?"

"Three hundred ninety five. Five hundred will be staying."

"What of you and I?"

"We're among those leaving. It's time for us to go home, Walt."

HANNAH - THREE

"There are eleven checkpoints in Froughton Forest before we reach my home," Nëven said. "I like the number 'eleven'. Not because is sounds a little like 'Nëven', in fact—my name sounds more like 'Seven', although not entirely, because the first 'e' is longer than the second. 'Eleven' is symmetrical, you see, but only as a number, not a word…"

Hannah was astounded by how much Nëven could talk and was quite impressed with how clever she was.

"How do you spell 'Hannah' backwards?" Nëven asked.

"The same as forwards," Hannah answered.

"You are 'even', like me. My brother, Artur, calls me 'even Nëven'. My sister, Vevila, calls me 'annoying'." Both Nëven and Hannah laughed.

They were travelling through the Outer Rim. Hannah had been here once before and the memory filled her with joy. Her family were travelling to Guame where Catanya led her on a wonderful adventure finding all sorts of trinkets and exotic treasures for sale at the busy stalls and markets. Here in the Outer Rim it was quiet, except for Nëven's talking. Up ahead, light was piercing through the treetops in a colourful arc of rainbow colours, illuminating the road.

"Do you see that?" Hannah asked.

"What?" Nëven stopped her talking to see where Hannah was pointing.

"Do you suppose we've found the end of the rainbow?" Hannah was intrigued. They reached the rainbow and it turned to orange. The girls jumped from their steeds and walked into the light filled clearing. Hannah watched it's splintered rays dance across the palms of her hands.

"I think there would be more colours if it were the end of the rainbow," Nëven explained.

"Perhaps orange is the only colour strong enough to pass through the trees and reach the ground." Hannah craned her head back, opening her mouth wide. She could just make out a hint of blue sky, the sun, and the light piercing through the treetops. "I think that is what it may be."

"Do you think orange is a strong colour?" Nëven asked.

Hannah thought it an interesting question. "Perhaps, when it comes to rainbows." Nëven looked up to the sky, squinting as she walked further into the path of light. "Your hair is orange," Hannah observed. "It looks strong."

Nëven smiled. "Auroch is orange. He is very strong." Hannah looked at the huge Dwyer bull named Auroch and nodded in agreement. She tried to think of other orange things. "And you, Hannah," Nëven said.

"Me?"

"You are of the Fire Realm. Fire is orange. That is strong."

Up ahead, Nëven's father turned about and looked at the two young girls as he walked beside Auroch. He snickered and shook his head. "The mighty fire dragons," he mumbled aloud but in the silence of the forest, Hannah could hear him quite clearly. Apparently, so could her mother.

"What of them?" Alessandra asked. Creighton flashed a glance back at her but did not answer. "What do you find amusing about our dragons?"

"Their absence," Creighton finally replied. Hannah thought he tried to say it in an amusing way. Her mother did not seem amused.

"And your own dragons?" Alessandra asked.

Creighton pulled on Auroch's reigns to slow him a little then turned to face Alessandra. Hannah and Nëven looked at one another, then to the adults. "The Spindlefax dragons are gone. They died defending our lands." Creighton pointed at Alessandra. "The Couldradt dragons—*your* dragons— have abandoned you. That is why your lands are threatened."

"So, you resent them for that?" Alessandra said. Creighton said nothing. "You resent *us* for that?" This time Creighton shrugged. "Have you broached this topic with my husband? Or my sister, perhaps?" Creighton urged his bull forward. "Wait!" Alessandra insisted. Creighton turned back at once, as did Nëven. Hannah looked at her mother—her face looked flushed. "If your people are harbouring resentment for my people, I need to know."

"*We* need to know!" Hannah contributed. Creighton and Nëven looked at her, then back to Alessandra.

"Yes, *we* need to know, before we travel through the Valley of Shadows and place our faith in you."

Hannah looked to Creighton. He flared his nostrils and rolled his eyes. Then he started to look a little uncomfortable.

"Perhaps we should camp here tonight and think about things," Hannah asserted. It seemed to be something an adult would say.

"I think that would be a smart idea," Alessandra agreed. She was frowning at Creighton. Hannah felt proud. Nëven look surprised.

"We'll be at the second checkpoint in a few hours. We can camp there."

"Is the checkpoint along the Outer Rim?" Alessandra asked.

"It's in the Valley."

"Then here will do just nicely." Alessandra looked at Hannah. "Thankyou, Hannah. A wise suggestion." She started unpacking her goods off the back of her horse.

Creighton turned about aimlessly, then huffed and puffed a little. Hannah looked at Nëven to get her take on the situation. She shrugged, suggesting she had nothing to offer.

Happy the conversation was over, Hannah loitered back to the orange blades of light and looked up again, letting them bathe her face. She thought about what Csilla had said to her the previous day—*I'm sure the god of fire wants to shine on your pretty little face before this summer is over.'* Hannah closed her eyes and let the sun glow through her eyelids. "Here you go then, it may be your last chance to find me in the forest."

"Who are you talking to?"

Hannah opened her eyes and blinked away the sunshine. Nëven was standing there. "One of the gods." Nëven looked up, squinting into the sun. She was wearing a necklace that had a large gemstone hanging from it, wrapped in macramé netting. The sunlight was throwing patterns in the stone. Hannah found it mesmerising. "Your necklace is beautiful."

Nëven stepped back from the sunlight and held the gemstone gently in her hand. "Oh," she exclaimed.

"What's the matter?"

Nëven was hesitant to say. She looked toward her father who seemed resigned to the fact that they were staying the night and was setting up camp. Nëven turned back. "It's my 'Earth' stone, also called a 'Jasper' stone. It's like the Juniper stones found along the old paths through the Valley. Those ones are the purple ones fired by dragons. But the green ones..." Nëven rubbed a thumb over it. "The green ones are *far* more fun. We dig them up, but they're hard to find and not all of us can use them. I think your Fire god was looking at it just now." Nëven looked to the sun again—this time with caution.

Hannah was most intrigued. "It looked beautiful with the sun shining through it." The colour of the stone intrigued her most. It was pale green and reminded her of foaming waves splashing against rocks in the ocean. The colours seemed to swirl within the stone. "When the sun was on it, I could see right through it."

"That's the secret of it," Nëven whispered. "Not everyone can *see through* with it."

Hannah was puzzled. That was not what she meant. "See through *what* with it?"

"Anything your heart desires. Anywhere you want. The stone can take you there."

"*Anywhere* you want?" Hannah did not understand.

Nëven was not listening. She was checking on her father's whereabouts again. Fifty feet away, Creighton was going over Auroch with a grooming brush. When finished, he placed the brush atop Auroch's saddle. Nëven swung back to Hannah. "Hannah, we are friends, aren't we?"

"Aye," Hannah smiled. She thought it nice Nëven already thought of her as a friend.

"Friends share secrets, don't they?" Nëven reasoned.

"I guess so…"

Nëven bit her bottom lip for a moment. "Watch this." She gripped the Jasper stone and vanished.

Hannah spun about, looking for Nëven. She was gone. She spun about again and there she was—right in front of her again, holding Auroch's grooming brush. Still gripping her Jasper stone, Nëven vanished again. This time Hannah caught a glimpse of her standing beside Auroch and the next moment, she was back again. Nëven pointed to Auroch. The grooming brush was sitting atop his saddle as before. Hannah was at a loss for words. She thought her own magic skills were getting good, but this was so, so much better.

Nëven put a finger to her lips. "Shh… this is our secret."

The god of Fire took his leave for the night. Hannah had caught glimpses of the sun's descent to the west before its rays disappeared from Froughton Forest all together. She wondered if Nëven's Earth god slept at night. Sitting cross-legged beside her new friend on her mother's blanket, Hannah felt the pine needles beneath her, pushing through the blanket. She played with a twig of pine, breaking it into ever-smaller pieces until so small, no more breaks could be made. This was all stuff created by Nëven's god. Hannah was pretty sure the Earth god was awake, even in the dark of night, because it seemed to her they were being watched.

Creighton would not allow a fire at first. He said fires were only safe at the checkpoints, which were well protected. Hannah thought Nëven's father to be as stubborn as her own father. *Mother knows how to deal with stubborn fathers.* Finally, Creighton relented and Alessandra built a small fire well clear of the road.

"I'm pretty sure father wants us to keep moving," Nëven said to Hannah.

"We won't be moving, Nëven. We'll be staying here tonight," Hannah explained. She was watching Nëven fiddle with the Jasper stone around her neck. Nëven spotted her and smiled. Hannah considered the fire again then turned back to Nëven. "Can I show you some magic of my own?" Hannah whispered.

"Yes, please!" Nëven said, a little too loud for her father's liking. He hushed her to silence.

Hannah checked her mother was not watching. She was away with her thoughts, gazing into the fire. Hannah stared hard at the fire and thought of which of her spells would impress Nëven without making too much of a ruckus and getting them into trouble. It was then she remembered Csilla's knife. Hannah drew if from her belt and held it to the side of the fire so she could see the flames reflecting off its fire-bronze and steel blade. Nëven watched and waited in silence, her green eyes widening with anticipation.

"Watch closely," Hannah said. She concentrated on the blade and whispered the spell Csilla had used. *"Fara gin parshin-ar."* Nothing happened. No ring of flame danced about the blade. *Nothing.* Hannah scrunched her nose. *"Fara gin parshin-ar!"* she said a little louder. Still nothing happened. Nëven giggled and Hannah felt her cheeks warming. *"Fara gin parshin-ar!"* Hannah almost shouted this time.

"Hannah!" Alessandra scolded. "Not here."

"Shh! Silence!" Creighton added.

The blade did not change at all. Nëven laughed out loud and fell to her side, as if to accentuate the complete hilarity of the situation. Hannah sheathed the blade, cursing herself for trying a new spell, rather than one she had already mastered.

"You need to both be quiet, *now!*" Alessandra said, standing and glowering over them both. Hannah spotted the sword in her mother's hand. She looked scared. Creighton was also standing in silence. His muscular hand gripped tightly to his sword. Hannah swallowed hard. The warrior's face looked as concerned as her mothers.

"Father?" Nëven said, her face painted in worry, forgetting to silence herself again. Alessandra squatted to the ground beside the Earth girl and placed a hand over her mouth.

Creighton slowly turned about. His back to the girls, he allowed his moss-green gown to fall silently to the ground revealing emerald body armour that flickered reflections from the fire. For a painfully silent minute the ӨhUidman stood motionless until, with the sound of a dull thud, his body jolted violently. Another thud and he jolted again and then a third time. Creighton fell to his knees and dropped his sword. Nëven screamed, but it came out muffled with Alessandra's hand now locked over her mouth.

Alessandra cast the other hand toward the fire. *"Fara Namon!"* she said. The flames vanished. The embers slowly died and in their fading glow, Hannah saw Creighton fall to his side. In the growing darkness, back toward the road, she watched the yellow glow of multiple torches shift briskly toward them.

Alessandra grabbed Hannah by her jacket's collar and dragged her to her feet.

"Run!"

Hannah did not need to be asked twice. She sprinted after her mother who was dragging the still screaming Nëven by the arm. Hannah glanced back at the torches, but her mother pulled her back into line. They hurtled away from Creighton in an unknown direction, stumbling over ferns and prickly bushes and side stepping trees that wouldn't shift. Alessandra positioned herself in front of the two girls, pulling both along behind her, taking the impact of the undergrowth and smaller trees she was punching through.

Hannah's fear grew. Nëven's screaming stopped but she was sobbing uncontrollably. The three of them were soon breathing heavy from exertion. After several long minutes they pushed out of the forest all together. Their aimless direction had seen them into a clearing of some sort. In the moonlight, Alessandra looked about, as if getting her bearings. Hannah baulked at the sight of her mother—"Mamma!" Her mother was scratched and bleeding all over. Her clothes were ripped from head to toe from the forest she had pushed through without any consideration for her own wellbeing. And she was shaking.

Alessandra stood between the two girls, clutching hands with each of them. Her sword was lost—most likely dropped when she grabbed the girls she was desperately tying to protect. The three looked back into the darkness of the forest. Approaching torches soon broke the darkness. The three girls took backward steps.

"Hannah. Nëven. When I tell you to run, you run back into the forest and find a dark place to hide in absolute silence. Find your way into the Valley.

Nëven, do you think you can find your way to the second checkpoint?"
Nëven did not answer. Hannah looked across her mother at her terrified
friend. "Nëven!" Alessandra shook her violently. Hannah had never seen her
mother like this before. "You've got a Jasper stone. I know you can use it. Try
your best to jump with Hannah. You can save your life *and* Hannah's. You
know you can."

The torches drew closer and were just moments from breaking through to
the clearing. Alessandra, Hannah and Nëven stood in the open field under the
merciless luminescence of the moon. The first torch reached the edge of the
forest.

"Exploda fara gin mara!" Alessandra shouted. The powerful spell made the
first torch explode in a blinding rage of light. The surrounding forest ignited.
The torchbearer wailed. "RUN, GIRLS!"

Hannah shifted past her mother to run but Alessandra's long arm grabbed
her at the last moment and drew Hannah to her body, hugging her close.
Hannah wrapped her arms around her mother, squeezing with everything she
had. She made a desperate wish to be gone from this place. Then Hannah felt
the soft touch of a hand on hers, drawing her from her mother. It was Nëven.
Alessandra broke her embrace and stood. From deep within her mother's
chest came a rumble as angry as a fire dragon. From the rumble came the
bellowing words of the same vicious Fireisgh spell—*'EXPLODA FARA
GIN MARA!'* Three more torchbearers broke the forests perimeter and one
at a time exploded as the first had done.

'RUN...' Alessandra's single word tore through Hannah's mind as a
thought.

Hannah and Nëven ran through the clearing, holding one another's hand
as tight as can be. Neither looked back. Hannah heard the metallic scything
sound of swords been drawn. Her mother's thoughts bathed her mind—*'I
love you beautiful girl.'* She ran with Nëven, faster still. *'Run my beautiful. Find
your sister. Find Catanya—'* Then her mother's thoughts fell silent.

Hannah heard heavy boots behind her, taking one step for every three of
her own and drawing closer. When so close she could hear the grunt of
exertion, Hannah and Nëven veered sharply into the forest. Hannah felt the
assailant's touch on her shoulder as Nëven spun about and locked arms
around Hannah, pulling her close. Hannah suddenly felt as if the wind had
been pulled from her chest. She was overcome with dizziness.

The two girls were standing next to Alessandra's horse by the side of the
road at the edge of the Valley of Shadows. Hannah fell, disorientated,

bringing Nëven down with her. *Voices... Torches...* Hannah blinked her dizziness away. Nëven was pulling on her arm, trying to drag her to her feet. Hannah looked down the road. Two torchbearers stood over Auroch. The Dwyer bull had been slain. The torchbearers turned from the bull and ran at the girls shouting deep, guttural sounds that were hauntingly familiar to Hannah. She had heard it often in past months as her father's legions fought to defend the borders of the Nuyan River. Hannah realised the attackers were Quag warriors.

"Mamma!" Shock hit Hannah like a bolt of lightning. Nëven was sobbing again at the sight of Auroch. It was the only thing that felt real. Instinctively, Hannah grabbed Nëven this time. Nëven was shaking like an autumn leaf moments before it dropped from the tree. "Nëven!" The Quag warriors were seconds away from them. "Nëven! GO!" Nëven gripped Hannah's arm and it happened again.

Hannah felt as if a great gust of wind had hit her all at once, from every direction. The thump to her chest left her heaving for air, and no amount of blinking would restore her blurry vision. Nëven continued to sob. Hannah was sure it was from more than shock or sadness—she was in pain. "Nëven?" Hannah rubbed her eyes and looked around into the dark of the forest. *Where am I?* "Nëven?"

"Hannah! Your knife..." Nëven wailed. Hannah was scared for her and scared the Quag would hear Nëven.

"They're over there!" shouted a deep voice. Through blurry vision, Hannah saw approaching torches once again.

Nëven yelled and lunged at Hannah, grabbing her.

THUMP!

Hannah was short of breath again. *Where are we now?* Strange thoughts swept through Hannah's mind at a million miles an hour. The thoughts were foreign and certainly not her own, and she could not shake them. They told her of a terrible pain in her chest. Hannah went to feel her chest but her left arm was stuck. She felt with her right arm. *There's no injury...*

"Hannah?" Nëven's voice tore through her mind making her jolt with astonishment.

"Nëven?"

"We're..." Nëven tried to talk but was struggling. Her thoughts came again. *"We're stuck... We landed in each other's jump and I'm hurt. Your knife..."*

Hannah reached for her knife. It was not there. She tried to speak but could not draw breath to do so. *"It's gone!"* Hannah spoke back with her thoughts. *"Why can I hear your thoughts but not your voice?"*

"We're stuck," Nëven repeated. *"One more jump and I'll pull free…"*

THUMP!

Hannah fell hard to the gravel ground and gasped. Breath finally came to her. She moaned, glad to have her voice back. She turned about, blinking her vision back into focus. There was a dim torchlight over her shoulder and she scampering away across the forest floor. She saw then that a Quagman's fist was not holding the torch. It hung from a tree above her. In the light, Hannah saw Nëven curled in a ball ten feet from her.

Hannah crawled to her on all fours. "Nëven!" She gently rolled Nëven onto her back.

Nëven's eyes opened and she stared at Hannah for a moment, then to the torch. "We're safe now," Nëven moaned. "We're at the second checkpoint." Then Hannah saw her knife—the one Csilla gifted her—protruding from the right side of Nëven's chest.

"Nëven—no!" Hannah cried. She took a hold of the knife handle. Nëven screamed from the pain. Hannah let go.

"What is going on here?" A deep voice demanded. Hannah spun, fearing the worst, until she saw it was no Quagman and for a moment, she thought it was Nëven's father. It was a big warrior with the same armour, gown, curly red hair and beard.

"Nëven's father is dead. My mother…" Hannah sobbed. The ΘhUidman grabbed Hannah by the arm and dragged her to her feet. "So you thought you'd kill Creighton's daughter."

Hannah's hands were bound with rope behind the trunk of an oak tree. Her head was flopped forward and she felt her black, matted hair dropping over her face. She had fought sleep through the night, but as the sun rose, she could fight it no longer.

Some time later, Hannah was startled awake when her feet were kicked out from under her. She could not fall, for her arms were bound too high about the tree but she felt the strain as they took the weight of her sagging body.

"Witches don't sleep." It was an ΘhUidman, yet not the one who found her standing over Nëven with Csilla's knife in her chest. "Are you a witch?" the man laughed.

Hannah got to her feet again but was too scared to reply and did not understand what was funny about the situation. She swallowed hard but her mouth was parched from thirst. Her lips tasted salty from spent tears. She glanced to her left. A small distance away, Nëven rested on a stretcher. Csilla's knife had been removed from her chest, but she had not moved at all during the night. Hannah closed her eyes and made a wish for Nëven to get better. She even tried to hear Nëven thought's again, but gathered it was her Jasper stone that had allowed them to do so previously. At the least, Hannah hoped that was why she could not hear her friend's thoughts any longer and not that she was too sick to think.

Morning aged into afternoon. Hannah could see the sun gliding ever so slowly over the dense treetops. The Fire god must have been looking for her, searching the forest from the skies. He was not able to penetrate through the trees here in the Valley of Shadows to find her. *Perhaps Nëven's god is hiding me here. Does the Earth god think I hurt Nëven?*

Two other ƟhUidmen riding Dwyer bulls arrived at the checkpoint. The man who was standing guard walked to meet them. "Anything?"

"I'll take it from here," said another ƟhUidman who had appeared beside Hannah. He was glaring at her. Hannah stared back. It was the man who found her the previous night. "What news?"

"We've found Creighton's body, Regan." The younger of the bull rider's said. "They made camp an hour west. Creighton's bull is slain by the roadside in the Outer Rim. No sign of the girl's mother."

"Any sign of Quag warriors?" the one named Regan asked.

"No, though it was definitely their doing. And we found this." The younger ƟhUidman handed Regan a scroll, which he unfurled and read. Regan looked at Hannah then continued to read. When he was finished, he stepped toward her again.

"You are Xavier's daughter?" Hannah turned her head away. She did not know what she should tell these men—not whilst tied as a prisoner to a tree. Regan sighed and walked to his comrades. "This is a sad state of affairs."

Hannah knew she was in trouble—big trouble. She thought of how Csilla's knife could have come to injure Nëven. To do so, she searched through dark, violent memories…

'Fara gin parshin-ar!' Hannah had tried to cast the spell Csilla had shown her, but failed over and over again, even when she was shouting the spell. Then they were attacked, and it was *her* fault. *I made too much noise.* She remembered Creighton warning her mother to keep going to the checkpoint.

We would have been safe here. Then there was the fire. *The fire attracted the Quagmen, as did my shouting...* Hannah refocussed her thoughts again on the knife. She remembered sheathing it in her pousse-plaited belt, but the belt had no scabbard. In the confusion that followed, Nëven had grabbed her and used her Jasper stone to save them both. *Just as mother told her.* Hannah knew that somewhere in the chaos of it all, she had come to stab Nëven in the chest.

The realisation made Hannah sink. Her legs seemed to give out and her arms took the weight of her body again. Hannah's eyes filled with fresh tears that tracked down her cheeks, her lips and fell to the forest ground at her feet. She looked to Nëven again and felt as if her heart was going to stop.

"That little girl didn't hurt anyone." Regan's voice was like a dream.

Yes, I did...

RED PASS

Nothing could have prepared Magnus for the sight of the Red River's blood-water bleeding into the tumbling waves of the Neverseas. *This is the blood I carry… The blood so many desire.* He wondered if others truly desired it, or was it Delvion alone who was mad enough to do so?

Here at the mouth, the Red River was drawn by the ocean rip beneath the surf, turned over and over then pummelled into a scarlet spray before fizzing away as pink foam, blushing cockles that freckled the otherwise white sandy shore. Magnus knew the Red River, formerly called the 'Little Traas River', ran red since Balgur was slain upon it twenty years ago. What he did not know was the effect it would have on him. He picked a pink cockleshell and rubbed its ribbed surface with a thumb. *A final reminder of Balgur's existence,* he lamented.

It had taken two days to reach the Red River at its end, but sighting where the river terminated gave Magnus a reference point as he and Catanya followed it upstream between the Black Cliffs and the Romgnian Mountains.

"This is where the 'Red Pass' begins," Catanya explained. Magnus looked at the gentle tapering of the mountain ranges either side of them forming a curved plain about two miles wide with black granite to one side and a less congruous formation of stone to the other. The Red River was at its lowest point. Magnus could hear the trickling of water. "We are days away from the Romghold, so there is no threat from that direction. The Black Cliffs however…"

"Worgriels and wyverns." Magnus said.

"Exactly. Still, I don't think they'll cross the river to get at us."

Out of caution, they stuck to the Romgnian Mountain side of the river.

"I can smell it," Magnus mumbled, sniffing the air around the Red River. Its blood-water had a scent—*a metallic, ashen scent.* It was the same scent others smelt on him. Magnus found the river alluring. If not on horseback he would have knelt to it and let his fingertips break the surface of the water. *What would it feel like?* Magnus asked Catanya if she has learned anything more of the river from the Couldradt Fire dragons.

"It's a place of remembrance." Catanya had been resting her head on Magnus's back as Tilly walked the Red Pass. She sat up in the horse's saddle, explaining some more—"They seldom talk about it, except Rubea. She was one of the few who weren't a part of the Battle of Fire, so is not so troubled by it. That and being young makes her curious." Catanya chuckled then paused before speaking again. "Further north at the Southern Plains, you'll see. I'll show you where Balgur fell. Here, the place speaks to you. I'm certain you will hear it." Catanya pointed northward, past Magnus. "The river will lead to the south-eastern border of Froughton Forest. I've been there numerous times with Rubea, but never this far south."

"Here is not the place to stop, then."

"No, it is not."

Magnus kept an eye on the peaks of the Black Cliffs until they travelled beyond them into the Southern Wastelands. The ground became a swirling mixture of dirt and dust, orange and rust, scooped by the winds, spinning into a formless brown haze that blinded them to anything more than a few feet away. Tilly tilted her head forward and kept a steady pace. The only reference point was the river to their left. The dust seemed to draw all moisture from the air leaving Magnus parched. He drew Marsala's coat around his body leaving only his hands and face to be pummelled by the dust like a thousand stinging needles.

By mid afternoon, Catanya insisted on taking her turn at the front of the saddle. Magnus said he would be looking over her shoulder and copping the wind all the same and that she may as well stay protected behind his back. "Besides, my beard affords me protection." Furthermore, having her hug him from behind gave him comfort. Magnus thought of when he passed into the wastelands via the Corville Pass long ago as a prisoner. Sarah had embraced him while he was in the sickening throes of Anunya. He had found Sarah so comforting. Little did he know at the time the sickness would continue, on and off, even to this day. If what Marsala said was true, his mixed dragon blood could do battle within him for some time to come. Would some resolution eventually be found? Would one Electus power win out over the other? Balgur told Magnus an Electus inheritance came with an obligation. Was he torn between conflicting obligations?

With nightfall came lethargy, but the winds waned and travel was easier for Tilly. Magnus sensed the mare was more than happy to get beyond the northern borders of the wastelands, and so they pushed through. The Red River guided Tilly through the next section of the Red Pass—the divide between the Corville Mountains to the west and the Romgnian Mountain ranges that continued unbroken to the east. Catanya shifted to the front of the saddle and nestled against Magnus's chest, getting well-needed sleep. Magnus felt little need for sleep. Waves of lethargy would abate with a flush of warmth bathing his muscles, mind and would-be-tired eyes. It was as if Balgur himself was saying— *"Keep moving"*.

Magnus kept one eye at all times on the peaks of the Corville Mountains until they passed beyond them and into the soft green pastures of the Southern Plains. As the sun rose the following morning above the Romgnian Mountain ranges, they had done several days worth of fair travel in a day and a night. Magnus looked behind him to the Corville Mountains one last time and thought he saw the figure of a man cloaked in black, high atop a mountain crag. Magnus turned away, unsure of what he saw and then looked back to the black figure a second time, but it was gone. To the north, however, he could just see the dark border of Froughton Forest.

Catanya woke, sat upright and pointed to the forest. She turned to Magnus. "Froughton Forest."

"Aye." Magnus smiled back.

"You're beautiful." Catanya continued her stare at Magnus until she drew his attention away from the forest and looked into her eyes. "You are. You're beautiful." A smile slowly crept across her face.

Magnus chuckled. It was enchanting to see Catanya content and it felt wonderful to be that much closer to home. He would have returned the sentiment, but instead, chose to bask in her flattery. He embraced her and right there by the Red River, he thought of the conversation they shared before Catanya was taken by Austagia to join the Irucantî. He repeated what he said to her then.

"We could run, Catanya."

Catanya smirked. "You know, I was thinking of that exact conversation. We had decided to go to the Ice Realm—to your mother's people." Her smile faded, her demeanour hardened. Magnus knew it reflected his own. Thoughts of his mother, of Catanya's mother, Hannah, even Xavier.

"And now, we just want to go home."

"Aye," Catanya agreed. "But we can't."

"Not yet."

"Soon, though."

Magnus turned from Catanya's eyes and considered the continuous range of the Romgnian Mountains. "How long until we reach the Romghold?"

Catanya followed Magnus's gaze. "It depends on our approach. By mid afternoon, Tilly willing, we should be directly beneath the Romghold. I think we should use the forest for cover once we reach it. A dragon can spot us from the mountaintop. If Liné and Rubea are there as Joffren revealed to you, they will be patrolling the borders from the air. I would guess that one will patrol the skies, the other will guard the temple."

Magnus gave an affirmative nod. It was sobering to think a dragon could be watching them at that very moment, wondering at their intentions. Magnus knew the closer they were to the Romghold, the more obvious their intentions would be. As they rode toward the fringes of Froughton Forest, Catanya gave Magnus a detailed description of the Romghold. He formed an image in his mind of the Temple of Fire—the temple he saw a brief vision of when he shared Joffren's thoughts back in Ba'rrat. In these thoughts, Magnus saw the two High Priests in the temple under protection of spells and two dragons guarding the temple doors. Catanya explained the training field, the accommodation quarters and other buildings laid symmetrically about a paved common. It was here they were headed—here they were going to confront the High Priests. This was Magnus's intention ever since Brue and the three Irucantî tried to kill him, but he was no closer to knowing how he would do it.

A mile from the southern border of Froughton Forest, Catanya insisted— "We should stop here. You need to see the river at this point."

They alighted and Magnus fed carrots to Tilly and served her water from the skin strapped to her saddle. Catanya took time to stretch her hamstrings and back muscles. Magnus simply cracked his neck to one side then walked to the river's edge. He squatted by the Red River and peered through the flowing water. It was opaque from its redness and only at its shallowest could the pebbles resting on the bottom be seen.

"This is where Balgur fell," Catanya said.

Magnus rolled forward onto his knees but kept his hands to himself, tempering his desire to touch the water. "He fell here?"

"Aye."

Magnus's thoughts were of Eamon. *Steyne… Where was he standing at the time? Was he far from Balgur? Why couldn't he reach him in time?* He thought of every possible scenario that could lead to Delvion possessing Steyne's sword and even then, not finding a way to prevent the lethal blow. He could only conclude there was more to the scene than he was able to piece together— more warriors, more violence, more at stake and… *more to the story than has been spoken.* Magnus recalled Marsala's words on the matter—*'You must learn Balgur's side of the story… Beyond Eamon's sorrow and Delvion's ego. With Balgur you'll find the truth.'*

Catanya knelt beside Magnus. He put a hand on her thigh, still gazing into the water.

"Some are afraid to touch it, others bathe, hoping it has healing properties," Catanya said.

"Have you touched it?" Magnus hoped she had. He wanted an excuse to do so himself.

"Joffren wouldn't touch it." Catanya seemed to come to a realisation of some kind as she said it. She stared at Magnus.

An involuntary smile came to Magnus's face. "You want to touch it now, don't you!" he said.

"I sure do. Same time?"

"Same time."

Both Magnus and Catanya reached fingers to the water's edge. With hands almost touching each other, their fingers breached the surface of the water. The effect was immediate.

Catanya's breath was caught. She was choking. Heat shot up her arm, through her body and filled her heart to the point of near explosion. She pulled her hand free and her breath returned. She took deep breaths to try and ease the heat in her chest but it persisted and starting radiating through her body. Catanya spun around, looking for Magnus. There was no trace of him anywhere. He had vanished.

"Magnus?" Catanya's voice ricocheted in her own mind but was silent to the world around her. She began to hear voices in her head, bouncing back and forth, each voice staking its claim for attention. Catanya tried to control the voices but they just became more confusing. She gripped the sides of her head and lay on the riverbank in the foetal position. *"STOP!"* she pleaded.

"STOP," a dominant voice spoke, subduing all other voices to a still-present background hum. *"Follow me as I go."* the voice said. It was an ancient, cavernous voice far beyond the age and depth of any person's. Catanya was sure it belonged to a dragon and here, with her fingers dampened by the Red River, the voice could only belong to one dragon…

"Balgur?"

"Come," Balgur said as if confirming who he was.

In one swift motion, Catanya was pulled deep into the Red River and drawn downstream. The great dragon was pulling on her mind, drawing her forth. She wanted to protest but they were moving so fast it startled her to silence. *This is not real, this is in my mind,* she told herself, trying to regulate her breathing, all the while knowing it was futile if she was in fact underwater.

"*Come,*" Balgur repeated.

Just go with it, Catanya. She asserted repeatedly that this must be a dream and like all dreams she would soon wake, unharmed.

Catanya was pulled through the river as it branched to the right along a narrow stream toward the Corville Mountains and then branched of again into a tiny rivulet that travelled beneath the mountain and through channels in the stone. The tiny waterway, barely more than a finger's breadth wide, worked its way deeper and deeper underground until it surfaced in a narrow tunnel, trickling down as a thin stream that seeped through more stone before finally dripping through the ceiling of a cave. Catanya knew she was not really there, yet her mind had travelled here for a reason.

"*Where are we?*"

"*In the Caves of Cuvee,*" Balgur said.

It was dark. All the voices in Catanya's head were silenced but one. It was a voice that was going to affect her somehow—*why else would Balgur bring me here?*

"*Listen,*" Balgur instructed.

Heeding the dragon's warning, Catanya concentrated on the one voice. It was a deep, insidious voice that jarred her mind in a way only one man's voice had done so before—when he spoke before his people in Ba'rrat's arena. "*Delvion…*"

Delvion's voice seethed with anger—with the need for vengeance. The bravado Catanya saw the Quag King flaunt in Ba'rrat was gone. It was replaced with absolute hatred. Through Balgur, Catanya sensed not so much his words, but the malice in Delvion's heart. The Quag King was embracing this malice to cope with the death of his second son—Crugion—and his own failure to obtain the one remaining Electus power he had hungered for since the Battle of Fire two decades before. Worse still, Delvion knew Bonstaph of J'esmagd was Magnus's father. Bonstaph had slayed his sons. Magnus was now the Electus. Delvion's need for vengeance against the J'esmagd family was more than palpable. His thirst for power had been reinforced with a ravenous hunger for revenge. Delvion was determined to see Bonstaph,

Magnus and all they held dear perish. This would pre-empt his final war against the realms of Allumbreve.

As quickly as she arrived in the malevolent Caves of Cuvee, Catanya felt herself pulled away. Out of the darkness of the Caves, Catanya could see again, albeit as a moving blur. Balgur led her back through the confluence of waterways to the Red River, northward to its termination at the Traas River and westward into Froughton Forest. Catanya felt a violent shudder as they entered and passed through what she could only guess was The Core of the forest. *Do the OhUid folk have wards protecting The Core's boundaries?* Catanya hoped she would never have to find out.

Balgur speared Catanya through a network of rivers, emerging from Froughton to the west via the Nuyan River. At speed faster than a diving dragon, Catanya was thrust through her homelands where she heard the chattering of her people and the shouting of war cries. She tried to grasp onto something here—a familiar voice perhaps—but is was not what Balgur needed to show her and she was pulled away before she could get a firm grip. Balgur's journey took them further and further north to the northern Realms End and into the Ice Realm. The Nuyan River became the Whytfé River and Catanya felt the water temperature drop rapidly. The Whytfé River entered the broad lake of the same name. Catanya was pulled through its depths. Its chilly waters saturating her mind, making her head ache from the cold. Beyond the Whytfé Lake, the river ascended the mountainous Ice Breach. The further they went, the more the river turned to ice until forced into separate rivulets that navigated through the Northern Highlands and finally terminated at the Ice Seas and its shores—the home of the Rhydermere.

The Ice Seas were beyond Catanya's dreams. At its surface, the crystal sea shimmered under a blinding white sky, but as Balgur and Catanya dove through the seas depths, the seas shifted through infinite shades of blue from sapphire to azure, cobalt to midnight, yet always keeping its crystal clarity. Looking up, Catanya watched powerful walls of waves furl over and bash against craggy chunks of pearl-white icebergs, then fold over and under in flowing perfection.

From the Ice Seas, Balgur led Catanya upstream through water channels that traversed streets made of white granite cobblestone, leading to a tall wall of ice. The ice formed the outer structure of some kind of fortress, or castle, or—*an ice palace?* Catanya considered. There was barely a moment to take in its form before she was drawn along waterways in the ice wall just as she was through stone in the Corville Mountains. The darkness returned and she was blind again, giving over to acute hearing. The cold ache in her head persisted but she tried to ignore it as Balgur drew her toward another voice as focused as Delvion's had been in the Caves of Cuvee.

It was the voice of a woman. It echoed as though projected through a great room in the ice palace. As she spoke, a thousand murmurs were silenced. Unlike Delvion, her voice was beyond fear and despair, beyond tragedy and remorse. She spoke concisely of plans and tactics. She knew what she wanted and her subordinates were listening intently. Her commands would be obeyed—that much Catanya knew. The voice spoke of the need for governance and to strip Allumbreve of all power not under the direct control of the Ice Realm. Catanya knew by the voice and location that she was hearing the woman Marsala spoke of—it was Magnus's mother.

"Alavia…"

As if to confirm what he had shown Catanya, Balgur's voice rang through her one last time—*"I have shown you two great threats to Allumbreve. Use discretion with this information."*

"I will," Catanya said. Her body, near frozen by the waters that traced veins in the ice palace walls, was thrust back the way she came. In a blinding, dizzying moment, Catanya was beside the Red River again, still shivering from the cold of the Ice Realm. She was kneeling beside the river, dry, with her fingers a hair's width from the water surface. It was as if she had never left but for the chill that lingered in her body on the hot summer day.

"Magnus!"

The moment his fingertips broke the vermilion surface of the Red River, Magnus was pulled down into its depths.

Completely submerged, he clawed frantically at the water, desperate to get back to the surface. Magnus's vision blurred and he began to panic. The more he struggled, the deeper he sank until his boots hit the riverbed. Straining at the end of his breath, Magnus's lungs heaved in protest until the scorching heat of dragon blood took control. His lungs were soon relieved of the burden to breathe at all. Magnus's vision began to return and the water became transparent.

The heat passed and Magnus felt invigorated. He looked up and could see the wavering silhouette of Catanya kneeling by the waters edge—her fingers immersed in the water. She appeared frozen in time. Magnus reached for her. Something knocked his hand as it swam past. It was a trout, swimming against the current toward a waterfall a hundred yards upstream. *What then…*

when you reach the waterfall?' Magnus realised it was a memory—a lamentation from the past. He looked up again, this time seeing himself standing on the opposite side of the riverbank to Catanya. His arm was outstretched—he was dropping something. A flower landed delicately on the surface of the water. It was a purple iris—*another memory…* Magnus looked down to the riverbed. Resting on a large stone was a bloodstained arrow. Blood rose from the arrow, swirled toward the surface and drifted downstream with the current, where it slowly dispersed into the red of the river. Magnus recalled—*the blood was Thioci's and the arrow was Quag. It had wounded the dragon youngling in Froughton Forest.*

A voice rumbled through Magnus's mind like gentle thunder from a brewing storm. He knew the voice—he had heard it once before at the clearing in the Valley of Shadows where he bonded with Thioci. He had dreamed of that voice ever since. *Balgur!*

"MAGNUS." Balgur's voice was all-powerful as though the brewing storm was now upon him, reverberating through him like a hammer striking a gigantic drum. But it was more than a thought. It came from the water itself, pulsing through the shimmering red.

"Balgur…" Magnus's mind whispered back, his own thoughts rippling through the water and echoing back to him. Small fish scattered and reeds sprouting from the riverbed swayed erratically. He looked to the large stone where the arrow sat, but it was gone. In its place was a Juniper stone. Magnus felt his breast pocket. His Juniper stone was gone. *I must have dropped it when I fell in.*

"Claim it. Take it back."

Magnus tried to move but his feet were fixed.

"REACH." Balgur's voice was growing more assertive. *"Just as we share thoughts—claim it!"*

Magnus knew Balgur was challenging him mentally rather than physically. Magnus reached for the Juniper stone, straining to free his feet so he could move toward it.

"You have power over this realm. Do not go to the stone, have it come to you. Take ownership of it. Claim it."

It seemed to Magnus there was a big chasm between being told what to do and knowing how to do it.

"It is only a chasm if you get lost in it," Balgur said, addressing his doubts. *"CLAIM IT!"*

Balgur's rumbling thoughts made the riverbed shake. Magnus could see the dragon's thoughts were having an effect on the physical world and yet, Balgur was not even alive in a physical sense. He looked once again at the Juniper stone. *Don't get lost in the chasm of thought. Just claim it...* He reached again.

"Where is the stone?" Balgur demanded.

"On the rock."

"Where should it be?"

"In my hand..."

Magnus looked at the stone, resting on the large riverbed rock. He then looked at his hand. There it was, in his hand, *where it should be...*

"There is no chasm," Balgur concluded.

Magnus placed the Juniper stone in his breast pocket. He was not entirely sure how he was able to retrieve it, nor why he was made to do so, but figured Balgur had his reasons. Magnus's impatience, though, was getting the better of him. He wanted to learn the truth of how Balgur came to be here.

"It was here that you fell... upon the Red River?" Magnus asked.

"Aye."

"How exactly did this happen? How did Delvion manage to slay you?"

"There is no need to dwell, Magnus," Balgur counselled.

"I ask as a good friend to Steyne, who laments his part in your death."

"Steyne had no part in my death. He was merely custodian of the sword destined to slay me."

"The fire-sword he allowed to fall into Delvion's hands?"

"The sword 'destined' to fall into Delvion's hands," Balgur corrected. *"Steyne's role was to make the transition happen. He just did not know this to be so."*

"Why would you not tell him and spare him the pain and guilt?"

"No Irucanti would have a will strong enough to deliberately see a dragon's life ended, fated or not—least of all Steyne."

Magnus agreed Eamon would never have made it to the Battle of Fire knowing his role was to facilitate Delvion in killing Balgur. But why would this be fated? Balgur's words only spawned more questions.

"When did you know this would happen?"

"The fire-sword was forged by Gilfieüg of Bowthwait with my assistance." Magnus knew of Gilfieüg. He was a renowned swordsmith. He was also Ganister's father. *"As the sword took shape, Gilfieüg and I shared a vision. This sword would slay me some day. It was ordained. It was inevitable. With this knowledge, it was shaped for such a purpose. It was forged in blue flame at the tip of my breath until the bronze was*

hardened more so than my scales. The blade was long and curved, and the blade's glyphs held wards that would assist with my transition."

"Transition? You mean… from a living dragon, to…" Magnus stopped himself short. Was it rude of him to pry further or was it his right to know? Either way, Balgur seemed forthcoming.

"We all make transitions at some point. I was simply gifted with the knowledge of the next stage of my purpose—to be here for our own Electus."

"But, it took twenty years to choose an Electus."

"It took that long for the dust to settle in the aftermath of the Battle of Fire. You are the Electus needed at this time."

Marsala's words played over in Magnus's head—*'Thioci acknowledged the Electus power within you, thanks to Breona, and decided you should live…'* Magnus then recalled Thioci speaking to Balgur and others of his kin through some kind of connection just before he passed. They all conceded Magnus was the right choice.

"I gather Thioci made you aware that I already carried Iisilée's blood. You agreed this was acceptable?"

"Aye. You are 'flame to ice'—a bridge between two realms. You will be the exemplar for what the Electi are capable of and in doing so, birth a Four Realm affiliation. This is paramount for Allumbreve's survival."

"But I do not know what powers I have from Iisilée."

"That you retrieved your Juniper stone moments ago was proof of her power. That was not of my blood." Magnus felt for the magic stone in his pocket. *"From the Red River, I have access to all the waterways of Allumbreve—Catanya has borne witness to this,"* Balgur explained. *"Iisilée has given you power over this realm. That is how you retrieved the Juniper stone."*

"It is true then…" Magnus affirmed. Marsala was right—about everything. But how was being a 'double' Electus going to help form a Four Realm affiliation and why was the affiliation so important? *"Is there feuding between the realms?"*

"Precursors to as much showed their face during the Battle of Fire. The strengths exhibited by the Electi of the other realms were overwhelming. Even the Irucantí were in awe. Their awe turned to ambition. The effects of this you have witnessed yourself."

"Aye." Magnus thought once again of the High Priests' campaign to end his life.

"You think of the High Priests." Balgur was reading Magnus's mind again. *"They have strengths you can draw on, for they are exceptionally well trained."*

"That sounds like a dangerous proposition." Magnus winced. He wondered where Balgur was taking the discussion.

"You will learn a lot from one of them, the other will be slain."

It was worse than Magnus thought. *"This is a prophecy? How will I slay a High Priest? Especially under the guard of two dragons."*

"Three dragons. Brue is with them now."

Magnus's heart sank. *"What then am I to do with three fire dragons protecting two 'exceptionally well trained' priests?"* Magnus asked. Balgur had told him long ago, as Thioci's blood drew him out of the darkness of death, that becoming the Electus came at a cost. *'An obligation,'* he had said. *A fate was handed to me...* Magnus recalled Marsala explaining—*'you survive challenges to meet your inevitable fate.'* Her words were beginning to sound like truth. *'Irony'* indeed... Magnus glanced back to Catanya who was still frozen in time, fingers piercing the water's edge.

"Catanya will be by my side. I don't want her life endangered."

"Neither does she yours. For now, remain together. You need each other for reasons beyond your mutual affection." Balgur's words pleased Magnus. He did not wish to be the overprotective lover. He simply could not bear to lose her. Anyhow, Catanya had saved his life more often than he had hers. Magnus reached a hand to her once again. This time, he drew closer.

"These waters will restore strength. Return here when needed."

"Aye," Magnus acknowledged Balgur's advice. Closer still he drew to Catanya. Just inches from her touch, Balgur spoke one last time.

"Heal wounds. Forge bonds. Be the greatest of the Electi."

Magnus's fingers reached Catanya's.

CLIMB - ONE

Their fingers met and they were free of the river.

Magnus and Catanya were kneeling—just as they were before touching the red water's surface.

"What just happened?" Catanya murmured, feeling Magnus's fingers with her own. "You disappeared just now. I..." her roving eyes found Magnus's. "Balgur..."

"I was in the river, looking up at you the whole time."

"I wasn't here. Balgur took me... on a journey."

"You were with Balgur too?"

"He showed me two great threats to Allumbreve. One is Delvion and... Magnus..." Catanya shook her head. It was not at all like Catanya to be lost for words.

"What, Catanya? What is the other threat?"

"The other is your mother."

"My *mother*?"

"I heard her conversation. Not so much words spoken as... I understood her intentions."

"I understand Delvion, but... my *mother*?"

Catanya explained how Balgur could penetrate the far reaches of Allumbreve through the waterways and from this, learned truths about Balgur and Alavia. "Your mother is in a position of power. Her people are listening to her."

"As their Electus?"

Catanya nodded. "Perhaps. It would make sense."

Magnus walked away from the riverbank. He needed to distance himself from the incredulities of the Red River, Balgur, Delvion and whatever it was his mother was up to. "What exactly is my mother doing?"

"I think she is angry, Magnus. Her manner seems calculated, determined and... cold."

"She thinks she has lost everything as she did once before. Perhaps she intends to do something about it."

As they continued on to Froughton Forest, Magnus explained everything Balgur had told him about confronting the High Priests, learning from one of them and his responsibility in bringing together the four realms. Catanya was in agreement with Magnus—the latter two of these revelations seemed so far-fetched they were not yet ready to deliberate on them. For now, finding their way into the Romghold and confronting the High Priests was more than enough of a challenge.

They reached Froughton Forest late in the afternoon and set up a temporary camp beside a freshwater stream in the Outer Rim. Magnus removed his cloak and boots and soaked his feet in the cool water. Catanya removed her lance and worked through a ritual of stretches before lying on a blanket to rest. Looking about at the trees, Magnus drew in the sharp scent of the pines. He welcomed the cool forest air that permeated through his Ferustir armour as reprieve from the summer heat. In the quiet of the moment, his thoughts turned once again to his mother. "Could you see where she was, Catanya?" Magnus had thought to let her rest but felt he needed to know.

"The visions were blurry, but I travelled well north of the Uydferlands until the rivers were all but frozen over. I could feel the cold... *ice* cold." Catanya sat up, wrapping the blanket around her. "Alavia was in an ice palace or sorts, speaking before a legion of people." She peered off as if in deep thought. "They are *her* people." She looked to Magnus. "They're in the Rhyderlands, north of the Ice Breach."

It did not really matter to Magnus where she was. If she were alive, he would find her.

"Magnus," Catanya emphasised. "Your mother was no subordinate. Her voice held authority. As I said, she is in a position of power. She is establishing her people as rulers, just like the Authoritarium."

Magnus tried to make sense of it. "Perhaps my mother has taken her place as Hasdereq's heir." Ice seemed to crawl its way up Magnus's spine forming the next, chilling question in his mind—"Could she have lifted the spell that masks her powers?"

"What would it mean if she did?" Catanya stared blankly.

Magnus shrugged—as much to shake the chills as to emphasise his uncertainty. "If she has lifted the spell from herself, she may have lifted it from me."

"That would explain your strange symptoms in Thwax, Magnus."

It would also explain my ability to retrieve the Juniper stone in the Red River... Magnus lowered his shoulders and shuddered the thought away. "We've enough to be concerned about right now."

Catanya seemed to linger on the thought a moment longer then stared up to the Romgnian cliffs. Magnus stood and dried his feet, then rested a hand on a pine trunk for stability as he pulled a boot on. It was a tight fit with his still-damp foot and so he let go, pulling with both hands.

"Hold it right there." Catanya's voice was sharp. Magnus froze and looked about. "Close your eyes."

"What?"

"I said, close your eyes." Magnus looked at Catanya. She frowned. "I didn't say look at me, I told you to close your eyes."

It was a game, Magnus decided. With a boot on one foot, he stood tall and closed his eyes. He could hear Catanya's feet stepping closer until she was in front of him.

"I need to tell you something. When we were at the artisans' camp, after we had gone to bed, I kissed another man." Catanya's voice was clear. Magnus heard a slight ring in his ears and his breath caught in the upper part of his chest. His eyes still closed, he reached for the tree for support again. His mind searched for reason in Catanya's sentence. He thought quickly of all the men he had seen at the artisans' camp and how and why this could have happened. He knew it was not for him to guess—it was for Catanya to explain. Then he thought of the Blacksmith's son. He could see at the time the young man had feelings for Catanya.

"Dale..." Magnus whispered. His eyes opened and reluctantly fell on Catanya—a reluctance that felt worse than the thought of the kiss. Her face was not nearly as composed as the voice of her confession. Her nostrils flared, her throat pulsed, and her brown eyes blinked repeatedly—each blink revealing more emotion than the last. Magnus could see she had mustered all her strength to say what she did. "Oh..." Magnus said. It was a pointless, useless word, but the sight of her distress was too much. He wanted to say, *'that's okay'* or *'I understand'* but it was not okay, and he did not understand. So Magnus stood, staring dumbly at Catanya.

"I need to tell you what happened," Catanya fumbled.

Magnus had never seen Catanya fumble words until now. He took some slow breaths.

"I left the women's sleeping tent in the middle of the night. Something was wrong, I..." Catanya hesitated. "I just had this feeling we had to get out of there. I came to look for you and happened across Dale in the blacksmith tent where he warned me we needed to leave." She rubbed her hand over the vambrace Dale has repaired. "He was hesitant to explain further. I kissed him..." Catanya crossed her arms over her chest, but kept her eyes on Magnus. "I kissed him to... snap him out of his daze."

"He was dazed because he has feelings for you."

"It was that obvious?"

"From when we met in the wheat field—yes."

"Oh..." Catanya dropped her gaze and swung a leg through a fern at her feet. "I just needed to know what he knew—*why* we had to leave."

"Did it work?"

Catanya looked up at Magnus. "Did what work?"

"The kiss."

"I guess so, yes. He knew you were the Electus. I knew then Delik must have known, too. And I knew *you* were in trouble. I left the tent and was captured."

"You were distracted."

"I was. I mean, what? NO! I don't know." Catanya frowned and scratched her head. "I was concerned for your safety, Dale and Willem's safety, and even Ivy's."

"Are you still concerned for their safety?"

"I'm not sure. With everything that followed, I've given it less thought."

"With Delik and the Quag dead, Dale and his family probably left the camp." Catanya nodded silently. Magnus walked to Catanya and wrapped his arms around her. She was clearly suffering more than he was over kissing Dale. "I do think you're responsible for cursing Dale," Magnus said, feigning a serious face.

"It takes more than a kiss to curse someone, Magnus." Catanya squinted the way she did when Magnus was playing games with her, only she did not seem sure he was.

"You underestimate yourself, Catanya. The next time Dale kisses a girl, he'll think of you—and every time thereafter."

"I think he'll get over it." Catanya rolled her eyes.

"I never did."

Catanya looked at him again and returned his hug. "I'm sorry, Magnus."

"You've nothing to be sorry about."

Magnus peered through the treetops and could see where the mountain vanished into clouds a mile high.

"Up there, where you're looking, is the Romghold." Catanya pointed, her other arm still wrapped around Magnus.

"So, you think it's safe to climb?" Magnus could not see a path up the steep cliff.

"Joffren and I made the climb many times." Catanya was still pointing. "The first took me an entire day. Each time we made the climb, I became more confident and stole time back." Catanya's finger traced its way up the Romgnian cliff in a zigzag pattern.

"I'll follow you, Catanya. I certainly can't see a path of my own."

"There is no path but in your imagination. Each climb was different. The path familiar was my conviction it could be done, even when it seemed impossible."

Magnus looked at Catanya as her words played over. "Do you believe that? By our conviction we can do the impossible?" Words Eamon once spoke on the matter came to Magnus—*Impossible…only if you believe it is'*. His words echoed through his mind, answering his question for him. Magnus reached into his breast pocket and drew out the Juniper stone. "Of course we can," he said.

"Of course we can," Catanya repeated, cupping her hands around his that gripped the stone. "But further to your last question, this climb will be more challenging than my previous climbs."

"How so?"

"We have no spikes and crampons." Catanya examined the souls of her boots. "Worse still, we need to climb during the night. I've not done that."

"Right." Magnus looked for the afternoon sun through the tall trees. "Because we don't want the dragons to see us."

"Aye. As I said, they will spot us from up there. And if what Balgur told you is true, Brue is one of them. We know what he thinks of you." Catanya winced.

"Balgur said to 'heal wounds' and 'forge bonds'," Magnus said dryly.

"I'm not sure Brue is the best way to start, Magnus." Catanya feigned a smile.

It would be a long night and they both knew it. Magnus and Catanya rested amongst the trees, both managing some sleep, and as dusk turned to dark they prepared for the climb. Catanya fed and watered Tilly and released the horse on the northbound Outer Rim road that would take her toward the town of Kreeluck, as Marsala had requested. Then they headed out into the night and across the Red River to the base of the Romgnian Mountain cliff face.

Magnus and Catanya made final preparations for the climb. Magnus buckled his scabbard tighter than usual and ensured Lucas's sword was secure. Eamon's long daggers remained sheathed one-a-side in their leg holsters. Magnus's packed duffle bag, with dried beef strips, dried fruit and a flask of water, was strapped across his back. Catanya secured her Ferustir's lance and throwing knives in the same manner. As always, she arranged her own knives to the front of the pouch in the left leg of her Ferustir suit, with Demi's blades to the back. She re-buckled her vambraces and greaves and checked the provisions in her own bag. Finally, she retied and double knotted her burgundy laces. Seeing her do so, Magnus followed suit and retied his own laces.

"Ready?" Magnus jumped on the spot a few times.

"Ready." Catanya smiled nervously and turned to the cliff face.

They started the climb. Magnus was grateful the summer day had left the cliff face warm and dry. He had learned from climbing the cliffs at the Western Margins as a child that cold stone soon worked your fingers into lethargy and wet stone was cause to cancel a climb altogether. Other than this, he left all knowledge and knowhow to Catanya.

"It's roughly a mile up to the clouds. The clouds there are consistent," Catanya spoke gently, not two feet ahead of Magnus. "Three hundred feet of cloud, then a mile further afterwards. If we are through the clouds before the moon shifts out of the Spindlefax constellation, we know we can reach the Romghold by sunrise. If not, we'll need to hide in the clouds for a day and resume our climb tomorrow night."

"Aye." Magnus tried not to think about holding on to the cliff face for a day, a mile above ground, waiting for the following night to come. Instead, he watched Catanya and followed her every move. He could see Catanya was pacing herself slow and steady, double-checking every placement of hand and foot before elevating to the next hold.

With the cloud cover above, it was impossible to discern time by the moon or stars. Magnus estimated they were half way to the clouds when he dared to glance about. A mile westward of the cliffs, the sky was cloud free and the moon cast blue light across the canopy of Froughton Forest's ancient pines and oaks. It was the most magnificent sight. Magnus looked then to the darkness of the ground far below, making his head turn in a spin. "That was a bad idea," he moaned to himself.

"Don't look down if you can help it." Catanya peered at Magnus. She released her left hand's grip, drew her fingers into a fist and cracked her knuckles.

"How are you travelling?" Magnus enquired.

"I'm good. It's different without climbing tools. Slower. I'll be glad when we're above the clouds. The moon will afford us sight. The closer we get to the clouds, the more I'm going by touch. I could make a fire orb but we'd stand out like a beacon.

Magnus had a similar idea but one that could work. Back in Ba'rrat, Sarah always had a small orb of blue light in her prison cell to stave off the darkness. It was far more discrete than the balls of amber a Fireisgh spell would induce.

"I could conjure a 'gypsy's eye'." Magnus knew the name and knew Sarah could perform all kinds of tricks with the 'eye' once created, including changing colours and intensity. Magnus knew none of this, but from his Gypsy magic lessons in Sarah's cell he could at least create one. "I think it could work."

"It's more subtle than a fire orb?" Catanya asked.

"I'm sure it will be. I can extinguish it immediately if you think it's not."

Catanya looked about, apparently considering the option. "Let's do it—for safety's sake. Plummeting a few thousand feet will be harder to reason with than a fire dragon."

Magnus was inclined to agree. Then again, he dreaded having to face Brue on the cliff face. A horrible vision came to mind of the long-tailed fire dragon scorching them both with flames. If it came to this he would leap over Catanya and try to envelope her, taking the heat himself. He had survived it unscathed before, but doubted Catanya would. In reality, he knew he could never cling to the cliff face amidst the excruciating pain of dragon flames. Even if he could, the dragon would take other measures to pick them off the mountain.

Once the nightmarish thought passed, Magnus whispered the gentle gypsy spell—*"Gan ni-sish bulniferé."* As with all gypsy spells, it needed to roll gently off the tongue as a whisper, else it would overpower itself and die before it was induced. A tiny blue spark—no larger than a pinprick—sprouted from intention and floated beside Magnus. He blew gently at the spark and it floated up a little way until it was beside Catanya. *"Ni-sish-sish,"* Magnus whispered, enticing the spark to grow to the size of a grape. Another whisper and it grew to that of a plum. The blue light from the gypsy's eye gave gentle illumination of a similar hue to the moonlight over Froughton Forest.

"Perfect," Catanya whispered and started to climb again.

Time passed and the ascent continued. The gypsy's eye kept to Catanya's left and occasionally, she would give it a nudge to move it about and help find her way. The clouds above were getting closer and with it, the stone cold and damp. Catanya slowed to a painfully slow pace, ensuring every grip was patent before moving to the next. Magnus sensed the slow pace meant they would not reach the Romghold before sunrise. It would mean searching for a ledge to rest on. Here, they could regain their strength, eat rations and, the gods permitting, get some sleep. Catanya apparently shared Magnus's thoughts.

"There are occasional outcrops but we need to find a crevice to rest in. I've seen them when climbing before. Some cut through the band of clouds. There are several deep crevices ahead."

"Can you remember where they are?" Magnus hoped she could.

"Aye. There's one back that way." Catanya pointed to her right and up. Fifty feet in that direction, there was a long ledge of stone jutting out a good five feet. "We've come a little more to the left than I wanted, but not too far. We could climb down a little and come back at it from below or we could—" Catanya fell silent and as still as if a spell had turned her to stone. A long, breathless moment passed then she looked directly up, into the clouds, no more than twenty feet away. Magnus continued to hold his breath, waiting for instruction. Catanya snapped her head toward him. "MOVE!"

Catanya reached high and hoisted herself upward, not waiting to assess the sureness of her grip. Magnus shadowed her, wondering what had her startled. "What is it?" he whispered between gritted teeth.

"Dragon!" Catanya hissed back. They were ten feet from the clouds. Wisps of mist floated down, dampening Magnus's face and limbs. Catanya reached to the gypsy's eye and flicked it up into the clouds where its weak light vanished. "Freeze, Magnus." Pinned to the cliff face, Magnus and Catanya were like a pair of statues. "Do not move. Not a single inch."

Then Magnus heard it. Two beats of a heavy drum, a sweeping sound and a sharp 'whoosh'. Less than a hundred feet to their left a dragon speared through the clouds. Its speed was phenomenal. Magnus's jaw dropped and his heart stopped. The dragon sped toward the darkness below and then— 'THUMP.' Its wings opened, tapering its decent. It flew out over Froughton Forest, casting a great, looming shadow over the blue treetops. The moon sparkled its reflection over the dragon's shimmering scales—a flashing contrast of blue and bronze that shifted with the beats of the creature's wings. The dragon banked to the left and came back around.

"Don't move. Face the cliff. She won't see us," Catanya whispered. Magnus did as told, fighting every natural urge to face the dragon. The only thing that pleased him in this moment was Catanya referring to it as a 'she'. *It's not Brue...*

By the increased frequency of beating wings, Magnus gathered the dragon was climbing again, half a mile to their right. A long minute later, the creature was over the mountain peak and gone.

Magnus and Catanya released their pent up breaths and were quick to move again. "Please be careful, Magnus."

"Aye."

"We've come too far to fall now."

"Aye."

Magnus followed Catanya into the clouds. Vision was dull, but by some miracle they came to a ledge that allowed them to sit and rest for a spell.

"What luck is this?" Magnus felt his own spirits lifting. The gypsy's eye drifted back toward them, affording a little light.

"This ledge is continuous. At some places narrow, at others it juts out up to five feet," Catanya explained. "To the south is the ledge we were under before Liné flew by.

"Liné?" Magnus asked.

"Aye. She's a beautiful dragon. Quick to temper, though."

Magnus chuckled and shook his head at Catanya's familiar tone. "You speak of them like friends. I just hope they don't try to kill us."

Through the haze of the cloud, Catanya shuffled over to Magnus. "I'm sorry. I guess they're so familiar to me, I..."

"That's okay." Magnus wrapped an arm around Catanya. They peered through the clouds. There was no clear vision to be had, least of all when sorting through conflicting thoughts. "You grew close to them in the Romghold, didn't you." Catanya nodded. "I do look forward to meeting Rubea." Magnus knew Rubea was her favourite—the young dragon she had grown to love.

Catanya closed her eyes and smiled. "Rubea is gorgeous." She looked at Magnus. "She'll love you. Especially when she reads my thoughts and learns of my love for you. Of that, she will be most excited."

"She'll do that? She'll read your personal thoughts like that?" Even as he said it, Magnus remembered the dragons in Ba'rrat were quick to assess Catanya and Magnus's relationship.

Catanya laughed a single laugh and shook her head. "Rubea's a little cheeky. You'll see."

After a few minutes recovery, Magnus addressed the next issue—"Shall we venture beyond the clouds and see if the moon has shifted beyond the Spindlefax constellation?"

"I think we can spare ourselves the effort," Catanya countered. "Even if by some miracle time is on our side, starting again with an early night will restore the cliff to warm and dry."

"Aye. And give us more of the night to cause trouble in the Romghold."

"Indeed." Catanya started to move. "We should find the crevice I told you about and rest."

"Then you can tell me more about the Romghold so I know what to expect this time tomorrow."

COUSINS

On the eve of the third day, the leading group of refugees from Brindle arrived in Thwax. They had rested on the second night and from the following morning, walked without further rest, just as Bonstaph had instructed them to do. Sarah travelled with the first group to leave. There had been minimal conversation among the travellers in her group—again, as per Bonstaph's instruction—*Be thirty sets of ears, not thirty sets of voices for other ears to find.*' Sarah could see Bonstaph had been very clever with his evacuation strategy. She would not have expected anything less from him.

The fifty extra people Bonstaph had accounted for were named the 'Perimetral' guard and were posted as scouts. They were all men and women he trusted. Sarah recognised many of them from the Fire Realm. Any others, Bonstaph knew from his days as Knight Commander. The Perimetral formed a protective barrier for the travellers. Sarah's group—the leading end of the migration—saw neither incident nor attack from any Quag warriors. In time they would know whether successive groups arrived in Thwax without incident.

If all groups arrived as they left, Sarah knew she had until sunrise to do what she needed to get done in Thwax. And so, with fog cloaking the abandoned ghost town on a moonlit night, Sarah stole herself away from her group as the last of them succumbed to sleep. Sarah headed straight for the jetty to get her bearings. *It has been a lifetime since I was last in Thwax.* The town looked even worse for wear than she remembered and its advanced state of decay made finding her way challenging. Soon though, she spotted the jetty. At the start of the Jetty was a wooden chair with a half-knitted shawl, knitting needles, and a ball of pale green yarn placed on top of it. It was a sight familiar to Sarah.

"Marsala…"

From here, Sarah was able to navigate the buildings, debris and abandoned streets to the small alleyway leading to a home she knew too well. Sarah knocked on the wooden door then looked away, drawing her cloak inward to shield from the cold, misty fog. It floated past her in milky strands like the tattered clothing of lurking ghosts. "Be off," Sarah mumbled. "You mind your dominion and I'll mind mine." With her back to the door, Sarah heard its small, square viewing-hole open.

"I didn't know you were coming and you're to blame for that—not I," the familiar voice said.

"It's nice to know I still have the ability to hide from you," Sarah said in a solemn manner she knew was not at all her usual self.

The door opened. Marsala looked Sarah up and down. "You've a story to tell, I see that much. And I sense it's not the sort I want to hear." The two women embraced. "It is good to see you, cousin."

"Aye," Sarah said. "It is good to see you, too." Sarah could feel the affection in Marsala's embrace, but also her trepidation. The two women entered Marsala's living area and Sarah fell, exhausted, into a chair.

"What has happened?" Marsala wrung nervous hands.

"Make me a meal and I'll tell you all about it. It has been far too long since I've tasted your fine food."

"You've changed, and recently at that," Marsala said as she disappeared through the curtains at the back of the room. "And entirely forgotten is was you who always cooked for me," she shouted after herself.

Sarah nodded in agreement as she scanned the room in contemplation. She spotted the black cat peeping through the curtain.

"Tilly," Sarah called, such that Marsala could hear her.

"No, that is my horse's name," Marsala's voice called back.

Sarah nodded again, still looking at the cat. "Blüflis," Sarah remembered— remembering also that the cat was a dark shade of blue only distinguishable from black in the sun. She doubted Blüflis spent much time in the sun.

"Aye," Marsala confirmed, returning with her tray of food and tea. She placed it on the table then sat and looked at Sarah. Blüflis assumed her position atop the tallest pile of books in the room.

"You're not alone," Sarah remarked. She could sense a presence in the home. It was not a recent presence, but a feeling someone else was here— now.

"Aye." Marsala leant forward and poured two cups of tea. "Downstairs in the back room."

"You are healing someone?"

"For a friend. He arrived yesterday. You need not concern yourself. I've given him something to make him sleep and aid with his healing."

Sarah knew she should leave her cousin to look after her patient—to put his needs ahead of hers—but that was the *old* Sarah. The *new* Sarah had an oath to fulfil.

"You need something of me," Marsala asked, sipping her tea then gingerly placing the cup on the table as though making a sound would disrupt Sarah's response.

"I need you to create a spell." The tone in her own voice seemed harsh even to Sarah.

"What kind of a spell, cousin?" Marsala said, mimicking Sarah's tone.

"I need a *Tenebris* spell."

"No." Marsala looked away and shook her head. "Dark spells such as that cannot be broken."

"I have sworn a gypsy oath, cousin. It is an oath that cannot be broken, nor fulfilled without your help." Marsala was still shaking her head. She pouted her lips like a child in defiance and began to scratch one of her knotted locks of coloured hair. "You have to do this for me, Marsala," Sarah insisted.

Marsala finally made eye contact with Sarah but continued to pout. "What is it for? What does it need to do?"

"Hide my presence in darkness, find another in the same and—"

"And?" Marsala's face intensified.

"And teach me a second Tenebris spell to take the life of a sorcerer."

Marsala's mouth searched for words. Sarah knew it would take some convincing. What she was asking her cousin to do, she knew, there was no coming back from. Eventually Marsala spoke—"Will you please eat some food?" she snapped, as though it were the only retaliation she could think of.

Sarah did as told, reaching for the soup bowl. She began eating the savoury mix of meat and vegetables. It was delicious, but she had no appetite. "Fennel… celery, carrot, lamb—"

"I will not waste my time arguing with you, Sarah." Marsala stood and paced about the room. Blüflis stared questioningly at the mystic, apparently not at all familiar with her agitation. "You must tell me what this is about."

"I do not wish to trouble you with such—"

"Such is much! If these Tenebris spells yield as intended, I may never see you again." Marsala was almost shouting. She took a breath to calm herself. Sarah kept eating her soup. "I cannot live never knowing why you would sacrifice yourself to such dark vengeance."

Sarah licked the saltiness from her lips. "This sorcerer killed Ganister."

Marsala's face softened. She came to Sarah and knelt beside her. They looked into one another's eyes. Sarah could see the eyes they shared—eyes that belonged to the sisters that were their gypsy mothers. She leant forward and rested her head on Marsala's shoulder. Marsala embraced Sarah again, only this time with true compassion. Sarah would like to have cried, but she was well spent of tears.

"What of your son, Sarah?" Marsala's voice had softened.

Sarah sat back in the chair again. "I will find Lucas, one way or another. He is out there somewhere."

Marsala remained on her knees. She seemed to sway a little and her eyes drifted.

"What is it?" Sarah asked.

"Lucas…" Marsala's word came as whisper from a distant thought.

"That's right—'Lucas'."

"Friend as a brother…fallen to darkness…" Marsala was mumbling.

Marsala knew something—Sarah was sure of it. "What do you know? What have you foreseen?"

"Cousin…" Marsala was shaking her head. "Who is Lucas's closest friend?" Marsala winced as she asked.

"Magnus. They are like brothers. 'Fallen to darkness,' you said. What do you know, Marsala?" Sarah was almost too scared to ask.

"Magnus carries Lucas's sword."

"How do you know this?"

"He was here. With another."

Sarah thought of when she last saw Magnus. It was the evening before escaping Ba'rrat. She looked at the empty seat next to her. "Catanya," she said.

"Aye," Marsala confirmed. "Not three days ago."

Sarah was at once pleased they were both safe, for the last she knew of Catanya was seeing her leave her and the other escapees east of Ba'rrat, in the farmer's cart, and heading back toward the Black Capitol's gates. But how did Magnus come to possess Lucas's sword? With a sigh of relief, Sarah realised Marsala's confusion—"That was Magnus's sword. They each have one, forged together by Ganister."

Marsala shook her head. Pity was written across her face. "I am aware there are two, but no, Sarah, the sword he carries is not his. It is Lucas's."

Sarah was quick to calculate. Bonstaph fought with Magnus in Ba'rrat's arena where Ganister was slain. That much she knew. If Magnus possesses

Lucas's sword, this is where he found it. Which meant Lucas either perished in the arena, or left without his sword. She doubted Bonstaph could keep Lucas's death from her. Another thing troubled her. It had been troubling her since she asked Bonstaph about it—

'What of this sorcerer?' Sarah remembered asking him.

'He fled with Delvion…' Bonstaph had replied.

'And what did you think, when you saw my husband's killer take his leave?'

'I cursed his name… swore I would kill him.'

It never seemed right that Bonstaph had failed to slay Ganister's killer. But if he knew the killer… If he knew the sorcerer… If Magnus had retrieved his sword…

"What are you saying, Marsala?" Sarah pointed at the mystic. "Do not mince words."

Marsala paused. Sarah hoped she was gathering her words into a neat arrangement of truth. She was. "I scried Lucas's sword. It spoke of his fall into darkness. Poison has addled his mind and he bends to the will of a master. That master could only be Delvion, cousin. No other has so dark a disposition."

Sarah stared hard at Marsala. "My son is the sorcerer?" She forced the words. "He killed my husband? His father?"

"Aye. Lucas is the sorcerer you speak of."

Sarah slumped, gripping tightly to the soup bowl in her lap. The room spun about in silence. The hatred Sarah was using as her emotional shield vanished in the silence. Her shield was gone. In its place was numbness so absolute that Sarah was almost sure she had died and joined the ghosts of floating fog outside Marsala's home. Only the aching beat of her broken heart told her she was still among the living.

"There will be no need for the Tenebris spells, then," Marsala said. Her voice came to Sarah as a muffled moan.

"The spells are essential." Sarah blinked away the fog. "As Lucas's mother, I bear responsibility. You shall bind out fates—"

"I will not conjure a spell so you can kill your own son."

"I still need a Tenebris spell to hide me from darkness and seek Lucas out. The second spell must bind our fates."

"You will not be able to kill him, cousin. Your heart will not yield to such a thing."

"I know this. There is something else you can do in its place. Something darker than the realm of spells."

"You want me to place a *curse*." Marsala was the one pointing now.

Sarah did not flinch. She knew a curse was as bad as murder, for it took away free will. "As long as I live, I will not allow Magnus, Catanya, nor anyone else to fall victim to this sorcerer of darkness—my son or not."

"Such a curse will bind you to a nightmare from which you can never wake." Marsala stared. Sarah would not yield and so waited for Marsala to do so. "Very well. I will prepare a Tenebris spell and conjure your curse, but you will need to place the curse yourself. This is not something that can be done from afar. You will need to seek Lucas out."

"Your spell will help me with that."

"Yes it will." Marsala blinked. She looked frustrated. "Now, for the love of the gods, will you finish your soup?"

Sarah left Marsala's home in the darkest hour of night—the hour before sunrise. It was the hour when restless sleepers rose and the ghosts of Thwax's past sank away before the rising sun exposed their unsettled secrets. Marsala watched as Sarah took her leave and vanished into the fog like an apparition.

Marsala picked the tray of half eaten food and tea off the table and turned toward the curtains at the back of the room. She looked at Blüflis who shot a judging glance at her. "Don't look at me like that," Marsala snapped, certain the blue cat knew she had used her mystic skills for ill will this night. Blüflis turned away, lifting her tail high as if to express her disapproval. "Hmph…"

Marsala was exhausted. Preparing both the twofold Tenebris spell and the curse used all her strength and it would be several days before she recovered enough to scry even the thoughts of a white-lipped tree frog. She left the living room and descended the narrow staircase to the kitchen with Blüflis twirling between her legs to get down first. In the kitchen, Marsala placed the tray on the kitchen bench. Blüflis leapt up and sniffed at the soup bowls. "Help yourself, so long as you drop the attitude, little lady." She turned about and jumped. A tall man was standing over her with a look of fury on his face.

"You're awake!" Marsala was startled. Blüflis arched her back, hissing at the man. "You frightened ten lives out of us," Marsala continued. "One from me and nine from Blüflis."

Joffren's face was clammy and his eyes an intense, pewter grey. He was unsteady, waving from side to side, knocking over bowls and cooking books.

"Careful, Semsü." Marsala reached for his shoulders to steady him. "When Färgd arrived with you strapped to his back, I feared the worst. But you've surprised even me—"

Marsala was cut short as Joffren's hands clasped around her throat, squeezing mercilessly. Blüflis leapt at Joffren, claws unsheathed, and imbedded herself into Joffren's face and skull. Joffren grunted in anger, released one hand from Marsala's throat, grabbed a handful of the cat's dark fur and hurled her across the room. The cat screamed until it hit a wall and fell to the ground.

Her vision darkening and her throat in excruciating pain, Marsala grabbed a heavy saucepan and swung it hard at Joffren's head, clocking him on the right temple. The Irucantî fell to the ground giving Marsala respite enough to cough her sight and breath back. Joffren recovered quickly, bringing a large kitchen knife sidelong to Marsala's throat, pushing her back against the kitchen bench where her head clanged against several hanging pots and bowls. Joffren pushed the pots out of his face with his spare hand. Marsala reached back to steady herself against the bench.

"What are you doing, you bald-headed priest?" Marsala shouted. "I'm trying to help you!"

Joffren's face hardened. His jaw clenched. His eyes were glazed and unfocused. He pushed the large knife harder against Marsala's throat. A haunting growl rolled from behind gritted teeth. Marsala felt the sting of the blade cut into her neck. She realised there was no reasoning with the priest and that his anger, mixed with his delirity, was going to spell the end for her. Her right hand held fast to Joffren's wrist and with the other she searched the bench behind her for something to swing at him again. She caught a brief reflection in a hanging copper pot as it swung by Joffren's bleeding head— there was a paring knife just a few inches from her hand.

In a flash, Marsala grabbed the knife and buried it into Joffren's neck. Joffren stumbled, dropped the large knife, and swung a fist at Marsala's face. She fell to the floor and Joffren fell on top of her.

When Marsala woke, she was lying prone on the floor. Blüflis was beside her, licking her bruised head. Marsala's jaw ached from Joffren's punch and she could not move. Turning her head, wincing at the pain, she could see Joffren's body lying on top of her. She scratched the mottled, colourful hair on her head and tried to open and close her jaw. "Ow…"

After a minute spent grunting and groaning, Marsala managed to pull herself out from beneath the priest who was close to twice her size. She felt Joffren's bloodied neck for a pulse. "Dead." Getting to her feet, she sighed. "Apparently, I did *not* fear the worst." Rubbing her jaw with one hand and carrying Blüflis with the other, Marsala left the kitchen and walked to the door at the rear of the house. Outside, the sky was a dull purple with an orange tinge beginning to push through the lifting fog. *Sunrise... I've been unconscious for nearly an hour...*

Marsala put Blüflis on the ground and went to a lean-to against the back wall of her home. Inside, she seated herself at a small table placed among dozens of potted plants and herbs. She took a piece of paper from a stack beneath a paperweight, a quill, and a bottle of purple ink. She wrote a letter that began— *"Dear Eamon..."*

When the letter was complete, Marsala cut a length of brown string from a long yarn with a knife. On the far side of the yard, Marsala opened a birdcage containing two Ahrona swallows and removed one of them. She carefully folded and rolled the note then tied it to the bird's right leg. In an Airisth dialect, Marsala whispered to the bird—*"Fana Eamon, ko quera...* find Eamon, post haste." She released the swallow and the small bird was quick to take flight, heading directly west toward Ba'rrat.

HANNAH - FOUR

Hannah was locked in a prison cage. She sat on the dirt ground cross-legged as far from the entrance as possible.

"How was the journey back?" It was an ΘhUidman posted to guard her. He was speaking with the one named Regan.

"Two altercations," Regan said. "The first after Checkpoint Four. Half a dozen outlaws tried to rob us. Can you believe it?" Both men laughed.

"Were you running a scuttle?"

"Absolutely. Three stage and four a piece."

"Ouch! I'm sure you made their day. What was the other altercation?"

Regan sighed. "More of those wretched worgriels."

"Curse them. Where?"

"A mile before Checkpoint Eight."

"Eight? That deep in the Valley? What in all of Froughton is going on?"

Regan shook his head, but had no words. He turned about and looked at Hannah. She'd been watching and listening, but was quick to drop her gaze. "As for this delightful little creature," Regan leant against the bars of the cage. "There'll be a peremptory commission, no doubt."

"She seems harmless enough. Are you sure she tried to kill Creighton's daughter?"

"I don't know… I just don't know. She's Xavier's daughter—I know that much."

Hannah looked furtively at Ragan again.

"So there are political implications, then." The other ΘhUidman glanced at Hannah then back to Regan, slapping his shoulder. "Better you than I giving testimony, Regan." With that, he left.

Regan stared dryly at Hannah as though trying to garner further truth about her somehow. Hannah kept her lips firmly closed and breathed through her nose, reminding herself not to talk to these untrustworthy people.

"You should eat, girl."

Hannah had eaten sparingly since entering her prison cage. She wanted to appear defiant and figured this was a good start. She did, however, drink water as it was given.

Regan turned about. Two other people approached but Hannah was careful not to look.

"Can we talk to her?" a girl's voice asked.

"I don't think you'll have much success, Vevila, but go ahead," Regan said.

"Can we talk alone?" a male voice asked.

Hannah sneaked a peek at the couple. *'Vevila'… That was Nëven's sister's name.*

"Very well," Regan said. "But you two stay until I return. She's not to be left alone."

"Aye," both the young man and girl said together.

"I'm holding you accountable, Artur." Regan pointed at the young man. "If you're to train as a 'Lochrator' in the new year, you need to practice assuming responsibility." Artur bowed respectfully. Regan walked off and Artur turned to Hannah, who was quick to look away.

Artur… Nëven's brother, Hannah deduced.

It was Vevila who spoke first. "Why did you try to kill our sister?" Her voice was angry and came as a hoarse cry. Hannah was terrified of being chastised any more and too scared to defend herself. She lifted her knees to her head and wrapped her arms around them.

"Vevila, silence yourself," Artur insisted. "You disgrace Nëven with your accusations. She already told you the girl was not to blame."

The hairs of Hannah's neck stood on end. *Nëven is talking? That must mean she is getting better! She can tell them, then, that this was all an accident.*

"Nëven blamed her Jasper stone for her injuries. How ridiculous! She's not fit to possess a Jasper stone and never will be."

"Your resentments are a bore, sister. Take respite of them so we can talk to the girl, will you?"

"Fine," Vevila spat the words. "You talk to her." She turned about, stomping the gravel at her feet. Artur lowered himself into a squat so his head was level with Hannah's. Hannah made a shifty glance at him, then to Vevila. There was no mistaking their relation to Nëven. They both had her red curls and freckly, pale skin. The brother had a gentle, rounder face like Nëven that reminded Hannah of a baked round loaf of bread. The sister was harder and more chiselled—as though carved from cold quarry stone.

"You've most likely gathered, we are Nëven's brother and sister." Artur said softly. "You are Hannah, yes?" Hannah said nothing. "Can you tell us exactly what happened to Nëven?" Still, Hannah kept her silence. She wanted to ask after Nëven, but did not want to open a line of conversation. Artur was persistent. "There's going to be a peremptory commission and if you cannot prove your innocence—"

"You'll end up worse than Nëven!" Vevila contributed.

Hannah closed her eyes while Nëven's siblings argued about Vevila's etiquette. A tear fell down Hannah's cheek and she felt its warmth roll its way down her neck. She sniffed once, blew a shaky breath and thought of the one thing that gave her peace—*Catanya*. Hannah knew if Catanya were here, things would be different. Catanya always protected her. If she were with Catanya, there would be no more arguments. Not between Vevila and Artur, not between Hannah's parents, and not with the ƟhUidmen. Catanya would set things straight and piggyback Hannah out of this horrible place. It was a lovely thought. Hannah squeezed her eyes shut and embellished it further in her mind, blurring the voices outside of her prison cage. Squeezing her knees even closer to her body, she could feel the iris in her jacket pocket push against her chest.

The following morning, Artur paid Hannah another visit. She had slept on and off during the night, but without the softness of a bed or warmth of a blanket, she was not comfortable. Kneeling beside the prison cage again, Artur handed her a large pottery cup of water. Hannah took it and drank it down without a word of thanks and handed the cup back to him. Then Artur gave her the bad news.

"A few hours ago, Nëven passed away."

"What?" Hannah stared wide-eyed at Artur. His face looked drawn and even paler than before. Hannah shook her head from side to side. *It cannot be true. It just cannot be...* "No, no, no..." Hannah repeated.

"The healer believes now it was not the knife wound that took her life," Artur mumbled. "She was broken inside. They blamed the Jasper stone. But Vevila and my mother..." Artur sighed. "With my father also dead, they are not listening to reason. They feel they need to blame someone. That someone is you."

Hannah was barely hearing Artur. Her thoughts were with her last moments with Nëven. With her special stone, Hannah's new friend had saved them both and taken them away from the Quagmen who killed Nëven's father and... *my mother*. Nëven had saved her life and Hannah had injured her in return. *Now she's dead!* Hannah felt dizzy. She vomited up the water she had just drunk.

"What is it? What happened to you both?" Artur asked.

Hannah looked at him through watery eyes. She was sick of not talking and felt sorry for him, for as much as she had lost a friend, Artur had lost a sister. "We landed in each other's jump!" Hannah sobbed.

"You *jumped* together?" It was Artur's eyes that widened now.

"One, two, three, four times we jumped. Nëven saved us from the Quag who killed your father and my mother." Hannah was crying. She was crying hard and now that she'd started, there was no stopping it. *Catanya, Catanya,* "Catanya!" Hannah finally cried aloud.

Artur reached through the prison cage bars and rest a hand on Hannah's shoulder. She continued to sob and rubbed her eyes with the balls of her hands. When she was done rubbing, she blinked her eyes into focus and looked again at Artur. Artur gave a nod. It was as though he somehow understood what he needed to know.

"I have something for you. I must go now and comfort my sister and mother, but I shall return." With that, Artur stood and walked away.

A short while later, Artur returned to Hannah's prison cage. She was glad to see him again, if nothing more than it being a change from the other OhUid folk who stared at her through the bars like she was a caged animal about to attack. Relieving the prison guard as he had the night before, Artur looked about, apparently making sure no others were present. He squatted by the cage again and looked at Hannah.

"Here," Artur said, feeding a clenched fist through the prison bars. Hannah hesitated. "Take it—quick!" Hannah offered an open palm and Artur dropped something into it. He closed Hannah fingers over the object before she had a chance to see what it was. "Hide it." Hannah sat back cross-legged and tucked her closed fist beneath her jacket.

"What is it?"

"Nëven's last wish. She wanted you to have it. I'll be outcast if anyone knows I gave it to you, but Nëven meant the world to me. Granting her last wish is the last thing I can ever give her." Hannah stared awkwardly at Artur. "Vevila is looking for it, but she could never wield its powers, else it would have gone to her, not Nëven. You can wield its powers and you should... as soon as you can." Artur stood and smiled as sad a smile as Hannah had even seen, then walked away once again.

Hannah spun about, her head facing away from the guard who was returning to his post by her cage. She pulled her fist out from beneath her jacket and prised open her fingers. In the palm of her hand, wrapped in macramé netting and still hanging from its string necklace, Hannah was holding Nëven's Jasper stone.

CLIMB - TWO

Wisps of cloud brushed the sheer walls of the Romgnian Mountain crevice carrying a bronze glow from the setting sun to the west. Catanya had been watching the dancing spectacle, imagining the misty tendrils were dragons flying about the skies in the final battle of Allumbreve. They were bringing an end to the Quag, the Authoritarium, and even erroneous members of the Irucantî in the same manner she had seen with her own eyes when the dragons destroyed Ba'rrat. They flew about the crevice extinguishing foes without restraint or pardon. *As only dragons can do…*

Catanya looked to her left. Magnus was still sleeping which pleased her. He had denied himself sleep most nights and even though he rarely seemed to need it, everyone had their limit—*even the Electus.*

Before he slept, Magnus told Catanya more of his conversation with Balgur at the Red River. It was a revelation that 'Steyne' was not responsible for the great dragon's death—that his sword was pre-destined to slay Balgur. She hoped Magnus would soon have the opportunity to share this truth with Eamon.

Catanya had spent much of the day reiterating the layout of the Romghold to Magnus. They would approach from the training field where her induction into the world of the Irucantî had started. To the east of the training field was the central, paved common. To the common's north was the Temple of Fire that towered high thanks to its four steeples. South of the common was a neat network of alleyways and two semi-circular lines of priest quarters—each a separate, small building. There were three larger buildings north of the common and adjacent the temple that formed the common kitchen, training hall and storage facility.

Details to the east of the Romghold seemed irrelevant other than the narrow crevice that split the eastern mountain face and ran a mile deep. "Dragons will not fit here, although their flames will funnel through and reduce to cinder anything that flees this way," Catanya explained. Nevertheless, through this crevice they would find the Dormiul Path that descended southward, and the Domult Path leading to the north face of the Romgnian Mountains and the Traas River—a river that flowed from

Froughton Forest to the Neverseas. Either the Dormiul or the Domult could prove a necessary escape route if necessary. The Dormiul Path certainly had when Catanya fled the Romghold on a fateful, rainy night not so long ago. When Catanya was satisfied Magnus had a clear picture of the Romghold in his mind, they had delved into their food rations. Catanya had then taken time to sleep.

Much of the day had passed when Catanya woke and found Magnus sleeping peacefully next to her. It seemed a good investment in a day spent waiting for the return of night. Then they could complete their climb to the Romghold fresh and focused.

Catanya looked again at the cloud of bronze dragons dancing across the crevice walls. The sun eventually waned and the dancing dragons turned teal before silently spiralling into a sombre grey. Catanya walked to the edge of the crevice. *Dusk...* The grey band of clouds spread over the eastern margin of Froughton Forest—the very clouds that hid them a mile up the Romgnian Mountainside. Catanya spread her arms and felt the warmth of the narrow crevice walls. *Ideal for climbing again*, she thought, yet there was an inconsistent chill within the crevice. The chill took hold at the nape of her neck. Catanya crossed her arms and looked about the crevice. The walls were beginning to frost over. The frost was growing, like climbing ice-blue vines spreading a winter chill. All about the narrow walls the frost spread upwards to the sharp peak of the crevice. It was not a normal occurrence—that much Catanya knew. She drew her lance and held its pulsing grip just shy of firm enough to ignite it. She followed the source of the creeping frost down the walls to... *Magnus.*

Magnus was still sleeping. His breathing was slow. The veins of his arms, thighs, face and neck were iridescent. Each vein pulsed with alternating, contrasting surges of amber and blue. Parts of Magnus's body were layered in a creeping frost and from where he rested against the crevice wall, the frost spread. Venous surges of amber would course through him intermittently as though reclaiming their territory. But it was Magnus's face that made Catanya reel. A hundred branching veins flushed with the same amber and blue. One moment a cheek's veins pulsed blue bringing with it frost, only to be vaporised as the veins turned amber with heat again. Catanya knew what it meant. It was just as Marsala said. Within Magnus, Thioci's blood was battling with Iisilée's for supremacy.

"Magnus!" Catanya shook his shoulders, only to have the frost take hold of her hands. She stood back, shaking her fingers free of the burning cold.

"Namon hama fara meo…" Färgd's spell worked, burning the frost from her hands. "Magnus!" She shook him again—violently this time. "WAKE, MAGNUS!" Magnus gasped a long breath and his eyes opened wide. Thick rings of flame shimmied down Magnus's body and limbs making him leap and then fall heavily to the stone ground. The rings of flames stripped his body of the blueness and frost but did not stop there. The flames spread from Magnus, across the stone ground and up the crevice walls. They moved in lines like a legion of soldiers, stripping away the creeping vines of blue and chilling frost. Magnus gripped his chest. He looked to Catanya and his eyes flashed a brilliant, sapphire blue like they had back in Thwax, only far more intense. He blinked and blinked again, winced as if in pain and shook his head. Magnus's eyes burned as bright as a fire dragon's before returning to their usual, blue-green colour. Magnus stared hard into Catanya's eyes, reached for her and held her face in his hands.

Magnus had woken from a dreadful dream. At first, the dream was familiar, like the dream he had in Ba'rrat just before Brue made his attack.

Lucas stared at him in silence. Magnus tried to explain, again, why he never returned for him in the Uydferlands. The more Magnus explained the more Lucas retreated into the darkness of his hooded robe. Now Jael was there in Lucas's place, beckoning him.

"Come," Jael said.

"Do you know where Lucas is?" Magnus repeated the question. Jael would not respond. She placed a hand on his chest. Energy passed between them—a feeling of elation. He looked into Jael's dark eyes and lost track of his thoughts. "Why am I here?"

"I can show you everything you need to know," Jael said, her voice smooth… knowing…

Magnus looked around. There was something… something he was meant to do, to know…

Jael was still there and was growing impatient. Her eyes sharpened. Magnus reached and placed his right hand on Jael's chest. His hand discharged teal and turquoise fibres of living ice that spread across Jael's Ferustir suit, up her neck, strangling her. Her eyes frosted over and her final breath left her mouth as a pale puff of mist. She fell to the ground, dead.

Behind her stood Alavia, dressed in her azure robe. This time, her white sword was sheathed at her side. This time, the legion of Rhydermere warriors was a thousand strong. Alavia smiled—pleased with what Magnus had done. This time, he had killed Jael…

"Magnus…"

"MAGNUS!"

Magnus gasped and his body heaved involuntarily. His mind and body swam in a sea of insatiable cold and his heart pumped heat fast and hard to counter it. Lying back against the hard stone ground, he gripped his chest, beckoning his fire-dragon blood to counter the cold.

Magnus looked at Catanya. His vision was foggy. He blinked again and again, squeezing his eyes and still, he could only make out Catanya as a spectre. A crack of white heat scorched his eyes. He grimaced, shook his head and looked again—his vision had cleared. He saw Catanya again. *Her eyes... her beautiful eyes.* Magnus reached for her, cupping her face in the palms of his hands.

I killed her... "I killed her!" Magnus mumbled. The image of Jael—*dead*— was still clear in his head.

"It's okay. You had a bad dream," Catanya's voice was soothing, but she looked confused.

"I killed her, Catanya," Magnus was almost shouting.

"Shh..." Catanya said, looking about, then back to Magnus, holding his hands in hers. "Who Magnus? Who did you kill?"

Magnus thought back to the dream. He had never told Catanya of his first dream, where his mother killed Jael. Now *he* killed Jael, and his mother was pleased. Magnus sighed and let his eyes close.

"Magnus..." Magnus looked back to Catanya and saw the panic-stricken expression on her face. "I think your mother has lifted her spell."

"What happened?"

"You froze over! The whole crevice... your whole body. You were blue and then, it was like the fire in you took over and... burned you out!"

Magnus got to his feet and steadied Catanya's shaking shoulders.

"Who did you say you killed just now?"

With some degree of clarity returning to him, Magnus felt awkward about the dream. "I was having nightmares, Catanya, it doesn't matter." As he spoke, Magnus looked to his right hand. A small vein, tracing from his wrist to the tip of his little finger, pulsed an iridescent blue.

Catanya grabbed his wrist, raising his hand. "*That* matters, Magnus."

He drew the hand into a tight fist. Heat came and the vein's iridescence changed to amber. His hand gave off a puff of vapour, then the vein faded to nothing. Magnus sighed. He was relieved he had some control over the condition. At least, he seemed to have control when awake. "I can control it," Magnus said. He studied Catanya who stood rigid. She looked entirely unconvinced. Magnus knew though that right here in the crevice, a mile below the Romghold and a mile above the Red River, there was nothing he could do. "I'm okay." He smiled and Catanya stared a moment longer before giving an almost imperceptible nod. Then she squinted and clenched her jaw.

"You know, when we get up to the Romghold to confront the High Priests and the dragons, we could both die." Catanya's words came as a punch, like she was forcing Magnus to face a truth they needed to acknowledge.

"Balgur said one High Priest will be slain, the other I will learn from. I don't think we'll die." Magnus knew he spoke with less certainty than Catanya and it was far easier to believe Catanya's prophecy than Balgur's. "We can only do our best." Catanya turned from Magnus and scooped her duffle bag from the ground with an aggressive, sweeping arm. "What choice do we have, Catanya?"

"None!" Catanya barked back. "We have none," she repeated as a murmur, her hands raised. "Look at us." Catanya looked over Magnus and then herself. Magnus knew what she was saying. The two of them were warriors in Ferustir armour. "This is what they've made us." She threw her bag hard against the crevice wall and drew her fingers into claws, grunting in frustration. "For so long I told myself—'become the warrior and there's nothing you cannot do'. Yet, no matter what I do, death comes for us. And here we are, literally on the precipice of death." Catanya sat cross-legged and slumped, head in her hands. "We should just go home. We should climb back down the mountain and go home. I need to see Hannah. I need to know she is safe."

Magnus leant against the wall and folded his arms. *Hannah...* He thought of her for a moment, remembering her smile, the spark in her eyes—*she must be seven now...* He felt Catanya's frustration and knew that to her, Hannah was no further away than a day's journey on a dragon. "Do you think Hannah is safe?" Catanya lifted her head and sighed. "Your mother wouldn't let anything happen to her, Catanya. Nor your father."

"They'd better not." Catanya extended a leg and leant forward to retie her lace. "Csilla," Catanya said.

"Csilla?"

Catanya swapped legs and retied the other lace. "Csilla won't let anything happen to her. If the Quag overrun Nuyan, Csilla will make sure Hannah is safe."

Magnus thought of Catanya's aunt whom he had never met until he, Lucas and Breona came skidding down the banks of the Nuyan River after the wyvern had attacked them. Csilla had charged her Uydfer archers to protect Nuyan's borders along the river and north of the Quarry. She was an extremely capable warrior—he was certain of that. Magnus stood over Catanya and offered her a hand. She took it and Magnus pulled her to her feet. "Let's get this done, Catanya. Then we can go home."

'Aye," Catanya conceded.

They walked to the cliff edge and peered again through the darkening cloud.

"I've just had a thought." A spark returned to Catanya's eyes. "There's an old priest in the Romghold I told you about named Trax. He's a caretaker of sorts. I've never seen him leave the Romghold so there's a good chance he's there. He's as smart as a whip, too."

"The one with the Ahrona swallows," Magnus recalled. "Would he be sympathetic to the High Priests?" Magnus asked.

Catanya bit a thumb, thinking things over. "Perhaps not. He's proud of the Irucantî traditions. I can't imagine he'd condone what's happened of late."

"Perhaps we may find him and ask?"

"If I do the asking, then yes—that may get us somewhere."

Magnus thought the spark in her eye resembled a glimmer of hope. "Let's do it, then." Magnus reclaimed his sword and duffle bag, but Catanya did the opposite—removing her scabbard and placing in on the ground. She came to Magnus.

"If there is a chance we're going to our deaths…" Catanya grabbed Magnus by his breastplate and pulled him close to her. "I want to go knowing I've known you, loved you… *made* love to you, Magnus." She released the buckles of his Ferustir suit and pulled the armour plates forward leaving his chest bare. She discarded his armour then gripped the bottom of her own chest piece and pulled it up and over her head, dropping it to the ground. She stood, facing Magnus, baring herself to him, waiting for his response.

Magnus extended both hands and they met Catanya's. Their fingers interlocked. They drew one another closer. Magnus felt Catanya's chest touch his, then she pulled away slightly and ran gentle fingers down Magnus's toned chest and abdomen. This time, there was no awkwardness or discomfort between them. Catanya took Magnus's hand and placed in upon her own chest. Magnus's heart raced. He looked over her beautiful body. In all the years they had known one another, they had never shared such physical intimacy. *Why now?* Magnus thought, but she had just said why—*because it may be the last chance we ever have…*

Magnus stepped forward and kissed Catanya. She drank his kiss with a passion that made him dizzy. Her lips and tongue were so sweet, her breath so warm. Magnus held Catanya by the waist, feeling the lines and curves of her body to the soft underside of her breasts. He dared to let his thumbs caress them. Catanya gently bit Magnus's lip and sighed.

"Are you sure?" Magnus asked.

Catanya had always yearned for this. Not so long ago, her father refused to let her marry Magnus, then the Irucantî insisted on her abstinence, but this moment was void of judgment. It was Catanya and Magnus and that was all it should ever have been. Catanya had never been surer of anything in her life. "I'm sure," Catanya replied.

Taking a hold of her hips, Magnus lifted Catanya off her feet. She wrapped her thighs around his waist and squeezed him tight, kissing him passionately once again before tilting her head up. Magnus lingered on the smell and the texture of her neckline down to the soft skin beneath her collarbones. Catanya pulled her torso back and Magnus supported her body with his arms. He kissed Catanya's chest, gauging her reaction, daring to explore further.

Catanya closed her eyes and drew a long breath between gritted teeth, overwhelmed by Magnus's touch. She squeezed her legs tighter around his waist, crossing her boots over one another. She looked back at Magnus. He stared into her eyes. There was a beautiful wildness to them—a surety that lay waste to any doubts or thoughts of predicaments beyond the two of them. *This* was the Catanya he loved—the powerful woman who put their needs first. Catanya wanted Magnus and knew he would never suggest the same without her initiation. That he was a gentleman only made her want him more. And in this moment, Magnus wanted her more than anything.

It was dark when Magnus and Catanya were finally ready to resume their climb to the Romghold. They had consumed more of their food and water rations. The whole time they ate, Magnus sat against the crevice wall with Catanya in his lap. Catanya looked at Magnus, played with his hair and caressed his bearded face. Her eyes seemed to have softened and had gentleness to them Magnus had not seen in a long time. Neither spoke much. Both were content.

The second half of the climb commenced. Catanya took the lead again, having orientated herself with familiar landmarks from her previous climbs. Once again, Magnus copied her every step and handhold. The stone cliff was warm and dry once clear of the clouds and the sky sparkled with the four realms of constellations against the pitch-black night. The moon was to the east beyond the cliff top, giving little light but the advantage of being able to climb in the shadows.

"We need to get as far as we can before the moon shifts into view. We'll be much easier to spot once it is," Catanya said. "I dare not use a gypsy's eye without the cloud overhead to cloak us."

"Aye." Magnus was a more confident climber this night. It was as though his body settled into a rhythm. With the clouds below, he could almost forget how far beneath them the ground was and imagine that perhaps, should they fall, the clouds would provide a soft landing.

Several hours into the climb, the moon showed itself. They were half way between the clouds and cliff top and the extra light greatly improved visibility. *To us and the dragons…* Magnus shuddered. He made a mental calculation of the hour in which Liné made her pass the night before. "Catanya. Are dragons creatures of habit?"

"You're wondering if Liné will pay us another visit? I've been thinking of little else."

"I've been thinking of other things as we go," Magnus confessed. Grinning, he glanced upward trying to get a take on Catanya's expression but her face was a silhouette against the moon. Then she shifted at just the right angle affording Magnus a view of her smirking face.

"Concentrate." Catanya smiled.

More hours passed without incident or sign of Liné, and with just over a hundred feet to go, the cliff bowed out over their heads.

"Follow me," Catanya whispered as quiet as can be. "Around to the right and up as we go."

The final part of the climb was more sideways than up, but a slow, careful hour later Catanya stopped just six feet from the mountaintop on a small ledge wide enough to hold them both. Magnus shifted beside her and Catanya placed her mouth to his ear. "We're here. Over that precipice is the training field. It is often illuminated at night. There may be dragons sleeping on the green. Magnus nodded, swallowing hard. "Are you ready?" Magnus nodded again. Catanya kissed him on the cheek. "I think we should take a look. That is all—just a look."

Together, Magnus and Catanya found safe footholds and hoisted themselves up until their heads peered over the Romgnian Mountain precipice to the Romghold's training field.

SCOUTS

Austagia walked the moonlit canyon of the Corville Pass. He was appeased by the shadow that flew overhead, for as long as he could see the dragon, the dragon could see him. While he scouted at ground level, Färgd scouted the skies, and it was the safest way to get this done. Low flying through the narrow ravine of the Corville Pass would leave both of them susceptible to a wyvern attack from above. At least with Färgd riding high, the dragon would spot danger before it spotted him.

Austagia, though, was not alone. As he entered the pass from the north, a Ferustir named Simeon entered from the south, accompanied by a dragon named Braug. Should nothing untoward be encountered nor discovered, they would meet midway along the ten-mile canyon.

Austagia was in search of answers to a great predicament. During the Battle of Ba'rrat, many Quag clansfolk fled, and of these, a great number succeeded in reaching lands north of the Black Cliffs, through the Southern Wastelands and into the Corville Mountains. Scouts saw Quag warriors and wyverns enter the Corville Pass. However, in the ensuing days, none had ventured through the northern exit of the pass leading to the Southern Plains, south of the four realms.

So where are they? Austagia frowned.

With Ba'rrat reduced to ruins after a five day offensive, Austagia had sent Ferustirs and dragons scouting for signs of a Quag army gathering in the Corville Mountains. Eamon had Färgd take Joffren to Thwax where the healer named Marsala would oversee his recovery—if it were at all possible for him to recover. Once Färgd returned to Ba'rrat, he, Austagia, Simeon and Braug volunteered for the Corville Pass scout. This was predicted to be the most dangerous scout mission, for if there was a hidden enclave within the pass, Austagia expected they would be in great numbers.

Walking from the northern entrance of the Corville Pass, Austagia looked for a hidden cave entrance in the towering vertical cliffs that separated the eastern and western ranges of the Corville Mountains. Austagia's thoughts, though, were elsewhere. His mind was troubled—far more than an Irucanti should ever allow one's mind to be troubled. He was thinking of Catanya. It was hard for him not to regret what had come to pass in the previous month or so, since he told Catanya that her lover—Magnus—was in fact the Electus. This had escalated into a deadly game of deception and confusion. What troubled Austagia most was Demi's attempted assassination of Catanya. *How did Demi even know where to find her?* All evidence seemed to suggest Joffren was the source of betrayal. But, again—*How did Joffren know Catanya was in Brindle?*

Austagia was missing something. His only confidant was Jael and they shared an unbreakable loyalty to one another. Their loyalty was forged over time, beginning when he found Jael years ago—an abandoned child beside the Traas River. She was only thirteen, traumatised and beaten having escaped from some peril she never spoke of, even to this day. It was unorthodox to take someone so young to the Romghold, yet Austagia vouched for her and gave her a home. He helped Jael heal and he taught her to read and write in both common tongue and *Fireisgh*—the native tongue of the Fire Realm. She learned the philosophies of the *Murata Fara*—the Irucantî book of teachings. She worked in the kitchens and with the gardeners. Each evening after supper, Jael took to the training field to train with Austagia under the glow of lanterns surrounding the field just as a Semsarian would during the day. Finally, after three years and having convinced the High Priests of her worthiness, Jael was inducted into the order of the Irucantî at the age of sixteen—a year younger than any other recruit. She became Joffren's Semsarian and Austagia was as proud as any father.

On a fateful night a month ago, Liné returned to the Romghold with Jael and the body of her dead dragon youngling—Thioci. Jael was once again traumatised and beaten, having once again escaped from some peril she was yet to speak of. It was then that Austagia realised how unbreakable Jael's loyalty was to him. That realisation came with a hidden message that Jael dared only share with Austagia. She handed him a bracelet. The bracelet was made of his family's traditional pousse-plaited leather. Then Jael whispered to him a fateful secret the elders of his order could never know— *'Whoever wore this bracelet is the Fire Realm's Electus.'*

That evening, Austagia summoned Catanya to his quarters. He spoke truths about the bracelet, about Magnus and about Catanya's mother wanting her protected. Austagia had promised Alessandra he would protect her. Bringing Catanya into the fold of the priesthood was meant to achieve this, but it had posed as great a threat to her life as the war in Nuyan perhaps would have. There were truths Austagia had not told Catanya or Jael, nor was he sure he even would. Such truths, therefore, remained within his heart—

One of them was the daughter he never had. The other was the daughter who filled her place.

Lost in thought, yet keen of eye, Austagia glanced upon a slim fissure in the eastern cliff face. From within the fissure, two ghostly eyes peered back at him. As soon as they did, they disappeared. Austagia waved a signal to Färgd, who banked to his left, came back around and assumed a figure eight flight pattern directly above Austagia's position.

Austagia squeezed through the fissure in the cliff face. On the other side, he was standing in a cave. It was narrow yet deep and widened the further he dared venture. He drew his lance. The cave grew colder and darker the further from the fissure he went. Worse still, there was a horrid smell. It was not the dankness from the weeping walls, nor was it the rotting remnants of half-consumed carcasses strewn across the ground. No, it was blood both old and new and a wheezing, hidden breath from something in the dark.

Austagia heard a distant cry. It was a single screech whose pattern of reverberation revealed a large, cavernous space further ahead. Then he saw the ghostly, unblinking eyes again. Further cries and more sets of eyes appeared. Austagia drew a tight fist around his lance, igniting it and revealing his presence with a loud crack and splaying of light from the bronze shaft between his fingers. Austagia swept his six-foot lance, using the pommel's light to survey the cave walls closest to him. To his left was a complete armoury stacked with Quag blades, archery weapons, spears, wyvern and warhorse saddles and more, stretching beyond his sight. He swung the lance forward again. Dozens of worgriels were coming at him fast and were soon making a deafening cry. He stood his ground as several leapt at him with jaws open and claws extended.

Austagia's lance tore through flesh, every blow culling another worgriel. The hides of the worgriels were too thick to thrust into and recover in time for the next one. The most efficient blows were short stabs at the throat and weighted sweeps at the eyes. Three were slain, then four. A fifth creature latched onto his chest armour with both front claws and drew its head forward with a wide, open jaw. Austagia thrust his lance deep into its throat. *Enough,* Austagia judged. The worgriels were able to draw too close to maintain a defence and a large pack were clambering over one another for the prize of being first to kill him. Austagia knew there would be no more cave exploring this day.

Soaked in worgriel blood, entrails and mucus, Austagia fled back toward the cave entrance, letting out a loud whistle in a pattern of four sharp sounds.

He repeated the pattern over and over again. The worgriels were catching him—some clambering across the ceiling overhead. Austagia leapt sideways then sprung off the cave wall, using his momentum to slay another black beast on the run. Another dropped from the ceiling, blocking his path. Austagia drew a throwing knife and buried it in the worgriel's forehead, pulling it free again as he passed the wounded beast. The deafening, collective screech was insufferable, but the narrow entrance drew closer. Moonlight pierced through the fissure in a thick beam of promising blue light. Six, eight, then ten worgriels overtook him and fell across his path. Austagia persisted with his loud whistling. The light through the fissure fell to darkness.

Austagia drew to a halt. A moment's silence fell across the cave. The worgriels knew they had him trapped, yet trepidation held them at bay, for prey is never more dangerous than when trapped. Suddenly, every pair of ghost eyes turned to the cave entrance. In the light of his lance, Austagia saw a massive paw reach through the narrow fissure. Claws gripped the rock wall and tore it apart, creating a gaping hole. Through the hole came Färgd's enormous head with open maw. A guttural thump formed in the depths of the dragon's throat. Austagia smiled, for he knew what came next. *"Namon suma feera meo..."* The quickly whispered spell protected Austagia from the roar that tore through the cave and would otherwise have ruptured his eardrums and reduced him to an unconscious mess. The worgriels' responsive screams were barely audible. Those closest to Austagia scuttled away. Austagia threw himself through the cave entrance, rolling beneath Färgd who stood on all fours.

Färgd shoved his head into the cave entrance again and released a torrent of fire. Austagia stood at Färgd's side, listening as the burning worgriels released their final, harrowing scream.

The Quag lair had been found.

MESSAGES

Eamon released the Ahrona swallow and unfurled the small piece of paper. He recognised the purple-inked handwriting immediately and read with anticipation—

"Dear Eamon,

This note comes with unfortunate news. Joffren is deceased. For two days I administered milk of elkwood, rhuderburry extract, Paragon weed and hourly thimbles of thöe. I placed a rather brusque Cantomine spell over him to hold fast his internal bleeding. He was at peace but this morning he woke, delirious and aggressive, and tried to kill me. I am sorry Eamon, but there was nothing I could do to stop the priest. I killed him in self-defence.

For too long you carried the burden of his blame for leaving him during his training, but I believe Joffren allowed his resentments to corrupt him. His blame goes with him to the grave and is no longer yours to bear.

Know that Magnus and Catanya are well and have one less threat to negotiate.

If you've time, please have someone come to assist with Joffren's burial—not for moral support, but to help me remove the tall priest from my kitchen floor.

My thoughts are with you,

Marsala."

Eamon scrunched Marsala's note into a ball and held it aloft in the palm of his hand. *"Fara ginparshin-ar,"* he mumbled. The paper ignited into flame and burned. He watched as the glowing embers floated gently off into the breeze of the night.

Eamon felt an eerie sense of quiet as he often did when learning of the passing of a friend. It were as though time paused so that he may sit upon the precipice between two worlds and for a moment, feel the soft breath of peace as that friend passed from one to the other.

"It is over, my old friend," Eamon whispered at the precipice.

Ba'rrat had been eerie these past few days. The town was brought to its knees under the fiery battle of dragons and wyverns, Ferustirs and Quagmen, amidst the backdrop of a city screaming in terror. But it was over. Austagia had taken the mantle of leader among his brethren in the absence of the High

141

Priests. Färgd had done the same among the fire dragons. Färgd, as the most elder dragon among them, was not to be questioned by priest or dragon and it was something many of the priests took a while to come to terms with. Three priests and one dragon had attempted to kill Magnus. Magnus had slain the priests. Brue had fled—wounded. In a way, it had played as a warning that the Electus was not to be reckoned with. *An unfortunate warning, but necessary,* Eamon believed.

Ash and black smoke rose from the scorched black granite buildings into the night sky. To the northeast, Eamon saw an approaching shadow gliding through the stars. It was Färgd returning with Austagia. Eamon sighed and pulled his stout smoking pipe and tobacco pouch from his duffle bag. He pinched a portion of the tobacco from the pouch and stuffed it into the pipe, then whispered the Fireisgh spell once again to ignite the tobacco. He took several long draws on the pipe's mouthpiece and expelled the smoke from his nostrils. "What a shame," he said. "What a terrible shame…"

"What is the shame, Eamon?"

Eamon turned and saw Jael approaching down one of Ba'rrat's narrow, cobbled streets toward the quadrangle at the Eastern wall where camp had been made. Eamon frowned. "I've regrettable news and regret having to tell you, Jael." Eamon knew Jael was Joffren's Semsarian before Catanya was. Although this all happened after Eamon's departure from the order, he had learned of such things from the conversations he had shared with Jael in the days following Magnus and Catanya's departure.

"What is it?" Jael asked. Eamon hesitated and Jael shifted with unease. "It's Joffren, isn't it?" Her piercing dark eyes knew.

Eamon buried a thumb in the chamber of his pipe, extinguishing the flame—he had no appetite for smoke, after all. "Aye. I just received message. He has passed."

Jael stood as if to attention—a pose that seemed to guard against her feelings. "If I were to guess, I'd say he died awake, rather than in his sleep."

Eamon knew this to be true. "Pray tell, why would you guess that?"

Jael looked to the ground in thought, then tilted her chin up to speak. "His conscience. It gave him nightmares when asleep—harmless enough. When awake… it was at odds with his convictions."

Eamon was intrigued at Jael's observations. "His 'convictions', you say?"

"Aye. He was devoted to our order, yet never at peace."

What of your convictions? The words hung to the tip of Eamon's tongue, but he resisted letting them go. Jael stared at Eamon. Her eyes were sharp—alert.

Jael was reserved, yet unyielding in her own convictions, whatever they were. Furthermore, Eamon sensed a quiet determination. He long believed ones eyes were windows to truth and somewhere in Jael's fine, dark eyes was a story that gave rise to such determination. He had wondered before now what Jael's origins were and wondered all the same how much Austagia knew of her past—before he took her into his care.

Eamon smiled. "You are a very perceptive woman, Jael." Jael's stare lingered before looking away at something that made her frown.

"What happened to you?" Jael called. Eamon turned. Austagia was approaching.

"We've found the Quag lair. It seems they are hiding in the Caves of Cuvee."

"You were in the Caves of Cuvee?" Eamon said. Austagia's filthy state suggested he had been somewhere disagreeable.

"Not intentionally," Austagia grimaced. "A fissure in the eastern cliff face along the Corville Pass gave access to a network of caves. Quag are storing armoury here. Packs of worgriels make access challenging." He rubbed a bruise on his neck and then appeared to notice something was wrong in his companions' expressions. "Jael. Eamon." He looked from one to the other. "What news in my absence?"

"Joffren has passed," Jael said. Eamon looked at his pipe, suddenly in the mood to smoke again.

"That is bad news, but… not entirely unexpected." Austagia licked his lips, as though cleansing his palate of distasteful words. He stepped closer to Jael. "How are you?"

"If it were *you* it would be a tragedy," Jael spoke without hesitation. Eamon thought she was making a point as sharp as her eyes. *Austagia was always her true teacher,* he thought. Austagia nodded. No more, apparently, needed to be said on the matter.

"We should return Joffren's body to the Romghold for cremation," Austagia suggested.

"Is he worthy of it?" Jael said, crossing her arms.

Eamon could see her point. Then again, Joffren had given his life to the priesthood—even if his final deeds were questionable.

"For the most part, I think so." Austagia spoke Eamon's mind. Austagia kissed a closed fist then opened it, placing a palm on Jael's forehead. Eamon smiled. A wave of nostalgia for the order passed through him. Austagia's gesture was a customary show of accord among priests. He remembered doing the same to Joffren when proud of his Semsarian's accomplishments. Eamon was quick to clear the thought. He relit his pipe.

"If Joffren is to return to the Romghold, I shall take him," Eamon said. "Perhaps Färgd could assist me with this." He needed to be sure Marsala was okay after her altercation with Joffren. Then, Färgd willing, he would accompany Joffren to the Romghold. A trip here would serve two purposes. Firstly, Eamon wanted to assess Magnus and Catanya's secret mission to return to the Romghold and confront the High Priests. The danger this posed had plagued Eamon since they left and yet, after the attempt on Magnus's life, no other could be trusted for support. As much as Austagia and Färgd had worked hard to establish order among the dragons and priests, Eamon knew the time would come where they would head home to the Romghold. He wanted to be there to support Magnus and Catanya when they did.

The second purpose to Eamon's trip was one suggested by Catanya when last he saw her—*'Make the journey to the temple… leave the fire-sword and with it, the priest who once was Steyne… perhaps if Joffren is well enough he can accompany you and together you can reach a mutual understanding…'* Catanya's words were of such wisdom at the time. He yearned for the closure, but it was to be a bitter journey with Joffren deceased. *We never will reach a mutual understanding…*

"I'm sure Färgd would be honoured. Are you happy to return to the Romghold?" Austagia asked.

"Aye. All things considered."

Austagia nodded. "When do you think you will arrive?"

"A day to Thwax. I need some time there, then two more days to the Romghold. Färgd will no doubt favour an approach from the east." Eamon knew Färgd called the east coast his home and a coastal approach would be more discrete than most others.

"The scouts will return to Ba'rrat within a day, giving me time to square things away here in Ba'rrat." Austagia looked to Jael. "We have to assume the Quag are spread throughout the Caves of Cuvee. With unknown exits throughout the Realms' southern borders, we'll soon need to run scouts all along the Southern Plains." Jael nodded in agreement. Austagia looked again to Eamon. "Several Ferustirs will remain here in Ba'rrat for the time being. I'll return with the others to the Romghold."

Eamon blew a steady stream of smoke from his nostrils again as he considered Austagia. Magnus and Catanya were well on their way to the Romghold now and so, he felt it was time to reveal their intentions.

Eamon asked to speak in confidence with Austagia and immediately sensed the priest knew he was about to learn something he would not like.

"Alone? You sent them to the Romghold *alone?*"

"Austagia, it was not of my doing. The Electus chooses to confront those who would have him dead. Joffren shared the knowledge with Magnus that the High Priests take refuge in the Temple of Fire under guard of spell and dragon."

"What *exactly* do they think they will do when they get there?" Austagia appeared visibly shaken which did nothing to appease Eamon's lingering doubts about letting Magnus and Catanya go alone.

"In Magnus's words—'see them repent or fall'." The words sounded grandiose to Eamon—much more so than when Magnus said them. Austagia looked ready to spit words of bitterness but Eamon got in first. "Think about it, Austagia. When these words were spoken, Magnus had just survived his most vicious attack since entering Ba'rrat. Yet it was not the Quag who attacked, nor Delvion, nor black wyverns, but *your* brethren, who were sworn to protect him... *and* a dragon!" Eamon knew he was shouting, but they were words of truth that needed to be said. "This followed an assassination attempt on Catanya's life—the most precious thing in Magnus's world—by the same order. All things considered, there was no more sane thing he could have done."

Austagia still looked shaken, but seemed to be seeing the bigger picture. "I see reason—I do. But it does not change the fact that even if they could get near the High Priests, they are dealing with something so beyond their understanding it will almost certainly lead to their end."

A long pause of silence passed between Eamon and Austagia. It was Austagia who broke the silence. "They will have the advantage of surprise. The High Priests won't be expecting them."

Eamon agreed. "This was Magnus's intention."

"And if others of my order learned of their intention, there would likely be another assassination attempt."

"Again, something Magnus foresaw."

"It seems he set forth with reason. Angry... Naïve... but with reason." Austagia shook his head. "We need to get there as soon as we can, Eamon."

"Very well, then."

Austagia was pacing, rubbing his chin. "Something is bothering me with this scene—the High Priests under guard of dragons. I wonder, under what pretence do the priests have dragons standing guard over them?"

Eamon had no answer, but figured Austagia was about to work it out for himself.

"Did Magnus say which dragons they were?"

Eamon thought on the matter and then shook his head. "No... no I do not recall him saying so."

"Liné." Austagia stopped his pacing. "Liné remained in the Romghold. She is with child. In her condition, her younger sister—Rubea—is likely to be in her company." Austagia's eyes widened and he drew a sharp breath. It was emotion Eamon had rarely seen in the priest. "The High Priests play custodian of a dragon's egg unto such time the mother wishes for it to hatch."

Eamon realised what Austagia was getting at. "If the High Priests hold the egg as collateral in trade for their protection..."

Austagia shook his head. "No. They would not be so stupid. Such folly would undermine all confidence in our order."

"You do not think they have it in them?" Eamon barked. "The same High Priests who sent your brethren here to kill the Electus?"

Austagia let out a long, exasperated sigh. It was a sigh of letting go, of finally acknowledging a truth, and of something else—"I know then where Brue is." Austagia anxiously kneaded the knuckles of a fist into the palm of his other hand, looking about the room, as if for a more desirable answer. He finally turned hesitantly to Eamon. "He is in the Romghold."

Eamon swallowed hard. "For why, Austagia, for why?"

"He is the father of Liné's unhatched child."

The pieces fell together in Eamon's mind. "Brue is driven spare with protective instinct. Enough to follow through on a promise—to kill Magnus for the life of his child!"

A deafening silence fell between them.

"This is why Brue tried to kill the Electus," Austagia said.

"He was blackmailed."

"No doubt, with Thioci's death as a catalyst, for Brue was also his father."

"I see," Eamon was beginning to see the full picture. "The High Priests convince Brue that Magnus is responsible for Thioci's death. They hold the egg, employing the deception that they're protecting it from Magnus, and then—"

"You have a fire dragon thirsty for revenge for the death of his son and now..." Austagia provided conclusion to their deliberations. "And now Magnus and Catanya enter the Romghold where Brue will be waiting to kill them."

TRAX

The training field was dark. Only the moonlight illuminated the field's perfectly manicured grass. At its centre was a large, sleeping hulk of a creature—*A dragon...* Magnus expected as much, but his heart sank nevertheless. Beyond the field to the north was the Temple of Fire. Sure enough, as Balgur had told him, there were another *two* dragons. One stood to attention at the top of a set of wide stairs beside the doors of the temple while the other dragon perched on one of the temple's steeples. This third dragon was the only one Magnus recognised—*Brue...*

The Temple of Fire had four steeples as Catanya had described—two at the front and two taller ones at the rear. It was on one of the taller ones that Brue kept his vigil. His extraordinarily long tail spiralled down the tower, mirroring the curve of an equally long hornpipe that wrapped around a tall parapet. What struck Magnus most about Brue's presence was his alertness. He was not at peace. He stood tall and rigid, turning his head about, taking in all the details of the night.

Magnus sunk back behind the precipice, pulling on Catanya's arm. She squatted beside him and studied his expression. "It's a long way back," she whispered, clearly seeing the dismay in his face.

Magnus gave a weak nod. He slowly rose, peeping over the precipice for a second time. He eyed Brue and the other two dragons again before focussing on the Romghold's layout. All was just like Catanya described. There were three buildings adjacent the temple. Across the common were the arrangement of small buildings—*the priest's accommodation*, Magnus surmised. He glanced one more time at Brue before squatting beside Catanya again.

"I recognise Brue atop the steeple. The other two?"

"Liné is at the temple door. Rubea is asleep on the training field. You've met her before," Catanya said. Magnus could not recall. "By the Nuyan River," Catanya clarified. Magnus remembered. She was the dragon who carried Catanya away all those months ago. Catanya retied her laces then pulled on the tongues of her boots. "We have to get to the buildings before sunrise."

Magnus looked to the moon, which was beyond the Spindlefax constellation and into the Couldradt constellation, soon to disappear over the horizon. They had about two hours before sunrise. After that, they would be easily spotted by a dragon taking flight over the cliff face.

"If we make a run for it—" Magnus snapped his mouth shut. Something was moving across the field above their heads. The thud of footsteps drew closer. Magnus winced. He could hear dragon scales sliding over each other like a hundred sharp blades gliding over sharpening stones. Magnus and Catanya pushed their bodies hard against the cliff face beneath a lip of rock that jutted over their heads. Six talons spilled over the lip, gripping tightly to stone. Each talon was two foot long. Magnus looked at Catanya. She mouthed a single word—

"Liné!"

Magnus's heart lurched. There was no heat to bathe the panic away. It was an unfettered emotion he had to endure. Liné thrust away from the cliff, making rubble fall across Magnus's face. Directly in front of him, Liné arched over, tucked her wings back and fell into a dive. As fast and silent as a shooting star, she shot down the mountainside and vanished into the clouds a mile below. The fire dragon had not seen them. Magnus released a long breath of relief.

"We have to go NOW." Catanya pulled Magnus up.

"Now?"

"Now! If her patrol is like last night, she'll be back in a few minutes. We can be across the training field in a moment. If we hesitate, we're done for."

Magnus had no counter argument. The anticipation of Liné approaching from behind terrified him even more than what he'd just been through. They peeked over the cliff face once again. Rubea was still sleeping. Brue was still atop the steeple, looking about.

"As soon as Brue is looking northward, we go," Catanya instructed.

"Aye. I'll follow you."

"To the back of the small buildings to the right."

"Whatever... I'm following you." Magnus stared at Brue. Worse case scenario, he figured he would have to confront the large dragon just as he had in Ba'rrat. This time, at least, they would have the solid stone buildings for protection against fire. Just as he was done reasoning with himself, Magnus saw movement at the temple doors.

Magnus and Catanya dropped again, peering as discretely as possible. One of the two doors had opened and a black-robed figure walked out. Brue looked down at the figure as it moved swiftly down the stairs and across the common toward the three buildings adjacent the temple.

"That's Trax," Catanya whispered. The figure walked a distance before disappearing into one of the buildings. With the priest out of sight, Brue turned away to the north.

"Go!" Catanya sprung up and over the lip of the cliff face and took off, fast and soft footed. Magnus was barely a step behind her.

The accommodation buildings were a hundred yards away but every yard felt like ten. Catanya made a direct line for the buildings. Magnus was right behind her. Neither glanced at Brue or Rubea. They reached the paved common and, in six more long strides, were there. Catanya reached for Magnus's arm and pulled him around the back of the building. He heaved for breath in painful silence and looked at Catanya. Mouth closed, she drew controlled breaths from flared nostrils. A moment passed and the night was still silent. Then the silence broke—Liné was returning.

Liné landed on the field, walked to the temple steps and up to the temple doors where she sat to resume her vigil. Brue looked down to her. On the grassy field, Rubea rolled over, shimmied about to scratch her back, then dropped to her other side and kept sleeping. Catanya led Magnus around the back of one, two, three buildings, separated by three-foot gaps. They peered around the eastern wall of the third building and looked directly across to the large building Trax had entered.

Catanya put her mouth to Magnus's ear. "That is the common kitchen. Trax is in there. This room here," she pointed a thumb at the small building they were leaning on. "That's my room." An awkward smile crossed her face and Magnus felt a pang of sympathy for her. This had been her home for more than six months before Austagia encouraged her to flee and find him.

They continued on.

Side-stepping along the eastern wall that shadowed them from moonlight, they reached the corner at the edge of the common. Magnus peered around the corner and back toward the training field to their left. They could see Rubea but the other two dragons were out of sight thanks to the temple being set back from the common behind the temple stairs. Directly across the common was the open entrance to the kitchen where Trax had entered.

"I'll do the talking," Catanya said.

"Should I... try to restrain him?" Magnus proposed. Catanya looked blankly at him. "Bad idea?" he deduced.

"Bad idea."

After exchanging affirmative nods they ran to the kitchen entrance. The common kitchen had six long tables in two rows of three, each with many stools placed upside down on top. The polished hardwood floor mirrored light from a single torch mounted in a sconce over a tall bench at the far side of the kitchen. Behind the bench and through a door in a wall to the left was a separate, brightly lit room. They shifted quickly to the bench and crouched behind it. The tinkering of pots and the sizzling sound of cooking food came from the other room, accompanied with the smell of fresh herbs and spices. Catanya hesitated then took a deep breath, stood and walked around the bench toward the door. Magnus sprang to his feet. Catanya looked back to Magnus and pushed an open palm at him indicating he should stay back. She stood in the doorway, looking inside. The tinkering stopped.

'Semsame," Catanya said, bowing her head politely. There was a long, awkward pause. "Are you well?" Magnus heard the sound of a pot being placed on a hard surface. He waited for the sound of a lance being unsheathed, but a voice spoke first—

"Are you alone?" The voice was drawn with trepidation.

"Can we talk, Trax?" Catanya said, not answering the priest. Magnus fidgeted, desperate to see the Irucantî. There was another pause—even longer this time.

"I gather you're not alone. Is… *he* here?"

Catanya took two steps back from the entrance, turning toward Magnus. The dark robed figured moved tentatively through the entrance. He paused in the doorway, slowly drew back his hood and followed Catanya's gaze toward Magnus. Trax walked past Catanya and came slowly toward him. Magnus kept his eyes on the priest, taking note of his lance that was sheathed over his left shoulder. Magnus's peripheral vision saw Catanya's fingers poised just inches from her own sheathed lance. She was readying herself for all contingencies. Rounding the bench, Trax approached Magnus. He was elderly, but moved lithely. Magnus stood with hands crossed to his front, wanting to suggest a peaceful meeting. Trax stood before him. The wavering torchlight made the Irucantî markings dance across one side of his bald head. He stared in silence for a good, long minute before speaking.

"May I see your wound?"

Magnus knew what he meant. It was the only scar his dragon blood had not healed—the scar Thioci gave him when he pierced him with his talon and gave him his dragon blood. Magnus raised his arm, baring the scar on his right wrist. Trax reached and held Magnus's arm, studying the scar. When he was done, Trax let his arm go and walked to the nearest table, removed a stool from its top and sat on it. He rubbed his brow, looking at Magnus, then Catanya.

"How have you survived?" Trax spoke quietly. Catanya took a stool to sit beside him. Magnus did the same.

"We fled," Catanya said.

"They *did* find you, though," Trax said. He turned to Magnus. "The wound you gave Brue is testament to that."

"Aye, they did," Magnus admitted. Trax sat tall. His eyes widened as if intrigued by him—by the *Electus*. Magnus wanted to put the priest at ease, so he spoke casually—"Luckily, Catanya found me first. I've her to thank for living this long."

Trax looked at them both again.

"We have supporters. Austagia, Jael, Färgd," Catanya said.

"You have Färgd's support?"

"More than that, he defends Magnus as the Electus and insists the priests and dragons support Thioci's decision," Catanya elaborated.

Trax gently tapped a finger on the tabletop. "And here you are."

Magnus sensed they were at an impasse. The spicy air from the kitchen seemed to thicken in the silence. Would the priest lash out and attack him or would he alert the dragons and the High Priests? Magnus and Catanya had to be prepared for either.

"There is a dangerous game being played here, Semsame," Trax eventually said, eying Catanya. "A game of ambition and deception. No matter the outcome, blood will be shed." He looked at Magnus. "For my part, I wish to do the right thing—right by the order, by the Couldradt Fire dragons, and by the people of the Fire Realm. I have sworn to do so as it is written—

'The fourth of four realms,
The last to bring bond and the power of fire,
May give over to one of their choosing,
Whose progeny shall forever inherit the power of the realm of fire…'

Magnus recognised the words from something Catanya said to him in the dungeons of Ba'rrat. It was something from the 'Murata Fara'—the priests' sacred book.

"It is of the dragons' choosing. Not the High Priests'," Trax continued. He gave an affirmative nod.

"And they have chosen," Catanya said. "Why then do Brue, Liné and Rubea support and guard the High Priests? Do they not know the truth?"

"They do know. But more has come to pass and a lot is at stake. Liné has born a child. As is tradition, the unhatched egg was delivered into the custody of our order for safekeeping in the chamber rooms beneath the temple."

"Safekeeping?" Magnus asked. It seemed to him that a dragon's egg would be safest with its mother.

"Aye. Over the years, Delvion has exhibited irrational means to try and obtain the last remaining Electus power for himself. Even a dragon's mother cannot be with its egg at all times."

Magnus understood. Long ago at the gates of Guame, Eamon told how Delvion killed Electus offspring and drank their blood in the hope of getting their power. Magnus cringed at the thought of him extracting an unhatched dragon for the same purpose.

"After the first new moon, the egg was supposed to be given back to Liné for her to begin her hatching ritual," Trax continued. "It was not. The egg is being held as collateral in exchange for *your* death." Trax studied Magnus. "If the egg is not hatched after the second moon, it shall never hatch at all. What's more, Brue is the father." Magnus and Catanya stared at one another, dumbfounded at the news. "As he was to Thioci," the priest added.

"More than one reason Brue tried to kill me, then," Magnus realised.

"No. One reason—blackmail," Catanya said. "If Thioci's death were your fault, he'd not have made you the Electus."

"Does Brue see it that way?" Magnus directed his question to Trax.

"I would say sly words have leant suggestion that Thioci need not have died and that you are to blame," Trax said. "I cannot see Brue acting as he did in response to blackmail alone."

"Why are you still here, Trax?" Catanya asked.

"I was waiting for brethren of sound mind to return." Trax looked at Catanya. "The egg is of great concern to me. It needs to be recovered and it is not something I can do alone."

"Once recovered, will the dragons turn on the entire order of Irucantí?" Catanya asked.

"If we three present the egg to Liné and Brue, they will perhaps see the High Priest's folly as their own and not representative of the entire order." Trax's eyes widened. "It could mean the difference between war and peace."

"Without the dragons, we'll never end the war with the Quag," Magnus said.

"That's entirely another matter and better addressed on the far side of our predicament."

Magnus was dressed in a black priest's robe, wrapped and tucked about his body the way all priests dress when not in Ferustir guise. Beneath the robe, he still wore Eamon's Ferustir suit with Lucas's sword strapped low across his back. Outside the robe, he wore Catanya's lance sheathed high across his back so as to appear as Trax did when he entered the kitchen half an hour ago.

Magnus, Catanya and Trax had been quick to plan their infiltration of the Temple of Fire. A small window of opportunity was upon them.

"Every morning before sunrise I bring a meal to the High Priests in the temple," Trax had explained. "Wards about the temple are lifted to allow my coming and going."

The plan was to have each of them, and the dragons, enter the temple whilst the wards were lifted. They were now ready.

"Shall we go over the plan?" Trax suggested.

"I enter the temple disguised as you, carrying the High Priests' morning meal," Magnus said.

"Move with purpose," Trax warned. "If Liné catches your scent, you are done for."

"Once in the nave, Magnus hurries to the *third* door along the eastern wall and lets me in through the healing room," Catanya added.

"Correct," Trax said. "By which point I've approached the temple as myself, also carrying a tray of food, thereby raising the alarm as to an imposter."

"Liné is closest and will be the first to follow you into the nave," Magnus said.

"I imagine Brue will be close behind," Trax added. Magnus shuddered at the thought.

"The commotion will alert the High Priests, by which time I will be hiding behind the statue of Balgur," Catanya said.

"Correct." Trax rubbed his palms together. "At this point, chaos will ensue. Brue will have spotted you, Magnus. Rubea will be the last dragon into the temple and the two High Priests will have entered the nave through the *second* door along the western wall."

"I will keep the High Priests from killing me," Magnus added.

"As I try to reason with Liné. If she knows you are the Electus, she may keep Brue from killing you."

"In the chaos, I will enter the *fourth* door along the western wall," Catanya said.

"Correct. Now listen closely, Semsame." Trax was wide-eyed again. "This door leads to a spiral staircase that ends at a curved corridor." Trax drew on the tabletop with fingers as he explained. "It will be disorientating, but know that at the end of the corridor, as it opens to a chamber, you face *south*. The chamber itself is circular with twelve doors evenly spaced about it as hours on a clock. Liné's egg was born at the midday hour, so her egg will be stored in the chamber room behind the *twelfth* door."

"Chamber room twelve—got it," Catanya confirmed.

"The doors are not labelled numerically," Trax warned. Catanya stared at the old priest. "The twelfth door is directly north—behind you as you enter the chamber."

"Directly north—got it."

"There is something more you should know, Semsame. A fire dragon egg born at the midday hour is a 'Zenith' dragon—preordained to be the most powerful of dragons. The sun is at its zenith at this hour—the most powerful hour of the Fire god—'Couldradt'. The last Zenith dragon born was Balgur."

"You're saying Liné's egg is to become the most powerful dragon born in hundreds of years?" Catanya asked.

"In five hundred years, yes."

"Got it."

"Hopefully, with the High Priests distracted by myself, the Electus and three dragons, Catanya will return through the fourth door with Liné's egg and the High Priests will have lost their leverage for favour." Trax's eyes shifted back and forth from Magnus to Catanya.

"We play things by ear after that," Magnus concluded.

"Indeed."

Magnus walked out of the kitchen and nearly missed the step. He stumbled slightly, recovered quickly, but continued to shake nervously. He steadied the tray of food that permeated more heat and stronger spices than usual— something Trax cleverly thought would help mask Magnus's scent.

With his hood pulled well forward over his face, Magnus took deliberate breaths to match his short steps as he tried to emulate Trax's walking style. He walked across the cobblestones of the common, eyeing a still-sleeping Rubea on the training field. The temple stairs came into sight, then the Temple of Fire itself. Liné was lying six feet from the tall, black doors he was going to walk through in just a moment. *"Move with purpose..."* Magnus remembered Trax's warning and quickened his pace, reaching the bottom step of the temple. He dared not look at Liné, or Brue, who was surely looking down on him at that very moment. *Does Trax take one or two steps at a time?* He cursed himself for not asking. He assumed the old priest took one step at a time whilst carrying the food tray, and so did so.

One, two, three, four... Magnus counted every step until he reached the top of the stairs. Liné stood tall and Magnus lifted his head without thought. Her amber eyes flashed briefly at him, then looked away. Magnus lowered his head again and moved quickly through the portico arch to the temple doors. One was ajar, but not enough to squeeze through with the tray. He pushed it with his foot and the bulky hinges groaned as the door opened the few extra inches he needed. Magnus was in the temple.

THE HIGH PRIESTS

Using the same foot, Magnus closed the temple door but was careful to leave it an inch ajar for Trax to follow him in. Turning, Magnus found himself in the temple's narthex. There was a second set of open doors just ahead. Magnus walked briskly toward them and peered in, realising at this point he was still carrying the tray of food. He cursed under his breath and placed the tray off to the side before entering the nave.

The nave took his breath away. The floor appeared to be a smooth surface of water as he stepped tentatively onto the black marble. *Haste...* he reminded himself. *Third door on the eastern wall...* Magnus sprinted across the floor to the third door and slid back the steel locking bolt. He entered the white-walled healing room. On the far side, he slid the second bolt and pulled that door open, too.

Catanya jumped through the door and closed it behind her, leaving this door ajar as well. Coming back through the healing room, Magnus pulled Catanya's sheathed lance from his back and handed it to her, then discarded the priest robes he was wearing and re-sheathed his sword over his left shoulder. They entered the nave just as an explosion of noise erupted through the temple doors from the narthex. Magnus and Catanya exchanged quick glances—glances full of hope and dread—and assumed their positions. Catanya leapt behind the white marble statue of Balgur at the back of the nave. Magnus came about and stood at the very centre of the vaulted room as Trax came charging through the second set of doors with Liné's bellowing roar and hulking body right behind him.

Trax leapt at Magnus and turned about when he reached him. "I just had a thought! Do something to show yourself!"

"What do you mean?"

You are the Electus! Show it!"

This was not part of the plan, but Magnus knew what Trax meant. Magnus clenched hands into fists and tried to conjure fire but was quickly distracted. He could see a second dragon entering the nave behind Liné—it was Brue. Trax intercepted Liné. She was half way across the nave floor with a horribly familiar burbling sound rising in her belly. Magnus knew what the sound was pre-emptive of and grew concerned for Catanya's safety should the nave fill with fire. *Will the statue of Balgur protect her?*

As Trax predicted, Rubea was entering the temple behind Brue. Then the second door along the western wall opened. Two black-robed figures moved like apparitions into the confusion. In a blur of fire-bronze, the two High Priests drew weapons and twirled them about in a fantastic display of skill. As their weapons drew still again, Magnus saw they were not holding lances—they were holding fire-swords.

As if reacting to the forsaken weapons, Liné twisted her head to one side and released her surge of flame over the High Priests. Magnus reeled from the searing heat. The flames wrapped around the priests but could not penetrate the air within two feet of them. Both High Priests were mumbling spells. Amidst the fiery attack, one of them pointed an arm at Magnus.

Assuming the worst kind of sorcery was to come, Magnus pointed an arm of his own back at the High Priest. The pores in his arms and hands bled seeds of fire that merged and spun into an eddy of flames about his arm. With a flick of fingers, the flames launched toward the priest. Before Magnus could see what effect they had, a dazzling white light filled the nave and Magnus was blinded. It lasted just a moment but his eyesight was slow to regain its focus. When he did, he saw the High Priests had moved into offensive positions and were whispering at a furious rate. One focused on the dragons, the other was looking at him. Beyond them, Magnus saw that the fourth door from the left was open—*Catanya got past the priests!*

Catanya sprinted down the spiral staircase that ended at the descending curved corridor. Trax was not lying—by the time the corridor opened into the circular chamber she was completely disorientated. There were twelve doors, evenly spaced about the cylindrical walls of the chamber, with little to tell them apart. The darkness did not help with the confusion. There were sconces mounted over each of the doors, but only seven of them had torches lit and dimly at that. They each cast strips of light across the chamber floor that would have formed a star-like pattern of twelve yellow blades if all the lights worked. It seemed odd that the temple above was magnificent and meticulous in every way when this hidden underground chamber was drab and neglected. Catanya saw this as a metaphor—*like the High Priests' who are virtuous on the outside, yet poisoned with ambition within.*

"Twelve doors…" Catanya shifted to the centre of the chamber. Even this far below ground level, the foundations trembled with the dragon battle happening overhead. "Focus." It was difficult to do so knowing Magnus was in the middle of it all. Catanya bounced on the balls of her feet. She spun about to face the corridor she had come down and looked directly at the door in that direction. "North. Trax said the twelfth door faces north."

Catanya ran to the door. There was no lock. She held the large brass knob attached to the chunky latching mechanism and lifted the latch away. The door pushed inward to a trapezoidal shaped room about ten-foot deep and broadening width as it deepened. The room was eerily sparse yet lit by a ring of six fist-sized fire orbs floating ten feet from the ground, surrounding the centre of the room. At this centre was a black marble plinth standing waist high with a shallow, spherical depression in its top. Within this depression sat a two-foot long, burnt-orange dragon egg. Catanya stepped into the room, walked beneath the ring of orbs and reached for the egg. There was no time to lose and so without a second thought, she held the egg between her hands and lifted it from the plinth. The egg was heavier than Catanya expected, but more surprising was the heat it radiated. She held it close to her body for fear of dropping it, walked out of the room, into the chamber and almost dropped the egg at the sight before her. Someone was standing at the centre of the circular chamber, partially hidden in shadow but with yellow strips of light highlighting the familiar features of her body and face. She was holding a single purple iris. It was *Hannah*.

"That will do it!" Trax shouted to Magnus after his fire display—ineffective against the High Priests as it was. Trax maintained his position between Magnus and the dragons. His arms were wide and he stared at Liné. Magnus saw Liné's eyes changing colour, flashing through a myriads of variations before settling on brown to match Trax's. He had seen the fire dragons do this before—first with Thioci and then again at the gathering in Ba'rrat. Magnus was certain it meant Liné and Trax were sharing thoughts. *This has to be a good sign...*

All of a sudden, Magnus's own thoughts felt as if they were being twisted. He felt confused and disoriented. He looked to Brue, who was circling around the eastern wall, focused on Magnus. Rubea was doing the same toward one of the High Priests in the other direction. The other High Priest was staring at Magnus, his mouth still moving rapidly. *He is making a mental assault...* Magnus deduced. He stared back, searching his own mind for an area yet to be dominated by the priest. He hoped he could establish a stronghold with which to anchor and work to regain control and block the priest from his head. A memory of Thioci came to mind. Färgd was there, talking to the young dragon. It was when they were at the eastern wall in Ba'rrat. He felt Färgd's joy as well as his sorrow and his acknowledgement that Thioci had chosen him to be Electus. He held fast to the memory, for the High Priest was quickly encroaching on the rest of his mind with sorcery. It was as if everything was becoming a mangled vortex of confusion. Magnus tried hard to resist the mental assault. Then came the heat.

Dragon blood raged through his mind faster than even before. Magnus concentrated on working with the heat—pushing back against the priest's sorcery, allowing his mind to burn the effects free. He kept pushing, but the High Priest was well skilled and his mental manipulations persisted. Magnus eyed the High Priests' fire-swords. He was of the understanding that only one such sword still existed—*Eamon's sword.* They were considered a curse and were all thought to be destroyed after Balgur was slain with Steyne's own sword in the Battle of Fire twenty years ago. *What madness made the High Priests bring those to the fight? Surely they knew they'd make instant enemies of the fire dragons?* Then, in some portion of his brain free from the priest's assault, it dawned on Magnus—*arrogance is their weakness. They don't believe their own dragons would attack them while they hold Liné's egg to ransom. Facing the dragons must have come as a surprise to them.* Magnus knew Liné's fiery assault on the High Priests was testament to this. *Good,* Magnus thought. *A weakness I can exploit…*

With his addled mind, Magnus fumbled awkwardly over his shoulder for Lucas's sword. Although it was partially made with fire-bronze, its most lethal component was fleu-steel, represented no ill will to Liné, Brue or Rubea. He clawed for the sword's pommel, slowly drawing it from its red scabbard with thumb and gnarled forefinger. The effort was excruciating with the High Priest's sorcery working hard against him. With a final effort and guttural yell, Magnus freed the sword and held it aloft. The High Priest reacted as Magnus hoped he would. The mental assault waned slightly and the High Priest raised his fire-sword. Both Brue and Rubea roared at him. The priest slipped his grip even further over Magnus's mind and Magnus felt a soothing shunt of heat clear away the weakening mental assault. Alas, and despite the dragons' aggressiveness, the High Priest came at Magnus.

The fire-sword came down so hard that Magnus nearly lost his grip parrying the blow. The second blow was an unexpected boot to the chest and the third was an open palm to his right temple. All three happened in the same moment. Magnus stumbled back, catching himself after a single step.

He cracked his head to one side and a snap of heat healed the beaten side of his head. More burning heat repaired a cracked rib.

My turn…

Magnus drove hard at the priest and dealt blow after blow, each caught or deflected as though the skilled Irucantî anticipated his every move. Magnus did not let up. If the priest made a single false move, Magnus would have him, but then—

"Slow… predictable… rigid…"

The priest shared thoughts as he critiqued Magnus's assault. *Such arrogance. Who do they think they are?* Anger boiled within him. These were the priests who commanded his brethren to kill him and Catanya, failed to defend the people they were sworn to and threatened the dragons of his realm. *Now he has the nerve to school me on my skills?*

"Power monger, liar, coward…" Magnus shared his own views.

The priest fought back and their swords sung as fire-bronze and fleu-steel made hard contact. Lucas's sword was strong and it would take a lot to break it, yet he was sure if there were a way, the priest would find it.

Trax shouted—"Magnus! Show Liné the mark her son gave you, let her know your mind!"

"A little busy, Trax!" Magnus shouted.

Trax spun about, pushed Magnus free of the High Priest and ignited his lance, taking over the fight.

Magnus turned to Liné. Her eyes immediately flickered to blue-green and he knew he had her attention. To his left, Brue turned to him. Magnus squatted, placed the sword on the ground and stood. *'I am sorry I hurt you back in Ba'rrat, Brue. But you did try to kill me.'* He looked at Liné and said nothing. He let his mental barriers ease.

Magnus recalled Eamon telling him to do the same in Ba'rrat when the fire dragons congregated to meet him. *'Remain open,'* Eamon had said. *'Let them see who you are.'* Magnus felt vulnerable at the time, but such doubts were a luxury he could no longer afford. To his right, Rubea turned her back on the commotion with the other High Priest and sniffed him curiously. Her mental presence was gentle compared to Liné and Brue's palpable fury.

Magnus let his thoughts fall on his memories of Thioci once again. It gave a good reference point for the three dragons as they probed his mind, looking this way and that. Magnus's mind then drifted to thoughts of Breona— *beautiful Breona…* He did not expect it and his heart heaved. The dragons drew on the memory of Thioci and the Astermeer who died alongside him. They learned all there was to know about their interaction, from Breona defending Thioci, to sharing intimate thoughts with him. From here, the three dragons branched away from one another in their respective searches through Magnus's mind.

Magnus felt Brue's mind transfix on every memory he had of Thioci. Brue was drawing on all Magnus had of the youngling's physical appearance as though extracting the memories for keepsake. He was clearly not looking for reason, but trying to satisfy the emptiness he felt from losing him. To Magnus, it did not seem to be working. He sensed a great pain in Brue—the same pain he had felt for losing Breona. He could see how much worse it was for Brue losing a son. The disdain Magnus felt for the long-tailed fire dragon dissipated in the same way it had when he rediscovered Eamon's friendship after months of hating the old man.

Rubea's interests were different. She flittered about his mind for a while, following her older sister's lead but then, Magnus felt her curiosity peak when she found Catanya in his memories. As Catanya predicted, Rubea was intrigued by their love, intimacy and long journey to reunite. Rubea realised she had met Magnus by the Nuyan River months ago and had watched him and Catanya at the time, never comprehending the pain caused in separating them. The fondness Rubea had for Catanya was obvious. Magnus sensed that a seed of compassion for him was born in the young dragon and that, perhaps, he had made an ally in Rubea if nothing else.

Liné was the most diplomatic of the three dragons and Magnus immediately became aware of how intelligent she was. She started with the facts and spared herself emotional attachment in her search for what she needed to know. Liné explored the story of Magnus meeting Thioci, how he shared his fish with him and then defended Thioci against Crugion and his men. She closely examined Magnus's relationship with Breona and from here, his mother. Finally, she scrutinised the process of Thioci choosing Magnus as the Electus. Only when she had learned the complete story did she allow herself to explore the intimacy Magnus and Thioci shared the following day during the last moments of Thioci's life—

'You traded your life for mine. Why did you do that?'

'My wounds were beyond healing. But yours I could repair. My role in this life is complete. Yours has just begun.'

'Thank you, Thioci...'

Liné's own mind was guarded and Magnus dared not intrude, but at the end of her exploration, a single thought whispered through his mind. It was a mother's pride for her son who gave his blood to save another.

The three dragons withdrew from Magnus's mind. A sense of peace came over him for as long as it took to realise the commotion was still occurring in the Nave. He spun about to find Trax defending himself against the superior strength and sorcery of the High Priest. Magnus reached for his sword but he need not have bothered.

Both Brue and Rubea came around Magnus and lunged at the High Priest. Trax leapt back out of harm's way. This time, neither dragon used flames. Brue knocked the priest to the ground with a fistful of claws and Rubea pinned down his fallen body. Brue was furious, but Rubea refused to move. She was holding the High Priest prisoner, keeping Brue from killing him. Magnus breathed a sigh of relief once again but as before, it was short lived.

"Where is the other High Priest?" Magnus ran about the nave, searching. He was nowhere to be found. He looked to Trax who pointed to the western wall. Magnus looked to the open door—second from the left—that led to the chamber below. Dread washed over him.

Catanya stared at her little sister.

"Hannah?"

It was a torturous apparition. She tried to convince herself it was a trick of the mind, most likely sorcery of the High Priests cunningly designed to draw on her most vulnerable traits as a distraction. The notion of such clever sorcery was farfetched, but far less so than the alternative—*Hannah is actually standing before me.* Yet there was too much to the vision only Catanya could possibly know. Hannah wore her pomegranate dress and Catanya's brown suede jacket. She could see the familiar freckle under her little sister's left eye, the dimple in her right cheek even when she was not smiling and the way she turned her feet inward when she was nervous. *It cannot be real…*

"Hannah?"

Hannah's nervous expression turned to fear. Her eyes widened. "Catanya!" Hannah shrieked, pointing to something behind her big sister. Catanya turned. A High Priest stood at the bottom of the spiral passage and swung his fire-sword cross ways at Catanya's neck.

Catanya dropped low to the ground, avoiding the strike. Swiftly and carefully, she placed the egg on the stone ground and then, in one quick move, she sprung upward, drew and igniting her lance, and caught the priest's second blow. With blades locked, the priest tilted his head forward and pulled back the hood of his cloak. The patchy light beams danced across his face and head that was almost completely covered in dragon markings. His eyes greyed over and Catanya knew the High Priest was making a mental assault.

"Namon penet animo meo." The spell shielded Catanya's mind from invasion. She knew any counter spell she could conjure would have little effect on this priest, so she would have to put all her strength into her lance. The priest, though, lowered his sword.

"You have no idea what you are meddling with, young Irucantî," the High Priest said. "The next age of Allumbreve will not be defended by dragons, it will be fought by men with the power of the gods." Catanya dared not turn from him yet was desperate to look to her sister again. The High Priest kept talking. "Who would you prefer to wield such power—the most elite of your brethren, or an outsider with no training… no affiliation with our order? You need to choose wisely."

"Thioci chose the Electus," Catanya replied. "What you think doesn't matter."

"Thioci's choice was not sanctioned by the order of the Irucantî, nor his elders."

"Thioci's brethren support him. Nothing you do or say will change that."

"You think I am arrogant, Semsame." The High Priest pointed his sword to Catanya. She lifted her lance, fidgeting nervously with its grip. "I read it in your eyes the day of your inauguration. I thought with time and training, particularly under Joffren's tutelage, you would tame. I was wrong."

"Joffren's self-righteousness has left him fighting for his life."

"Impressive! I did not think you had it in you."

"It wasn't me. It was the Electus you're so desperate to kill."

The High Priest laughed the most condescending of laughs. "My arrogance pales next to your naivety. We gave Austagia credit for his ability to find wayward recruits after bringing Jael into the order. This time I see, his judgment was clouded."

Catanya sneered deliberately. "Is teasing me your best comeback?"

The priest clenched his jaw—his grey eyes now a dark, dangerous glare. "There's not a loyal Irucantî alive who will support Thioci's choice."

"There were three Irucantî who opposed the decision." Catanya tilted her head to one side, keeping her gaze on the priest's unblinking eyes. "Can you guess who killed them?" She mimicked the priest's glare. "Brue supported them, acting under duress, then flew back here licking his wounds with his long tail between his legs."

The High Priest shook his head slowly. "Brue would like another chance to revenge Thioci's death. I'm sure he's getting that chance as we speak."

"I think Brue will be preoccupied with you once he and Liné get their egg back." Catanya pushed the egg away from her with one foot—it gently rolled toward the centre of the chamber floor. She turned for the briefest of moments and saw that Hannah was gone. She looked back again, her eyes darting around the gloomily lit chamber, but there was no sign of Hannah anywhere, yet no open doors she could have fled through.

A sharp sound alerted Catanya to the Priest swinging his sword again. Catanya caught the blade with her lance. Both fire-bronze weapons sparked. The sparks dissipated with a whiff of smoke that was telltale of the dragon forging built into them.

"A fire-sword. You priests are full of lies." Catanya spat her words through gritted teeth. She was sick to death of deceptions and false piety, the stuff of which had cost her enough and nearly her life and now—*Hannah?* Catanya dared not look for her sister again. She struck back.

Twirling her lance and drawing a throwing knife with her right hand, Catanya shifted into a series of attack combinations. The first two Joffren had taught her, the third was one she devised herself. She swung one end of the lance at the priest's neck then stepped forward for a double thrust to his chest then abdomen, then pulled the lance back to fend a predictable, retaliatory thrust of sword. *Combination one.*

Catanya repeated the move, but swung the lance back handed to the face between thrusts and finished with a boot to the chest, knowing the retaliatory thrust would come slower this time—which it was. *Combination two.*

Catanya came again, this time stepping twice toward the priest with a backhand thrust, bringing her right elbow toward his face. The priest took the bait. He drove an upward sword thrust intended to sever her arm at the elbow, but Catanya was ready—the right-handed grip on her lance was false and instead, it held her knife blade forward. She drove the blade toward his chest. The move saw her vambrace take the blow of the priest's sword, and her knife would now end the priest's life as she sunk into his black robes and between his ribs. Her knife though, could not break through the priest's robes. The priest had a knife of his own and he swung it down, driving it into flesh to the right of Catanya's neck.

Catanya stumbled back. Her knife slipped from her hand, hitting the ground with a muffled, dull thud that was barely audible above the constant ring in Catanya's right ear. Her left hand was still firmly gripping her lance but her balance was off. The chamber seemed to be tilting over to her left. Her feet stumbled, struggling to keep her upright.

"CATANYA!"

Catanya heard her little sister's scream but it was not real—it was a dream of sorcery, or perhaps her own delirity. Either way, it gave her strength. Catanya swung the lance at the priest, making him pause his advance. She reached up with her spare hand and took grip of the knife handle. It was buried in the thick muscle over her shoulder blade. Catanya looked at the High Priest—one of the two leaders of the Irucantî—and screamed a long scream at him as she pulled the knife free of her muscle, dropping it to the ground. It its place was a bloody wound. She felt the warm blood cascade down her chest to her abdomen, and down her spine to the small of her back. The priest discarded his black robe, revealing his own Ferustir armour—the armour that protected his chest from Catanya's knife.

"Not fair," Catanya mumbled as she stumbled back a few steps.

The priest came at Catanya again. His bronze sword danced through the dim chamber and Catanya fended blow after blow. She winced from pain and frowned with frustration, for even with the dizziness dissipating, she could not find a weakness in the priest's attack—until she did.

At one stage the priest shifted his sword into his right hand, freeing his left hand to crack each knuckle of his fingers against his chest plate. Was it an old injury? Had age seized his joints, making endurance his weakness? Whatever the cause, the priest was fallible. Where there was one ailment, there was likely more, and the thought gave her hope. Catanya knew she was losing a lot of blood, but she was not bested yet. She attacked hard and fast.

Her lance seemed to lighten in her hand with her renewed determination. She parried the High Priest's blows and struck out with her own, making contact several times across his armour, but never his flesh. Nevertheless she came again and again. At one stage Catanya coiled her lance about, making the sharp side of the blade score the priest across his brow, cutting him deep. The priest paused and so Catanya backed down. He touching his red stained face with a finger and examining the blood. It occurred to her it was likely the first time the High Priest had been injured in a generation and perhaps the shock would unbalance him. Catanya was wrong.

The priest retaliated. He swung high and Catanya fended it off. A kick to the chest threw Catanya off balance. She was standing in a puddle of her own blood and slipped. Her legs came away from under her and she landed hard on her back. The priest was quick to stand on her left arm, forcing her lance from her grip. It rolled away and extinguished itself. The priest held his fire-sword to her armour-plated chest.

"A weak spot in all Ferustir suits is off centre to the breastbone." The priest pushed his blade angled to Catanya's chest. She heard it tear through the fibres of her armour and felt the cold bronze against her skin. Catanya stared at the priests darkening eyes—the eyes of a hunter about to kill his prey. In her peripheral sight, she saw a dark shadow flying down the corridor toward the chamber where she lay beside Liné's egg.

"Drive a good blade at the correct angle…" the priest pushed the blade harder and Catanya felt its tip pierce her skin. She grunted. The priest continued—"And you've found the heart of the Ferustir."

The dark shadow was then at the priest's back. It was Trax. He drew back what appeared to be the other High Priest's fire-sword. Catanya concentrated on the High Priest's eyes, not wanting to give away Trax's presence.

With a violent jolt, the High Priest stumbled forward over his sword. Catanya grunted as the priest's body weight drove his sword deeper into her chest. She gripped the sharp blade with her free hand to halt its progress. The High Priest fell to the ground beside her—a sword protruding from his back.

"There's a weak spot off centre to the spine as well, Semsame." Trax squatted at Catanya's head and drew the sword from her chest.

"I know about that one," Catanya mumbled. She looked to her right and saw Liné's egg. Reaching to it, she drew the egg closer, hugging it into her wounded chest. Catanya took a deep breath, released it and smiled at Trax who smiled back to her.

"Hannah?" Catanya mumbled. The ceiling began to spin and so she shut her eyes, letting herself drift into dreams of her sister.

Hannah…

REUNION

Färgd flew from Ba'rrat to Thwax. *"When we arrive, make haste with your visit, Eamon. I'm more concerned with the wellbeing of the Electus than with Joffren's demise."*

Eamon agreed with the great dragon and yet, haste made him anxious. It did not help to be riding a dragon for the first time in two decades. Had he forgotten the power of the great beast? The height gained with each beat of scaled wings? The strength needed to hold the saddle horn and the awkwardness of his legs strapped fast in stirrups? *No*, Eamon mused. *One never forgets the experience of riding a dragon.* It was the phenomenal speed Färgd flew at that frazzled Eamon.

"Westerly trade winds." Färgd explained. *"They lend speed to our cause. The summer thermals are advantageous as well."*

"Give yourself some credit, Färgd."

They arrived in Thwax late in the morning, landing in a rubble-strewn street.

"I'll return within the hour," Färgd explained. *"There's a steer destined to be my breakfast in the field a mile back."* He took flight again.

Eamon wasted no time getting to Marsala's home.

"I got here as fast as I could."

Marsala closed the viewing-hole and opened the door. She embraced Eamon. "Thanks for coming."

Eamon stood back and held Marsala's face in gently cupped hands. She had a purple bruise over the right side of her jaw and more bruising around her neck. He gently stroked her jaw with a thumb making Marsala wince.

"Joffren did this?"

Marsala nodded, then leant forward and gave Eamon a soft kiss on the lips. "Come."

At the bottom of the stairs, Eamon turned into the kitchen. Marsala came in behind him. There was a blanket covering the top half of Joffren's body that lay on the kitchen floor. The kitchen was otherwise clean and in order with the exception of a cooking pot that had a large dent in the side.

"I did what I could," Marsala explained. "Turned him about and cleaned him up, read a passage from the 'Murata Fara'." Eamon looked at her. She shrugged. "It seemed the right thing to do."

"The man tried to kill you, Marsala. You don't owe him anything."

Marsala flashed a condescending glance at Eamon. "A dead priest in my kitchen is one thing. Having his spirit lingering is *not* something I need. I sent it on its way."

Eamon looked around the kitchen again, allowing old memories to wash over him. "It's been a while."

"And a lot has changed for you in this time." Marsala stood in front of Eamon and held his hands. "You did it, Eamon."

"Hmm?"

"You found him. You *guided* him. You did what you set out to do all those years ago."

"You met Magnus, then?"

"Aye."

"He's the right choice, isn't he?" Eamon felt proud—as if he was describing his own son.

"He is worthy of being your Electus. And young Catanya… she is quite the fateful addition."

"I will say, Marsala, she is the only person who has left me speechless besides you."

Marsala smiled. "Go up to the living room. I'll make supper."

"No need. A glass or two of your finest red will suffice."

"You are speaking my language!"

Marsala stepped into the corridor at the bottom of the staircase and opened a cupboard. She removed a dusty bottle and two small pewter goblets then started up the stairs with Eamon close behind. Half way up she stopped. Eamon considered her.

"Do you remember the Beckford incident?"

Eamon laughed aloud. "How could I forget?" He thought of the incident from about eight years before. Eamon had returned to Allumbreve after a two-year journey beyond the Neverseas. After docking at Ba'rrat, he travelled to Thwax to see Marsala. When he arrived, there was a middle-aged man having an argument with Marsala in the street out the front of her house. "That Mr Beckford was convinced you'd cursed his wife!" Eamon chuckled.

"His wife had left him after learning he was having an affair," Marsala contributed. He couldn't for the life of him imagine it reason enough to leave him. 'Must be the town mystic has put a curse on my wife'." Marsala shook her head and resumed her climb up the stairs. "Do you remember what you said to him—when you came across us arguing in the street?"

Eamon thought back. Mr Beckford was red faced with anger at the time. Though, he could not for the life of him remember what he said.

"He reached beneath his cloak and pulled a knife," Marsala said as if to jog Eamon's memory.

"Only it wasn't a knife!" Eamon remembered.

"It was a sweet potato!" Eamon and Marsala said together, laughing hysterically at the top of the stairs.

"Do you remember what you said?" Marsala was crying from laughter.

"Aye," Eamon remembered as he wiped away a tear of his own. "I said, 'you've got clout, brandishing vegetables in such a manner, but if you'd kept your vegetables in their pockets, your wife would never have left you'!"

They both laughed heartily again as they settled into the leather chairs in Marsala's eclectic living room.

"If only he'd known the truth!" Eamon said.

"Well," Marsala shook her head. "His wife did come to me first." She chuckled a final time as she poured red wine into the small goblets, handing one to Eamon. He held her hand as she did.

"I am sorry, Marsala. I truly am." Eamon deeply regretted putting Marsala's life in danger by sending Joffren to her. With Joffren's muddled state of mind he should have thought of the danger he posed. "It was short sighted of me to send Joffren to you." Marsala looked deep into Eamon's eyes as though studying her old friend for the first time in a long time. Her eyes softened. The gentlest smile came to her face. "I was desperate to save him. I was hoping I could—"

"Eamon," Marsala interjected.

"I should have known, I should have anticipated—"

"Eamon." Eamon looked at her. She took his bearded face in her hands. "It's okay. I'm fine. Joffren was your Semsarian. Your protective instincts for him are to be expected. This is not something else for you to endure."

Eamon sighed, thinking of recent events. "Over the past while, many ghosts from my past have come back to haunt me, Marsala. In daylight hours, no less."

"Things do have a way of resurfacing. I think it's a good thing—clarity precedes closure."

Eamon returned Marsala's gaze. "I'm without words once again."

"Good. Drink your wine."

Eamon sipped the wine. It was as wonderful as he remembered and lifted his spirits. *Rhuderburry wine...* It was a fair bet to say he and Marsala were the only folk in all of Allumbreve who had savoured the broody, red-grape wine. Marsala saved the wine for Eamon's company and it was he who gave it to her when he returned from abroad. He also gave her three pounds of rhuderburry extract—a potent medicine Marsala had skilfully mixed into many of her potions. From where he got it from exactly he kept to himself. He drank the wine and drank in the sight of Marsala—it was so good to see her again.

"You'll still not tell me where rhuderburries come from, will you?" Marsala jested.

"One day I'll show you." It was always Eamon's response and Marsala always rolled her eyes as he said it.

They sat in silence, enjoying one another's company for the little time they had left, knowing Färgd would soon return. Soon though, Marsala's demeanour began to change. She sat up in her chair, toying with her goblet. Her shoulders stiffened and a frown came to her face.

"What is it Marsala? You seem vexed beyond the dead man in your kitchen."

"Did you know Ganister of Bowthwait?" Marsala asked.

"Aye," Eamon said, knowing the Bowthwaitman perished in Ba'rrat's Arena.

"I know he is dead. Did you know his wife is my cousin?"

"Not that I recall."

"She visited just days ago, bringing the news with her. Her son—Lucas— was as a brother to Magnus."

Eamon listened intently, sensing there was a darker side to the story beyond Ganister's death. "Go on."

"Lucas is in a dark place, wielding a dark power. He is a sorcerer under Delvion's control, but I do not know how he got such power. What I do know from my time with Magnus is that he will bend the will of fate to save his friend."

"Will Magnus sacrifice himself for his friend?"

"The Electus will sacrifice what Allumbreve needs of him, perhaps even himself, to protect Lucas—yes."

An hour had passed when Eamon heard Färgd landing heavily at the bottom of the hill behind Marsala's home. Together, Eamon and Marsala carried Joffren's body out the back door and over to the dragon. Marsala helped him tie Eamon's former Semsarian to the rear of Färgd's saddle.

"Take care of yourself, Eamon."

"And you, Marsala."

"You've begun the second most important part of your life—the life for which I renamed you 'Eamon'. Do your best," Marsala instructed.

"Thank you. Perhaps though, this will be the most important part of my life—don't you think?"

Marsala shook her head. "No. That comes afterward, when you return and show me the world you've seen beyond the Neverseas."

"That sounds wonderful."

"Then we can pick rhuderburries together."

They embraced and kissed one another fondly. Eamon climbed into Färgd's saddle and strapped his legs in. In one powerful thrust, Färgd launched into the sky and Eamon waved to Marsala who disappeared into the fog below.

"To the Romghold, Färgd."

"We shall bring order to the Irucantî once and for all."

Beyond the Neverseas, Eamon thought to himself, thinking of Marsala's parting words. *If she only knew of the world she wonders…*

LINÉ

Magnus placed a hand on Catanya's forehead, stroking the hair from her face. With his other hand, he was firmly pinching the deep cut between her shoulder and neck, trying to stop the bleeding.

Catanya was lying on the white marble table in the healing room, yet to regain consciousness after her fight with the High Priest. The priest was dead and Liné's egg returned to her. Trax had seen to it that the remaining High Priest was locked in a holding cell at the far east of the Romghold under guard of a very angry dragon—Brue. Magnus was glad Brue had redirected his anger. The other two fire dragons stood at either door of the healing room. Liné was at the outside door, her egg with her, and Rubea was in the temple nave, seated at the third door along the eastern wall. After rescuing Liné's egg, the dragons were now honouring Catanya by protecting her.

Trax came bursting into the healing room from the outer door, carrying two arms full of stuff. "She will be okay, Liné, I promise you," he said before shutting the door behind him. He looked to Magnus. "How is she?"

"Stable," Magnus said in his calmest voice. Inside he was fretting. He hoped Trax was a good healer.

"I have everything we need," Trax said. "The healing room is usually well stocked, but we shouldn't be left wanting for anything. Firstly, let's stitch that wound, then we can assess the chest injury."

"She's lost a lot of blood," Magnus's voice wavered. He coughed to clear his throat. "And her chest—"

"Yes, we'll get to that, *Semsdër-fatel.*"

Magnus nodded. "Just tell me what to do."

Trax opened a draw in the small white table at the centre of the healing room and removed a white cloth, unwrapped it and selected the finest of many needles. "No need for too large a scar." From a roll of fine cotton threading, he snapped off a six-inch length. Next, he popped the cork off a small bottle and scooped some of its oily contents with fingers. He ran the threading between his oily thumb and forefinger, making the thread glisten. "And no need for infection." He finished his prep by threading the needle, taking the needle to a candle on the table and putting the needle to its flame until it turned red-hot.

Trax came to Magnus and stood at Catanya's head. "I've got it." He took Magnus's place, pinching the wound himself. He nodded toward the table. "Perhaps if you could run some of those cloth sheets through the warm water and clean the wound for me as I stitch."

"Aye." Magnus did as told, soaking four cloth squares and squeezing the water out, then gently wiping the blood away from Catanya's wound. As he did, Magnus could see how deep the cut had gone.

"It is a deep cut, but we Irucantî do heal well." Trax concentrated as he pushed the sharp needle into Catanya's flesh and began the process of stitching the wound closed. Catanya moaned gently. "That's a good sign," Trax added.

"You *do* heal well?" Magnus asked, stroking Catanya's forehead again.

"Aye. As Semsdër-fatel, you should know our secrets." Trax glanced at Magnus then returned to his stitching. "During our inauguration, we receive the sacrament of Couldradt blood. Nothing as extreme as you have, of course, for our blood is still our own… please wipe again." Magnus did as told, clearing blood away from Catanya's partially stitched wound.

"I know this," Magnus said. "Catanya went through the process of Anunya just as I did." He did not mention his own process of Anunya was an ongoing affair.

"Aye. It is good you've had her to learn these things. Our sacrament provides us with enhancements. One of which is that we heal well. Though, not as well as you, I imagine." Trax glanced at Magnus again.

Magnus considered the old priest. He was sure he could trust him but was wary about revealing his Electus strengths. Still, Magnus considered that every person in Ba'rrat's arena was witness to his healing potential after Briet nearly killed him. Furthermore, many an Irucantî was witness to his healing powers after his Juniper stone altercation with Joffren at the Eastern Wall. The stone had enabled their bodies to merge as one, share thoughts and memories and then pull free once again. The process left Magnus unscathed after his Electus blood worked its magic with a display of shimmering light about his body. Joffren almost lost his life and as far as Magnus knew, was still fighting for it.

"I survived six months and a hundred battles in Ba'rrat's arena. On many occasions I was wounded beyond reason to heal. I'm here to tell tale of it, thanks to Thioci."

Trax smiled as he completed Catanya's stitching with a knot. He returned to the table and washed his hands in the bowl of water. "I am glad to have lived long enough to make your acquaintance in my time, Semsdër."

"Well, I'm glad you were here to support us. Tell me though, what does 'Semsdër-fatel' mean?"

"Ah!" Trax's eyes lit up. "*Semsdër* is a derivative of *Semsdi*—'teacher'. *Semsdër* means 'leader', *Semsdër-fatel* therefore means 'fated leader'. Am I the first to call you as much?"

"Yes, you are." Magnus found the title disconcerting. Was the Electus preordained as the 'fated leader' of the order of the Irucantï? If so, he was beginning to understand why they wanted one of their own in such a pious position. He took no interest in the role himself and knew for certain Catanya would baulk at the idea of him doing so.

"Then I am honoured all the more to be the first to say so!" Trax said. "Let us tend to Catanya's other wounds." Trax retrieved a folded white gown from the end of the healing table.

"I can dress her," Magnus insisted. He took the gown from Trax and draped it over Catanya's body, then set to task removing her Ferustir suit with discretion.

"You are a gentleman as well," Trax remarked.

After a few awkward minutes, Magnus had Catanya's chest armour removed and set to task unbuckling her vambraces and rerebraces. Trax then examined the wound in her breastbone.

"This one is not as deep. The sword may have pierced a lung, but she doesn't struggle for breath or cough up blood."

"She was coughing blood a week ago from an arrow wound in her back."

Trax helped Magnus roll Catanya to her side so he could examine the arrow wound in her back. It was beginning to scar over.

"The wound has been cauterised… from iinside." Trax eyed Magnus then looked back to the wound. "See here, the thin ring of residual burn about the wound." Trax pointed to the ring of dark, burned flesh less than a quarter of an inch thick. "That would be far thicker if cauterised from the outside. Your handiwork, I assume?"

"Aye. I can heat metal and reshape it with thoughts. I did so to the Quag arrowhead."

"Indeed…" Trax traced the wound with a finger again. There was a second, thin black ring around the burned flesh. Trax scratched at the black marking and tasted his finger before spitting on the ground. "Poison."

"Poison?" Magnus was alarmed. "The Quag arrow was poisoned?"

"Aye. You must have burned it out when you removed the arrow."

"There is no residual poison?"

Trax shook his head. "She'd have fallen ill long before now if there was. I will stitch her chest wound and affect a Cantomine spell to halt any internal bleeding, then leave you to apply healing wraps to her other cuts and bruises."

Magnus breathed a sigh of relief. "Thank you, Trax." He offered his hand.

Trax stared at it, apparently unfamiliar with his informal gratitude. He eventually shook Magnus's hand, smiling. "You are most welcome."

Trax stitched Catanya's chest wound then prepared a selection of cotton cloths soaked in healing oils and left them sitting in a stone dish on the small table. He excused himself and left the healing room via the internal door where he started a conversation with Rubea.

Magnus gently cleaned Catanya's nicks and scratches in her cheeks, brow and chin. He was slow and methodical about it, looking at the detail in her olive complexion, her dark eyebrows, red lips and the widow's peak of her black hair. He felt the scar in her left earlobe and the priest markings over the left side of her head. Her hair had grown a little more over the markings— Catanya's attempt to distance herself from the priesthood.

"Hannah..." It was Catanya's first sign of consciousness. She mumbled her sister's name over and over and her face tensed.

Magnus rest a palm over her forehead. "Shh..." He kissed her. She breathed easy again. He drew in the scent of the healing oils on her skin, but could no longer smell jasmine thanks to Marsala lifting the tracking spell Joffren had put on her—the spell that enabled Demi to hunt her down. The thought of Joffren doing this left Magnus conflicted over whether to hope the priest would recover from their Juniper stone altercation. Magnus stroked Catanya's hair for a moment then attended to all her bruises and cuts, placing the healing wraps over her body, arms, thighs and legs.

"Semsdër..."

Magnus blinked himself awake and sat up. He had fallen asleep, draped over Catanya's abdomen.

"She is stable," Trax said. "You should leave her to rest."

"What more can I do?" Magnus blinked the grogginess from his eyes, wondering how long he had been asleep.

"Nothing as far as Catanya is concerned, but we are not out of the woods yet. The surviving High Priest is a very dangerous man, guarded by a dragon who is undecided as to his feelings for you." Trax stared at Magnus and pointed to Catanya. "I suggest you leave me to attend to her. Meanwhile, you see what you can do to form an alliance with Brue because if that priest finds a way of escaping, Brue is our greatest chance of overpowering him. Come."

Magnus followed Trax out of the healing room and into the daylight. Liné sat at the door with her right foreleg hugging her egg. Her piercing amber eyes looked Magnus over.

"I've prepared food for you in the common kitchen." Trax looked at Liné then spoke quietly to Magnus. "Perhaps discuss things with Liné for a start to familiarise yourself with dragon etiquette." Trax nodded politely then excused himself and went back into the healing room, closing the door behind him.

Magnus stared at the door for a moment. He wanted to help nurse Catanya back to health but knew he needed to trust in the old priest and so, with great reluctance and heeding Trax's advice, he turned and gazed into Liné's eyes.

He thought of everything he wanted to say—everything he *should* say to Thioci's mother. Liné's large eyes flickered through a series of colours until they were the same as Magnus's once again. Magnus opened his mouth to speak and then shuddered, realising Liné's presence was already permeating through his mind, melding her thoughts with his. It was sudden and intimate and made him feel vulnerable. Liné had none of the doubts that plagued his mind, though. Magnus wondered if he would measure up to her expectations and perhaps she would think him not worthy of being the Electus.

"Why are you not worthy? Have you changed so much since Breona vouched for you?"

Liné's confronting question triggered a myriad of uncomfortable memories in Magnus's mind. *Father, Xavier, Trager, Delvion…* All these men had, at some stage, made judgment on him. He had often run their conversations over in his mind and the endless nights caged in the dungeon beneath Ba'rrat had allowed him to fester on their judgments. Then he remembered the last time he saw his father and how proud he had been of him, which made him feel a little better.

"That last thought serves you no better." Liné's thoughts startled him from his reverie. *"Show me your mind free of the opinion of others."*

"Have you an opinion of me?" Magnus wanted to get an idea of what Liné thought of him as the Electus.

"So what if I have?"

Silence fell between them as if to emphasise Liné's point. *"So what if she has put value on my worth? It changes nothing."*

"That's better." Liné swung her huge head around, touching her nose to Magnus's forehead. Magnus felt the coarse touch of her scales and the smoky warmth of her breath. He was then drawn deeper into the dragon's thoughts. It was as though Liné took Magnus by the hand and led him in to explore. Magnus trod as tentatively as he had within Thioci's mind shortly before he died, but this was different. The depths of Liné's thoughts seemed endless and without the darkness and delicacy that accompanied Thioci's passing. Her thoughts intertwined with memories and emotions spanning centuries of time. There were the scars of painful memories, many healed with time and some in the process of healing. Each contributed to the dragon Liné was. It seemed, though, that the accumulation of such a vast span of knowledge had not jaded her. She held no resentments, although for some things she was sceptical. Above all, Magnus saw Liné was *wise*—an attribute she acquired from time, experience and an open mind.

As Magnus retreated from Liné's mind, he felt humbled. If every dragon's depth of thought ran so deep, there was a world of knowledge he could draw on.

"A world of wisdom, Magnus," Liné reminded him.

"Aye." Magnus smiled.

Magnus shifted his gaze from Liné to her egg. A burnished-orange colour, it sat in the safest haven in all Allumbreve—in the fold of its mother's arm. "May I?" Magnus asked. He was sure Liné would be able to read his honest intentions. She extended her foreleg, exposing the egg.

Magnus dropped to a knee and extended an arm to touch the smooth, satin-finished shell. The shell radiated heat—a *lot* of heat. It was not the surging burn of dragon blood he was used to, it was more like a stone lifted from the embers of a fire that still holds fast to its heat. *Like a Juniper stone,* Magnus considered, only the egg was a living, evolving thing and the heat came in pulses, beating with the unborn dragon's heart. *'A Zenith dragon...'* he remembered Trax explaining. Liné's pupils pulsed. Magnus was reluctant to let go, but feared he may enter the mind of the unborn dragon. A creature still developing, he felt, should not be exposed to his curious thoughts. He took a step back and looked up into Liné's eyes again. *"Thank you."*

"Thanks to you and Catanya for bringing him to me."

"You're most welcome."

Magnus stepped away, unsure of the common courtesy when departing the company of dragons. He nodded politely, walked around the side of the temple and down the wide steps to the common. Part of him felt that Liné was still with him, in his mind, though he could not be certain. Whatever it was, he felt glad of taking the first step in forging a relationship with her.

From the common, Magnus looked down the long path to a row of three prison cells. The High Priest that survived the siege of the Temple of Fire was in one of them. Seated in the middle of the path, was Brue.

Magnus walked from the common down the eastern path toward Brue. The long-tailed dragon turned away, as if wanting to avoid conversation. He lifted a paw to his face. As Magnus drew closer he realised Brue was trying to hide his nose—the nose Magnus had badly wounded in their altercation back in Ba'rrat. A sickening wave of guilt washed over Magnus, soon replaced with a hot flush of resentment when he recalled, for the thousandth time, the memory of Brue scalding him with his flames. It was no good—Magnus knew this. Brue and he needed to make amends. They needed to move on. He decided to make a passive attempt at conversation.

"Thank you for your help before." Magnus was not at all sure what to say. *"In the temple, I mean… with the priest. I'm pretty sure he would have got the better of me."* Hearing his own words, they sounded rather shallow, particularly as he knew what the pressing issue between them was. Magnus took a breath and gathered better words. *"I am sorry for your loss, Brue. From what I know of Thioci, he was magnificent. And… well… he saved my life. I hope someday you can teach me more about him."*

Magnus hesitated a moment, hoping to get some acknowledgement for his efforts, but it never came. With an awkward nod, he turned and walked toward the common kitchen. He felt pleased with himself for making the effort with Brue, even if the dragon was not interested in getting to know him. *And why should he?* Brue had just got his unhatched son back and was standing guard beside the man who held him to ransom. *Another time…*

BRUE

Catanya's breathing was stable and her heart rate strong, but she was still unconscious. Having eaten, Magnus sat vigil with her in the healing room for the rest of the day. He checked the wounds to her neck and chest and was intrigued with how well they were healing over. It was nothing at all like his own healing abilities, but certainly better than could be expected from medicines and healing wraps alone.

Catanya continued to mumble. A lot of it was incoherent. Sometimes she called for Magnus, but she was most stressed in her unconscious state when she called for Hannah, which was often. Magnus wondered what the High Priest had put her mind through in the dark chamber beneath the temple. Be it a mental game or for real, he knew if Catanya thought her sister was in trouble, she would head for Nuyan as soon as she was well enough to leave. At this stage, he hoped it encouraged her to regain health.

Trax split his time between monitoring Catanya's wellbeing and checking the security of the High Priest locked in the prison cell. As evening came, Trax returned to the healing room with supper and looked Catanya over again.

"Catanya is safe and stable, Semsdër," Trax assured Magnus. "You should retire and rest in her room beyond the common. If there is a change, Rubea or I will let you know."

"It seems every time Catanya and I are separated, some disaster befalls us." Magnus thought of the artisans' camp where they were taken captive. "I'm happy to rest here, on the floor." He turned his attention to Catanya again, needlessly adjusting the healing wrap over her shoulder wound.

"Very well, I think I will check on our prisoner again." Trax slipped out the external door once again.

Time passed and Catanya seemed to settle. The air in the healing room became cool and Magnus took it as a sign that outside the windowless room, their first day in the Romghold was coming to its end. Magnus could hardly believe it was only a night ago they were still climbing the cliff face—so much had happened since then. He laid a blanket over Catanya and opened the external door to let fresh air in. With the door partially open, Magnus saw

Brue strolling toward the training field. The setting sun in that direction rolled its reflection across his bronze scales and his long talons clicked across the common's cobblestones. To Magnus, Brue seemed more settled than the night before when he stood upon the towering steeple. The urgency in his manner had waned, his need for alertness abated. Magnus gazed until the dragon had moved beyond the temple walls and out of sight.

"Go."

Magnus glanced at the source of the voice in his mind—Liné. She was still holding vigil beside the healing room door. Her burning amber eyes were slightly open and against the shadows of the dying light of day, they glowed like furnace doors left ajar.

"Go to Brue. Resolve your differences."

Magnus glanced back to Catanya, who was still sound asleep, then closed the door behind him. He nodded to Liné and made his way around the temple, rubbing thumbs nervously over tight fists. To his left he could see Trax had taken Brue's place overseeing the High Priest's prison cell. He was seated on one of the kitchen stools, reading a book. Further along the temple steps, Magnus looked through the open temple doors, through the narthex and into the nave, were Rubea was still guarding the inner healing room door. She too cast a fiery glance at him. There was nothing more for Magnus to do. All was at peace and everyone seemed safe. And so then, Magnus looked over the training field.

The green lawn of the field was streaked with golden beams of afternoon light and the soft lime glow of the lanterns. Pink gladioli bloomed at the perimeter attracting a dance of summer bugs. At the far side of the field, perched atop the cliff, was Brue's large silhouette, peering out to the setting sun. Balgur's words from the Red River came to him again—*'Heal wounds, forge bonds.'* Magnus walked across the field. When he reached the cliff face, he sat to Brue's left in silence. Together, they watched the sun shift beyond the vast expanse of Froughton Forest.

Magnus sighed as the sun stole away the violence of the previous night and in its place, gifted an evening of peace. He wondered how many magnificent sunsets Brue had seen from this precipice in his long years. He imagined the dragon's memories spanned centuries as Liné's did and in time, he hoped to bridge his differences with Brue. For now, he would sit beside him in peace.

Dusk turned to night. Trax allowed the training field's lanterns to continue glowing as Magnus and Brue continued to sit beside one another in silence. Neither shared a thought. The silver constellations slid across the sky and Brue tilted his head upward, watching their procession for endless hours. Magnus did the same, but as his neck grew sore, he lay back and continued his watch.

What a thing, he dared to think. *To watch in awe, the stars for a night.* As the night aged, the moon moved and Magnus's eyes grew heavy. He glanced to Brue who was still stargazing. Magnus followed his gaze toward the Couldradt constellation—*Brue's namesake's constellation.*

Magnus sensed Brue was longing for something and considered what it may be he longed for. Perhaps he longed for the heavens of his kin, among the stars with the god of fire. It was this god who gave the Couldradt Fire dragons life to guide and protect the people of the Fire Realm. *'Sworn in guardianship.'* Magnus's father would quote from his large brown book—the 'Couldragda'. *'Four breeds of dragons bestowed upon the realms, one for each, sworn in guardianship.'* Was Brue longing to join Thioci in the stars? Was he longing to return to the Fire Realm and his people? Was he regretting his assault on Magnus? Whatever it was, Magnus decided he would not leave Brue's side. *Heal wounds...*

It was something Magnus had never done before—remain awake for an entire night to consider nothing more than the world around him. He had done it, and in the company of a fire dragon. *'Good morning, Brue,'* Magnus considered saying, but only thought it in the silent crevices of his mind. It felt presumptive to assume he had proven worthy of Brue's trust from a single night's vigil. As the sun began to warm his back, Magnus heard the soft padding of footsteps across the training field. Trax came and stood between him and Brue.

"Good morning Semsdër. Good morning Brue," Trax said in a gentle manner as if not wanting to disrupt their vigil. "Would either of you care for a morning meal?" Magnus felt a delicate brush of thought cross over him that he gathered was meant for Trax. Trax tilted his head to Brue and gave a single nod, then turned to Magnus.

"No. But thank you."

"Catanya is recovering well. I shall inform you when she wakes."

"Thank you, Semsü," Magnus replied, using the formal Irucantî address for the first time.

Trax's eyes moved from Magnus to Brue and back again. "With respect, 'Semsame' is more appropriate." He smiled then left.

Magnus felt a second brush of thought from Brue. It was subtle, yet tainted with feeling. Was Brue sympathetic to Catanya's condition? Did he respect Trax's insistence that Magnus address him with a familiar title? Magnus checked himself and tempered his thoughts—this was not about him, it was about Brue.

The day passed slowly. The sun reached its zenith and passed into afternoon. Magnus found his mind wandering back to Balgur at the Red River. *'The High Priests are exceptionally well trained,'* Balgur had said. *'You will learn a lot from one of them, the other will be slain.'* Balgur was right to predict the death of one High Priest. *Now, I am to learn from the other?* The thought seemed ludicrous to Magnus. How was he to go about this? Through a haze of doubt, Magnus strategized. First, he would need to reason with the High Priest and try to figure out whether he would try to kill him the second the prison cell door opened. Magnus shook his head. He could not see it working. Even with three dragons, Trax and a fully recovered Catanya supporting him, the High Priest would seize the chance to fight back. *The only way this will work is to negotiate with him,* Magnus decided. The priest would want something for himself—of that Magnus was certain. Could they find common ground? Could the process be of benefit to both of them?

"You must be careful." It was Brue. His thoughts were directed at the forefront of Magnus's mind—sharp with warning. *"He cannot be trusted."*

Magnus's mouth dried and his tongue became so woolly he doubted he could respond in physical words if he tried. But this was the opportunity he had waited for—to communicate with Brue. *"Should I give him the benefit of the doubt?"* he asked.

"You'll not get a second chance if you're wrong," Brue responded.

Magnus tried to contain his excitement—Brue was speaking to him. He wanted to forget about the danger of the High Priest but he knew if Brue was breaking his silence over the matter, then the matter needed his attention. Balgur's prophecy or not, Magnus would not gamble with the lives of those in the Romghold without Brue's support.

"You're right. I'll afford him no such benefit without your consent," Magnus shared as a thought.

Silence fell between them but a short time later, Brue spoke again— *"Catanya will recover?"*

"*Aye.*" Magnus looked over his shoulder toward the temple. Liné was still guarding the entrance to the healing room. She turned and looked at him. "*I'm sure she will wake soon,*" Magnus hoped.

"*In the meantime, will you keep sitting with me?*" Brue said.

Magnus smiled and breathed a gentle sigh of relief. "*Aye, Brue. I will.*"

RACE TO THE ROMGHOLD

Färgd was riding the afternoon thermals along the Romgnian coastline. Eamon looked to the western skies at a small black dot in the distance. It was coming toward them from the Corville Mountains.

"Wyvern?" Eamon squinted, trying to discern what manner of creature it was.

It took a moment for Färgd to confirm. *"Nay. That's Braug."*

"Thank the gods. I've had a gutful of Delvion's black rats."

"Black rats... I quite like that description."

"I'm glad you approve, Färgd."

Eamon looked over Joffren's body tied firmly across the saddle behind him. *It will be good to see this chapter over, for there are far more pressing concerns afoot,* Eamon lamented. He was hoping he would make it to the Romghold before Magnus and Catanya ran into trouble. Anxiety churned in Eamon's stomach. He coughed it free and mumbled under his breath—"Hope for the best, Eamon... hope for best."

Soon, Braug's flight path intersected them. Eamon could see he carried two riders—Austagia and Jael. Braug banked to the north and fell into flight formation with Färgd. A wave of nostalgia washed over Eamon and not for the first time. He had not ridden a dragon for two decades. Flying in formation was yet another memory. The two dragons quickened their pace. Braug took the lead, allowing Färgd to conserve energy in the younger dragon's slipstream.

"At this rate, we'll arrive at the Romghold by sunrise," Färgd deduced.

"Excellent." Eamon crouched low holding the saddle horn beneath his bearded chin.

Shortly before sunrise, the two dragons banked seaward to keep their distance from potential roaming eyes in the Romghold. They ascended to help shave speed and, once almost still, hovered with wings spread to their sides. A mile below, Eamon could see the Romgnian mountain peaks. Atop the westward reach was the magnificent apparition of a foreboding castle designed to ward off unwanted, airborne visitors. Countless steeples sprouted from the rock bed like stalagmites. The Castle windows were dark like the vacant eyes of skulls. Connecting the steeples were buttresses as convoluted and complicated as the wards and spells used to create the deception in the first place. *Deceptions and apparitions… the enduring trait of the Order of Irucantî.* Eamon shook his head. *Such a shame…*

"We shall lead and you follow," Austagia said.

"Aye," Eamon replied.

Braug tucked his wings and dove toward the Romghold like a crossbow bolt set loose. Austagia sat low in the saddle with Jael's torso sculpted behind him to minimise drag. Braug punched through the translucent ward-wall, giving away its presence with a shimmer. Braug then disappeared into the true Romghold below. It was Färgd's cue. Eamon squatted low as Färgd's serpentine body arched over and fell forward. Eamon shuddered as they punched through the ward-wall. The Romghold revealed its familiar repose to the former Irucantî once known as 'Steyne'. Eamon instinctively reached for his fire-sword that would have been sheathed behind his back many years ago as a Ferustir. His searching fingers failed to find the pommel, for the fire-sword was wrapped in suede cloth and strapped among his belongings behind Joffren.

"Curses," Eamon muttered. He glanced back and eyed Joffren's body. He imagined his former Semsarian was awake, returning to the Romghold with him. The vision passed as quick as it came. Eamon faced forward and thought no more of it. He combed his eyes over the Romghold through the dim morning light—light his old eyes found more difficult to navigate than night itself, for the moon was waning and the sun was yet to reveal itself. *Like the precipice between life and death that Joffren has navigated.* Eamon wondered if the precipice had been foreboding for Joffren. *Unsettling at the least, I imagine…*

In the inky dawn, Eamon recognised Braug's gliding body approaching the Romghold's common. He could see two other dragons. One was to the east of the Temple of Fire—*Liné.* The other was at the cliff edge of the training field—*Brue.* Neither Rubea nor the High Priests were visible. As they drew close, Eamon saw a Ferustir seated beside Brue on the training field. *Who is that?* Another priest exited a temple side door near Liné just as Braug landed. Austagia and Jael leapt from Braug's back and ran to the priest with lances drawn.

With their presence known, Färgd threw caution to the wind and landed quickly beside Braug. Forgetting Joffren, Eamon alighted and ran to join Austagia and Jael. He breathed a sigh of relief when Austagia embraced arms with the priest. Jael did the same and then the priest looked wide-eyed at Eamon.

"Steyne!"

Eamon squinted in the dim light, then nodded as he recognised the man. "Trax. It's good to see you."

"I never in all my years thought I would ever—"

"And I never thought I would see this place again," Eamon interrupted. He peered over to the training field, where Brue sat in silence with the Ferustir. "Who is that?" he mumbled to himself.

"That's the Electus," Trax said.

"That's Magnus? With Brue?" Eamon looked to Austagia and Jael who appeared as surprised as he was, so he looked back to Trax. "Catanya... where is Catanya?"

"I have just come from her. She is in the healing room."

"What is her condition?" Austagia asked abruptly and started walking toward the temple. Trax was right behind him with Jael and Eamon following.

"She is stable, yet lucky to have her life after her altercation with a High Priest."

"Where are the High Priests now, Semsame?" Jael asked.

Trax turned his head to Jael as he walked. "The one who injured Catanya is dead. The other is in a holding cell. Braug seems to have found him." Trax pointed. Eamon looked. Braug was staring into the holding cell with a deep growl rising in his belly.

Magnus and Catanya did it... Eamon smiled to himself. A feeling of delight rose in his heart.

Austagia and Jael reached the door that Liné was guarding.

"The healing room?" Eamon remembered.

"Aye," Jael confirmed. Liné stood, blocking their access to the room. *"WHAT ARE YOUR INTENTIONS?"*

Eamon stumbled in his step at the savagery of Liné's thoughts. He gathered she was examining each of their minds to ensure they meant Catanya no harm. *Good...* Eamon was glad for the dragon's allegiance.

Austagia whispered words to Liné that seemed to appease her. She let him into the healing room. Jael had her say and Liné let her pass, too. She was not, however, letting Eamon pass.

"You've a familiar scent, yet not one I've known for some time." Liné's eyes flicked through a myriad of colour changes but reverted to their natural burning amber. Eamon took a courteous backward step.

"You do know me, Liné." Eamon feigned a smile then turned about, hardly in the mood to explain himself. *In this place, there's no leaving the past where it belongs.*

Walking back down the temple steps to the edge of the training field, Eamon stood and crossed his arms. The sun rose over the eastern mountain peaks. It's tangerine glow shone over Brue and Magnus who sat peacefully together at the cliff edge on the far side of the field. Together, they both turned and faced the sun. Magnus looked at Eamon and smiled. Eamon smiled back and in that moment, all seemed well in the world.

IRIS

Catanya opened her eyes, blinking away sluggishness and blurry vision.

"Magnus?" Catanya shouted, lifting her hips from the hard bed, groaning from the pain. She lowered herself again. "Hannah?" Anxiety gripped her chest making breathing a chore. She looked about the room. *The healing room... Is this a dream?*

"Rest, Semsame."

The voice was too familiar—"Jael?"

"Aye. Just rest."

Catanya sat up, clenching her teeth at the pain and effort. She looked herself over, spotting the familiar oil-soaked wraps and white robe. It was just as she had been after her 'cleansing' on the training field long ago and numerous times after gruelling training sessions—though never as bad as the first time and this time.

"Have you seen Magnus?"

"He's fine. He's outside with Brue. Rest, Catanya."

Catanya looked about the softly lit room, drawing in herbal scents that were comforting, yet disconcerting. She blinked and blinked again. Her eyes were slow to focus but when they did, they found Jael. "How long have I been here?"

"A few days. Austagia and I arrived yesterday. Eamon as well."

Catanya nodded and forced a breath from her aching chest. She propped herself back on her arms and looked at Jael again, squinting her right eye. "Did you say Magnus is with *Brue?*"

Jael stared blankly. In time the blankness gave over to a wry smile. "It seems they've made amends."

Catanya stared a long moment at Jael. She had the same calculating manner about her that she had when they shared vigil over Joffren back in Ba'rrat. Catanya spun her body about, holding the robe over her chest and letting her legs dangle over the side of the table. She chuckled. "There's the Jael I know."

"What does that mean?" Jael asked, a deadpan expression on her face.

Catanya licked the dryness from her lips then spotted the cup of herbal water on the table. She reached across to it, wincing at the effort and drunk from the cup. She decided not to reply to Jael's question and instead, finished her drink and asked her own question.

"What of Trax?"

Jael pushed a tongue into her cheek and squinted. Her answer was slow to come. "He's been busy. Attending to your needs, overseeing the surviving High Priest who is now a prisoner, and ensuring the Electus and Brue don't kill one another." She stood and made for the external door. "You're in safe hands. Rubea has guarded that door since you were carried in here three days ago." She pointed to the internal door, then to the other. "Liné has guarded this door. It seems you owe many a debt of gratitude."

Catanya clenched her jaw tight. It hurt as much as the rest of her body. She decided it would be in poor taste to punch Jael in her condescending face. "Thank you, Jael, for your part in my recovery." She pulled her best derisive smile.

"Think nothing of it, Semsame." Jael smiled coyly. "Oh… one more thing. Joffren is dead. Eamon insisted you were present for the funeral." Jael turned and left the healing room.

With Jael gone, Catanya slumped forward, dropped the cup and buried her face in her hands. *Joffren…* She sniffed back tears and drew on the scent of, among other things, jasmine oil. *Jasmine…* The smell evoked memories of Marsala lifting the tracking spell Joffren placed on her. She looked to the small white table again and remembered the note Joffren had left her on that very table after her cleansing. "*Fleatermara.*" She remembered was written on the note. "Righteous." The scent of jasmine turned to bitter bile in her throat. Swallowing it back, Catanya lifted a leg and kicked the small table across the room, sending its contents flying. Though it pained her, it felt good doing it all the same. She thought again of something that had haunted her delirious dreams for the past three days—*Hannah!*

Catanya lowered herself over the table edge, easing her feet to the cold ground. She dressed in the white robe and stumbled toward the internal door, opened it, and was greeted by Rubea.

"*Semsame!*"

"*Rubea.*" Catanya was glad to see her, grateful for her protection, but needed to know… needed to see…

"*You are well! I'm so glad!*" Rubea rose, shifting her weight between back feet excitedly, then lowered her head to meet Catanya.

"Thank you, I am." Catanya rest her forehead on Rubea's nose and bathed in the dragon's thoughts. Rubea plunged through hers.

"Oh! You have been through quite the ordeal."

"I have. I really need to go down to the chamber, Rubea."

"You risked your life to save Liné's egg. When it hatches, he will be kindred to you."

Catanya pulled away, stroking Rubea's snout affectionately. "Thank you," she said aloud and stumbled toward the fourth door from left along the western wall. *I need to know…*

Catanya balanced herself along the bronze railing as she descended the steps. Each one seemed to be a little easier than the last as the blood returned to her limbs and the pins and needles abated. At the bottom of the stairs she followed the curved corridor down to the chamber. Here, the air was thick and the light dim. Scanning the surrounding walls, Catanya saw that only five of the sconces over the twelve doors still held a lit torch, casting their yellow light beams across the even-darker chamber floor.

"Hannah?"

Catanya reasoned with herself as she did before that it was a trick—the High Priest playing with her mind. Still, there was a feeling in her heart beyond reason telling her it was something more. The hairs on the back of her neck pricked up and tracked a shimmer down her spine.

"Fara mi parina!" Catanya shouted the spell. The five torches flared angrily, illuminating the chamber. In the pulsing light, Catanya saw a small object at the very centre of the chamber floor. She stepped and stumbled across the floor toward the object. She knelt beside it and took it tentatively between her thumb and forefinger.

It was a dried iris.

Her dried iris.

The dried iris Hannah had been holding.

A CONFESSION

It was a success. All twelve groups of refugees had made it safely to Thwax without incident. *Three hundred ninety five souls free from the Quag slave-mongers.*

Bonstaph climbed a short way up the eastern side of the Corville Mountains so he could survey the entourage of travellers as the last of them made their way northward out of the Southern Wastelands. He could breathe a little easier now, knowing Ba'rrat and the well-managed troubles of Brindle were a long way behind them.

Among the company were the 'Perimetral' who were vigilant in their protective detail of the travellers. Once north of the Black Cliffs and into the Southern Wastelands, the refugees had moved as a huddle, keeping the children and elderly shielded as best they could from the unforgiving sandstorms. The Perimetral formed a protective ring around the travellers. Now clear of the wastelands, the Perimetral formed a mile-long line once again, guarding the refugees from the eastern margin of the Corville Mountains. They were about to embark on the last leg of their journey together—through the Southern Plains to the Plains Lake at the border of Froughton Forest.

Two things about this leg of the journey troubled Bonstaph. The first was a demon from the past that had returned to haunt him. Out of nowhere it would appear, drawing Bonstaph into a blaze of violent memories. At times, the demon came subtly—as the smell of blood or the sound of war cries. Later, the memories hit like the crack of a whip and left a lingering paranoia that was hard to shake. It got the better of him just once. A tap on the shoulder from one of the Perimetral guards made him reel, draw sword and stop just short of severing the scout's head. Those witness to it dismissed the incident as a reprimand for the scout's informality. Since then, Bonstaph was vigilant—he had to avoid confusing fiction with reality at all cost. *The past is in the past,* he told himself. However, migrating north along the Red Pass *was* walking into the past. The Red River was testament to it.

Bonstaph was not there when Balgur fell during the great battle, slain by some incomprehensible twist of fate. Bonstaph was further afield leading the Knights of the Realm into the battering ram of Quag legions. Ganister was always by his side in his position of 'Commander's Arm'. He would have liked to have Ganister by his side once again. He *wished* to have him by his side. More than anything, Ganister would have helped with the second troubling issue of the journey—*Sarah*.

Sarah had been even more aloof since reuniting with Bonstaph in Thwax. Her presence had become unsettlingly dark, as though her remaining threads of life had been traded for something malevolent. Bonstaph wondered if Sarah had worked it out. *A gypsy's intuition runs deep. It was only ever going to be a matter of time.* On his travels from Brindle, before meeting up with Sarah again in Thwax, he had decided she should learn the truth about Lucas from him. But her aloofness, together with his responsibilities to the refugees, made it difficult to seize the opportunity. Or at least, that was the excuse he gave himself to avoid the inevitable.

Bonstaph looked on as the last of the refugees moved beyond the Corville Mountains and into the Southern Plains. Sarah had been walking toward the rear of the travellers since leaving Thwax. This morning though, Bonstaph had not seen her. He looked to his right at one of the Perimetral guards a hundred yards back. When he had his attention, Bonstaph pointed to his eyes with two fingers then to the road back to the south. The guard looked about, then back to Bonstaph, crossing his arms overhead—there were none left behind.

Where is she? Bonstaph signalled to the guard to move on, who did the same to the next man down the line and so forth. With a sigh, Bonstaph took a step down the mountainside to join the others. Then he heard something. He froze. It was the sound of a small stone tumbling down the rocky mountainside overhead. Something had moved it. *Something* was above him. Bonstaph looked up but saw nothing. He cursed under his breath, knowing he would have to find out what it was. If there were a group of Quagmen or a storm of wyverns perched high on the mountainside, waiting to ambush them, it was better to learn of it now rather than later.

Bonstaph felt for the pommel of his sword—now a proper, hardened steel sword that Brindle's committee kindly gifted him before leaving as a thank you for his service. He pinched it half an inch free of its scabbard, keeping it loosely sheathed. He then took tentative steps up the side of the mountain, careful not to loosen any rocks that would tell tale of his own presence. The climb was steep but seventy yards up, the ground levelled out to a track at the base of a sheer cliff that shot almost directly up half a mile before tapering back again. The track was barely a goat track and disappeared about a corner to the west a hundred feet away. Bonstaph deduced—*Whatever was above me is now around that corner.*

Bonstaph started toward the corner, drawing his sword with a firm left-handed grip. He reached the corner and rounded it. A further hundred feet on, he glimpsed a dark purple dress disappearing into a gap in the mountain wall.

Sarah...

Bonstaph ran. He reached the gap and saw it was a cave entrance—*an entrance into the Caves of Cuvee, no doubt.*

"Sarah!" Bonstaph grunted through closed teeth. He peered into the darkness and saw the glimpse of a shadow moving about. Sarah stepped out into the light of day and stared at Bonstaph. "Sarah, what are you doing?" Bonstaph looked about warily and then back to Sarah. "Talk to me, Sarah, please."

Sarah slowly shook her head. "We are past that now." She turned back toward the cave.

"Sarah... wait. There's something I need to tell you... about *Lucas.*"

Sarah stopped but did not turn to face Bonstaph.

"The sorcerer..." Bonstaph swallowed hard. This was impossible. To think he was about to destroy her in this manner and yet, he knew she had to know. "The sorcerer is Lucas, Sarah." He knew she had to know from him. "Lucas is the one you've oathed yourself to kill."

Sarah was motionless. Bonstaph waited. A long, silent moment passed without a word and then, without looking back, Sarah began to walk into the cave again.

"Sarah... *Wait!*"

"Commander?" Bonstaph turned about. Walt was there. He was standing back at the corner. "What are you doing, sire?"

Bonstaph snapped his head back to the cave. Sarah was gone. He looked back to Walt. "Keep everyone moving, Walt. I'll catch up."

"You're not going in there—"

"Go! I'll catch up."

Walt nodded unconvincingly, turned and left. Bonstaph ran into the cave after Sarah. Plunged into darkness, he rubbed his eyes free of the sun rings blemishing his vision then continued on. The darkness soon became absolute. He had to feel his way with his right hand against the cave wall that was eerily smooth to the touch. It did not feel naturally formed, but as though it was burnished with seams than ran diagonally in smooth waves. *No man-made tool did this, yet it is not naturally occurring.*

The deeper he went into the cave the more Bonstaph's footsteps echoed, suggesting the cave was widening until he came upon a broad intersection. His hand felt an opening to the right. Further around he found another opening, then another and another. A fifth opening he deduced to be the one he entered though he could not be sure, and so he counted back five, holding fast to this entrance for fear he may lose his orientation and never find his way free of the caves again. There was absolute silence and the darkness seemed to close in around him. He stood as still as a statue, frozen in time, holding fast to the tunnel wall he hoped would take him out.

"SARAH!" Bonstaph called just once. It echoed a long, endless pulse down each of the five tunnels. He listened until the final echo petered off to nothing.

"Do not follow me, Bonstaph."

Sarah's voice startled him. She was right there at the junction of tunnels. Bonstaph opened his mouth to reply but Sarah cut in first—her voice darker than the Caves of Cuvee.

"Where I go, there is no coming back."

With that, Sarah was gone.

PYRE

In the healing room, Catanya discarded her white robe and dressed in her Ferustir suit again, buckled up its ancillary pieces and sorted her weapons. She double knotted her laces then tucked the iris into her chest armour beneath her left collarbone. *I will see you soon, little sister...*

Standing tall, Catanya made for the external door. Liné was waiting outside just as Jael had said.

"Semsame," Liné greeted her.

"Liné. Thank you for protecting me."

"The gratitude is mine. You saved my unhatched child. I am forever in your debt."

"You owe me nothing. Your child should never have been used to blackmail you and Brue. Liné, have you seen Magnus?" Catanya did not want to sound abrupt, but she was determined to leave the Romghold with the speed and discretion with which she arrived. Only one thing mattered to her—finding Hannah.

"On the training green, Semsame," Liné instructed.

"Please... Call me Catanya."

Catanya walked to the front of the temple and stopped dead at the sight before her. There were a dozen Ferustirs and the same number of fire dragons standing about the common. Among them were Jael, Austagia, Trax and Eamon. Austagia spotted Catanya first and came running toward her, followed closely by Eamon.

"Catanya! You're awake." Austagia placed his hands on her shoulders. She could feel the relief in his touch.

"Aye, finally." Catanya smiled, eyeing Jael and wondering why she had not told Austagia as much.

"Catanya!" Eamon had no time for formalities. He hugged her. "So good to see you well!"

"Thank you, Eamon. It's good to see you, too. What is going on here?"

Eamon and Austagia stood back. "See for yourself." Eamon pointed toward the training field.

Catanya walked down the temple steps onto the common and looked across the field. Her jaw dropped at the sight before her. As a silhouette centred to the amber setting sun, Magnus and Brue stood in profile, bowing their heads to one another—Magnus with his head against Brue's nose, his arms holding the long snout of the large dragon. It was a most unexpected, yet beautiful sight.

"They have not left one another's side for three days," Eamon said.

"Jael said as much, I just didn't believe it." Catanya felt her emotions choking her, part of which was her ever-present thoughts of Hannah.

"Jael spoke to you?" Eamon asked quietly.

Catanya looked at him, then back to Magnus and Brue. "It doesn't matter. This is good news." It was more than she could ever have hoped for. She looked over to Liné, whose smouldering eyes squinted back. Catanya waved in acknowledgment.

"This is a good thing... A wonderful thing," Eamon whispered.

Catanya knew exactly what Eamon was saying. "Magnus shows compassion."

"Aye, Catanya, he does." Eamon took Catanya's hand and squeezed it enthusiastically. "Forgiving the dragon that tried to assassinate him. A meeting of the mind of two great warriors." Eamon leant in and whispered to Catanya—"This could save the relationship between priests and dragons."

"Let's hope so."

"Not a bad start for the Electus." Eamon squeezed Catanya's hand again.

"You've always known Magnus was the right choice, Eamon." Catanya smiled.

"Aye. I have."

Magnus learned more about the world of dragons in a day than he had in all his life. Brue had finally opened up to him. Every nook, cranny and crevice of the dragon's mind was a revelation and Magnus accessed it all. At first he thought Brue was revealing too much. He then came to realise that dragons did not think of their minds and memories as their own—they were part of a greater collective. Brue took Magnus beyond the threshold of his own memories and through kaleidoscopic arrangements of the memories and thoughts of other dragons. These in turn guided Magnus through further thresholds and so on and so forth. Brue was one part of an endless collective consciousness.

"Could I lose myself here?" Magnus considered.

"Breathe," Brue whispered back.

Magnus did as told. He took a slow, deep breath and concentrated on more grounded things—the breeze on his face, the touch of Brue's scales on the palms of his hands and the soft grass beneath his boots. As fast as he entered, he withdrew from the collective consciousness of dragons and was back in his own mind. Another breath and he re-entered the labyrinth once again.

"Wow..."

Brue steered Magnus through one threshold where he came across everything that was Thioci. Magnus saw how he was entwined in the young dragon's fate even though he only shared the last days of Thioci's life. Magnus could see himself by the youngling's side and understood now that it was not darkness Thioci passed into, but an infinite abyss of shared thoughts and memories. Thioci's last breath of life—the final rustling of autumn leaves—was in fact the tinkling transition from physical form into the stars beyond. Infinite in number, the stars embraced Thioci's consciousness and were all the more magnificent for doing so.

Magnus witnessed an age of memories in the blink of an eye. It left him questioning— *"What use is all this to you?"*

Brue's response washed through his mind like a smooth flowing river— *"Wisdom..."*

Magnus withdrew, feeling humbled.

"Wait. You are a part of the greater plan, Magnus. Come see." Brue drew Magnus into his thoughts one more time. *"Look again. Think of what matters to you."*

Magnus immediately thought of Catanya, his parents, Lucas and Eamon. In an instant, Magnus was pulled through a different threshold of thought and into his own kaleidoscope formed of the most seductive shades of bronze and ice blue shifting over one another like the scales of dragons. From the bronze and blue, every colour imaginable was born. As he moved through the spatial spectrum, each colour was a memory, a thought, an idea or a dream he had experienced at some stage of his life. Each of these was a creation that was somehow linked with that of every Couldradt fire dragon—present and past. Magnus was overcome by the realisation.

"You are a part of all this, Magnus. Thioci made you so."

"And others—Catanya? Eamon?"

"All living things are linked together. You have merely been given a tool to make it easier to see. We each form a unique link. In the realm of consciousness, there is no hierarchy—no pyramid of importance."

Magnus withdrew with a breath once again. His eyes bathed in the amber sun that was starting to set again over Froughton Forest. Brue lowered his head. Magnus rested his hands on the dragon's nose again—scarred from the sword he himself had driven through it. He bowed forward, letting Brue know how grateful he felt. *"Thank you."*

"Thank you, Magnus."

Magnus rose again. Brue stood tall and his eyes burned like a blacksmith's forge. Magnus caught his reflection in the glimmer of Brue's pale underbelly scales and gasped. His eyes were just like Brue's—burning fires of a forge.

Magnus turned toward the common. Two-dozen pairs of eyes were locked on him. Half were Ferustirs, half were dragons. With vision far sharper than usual, Magnus looked at each of the faces in turn, making out every detail— every nuance of expression. Among the faces were Austagia, Jael, Eamon, Trax and… *"Catanya!"*

"She is well!" Brue was as happy as Magnus.

Magnus and Brue walked across the training field. Catanya came to Magnus, wincing from pain she obviously still harboured. Magnus embraced her gently. "I'm so glad you're awake." He studied her for a moment. She seemed pleased to see him, but something was troubling her. "Catanya, is everything okay?"

Catanya glanced about, aware as Magnus was of the many eyes on them. "It can wait, but Magnus… if you thought your eyes were different in Thwax…"

"I know." Magnus squeezed his eyes tight and blinked several times. The peculiar sharpness to his vision faded and became normal once again. A dragon appeared to his left, nosing him in the shoulder. It was Rubea.

"We've not been properly introduced." The curious dragon looked from Magnus to Catanya and back again.

Magnus smiled at her. *"Hello Rubea. I am Magnus."* He felt he should indeed properly introduce himself.

"Oh, I know who you are."

Magnus smiled at Rubea and glanced back to Catanya. "Should we go somewhere to talk?"

"It's okay. It can wait," Catanya assured Magnus.

"What have you got to say for yourself, Magnus?" It was Eamon. He spread his arms and collected Magnus and Catanya into a hug. They exchanged smiles. "Never mind, we can discuss things later, dear friend." Eamon stood back and looked Magnus over, shaking him excitedly by the shoulders. 'So proud… so proud…" He looked at them both. "You did it. You said you would and you did it. Trax has told me all. What a tale! And what a pair you two make!" Eamon turned to the field behind Magnus. "Brue!" he said. He excused himself and walked to the long-tailed dragon.

The rest of the Ferustirs and dragons fell into discussions. After a while, Austagia called for attention.

"It is good we've returned to the safety of the Romghold. There are matters, however, we need to address. All but one of these matters can wait until tomorrow. A priest's pyre will be prepared at the northern end of the training field for Joffren. Those who so wish may convene at the temple for reflection in one hour. At midnight, the pyre shall be lit and the verity light shall burn its course. In the meantime, a meal is prepared in the common kitchen."

Many of the dragons took flight and headed over Froughton Forest. Magnus gathered they sought game to satiate their own hunger. Most of the priests moved toward the kitchen, some catching Magnus's eye and giving a nod as they passed. He took it as a sign of respect and yet, it was not respect he wanted. He just wanted to trust that none of them would try to kill him.

Catanya took Magnus's hand. "Come. I want to show you something." Catanya led Magnus to the small stone building of her personal quarters. She opened the door and removed a small lantern from an outside hook. "Come." Catanya led Magnus into the small room. He looked back across the common. Austagia remained behind and was talking to Eamon. Jael shared their company but her eyes were on Magnus.

"Magnus," Catanya said, shutting the door.

"This was your room?" Magnus looked around. He was most curious. It was neat with a small table and single chair at its centre. There was a narrow bed along the far wall with a bow and quiver of arrows leaning against the foot of the bed. "I like it." Hanging from a brass hook on the back of the door was a robe made of black, burgundy and white silk with gold embroidery weaving throughout the design. "Magnificent."

"Magnus," Catanya repeated. He looked at her. Only now did he notice the anxiety in Catanya's face.

"I'm so sorry, Catanya. I was distracted. What is it?"

Catanya reached beneath her chest armour and presented a flower. Magnus smiled, but Catanya's face told this was no romantic notion. "I found this…" Catanya forced the words. She held the dried, pressed iris to Magnus's face. "I found it on the chamber floor beneath the temple. Hannah was there, Magnus. Hannah was standing there, holding *this*."

"When was she there?" Magnus could not get a bearing on what Catanya was saying.

"I saw her when I rescued Liné's egg. Then the High Priest arrived, we fought and... Hannah vanished."

"Are you sure?"

"I went down to the chamber when I woke up just now and found this flower—*my* flower. It's from my own diary that I kept in a dresser in my bedroom back in Nuyan."

Catanya and Magnus stared at one another in silence until Catanya sighed and closed her eyes, lowering the flower. Magnus reached for her shoulders to appease her, but she turned away and began pacing the small room. "I know this sounds ludicrous but I know what I saw. It was Hannah."

"Could it have been a spell, or an enchantment by the High Priest to distract you? I wouldn't put it past them—"

"No. I thought that when I woke earlier. That's why I had to go see for myself. Then I found this!" Catanya held the iris up again. "That priest is long dead. Trax killed him. And I'm pretty sure he didn't conjure a flower from the afterlife."

Magnus took the flower from Catanya. He looked it over. It was certainly dried and pressed and looked as if it had been for many years. Catanya sat herself in her chair, folding her arms across her chest. She wiped the tip of her nose with the palm of her hand and sniffed.

"This was your flower?"

"You gave it to me. It was one of the first you ever picked for me, from your side of the Nuyan River."

Magnus remembered the story. She told it to him before they parted ways at the same river long ago. "You put them in a pitcher... in your kitchen."

"All but one," Catanya smiled awkwardly. "I knew they wouldn't last forever, so this one I pressed in my diary. I *know* it's the same one—I used to look at it each night before going to bed. I know every petal. Look, the second petal has a black inclusion through it..."

"And Hannah knew of it?"

"Yes. It was our secret. I would..." Catanya sighed. "I would tell her stories about you. I would tell her how much I loved you and how we were to be married." Catanya smiled at the memory. "Hannah would stare at the flower with those big, brown eyes of hers."

Magnus was more than touched by Catanya's story and could see she was convinced it were true. *But... Hannah in the Romghold?* If it were true, where

would she have gone? He could only think to make a weak suggestion—
"Perhaps Eamon could help us look around. I don't know of anyone better
suited to solving a riddle." Magnus smiled weakly, knowing his idea was lame
at best.

"Perhaps. But I don't need him thinking I'm crazy. I can see you think I'm
crazy."

Magnus handed the flower back to Catanya. "I've seen enough crazy to
know you are not, Catanya. If you say this is your flower, then it is. Which
means Hannah has been here."

"I need to find her, Magnus. If not here, then at home in the Uydferlands.
This is a sign if nothing else. I have to know she is safe."

"All the Irucantî should be returning to the Fire Realm now and finishing
this war."

"They will be deliberating for days, weeks, perhaps even months. I could
be there by tomorrow night. Rubea will take me." Catanya huffed. "She
brought me here all those months ago. She can damn well take me home
again."

Two dragons stood either end of the pyre. One was Rubea, the other a male
dragon named Altair. The pyre was made from a tall stack of dried pine logs.
Joffren's body rested atop the pyre on a bed of pine needles. He was dressed
in his formal silk robe—the same robe he wore during Catanya's
inauguration. The priests walked about the pyre, throwing gladiolus flowers
onto his resting body.

'Gladiolus…' Catanya remembered Joffren explaining during her
inauguration. 'The flower of strength, faithfulness and honour.' Joffren had so
honoured these virtues, as he had honoured all the rituals and philosophies of
the priesthood. At the time, 'strength' was the only virtue Catanya believed
she possessed. On reflection, she thought her time as Joffren's Semsarian had
taught her 'faithfulness', but not faithful to the order of the Irucantî. Catanya
had been faithful to her own beliefs in what was right and wrong. Yes—she
was convinced that her training had been her personal test of faith in her own
beliefs. So now, as Joffren was about to be sent to the realm of the gods,
'honour' was the virtue Catanya was unsure the gods would recognise in her.
Still, two out of three isn't bad, Catanya decided.

Beyond the virtues of the gladiolus flowers, there was another that
spooked Catanya more—'Fleatermara'. On her first night in the Romghold,
she asked Joffren what he believed her purpose for being here was. He had

said 'righteousness'. It did not sit well with her at the time. Even now it felt wrong. Catanya decided to let that virtue burn at the pyre with Joffren.

Rubea and Altair opened their jaws and let jets of flame consume the pyre. The night was filled with heaving fire that sucked angrily at the cool evening air. Sharp yellow tails of flame reached for the stars, their final rise in the form of oily, black smoke typical of dragon fire.

The pyre still burned hot when Catanya turned away. The heat had brought tears to her eyes. She saw that Eamon shed tears as well and wondered if he too used the heat as his excuse. They looked at one another, each knowing how the other felt, having said their bitter farewells to Joffren. He was Eamon's Semsarian. He was Catanya's Semsdi. Could things have turned out better for Joffren? Catanya thought she would never know. She was content, though, that he was honoured with a proper Irucantî funeral. *He would have wanted that.*

With the funeral over, Eamon had one last thing to do. He hoped it would give him closure on the other, equally bitter death he had long carried the weight of responsibility for. Once this was done, he could finally put the name 'Steyne' to rest.

Magnus had been kind enough to bring the suede wrapped fire-sword to Joffren's funeral. He also insisted he have a word with Eamon before entering the Temple of Fire. Magnus spoke the truth of the sword and its fate known to only Balgur and Gilfieüg—the swords forger. It was a revelation Eamon was ill prepared for.

"So then, it was always destined to kill him," Eamon said aloud to see if the words would ring of truth.

"Balgur told me himself. It fact, the sword was shaped to do so. Its glyphs held spells that would protect Balgur as he transitioned to…" Magnus seemed unsure how to explain it.

Eamon saw both truth and concern on his face. "I know what you're saying, Magnus. It seems then, Balgur believed it was best I did not know this for all the years I carried the sword."

"Aye. It was a cruel thing, Eamon. But if you'd known, would you have let the sword fulfil its fate?"

At last and with a sigh, Eamon understood. "Most certainly not, Magnus. No, I would not. I would have destroyed it long before it was able to fulfil its fate."

"Using you for such a task seems so deceptive." Magnus shook his head.

"Yet, Balgur trusted that when the time came, I would know what needed to be done. And... I guess I did."

"What do you mean?"

Eamon thought matters over in the manner he often did when they occurred so long ago. Memories would come to him glazed with emotion. He would dwell for a moment, allowing the glazing to melt away so the memory could stand on its own. Often, it was difficult to make the separation. *Torture for the poet in my heart,* Eamon chuckled.

"What is it, Eamon?" Magnus was ever inquisitive.

"I was a priest and this was my sword." Eamon looked at the wrapped object in Magnus's arms. "We of the Fire Realm don't name our swords like the Rhydermere do. Indeed, what name would be given to a sword with such a fate?"

Eamon could see the battle now, as clear as if he was there again. He was on the Southern Plains, by the Little Traas River. "Balgur had fallen upon the river and was wounded after a well-staged attack by the Quag. When first my eyes found the scene, Delvion was standing over Balgur. In his flamboyant manner, Delvion called for the attention of all as he held his poisoned black blade over Balgur's head. I was cornered, fending off the enemy upstream from Balgur. I hurled the sword. I aimed it true, Magnus. It made a path for Delvion's heart. Then it happened." Eamon ran the event through his mind for the millionth time. "It was as if Balgur *told* him..."

"Told Delvion what?" Magnus asked.

"The way Delvion paused his black blade. He looked into Balgur's eyes and squinted. Balgur was telling him. I never understood until now." Eamon remembered Delvion's face. He was attentive—listening to the great dragon. "Delvion was *told* to seize my sword. I always put it down to some dark intuition the man possessed."

"How did it happen?" Magnus asked.

"Delvion looked from Balgur to me. My sword came to him, it..." Eamon struggled for the words. He had never described the incident in such detail before—not even to Marsala. "Delvion released his poisoned black blade. It was the blade that would have cursed Balgur in the afterlife. With the same hand he caught my sword."

"He caught a sword that was thrown at him?" Magnus's eyes widened.

"A million times I've played it over in my mind. There was intervention at play and Balgur was that intervention. It was fated as Balgur told you it was, Magnus."

"You need not say anymore, Eamon. I know what happened next."

Eamon looked at Magnus. He was grateful to have him there, now, when he was about to put the sword to rest. "Thank you for telling me, Magnus."

"You're welcome."

Magnus reached for Eamon's hand. Eamon gripped it and hoped Magnus could feel what he meant to him in the firmness of that grip. Together, they walked up the temple steps. Catanya was waiting for Eamon, as well as Austagia and Jael. Trax opened both sets of doors leading into the temple nave. Austagia took the lead with Magnus following, carrying the sword. Eamon let go of Magnus's hand and followed with Catanya to his left. She took his hand in Magnus's place. Jael was to his right. For the first time, Eamon laid eyes on the enormous, white marble statue of Balgur. His breath caught at the sight. He had forgotten how large Balgur was—how *magnificent* he was. Eamon's knees began to shake and he almost fell. Catanya and Jael caught him by the arms and steadied him.

"Are you okay, Eamon?"

"Thank you, Catanya. I am fine. I just need to pause a moment."

Magnus turned, concern on his face.

"I'm fine, Magnus." Eamon forced a smile, though knew he need not have in this company. Magnus smiled back.

Eamon took a deep breath and peered up to the dragon's enormous head. The statue appeared so life-like. Balgur stared down at him. His eyes, though polished white marble, came to Eamon as the sun orbs they once were—the same eyes that would change colour to match his. Eamon's mind flushed with the memories they once shared. He heard Balgur's drumming voice peeling through his mind with surety only a dragon purveyed. Eamon wanted to talk to him. He wanted to say he was sorry. Fate or not, he had played his part in allowing the fire-sword to slay Balgur. Fate or not, he could not save him. He was most sorry for that.

Tears came, blurring Eamon's eyes. He stepped awkwardly down the stairs to the nave floor with Catanya and Jael supporting him. He felt old. He felt tired. For too long, Eamon had harboured regret for Balgur's death. Magnus caught his eye. Eamon blinked the tears away and looked at the young man before him. Magnus was the reason 'Eamon' existed. 'Eamon' took the place of the priest named 'Steyne' and played his part in a new chapter in Allumbreve's history as Magnus became the Electus.

"I am so glad you are here, Magnus." Eamon breathed through a smile but it came out as a sob. "I am glad all of you are here." He looked to his other companions.

"We are honoured to be here, Eamon," Austagia said.

Magnus lifted the wrapped fire-bronze sword to Eamon. Eamon peeled back the cloth and lifted the sword with delicate fingers at either end. Then he wrapped his left hand around the pommel, feeling the familiar indents in the leather grip—indents made by his own hand. He carried the sword to the base of the statue, placing it upon the bronze plaque at its base. He read the inscription in the plaque—*"Balgur Qewrum Fara*—Balgur King of Fire." He read the smaller script beneath—"Born of fire in the northern Fire Realm. Died at the Battle of Fire, aged five hundred and eighteen years."

Eamon rest a hand on the front right middle talon and gave it an affectionate pat followed by a final nod. "Farewell, old friend."

A CURSE

Sarah's fingers dragged along the black granite walls of the tunnel. She felt the markings where worgriel teeth and claws had scraped and chipped through the ages, forming endless convolutions of narrow tunnels beneath the Corville Mountains. Sarah gave the foul creatures credit for their tenacity. It was a quality she was tapping into. She was being tenacious. She needed to be for the Tenebris spell to work. If she lost focus, the heavy spell would soak all her strength and kill her.

Marsala's Tenebris spell was dangerously effective. She had passed two packs of worgriels in the tunnels—so close their clammy black skin brushed past her—yet they never saw her. They never even drew on her scent, her body heat or the sound of her footsteps. The effectiveness of the spell, however, was doing more than just cloaking her presence. With her focus always on thoughts of her son, the spell was guiding Sarah to him.

Lucas...

Lucas...

Lucas...

Sarah was not thinking of the countless hours spent walking the worgriel tunnels that interconnected the Caves of Cuvee, for thoughts deviating from Lucas would compromise the Tenebris spell. She knew too, there was no way the tunnels were navigable by humans without spells. Three times so far the tunnels had opened into caves completely void of light. Each cave was either a breeding ground for worgriels or a graveyard of animal remains—the leftovers from worgriels feeding. Each cave became a junction to more tunnels. With each turn and step, Sarah knew she was getting closer to Lucas.

Lucas...

Lucas...

Lucas...

Hours passed and once again, Sarah could hear the scampering of claws approach—*more worgriels*. However, this time was different. The scampering was accompanied by the dull, rhythmic strike of boots—*men*. The strikes were awkward and heavy, as though the men were tall and heavyset, struggling in the narrow tunnels—*Quagmen*. Sarah drew her body hard against the tunnel

206

wall. The worgriels brushed past followed by a legion of Quagmen. Several bumped into Sarah and were mystified by her invisible presence. Sarah fell in behind them.

The procession of undesirables walked on and on, crisscrossing through tunnel after tunnel. Eventually, they came to an enormous open cave that was well lit by two means. Firstly, a dozen or more hulking black chandeliers hung from great chains bolted into the cave's granite ceiling and secondly, a huge beam of white light came from a cavern that rose hundreds of feet to the open sky above. Sarah looked at the natural light and craved to stand under it. The thought caused her to feel lightheaded. Strength drained from her body. The Tenebris spell was using Sarah's unfocused yearning to draw energy reserves from her. She leaned against the wall beside her and noticed her shadow beginning to appear.

Sarah refocused. *"Telburrow Moosha Canfligetis..."* She reinforced the Tenebris spell, refocused her strength and thought of nothing but Lucas again. Her shadow began to fade.

Peering across the vast, open cave, Sarah absorbed the scene before her. The floor of the cave was several hectares in size and was bustling with industry. There were countless forges and as many anvils where muscular Quag blacksmiths wielded tongs and hammers in the manufacture of weapons and armour. Other Quag warriors were stockpiling spears, black blades, shields, maces and other dreadful looking weapons Sarah had never seen before. There were saddles and chamfrons for warhorses and wyverns, bedding for the warriors, and barrels containing food and wine.

The smaller caves Sarah had passed through may have been the breeding grounds of worgriels, but here was the breeding ground of a massive army. It was like Ba'rrat all over again with one malicious difference. There were two long rows of cages, thirty or more to each, holding two different breeds of vile creature. The first row of cages held young wyverns that paced about in confinement, hissing at anything that came near. The second held huge worgriels. Unlike the wyverns who were one to a cage, the worgriels were two to a cage. In some of the cages, one or both worgriels were dead. In the remainder, the two worgriels were fighting tooth and nail for the right to be the survivor. It was a ghastly sight, but Sarah could see what the Quag were trying to achieve. *They filter out the weak, keeping the strong stock to help in battle. But why do some cages hold two dead worgriels?*

Sarah focused again, letting the Tenebris spell wield its magic—to show her where to find Lucas. On the far side of the cave, eight tunnel entrances were visible. One of them was different. The dark light within shimmered in a hazy shade of amethyst. Sarah felt a yearning to go that way. In ghostly silence and with the presence of an apparition, Sarah glided down the incline, across the cave floor, toward the pull of the amethyst haze. She entered the tunnel unnoticed.

Voices… The voices echoed as a murmur, but as Sarah got closer, she could discern words beneath the echo.

"Keep petty grievances out of this." The voice was deep and commanding. "Remember 'Dephkeep Law'. You may challenge a direct superior for position. If you fail, your life is forfeit."

"Remember this… I may be Quag but I'm not of Dephkeep blood. Besides, we are no longer on the burning lands of Dephaer. This is Allumbreve."

"Regardless, rules apply."

"Who is this sorcerer, anyway?"

"Forget it, Muldig. You may be twice his size but he's ten-fold deadlier than you."

Sarah turned a corner and came upon a small, well-lit cave. Two large Quagmen were talking. Sarah shifted back a little and watched proceedings.

"That 'Gretarior' is just not right," one said. "Up here." He pointed to his head.

"He's *not* your direct superior," the other said. "Since Crugion died, Delvion's invested everything in this sorcerer. That means if you've grievances with the sorcerer, you've grievances with Delvion. Understand?" He tapped his comrade firmly on the head. "I swear you're as dumb as muck, Muldig."

Gretarior? Sorcerer? Sarah shifted around to gain a better view.

The two Quagmen were quick to stand to attention as a tall man— possibly six foot five—came into view. He was dressed in finely smithed and burnished armour with even finer engravings in the metalwork. The black ensemble was draped with a cape so dark a purple that, like Blüflis, it was almost black. The man had thick brows, a strong jaw and an obvious underbite.

Delvion! Sarah gathered.

She fumbled beneath her dress for her blade but froze at a second, even more ominous sight. Following Delvion was another man, though more a ghost than a man. He was cloaked in a black robe that covered every trace of his body and face. The figure stood beside Delvion and drew back his hood revealing his pale face, steel-grey eyes and thinning, curly blonde hair. Sarah had no doubt—*Lucas!*

Oh, Lucas...

Sarah struggled to focus and felt weak. She took a breath and stared directly at her son. Lucas's head turned toward her. His lifeless eyes locked on her. *Can he see me?* Sarah took a step back. Lucas turned his head slowly to the two Quagmen whom Delvion was talking to.

"What of the blood mix?" Delvion asked one of the Quagman.

"My King, you had best ask the alchemist..."

"I am asking *you.*"

"Sire, progress is slow. The worgriel's take to the wyvern blood but..."

"But WHAT?"

"But... it makes them an awful lot stronger, more savage, until... they die."

"They *die?*" Delvion's nostrils flared and he clenched his jaw, revealing his lower teeth.

"The alchemist says he can make it take, but never for more than a few hours. The worgriel will always die. The females even quicker than the males."

Sarah listened but her eyes were locked on Lucas. It was as though he sensed her presence somehow, for his focus wandered occasionally in her direction. His face remained expressionless.

After a moment's silence and chin rubbing, Delvion spoke again—"I do not care if the worgriels only live for a few hours. If what you say is true, that will have to do. Be off." The Quagmen hurried away. Delvion glanced at Lucas. "How you took to the wyvern's blood, I do not know." Lucas glanced to the ground. "Look at me!" Delvion demanded. Lucas slowly looked up to the Quag King. "My alchemist has administered wyvern blood to men far stronger than you. None have survived more than a few days. What more is there to your conversion?"

Sarah held her breath. *Wyvern blood? I thought Lucas was poisoned?* She waited to hear Lucas's reply—to hear her son's voice. She yearned to sense something more of her boy than the ghost standing here now. But Lucas said nothing. He raised an arm. A black mist formed around his hand and with a flick of his long, skinny fingers, the mist twisted over itself forming syrupy black tendrils that wafted toward Sarah's face. She took another step back, avoiding the dark matter.

Frustrated, Delvion turned and walked back the way he had come. Sarah pushed hard up against a rock wall and watched the black matter snake toward her. An inch shy of her face, Lucas lowered his hand. The matter dissipated. He seemed to stare into Sarah's eyes for a lingering moment then turned to follow Delvion. Sarah followed at a distance. She whispered the Tenebris enhancement again, keeping herself invisible in the virtual darkness of the tunnel. A little way along, Delvion turned and pointed a finger at Lucas.

"My scouts report that a contingency of refugees from Brindle have passed into the Southern Plains. Bonstaph of J'esmagd leads them. That man murdered both my sons. I want him dead. Soon, we shall release the infected worgriels. They only need to survive the attack. Have your wyvern queen come. I have a deed for you."

Delvion looked beyond Lucas in Sarah's direction and squinted his dark, deep-set eyes. Sarah held her breath. The Quag King looked back at Lucas, then turned and walked away. With his back to Sarah, Lucas continued on down a different tunnel. Sarah followed.

Lucas entered a small, hemispherical room through an opening in the tunnel. He lay down on a simple makeshift bed of roughly sewn sacks and remained still, staring at the stone ceiling. Sarah stood directly behind him.

"I know you're there," Lucas said, his voice monotonic and scratchy. Sarah said nothing. She held the words to Marsala's curse on the tip of her tongue as she tried to find cause to avoid saying it. "Have you something to say?" Lucas continued.

Sarah could not help herself—"Have *you* something to say? About your father?" She squatted behind Lucas. A part of her wanted to stroke her son's hair, a part wanted to place the curse on the sorcerer who killed her husband.

"Father..." Lucas mumbled.

"Your father is dead, Lucas."

"Delvion watched his son die. No man should watch his son die."

"Sympathy for Delvion comes to you before regret for your father?"

"Father..." Lucas mumbled again.

"And now Delvion wants you to help him kill Bonstaph? Then what?"

"It's just the beginning..."

"Magnus? Catanya? Your mother?"

"I am reborn to a new mother."

Sarah's heart heaved. "What... what do you mean?" Her words dribbled from her tear-soaked lips. "*I* am your mother, Lucas."

Sarah gripped the sides of Lucas's head. She immediately spoke the first part of Marsala's curse. They were a poisonous collection of dark words from an ancient age—from the darker side of the Paragon era, long ignored in the recollections of nostalgia and unwritten in legends and scripts. These words were the stuff only mystics like Marsala knew and dared not whisper, except for the needs of a desperate cousin. The words were short and sharp and designed to take hold of Lucas's mind like the grips of a vice. Lucas's eyes widened and his pupils pulsed furiously. He tried in vain to fight back.

Confident the curse would keep Lucas well restrained, Sarah whispered words to lift the Tenebris spell. She knew she could not perform the other components of the curse while the Tenebris spell drew so much of her energy. Her body's true form took shape and her shadow fell into view across Lucas's body. Sarah felt her strength return. Lucas stared up at her.

"Mother?" His voice seemed a muddle of recognition, confusion and horror.

Sarah spoke the next part of the curse. She gripped Lucas's head harder, closed her eyes and entered her son's mind as tentatively as handling a newborn baby. Such a thing was heresy for a gypsy to do to a loved one, but the mind Sarah saw was hardly her son's—it was utter bedlam. The wyvern venom had poisoned his mind, monopolised his thoughts and used every piece of self-doubt and self-judgment Lucas possessed as a vehicle to convey a dark perspective of the world.

The first thing Sarah desperately wanted to know was how this all happened. She searched through Lucas's memories, right back to when she last saw him. Together with Magnus, he was fleeing toward the Crescent Woods, then through the woods and across the plains toward the Nuyan River. On these plains the wyvern attacked. It poisoned Lucas. A healer was quick to draw out the creature's venom but traces of it remained. The wyvern had entered Lucas's mind—briefly and inconspicuously—nourishing seeds of self-doubt that tormented and festered, creating an ideal host for the poisonous traces of venom to exploit. It was slow at first, but the darkness proliferated at an exponential rate. Sarah saw this proliferation through a journey of cascading thoughts, each darker than the last, reflecting like mirrors on one another until reason and logic were lost. Perplexed by malignant madness, Lucas fled to the Corville Mountains.

At the peaks of the desolate mountains, Lucas came upon a nest of black wyvern whelps. The nest offered relief from the cruel winter winds and so he lay here to rest. The wyvern queen returned to its nest and attacked Lucas. In the attack, the wyvern scried his mind, recognising the poisonous work of another wyvern. She assumed Lucas was serving a purpose and spared his life, supplementing his poisoned body with a fresh infusion of venom.

Time passed and the wyvern queen watched on as Lucas suffered, inching ever closer to death. The queen used her barbed tail to pierce Lucas's stomach and infuse him with her wyvern blood in an attempt to revive him. Lucas recovered but within hours, his body rejected the blood. Finally, having fed the whelps in her nest, the queen also fed Lucas the whelps' milk. The milk provided nourishment and strengthened his body so it could resist the lethal side effects of the venom and rich wyvern blood, all the while exploiting their strengths.

Sarah reeled in horror at what she was seeing. This wyvern queen's milk was the sole reason her son had survived so long where Delvion's experiments with wyvern blood failed. *But how did he come to be in Delvion's service?* She continued to search Lucas's memories.

Having recovered yet transformed, Lucas was left to wander the Corville Mountains alone. No other wyvern harmed him, for they caught the scent of the queen. Delirious and mad from his second and unrestricted dose of wyvern venom, Lucas journeyed across the Southern Wastelands for days until he emerged through the blinding dust at the Black Cliffs of Ba'rrat only to be greeted by a group of patrolling Quagmen and their tamed wyverns. The Quagmen meant to kill Lucas, but their wyverns formed a protecting barrier around him. The situation was reported to Delvion whose attention was sparked, particularly when he learned Lucas was the son of his new prisoner—Ganister.

Delvion now had the perfect disciple. Lucas had a poisoned mind waiting to be twisted and manipulated and he had forged a unique bond with the wyverns. Furthermore, he had the son of his enemy as a faithful servant.

Delvion had his sorcerers teach Lucas to exploit his dark power and become a sorcerer himself. As Lucas quickly mastered one sorcerer's skill set after another, he would kill them, not allowing them to get so close as to learn the true formula of his strengths and abilities. Delvion was unperturbed and prepared to sacrifice his sorcerers in order to build his disciple's powers. After all, Delvion's vision was to replicate Lucas's powers for himself and his men now that the final Electus had been chosen, stealing away his last chance to obtain the powers of dragon blood. Until now though, Delvion had failed to learn Lucas's secret as to how he survived both the wyvern venom *and* the wyvern blood.

It took some time for Sarah to recover—not from wielding the second stage of the curse, but from learning what her beloved son had been through and what he had become. Still gripping his head, Sarah found herself stroking his fair hair. It was a paradox and she knew it. He was the boy she loved yet all at once despised.

Having seen every portion of Lucas's thoughts, Sarah knew it would take a team of sorcerers an infinite amount of time to isolate and remove the poison and retrain his darkly shadowed mind. More so, with the wyvern queen's blood and milk binding him together, what would be left of him if they did? Sarah had no choice—she had to employ the third part of the curse and it would be the most demanding on her.

The third part of the curse was to conditionally control Lucas's mind. It worked on two levels. Firstly, Lucas would become at odds with his sorcery, forever question its use, and never find peace in its power. Secondly, if Lucas were to ever kill Sarah, he too would die. *A child who sends both parents to the grave has earned a place beside them...* Sarah believed. *Perhaps then, when we stand before the gods in the afterlife, I may trade what merit I have to earn him a place in the stars...*

Before placing the final part of the curse, Sarah recalled her wish to Marsala—*'The curse must bind our fates.'* Then she recalled Marsala's warning—*'Such a curse will bind you to a nightmare from which you can never wake.'*

"So be it..."

Sarah looked into her son's steel-grey eyes one final time. He stared back. Incredulity pulsed through his thoughts. *He knows what is to come,* Sarah observed.

The words of the curse rolled from Sarah's tongue. Her tears fell into Lucas's eyes, clearing the grey shadow and revealing their natural green. For a moment her son was there, looking at her, but his eyes soon greyed over again and his face contorted into its former malice. Examining Lucas's thoughts once again, Sarah could see the curse working. The mirrors of darkness perpetuating his mind of madness were twisting and turning inward toward layers of reason and logic—reason and logic taught to him over a lifetime by Sarah and Ganister. Lucas would now be forced to watch rather than retreat to his shadows. He would forever be in a state of reflective unrest, spectator to his dark deeds—*against his will.*

Sarah spoke the final words of the curse that bound her to Lucas. Speaking them revolted her, for they were words as poisonous as the wyvern venom that ruined him. Lucas's mind now harboured a dormant sickness that would bloom should Sarah die at his hands, causing his own death.

Sarah leant forward and kissed her son softly on the forehead. "I love you, my son. I'm sorry for your fate. Search for light. Only then will you find rest." She let Lucas go, stood, and walked away.

"Telburrow Tramblo Canfligetaris…" Sarah restated the Tenebris spell with a slight variation. It was something Marsala had insisted she learn. It would get her out of the Caves of Cuvee. *Perhaps,* Sarah considered, *it will help me find the refugees on the Southern Plains and warn them of the worgriel attack.* Instead of focusing on Lucas, she now focused the Tenebris spell on finding the man Delvion wanted to kill—*Bonstaph.*

A PRISONER'S ADVICE

Magnus held Lucas's sword, pointing the blade at the Ferustir. He did not trust him at all. For a whole day, the priest had thwarted every move Magnus made to overpower him.

"Again," Austagia commanded.

And again and again and again, Magnus sighed. It was ridiculous. *One hundred fights in Ba'rrat's arena and I never lost a single one. I even bested Joffren...* He realised then that he did *not* best Joffren. It was Catanya who fought the rogue priest while he snuck up on him with the Juniper stone—at Eamon's suggestion— and overtook Joffren's body and mind, then was able to recover where Joffren was not.

For a whole day he had been on the training field sparring against Simeon. Both of them were dressed in Ferustir armour, though Simeon need not have bothered. Every bout ended the same way—Magnus injured or yielding. The simple truth was he could not match Simeon for training and skill. Far more frustrating for Magnus was the feeling that any respect he had earned by making amends with Brue was surely waning. At some stage, every Irucantî in the Romghold had watched him spar and fail. Catanya had offered Magnus advice on technique, as had Austagia and even Eamon. They all saw flaws in Simeon's methods but Magnus could not see it.

It is hopeless... Magnus conceded.

To her credit, Catanya had given Magnus a few days grace. Magnus knew she wanted to leave right away to find Hannah and he intended to go with her. Austagia convinced Catanya that Magnus needed to use this valuable time to train—at least for a few days. Magnus felt terrible about it. He should have sided with Catanya and left right away just as he should have bested the priest in sparring as he had done to every Quag warrior who had ever threatened his life. *Except for Briet...* Thinking of Briet was his undoing. *The only way I can best Simeon is by using my Electus powers, as I had to with Briet.* However, Magnus knew using his fiery powers was hardly sparring—*I could kill him.*

"Again, Magnus," Austagia insisted.

Frowning at Austagia, Magnus sheathed his sword and approached Simeon. He had been sparring with the priest for eight hours straight and decided it was time to ask him directly for some help. "Give me some pointers, please."

"What would you like to know?" Simeon answered. His face was expressionless.

"You know what I'm going to do before I do it. The more we spar, the more flaws you find in my technique. I'm getting more predictable and less inclined to best you each time." Magnus spread his arms wide, admitting defeat. "If you have any pointers for me as to how I can best a priest, please tell me."

Simeon looked at Austagia who nodded to him then he looked back to Magnus and sheathed his lance. He stood rigid with feet wide and hands clasped behind his back. Magnus wanted to slap him for his conceited posture. When he spoke though, Magnus was surprised at his directness.

"It seems you should be fighting with two swords rather than one. Your strength outmatches the light sword you wield. Secondly, you look for weakness in my technique. This is something an opponent can feign and use to trap you, should you try to exploit it. It is better to look for patterns in an opponent's technique and predict from this. It is harder for an opponent to fake strengths than weaknesses. Finally, if I may say so, do not concern yourself with them." Simeon pointed to the common where three priests had taken time out to watch his sparring. "And do not concern yourself with this." Simeon prodded Magnus's forehead. "Clear your mind and fight to win."

Magnus realised he was standing with his jaw open and snapped it shut. "Thank you." It was all he could think to say.

"Perhaps we could take time to rest?"

Magnus was sure the priest was saying it because he was bored as much as he was being polite. "Good idea. And thanks again." He nodded to Simeon and walked toward Catanya, ignoring the fact that Austagia was in clear earshot. "Help me, will you? The sooner I get this, the sooner we can leave."

Catanya crossed her arms. "For six months I endured my training here in the Romghold. Never was a day shorter than yours was today. In fact, on my first day of training I gave up… declared that I was going home!"

"How did that go down?" Magnus was curious.

"Ask Austagia."

Magnus peered reluctantly at Catanya's uncle.

"Have a meal and we'll resume training tomorrow," Austagia said.

Magnus looked back at Catanya who smirked. "Aye. It was something like that."

Magnus and his companions joined Eamon, Jael and Trax in the common kitchen for a meal. Three priests were working to feed the now thirty-strong congregation. Most were still dressed in full Ferustir armour. Magnus looked around. He was sure if he faced off against any one of these priests—without using Electus strengths—he would fare no better than he had against Simeon.

"Don't look so despondent, Magnus." Eamon slurped at his bowl of soup. "You bested three of these warriors in Ba'rrat, if you remember."

"I brought a roof down on top of them. That was hardly besting them."

"You saw an opportunity and took advantage of it. No different."

Magnus felt Jael and Austagia's stares and wanted to end the humiliating conversation. "I'm fine, Eamon."

"You're among friends now, no need to worry."

"That's what you said when we dined at the Hugmdael Inn. Do you remember that one?"

Eamon grumbled then retorted. "It's far less likely a handful of Quagmen will march into this kitchen and besides, the food here is immeasurably better." Magnus could not help but laugh and Eamon laughed with him, drawing attention to their group.

"I do not think this is a laughing matter." It was Trax. He was seated directly opposite Magnus and stared straight into his eyes. The drone of conversation in the common kitchen dulled to silence. Trax stood and projected his voice.

"Less than a week ago, Magnus, Catanya and I hatched a plan to bring down the two most dangerous priests of our order. It worked. Liné's egg was returned to her and the surviving High Priest is restrained in a prison cell. I want you all to take a look at the three of us. I am an old man. Catanya is our youngest Irucantî and Magnus has no formal training in our ways. And yet we succeeded. How? We fought together and we fought with heart. This same heart led Magnus to bridge the gap between he and Brue. You all saw this for yourselves. Magnus has never so much as ridden a dragon—am I right, Magnus?"

Magnus played with his fork. "Aye. I have not ridden a dragon."

"And yet he trains amongst us, searching for ways to replicate our methods of combat without resorting to using his Electus strengths— something he hid for one hundred battles in Ba'rrat's arena." Trax walked around the table and stood in the middle of the room. "Ba'rrat was Magnus's cleansing and not one of us are envious of it. I would wager that if his life were on the line, or Catanya's, or mine, Eamon's, or any of yours, we would have seen a very different fight on our training field today. Magus fights for others. He fights with *heart*. That is why Thioci chose him as our Electus."

Magnus glanced at Catanya who took his hand and clasped it tightly. Trax looked directly at Magnus. "Semsdër-fatel, do not judge yourself by how we spar. Should battle come, I would place my life in your hands."

"What Trax says is true." It was Simeon. He stood at a table at the far end of the room. "Magnus fought today like he was trying to learn our technique. Each of you saw him sparring. I am sure every one of you saw the obvious."

"He was holding back," a priest said, seated at Simeon's table.

"Who else saw this?"

Magnus looked around. Every priest raised a hand.

"I too would put my life in your hands," Simeon said with a bow and seated himself again. Many of the priests nodded in agreement and they all returned to their conversations.

Jael leaned toward Magnus and spoke softly. "I saw you fight in Ba'rrat's Arena. Austagia and I entered the arena to protect the Electus, yet you held your own and fought with us as a warrior." She glanced at Catanya then turned to talk with Austagia.

Magnus buried a tongue in his cheek. He knew he was supposed to appreciate Trax, Simeon and Jael for defending him, but he still felt he was being weighed and measured by their standard. He was beginning to realise why Catanya resented these people so much.

Magnus leant toward Catanya and whispered in her ear. "We leave here tonight." He stood, letting her hand go and marched out of the kitchen, knowing Catanya's eyes were following him. He walked eastward from the common along the cobblestone path, trying to ignore his plaguing thoughts about the day wasted in the Romghold. He felt a fool for making Catanya wait. They had done what they came to do and were wasting days when they could be fighting the war back in the Uydferlands.

Magnus kicked a pebble at his feet. It skittered across the cobblestones, off the path and clanged across the iron bars of the High Priest's prison cell. Out of the cell's darkness, a hand reached through the prison bars. Long fingers grasped the pebble and held it a moment before drawing the arm back into the cell. Wondering at first why the cell was unguarded, Magnus gathered there were likely a myriad of wards keeping the High Priest behind the hardened steel bars. He approached, trusting the wards would protect him. At the cell door, Magnus peered in. A single lamp from the path shone dim light through the bars, illuminating one half of the High Priest's face.

"All of Allumbreve held in such a simple thing," the High Priest said, examining the pebble in the light. He turned it about, examining the detail. "It serves to reflect on such things at times."

Magnus studied the priest's features in the broken light. Unlike the other priests, whose dragon markings covered the left side of their heads, this High Priest had markings over his entire bald head. He wondered if it meant he possessed greater power than the other priests. Perhaps it was ornamental like the great statue of Balgur in the Temple. To Magnus, he certainly looked more intimidating. He remembered the first time he ever saw a priest. It was Austagia, back at Catanya's family home before he took her away from him. Magnus found Austagia so intimidating at the time. Now, he saw him as most other men. He took a step closer to the High Priest.

"I underestimated you," the priest said. Magnus looked but said nothing. The priest's eyes shifted to Magnus and seemed to lock on. Magnus felt no disturbance in his thoughts but nevertheless, he was wary. "I can take time to reflect on you now."

The priest's stare continued, making Magnus feel awkward. He looked away and saw Catanya walking toward him. Eamon was there and took her by the arm. Catanya turned and Eamon spoke. Magnus imagined their conversation—*'Leave them to talk, Catanya, he is perfectly safe.'*

"I see the young Irucantî survived. This pleases you?"

This time, Magnus let his eyes fall darkly on the High Priest. His mouth filled with sharp words, but he swallowed them back. "Does it please *you*?"

"Your first words are not of derision, nor contempt. That pleases me."

Magnus started to walk away. He found the priest's indifference to Catanya too much to stomach. Furthermore, he sensed he was in for a pretentious debate that he was not in the mood for.

"Electus. We need to speak," the priest called after him.

That's more like it. Magnus turned and approached the door of the cell again.

"We should speak candidly to one another." The priest rose to his feet.

"We should."

"I imagine you intend to return to the Uydferlands. To defeat the Quag army."

"That is my intention. Why was it not yours when they first attacked?"

"It is a complicated matter."

"Just as well we're speaking candidly to one another."

"Indeed." The Priest arrived at a pause.

There it is—the calculating mind at work, Magnus observed. "Look, if there's a reason we should not be protecting our people, you need to tell us before we go to our deaths." Magnus was hoping the priest would get to the point.

"There are several reasons. Will you afford me the time to explain each of them? Only then will you see the dangerous predicaments we have been facing."

Magnus sat cross-legged on the ground beside the prison door and waited for the High Priest to explain.

"Firstly, the battle in the Uydferlands is a *ruse*. To understand the purpose of this ruse, you need to understand why the Romghold exists. Do you know why the Irucantî have long resided in the Romgnian Mountains, so far from our homelands of the Fire Realm?"

The first thought that came to Magnus's mind was his father's contempt for the dragons not being in the Fire Realm to protect their people. It was not until the war broke out that Magnus gave it any real consideration himself and then, he wondered why they were not returning home. He had a feeling he was about to find out.

"For their own protection?" Magnus answered.

"Yes. Quag armies cannot breach the Romghold. The closest they got was the Southern Plains during the Battle of Fire. If such a battle were waged on the plains of the Fire Realm, we may have been destroyed."

Magnus thought it made sense. Then again—"If people of the Fire Realm have managed to hold the Quag armies at bay in the Uydferlands, why would you have any trouble defeating them?"

"Because this is not a war. As I said—it is a ruse."

"In what way?"

"Delvion places just enough warriors and wyverns to keep Xavier and his soldiers busy—extremely busy, but no more. He hoped this would create a knee-jerk reaction, leading us to mount a defence and empty the Romghold of all our resources. Then a true war would start."

"What do you mean?"

"The Caves of Cuvee harbour Delvion's true armies. All manner of man and beast, numbered in the thousands, lie dormant, waiting to attack. Such caves have many exits throughout Allumbreve as far north as Froughton Forest and as far south as the Black Cliffs. Once in motion, Delvion's armies would prevent a retreat to the Romghold, force us to fight in open combat and most likely destroy us."

Magnus thought of the worgriel attack in the wheat fields near Brindle. The blacksmith—Willem—spoke of three known exits in the Black Cliffs at Ba'rrat, Brindle and Thwax. As for Delvion's armies hidden in the Caves of Cuvee, Austagia told Magnus he had discovered their presence in the caves just days ago. Magnus was about to question the High Priest about his secrecy on the matter when he recalled something his father used to say to him— *'He who withholds information from you considers himself your master.'* Magnus scanned the priest over, wondering what other secrets he was yet to learn.

"So, you believe this 'ruse' is to draw you into an even greater battle?" Magnus asked.

"Greater than the Battle of Fire. The real destruction of the Fire Realm would follow."

Magnus nodded to suggest he understood and yet, he was no closer to trusting the priest who ordered his assassination and blackmailed Brue and Liné.

"What were the other reasons for holding back? You said there were several."

"You'll need patience to understand this. Do I have your ear?"

"Aye."

"Twenty years ago, during the Battle of Fire, all of Allumbreve learned a powerful secret."

Magnus knew what he was going to say. This is what Joffren revealed to him when he infiltrated his mind with the Juniper stone. Joffren revealed how the High Priests desperately wanted the power afforded the Electi of the other realms. "The existence of the Electi," Magnus said.

"Exactly," The High Priest agreed.

"You wanted it for yourselves."

"That is how is appears—yes. This is where you need to listen."

"I'm listening."

"There is a potential civil war brewing among the realms. A silent power struggle ensues. The realms of Ice, Air and Earth build strength through their Electi and are able to use these powers, once afforded to dragons alone, at their discretion. While these three realms appear to have hidden away from the world, we have learned they are each breeding a race of Electi warriors— descended from their chosen ones."

Magnus had no knowledge of the Air and Earth Realms but knew what he said was untrue of the Ice Realm. He and his mother were the only Ice Realm Electi remaining. Magnus wondered if the High Priest was ill informed or building a ruse of his own to justify his ambitions. He did not believe the priest to be ill informed. Nevertheless, he decided to humour him.

"You find this a threat? Ours is the only realm with dragons to fight for us."

"Perhaps. But are we to trust their Electi to be as virtuous with their powers as their dragons once were?"

"Were the Electi not chosen for their virtue?"

"Generations have passed since their original Electi were chosen. We face the progeny of such chosen ones. Are the virtues of their forefathers inherited along with their powers? Virtue can be a struggle for those born into power." What the priest said made sense but the thought was unsettling. "It does not rest well in the mind, does it?"

It did not rest well in his mind. Then again, no matter how Magnus saw it, the High Priest craved for power. "You didn't answer my question. Why do you need such power when our dragons are still strong?"

"If our dragons are defeated by Delvion's army and you, the Electus, are our only source of such power, we become vulnerable not only to the Quag, but against a multigenerational army of Electi."

Magnus thought he knew where the High Priest was going with his explanations. "So you think the Irucantî need to create an Electus and breed an army of Electi, ready for the inevitable?"

"We tried to convince our dragons to create multiple Electi from highly trained Irucantî. Our purpose was always to be the greatest warriors and forge the closest relationship with our dragons. By keeping Electi within our fold, we keep that relationship going. However, our dragons insisted—there would only ever be one Electus chosen by them. Conceding, we urged them to make a choice. The dragons insisted this was a process to be decided in its own time."

Magnus's mind was turning over everything the High Priest was telling him. Things were beginning to make sense, but far from everything. "I was chosen as the Electus. You tried to assassinate me. You tried to assassinate Catanya! Where does this fit in to your plan?"

"Word spread throughout the lands of an exceptional slave-warrior in Ba'rrat calling himself 'Balgur'. This gained our attention—particularly after Thioci's death. With no clear knowledge as to your origins or motives, you were considered too dangerous. Once eliminated, there would be no choice but for our dragons to choose another Electus—preferably from our superior order of warriors." The priest paused. "As for the young Irucantî, she was of no concern to us. That was Joffren's decision."

Magnus thought the priest's reasoning was cold-blooded, yet sound. There was more that needed answering, however, before he could accept the priest's words.

"How was holding Liné's egg for ransom going to work for you?" Magnus was sure the High Priest would be at a loss for words at this point. It would make everything he said until now a complete farce. The priest, though, seemed to have an answer for everything.

"Only Liné and Brue knew of your existence, being parents to the deceased youngling—Thioci. They would never support your assassination. By withholding their unhatched egg, Brue became more... amenable. The rest of the dragons left for Ba'rrat under the pretence they were bringing down Delvion."

Magnus stared hard at the High Priest. He could not believe the boldness with which he confessed to manipulating Brue. Catanya had described the High Priests as arrogant. He saw it himself in the Temple of Fire, but only now could Magnus truly put it into perspective. *They truly believe they are of a higher order than even the dragons.* Magnus remembered what Brue told him— *'We each form a unique link. There is no hierarchy—no pyramid of importance.'* This was in such contrast to the High Priests' beliefs.

"Desperate times called for desperate measures, Semsdër-Fatel."

"You never considered the consequences once Liné got her egg back?" Magnus could not take his eyes off the priest—curious to hear his answer.

"It was a means to an end. As I said earlier, I underestimated you. I also underestimated our youngest recruit." The priest looked down the path to where Catanya was pacing back and forth, biting her nails nervously while Magnus spoke to the priest.

Magnus ran everything the High Priest told him through his mind. As much as he disagreed with his methods, what he said at least made sense. This whole debacle began back in his homelands. Magnus remembered being in his family kitchen with his mother and father. His mother had just ridden half the length of Realms End—from Overpell to Froughton Forest—and discovered the guards had left their posts. Magnus later learned it was the Authoritarium who afforded Crugion, Briet and the rest of the Quag access into the Fire Realm.

Magnus wondered—"What are your concerns about the Authoritarium? Was it not them that told you and the dragons to cease their guard of Realms End years ago and then remove the knights from their posts prior to this 'ruse' of a war?"

"It was. But there is no need to be concerned about the Authoritarium. They have been destroyed."

"Destroyed? By whom?" Magnus stood with his face at the prison cell bars.

"I thought you of all people would know." The priest came to the bars and stood nose to nose with Magnus.

"Why would I know?"

"It was the Rhydermere who killed the elders of the Authoritarium. And it was *your mother* who killed Trager—their leader."

Magnus took two steps back from the cell door. "You are lying."

"The Rhydermere have placed Guame under martial law. Your mother declares the Rhydermere 'rulers of the four realms' with herself as their leader." The priest gripped the bars of the cell door and pulled himself forward. "You can see, then, my concern when the Electus of our realm carries the blood of our new enemy."

'ONE'

"Did you kill her?"

Lucas stood in Delvion's chamber. To Lucas, it was darker than any other crevice, tunnel or shadow within the Caves of Cuvee. The darkness shifted with Delvion. Wherever the Quag King went, the darkness followed and it *always* summoned Lucas—drew him to Delvion such that he rarely left his side, except to sleep.

"I said, did you kill her?"

"I couldn't do it." Lucas felt his words wheeze from his mouth—heard the weakness in his own conviction.

"*What* did you say?" Delvion flashed his dark, deep-set eyes at Lucas. They usually penetrated his mind and ran inventory on his peripheral thoughts. Delvion was never able to penetrate his mind to the real truth behind his strength. His sorcerers could, but Lucas saw to it they would only get so far before he killed them. This time, Delvion was struggling to get in at all. He squinted—confirming his control over Lucas had slipped for a moment.

He will be wary until he regains control...

"Come. We shall do it together."

Lucas followed Delvion through the primary corridor leading to the armoury cave. His eyes glanced to the floor at Delvion's feet, watching the tips of his black blades protruding from his large, dark cloak. He knew in a moment he could take possession of the Quag King's blades and drive them through his back, his heart, and out through his chest. He considered the option as he always considered such clandestine things—in the shadow of his darkest thoughts. This shadow had always been there, even as a child. It was a place to tuck away darker thoughts of self-doubt and derision from those who thought they were better than him or doubted his abilities. It was often easier than proving them wrong. When poisoned by the wyvern in the Uydferlands, Lucas was drawn to this place. He developed an insatiable desire to linger on his darker thoughts and, for the first time, he was not alone. The wyvern had found his shadow. From here, Lucas's world seemed to cave in around him. Then he met *her*.

The wyvern queen...

He was close to death when the queen infiltrated his mind, acknowledging Lucas's pain. She nursed him back to health. Lucas had felt the fierce strength of her blood and the maternal warmth of her milk flood his decaying body and breathe new life into him. The queen found Lucas's shadow and presented it to him—reminding him of every dark thought he had ever had. She taught him how to use those thoughts. They could provide him with a dark, satisfying strength. Delvion had exploited this strength, but would *never* know its source and never truly know the bond he had with the queen.

Delvion strode across the cave floor to a rack of freshly forged *domblaus* blades—'black blades'. These bulky, burnished blades were slightly curved, sharp and waiting to be stained with wyvern venom. During battle, the Quag would lick the blades to elicit hallucinations and trigger *gretaro*— 'war-rage'. Lucas had the same venom coursing through his body at all times. Delvion's men called him *Gretarior*—'War-rager'. It was not considered conducive to be in this state on a regular basis and indeed, Quag warriors would steer clear of their common clansfolk following battle until the effects of the venom wore off to ensure their 'rage' would not lead to collateral damage. To Delvion's men, Lucas was collateral damage waiting to happen.

Delvion drew one of the domblaus blades from the rack and handed it to Lucas. "Take it."

"I need my sword."

"It is gone. Take it." Lucas did as told, holding the black blade as one would a dagger. "You've a choice. Use sorcery or a blade. Either way, you must show loyalty." Delvion pointed to a tunnel feeding off the far side of the cave. "It is time. Kill her."

Lucas looked to the ground again. He retreated into his shadow. The queen knew he was there—he could hear her thoughts as she could his. "I cannot," Lucas mumbled.

At the click of Delvion's fingers, two Quagmen approached Lucas with blades drawn. Lucas pointed a finger at the larger of the two men and let anger brew in his hidden shadow. It brewed thick and dark until it began to seep from his mind, through his body before finally leaching from the pores in his hands as a shadowy black mist. It felt so good—like he was expressing his inner pains without the need for words. The mist took shape forming their poisonous black tentacles. Something though, was not right.

Lucas looked at the sorcerous black strands coming from his hands and suddenly they appeared as living, writhing creatures of death. The large Quagman saw the black magic and was quick to step away from Lucas. His companion backed away too. Barely noticing their retreat, Lucas caught a vision of what he was doing. He was outside his own body, watching a phantom-like reflection of himself frothing and foaming with anger, the syrupy vines of blackness oozing from his grey, clammy skin. It was a revolting sight. Startled, he found he was inside himself again and shook his hand frantically until the black poison vaporised.

With the threat gone, one of the Quagman bounded at Lucas. Lucas refocused. He was back in his shadow. The black mist was quick to reform and morph into the sickly black matter. It leapt at the Quagmen, wrapping his limbs and torso, entering his mouth and nostrils, blackening over his eyes. The Quagman fell in a convulsive heap. Lucas felt every morsel of the warrior's pain until the Quagmen took his last breath. The second Quagman backed away and Lucas dropped to a knee, exhausted in a way unfamiliar to him. The caged wyverns began to howl. Lucas shut his eyes and drew on their dark thoughts, using them to replenish his strength. With the Quagman dead, the pain subsided. Lucas could not understand what had just happened but was glad the terrifying ordeal was over.

Delvion growled—"You *will* kill her and prove loyalty to me. You are no longer dependant on her." He marched to the centre of the cave floor. "Bring her in!"

Lucas reeled. *NO!*

Through a broad tunnel on the far side of the cave, six Quagmen entered pulling chains. The chains were connected to a broad wooden cart that slowly rolled into view. Atop the cart was a huge, hulking, black mass of a creature, chained fast to the cart.

"NO!" Lucas screamed in the shadow of his mind. A single tear fell across his right cheek. The black creature tensed her thick, leathery muscles and tried to flex her barbed wings. She opened her big yellow eyes—her crescent-shaped irises pulsed when she recognised Lucas. Her thoughts groaned through Lucas's mind. She was half terrified, half furious. The wyvern queen was quick to find Lucas's shadow and bath him with her maternal affections.

She understands…

Delvion approached the queen and examined her. "The queens can never be tamed," he said. "Ever the shame. They are the most powerful wyverns and would make great steeds in the final battle for Allumbreve." Delvion stepped away from the wyvern.

Lucas came to her, placing a hand on her thick brow. Her eyes remained fixed on him. He knew if she begged for her release he would see it done, but the queen does not beg. The queen protects her children, removing them from harm at her own expense. The wyvern swam through Lucas's mind. She knew it was over for her. She knew this was the last chance she had to protect the adopted child she saved from certain death in the Corville Mountains.

Lucas closed his eyes and let the queen examine his thoughts. She found something—something that was not there before. Lucas saw what she saw. There was something locked onto Lucas's mind, manipulating his will. The queen's mind darkened over—how dare something warp the mind she had nurtured? Her body heaved, straining the chains to their limits. The Quagmen worked to reinforce them.

"Kill her!"

Lucas felt Delvion's darkness weighing on him. The queen continued her feverish mental assault, searching through Lucas's mind, desperate to find answers. She was like a mother searching for a missing egg, scrounging and foraging through undergrowth, a race against time before a predator found it first. Suddenly, there it was…

"A CURSE!"

The wyvern tugged and pulled at Lucas's mind, trying to free it of the curse's mental manipulations, but it was hopeless. The curse was of words far beyond her comprehension. Furthermore, the curse bound Lucas's fate to another. Whom he was bound to was cloaked from sight as part of the curse. The wyvern was relentless. She was not able to lift the curse but she was fixed on revealing its maker. At least with that, the child she had saved from certain death in the Corville Mountains could seek his revenge.

Then she found it.

The curse wielder's identity was cloaked by no more than a memory lapse, fastened with the after-effect of a Tenebris spell. This was something the wyvern queen *could* overthrow.

"Kill her now! Prove your loyalty to me!"

Delvion's darkness was suffocating. Lucas needed to find his shadow. He needed to retreat to the one spot only he and the wyvern queen knew about. However, the queen was still feverishly at work in his mind, untangling the effects of the Tenebris spell, making his retreat impossible.

All of sudden, the queen was done. The cloak was lifted. Lucas's memory returned. He saw her face as clear as if she was there with him now—the face of the one who cursed him—the face of the one he was bound to against his will.

"Mother!"

The wyvern queen rested. Her foraging and mayhem had left Lucas's mind raw and dishevelled, torn and tattered. He needed a moment to himself. *Just a moment...* It was all he needed to collect his thoughts and grasp what had just happened. But his hidden shadow was gone. *She* had torn it to ribbons in order to rip the Tenebris spell clear of his mind. It was worth it though—to know whom to avenge. From now on, there would be no more shadow for Lucas to bottle resentments and dark thoughts. From now on, Lucas would have to declare himself.

Delvion was upon Lucas like the darkness of death itself. Lucas could hear his breathing and felt the weight of his stare on the back of his neck. The wyvern's yellow eyes moved from Lucas to Delvion and back again. Her muscular shoulders began to roll forward rhythmically, pushing on the chains.

She will try to escape. It is now or never...

Lucas glanced over his shoulder to assess exactly where Delvion was standing then squeezed the thick pommel of the domblaus blade in his left hand. In one swift move he lifted it and stabbed it deep into the wyvern queen's skull. He held fast to the blade, soaking in her fading death scream, letting her pain wash through his body and mind. He was not alone—every caged wyvern in the armoury cave screamed in unison, sharing their fury and sorrow for the death of the queen.

Farewell, mother...

When the collective screams of pain and sorrow finally subsided and all was silent again, Lucas released the blade and collapsed to the floor, convulsing and sweating from the excruciating ordeal. His throat was parched and sore and he realised that he had been screaming with the wyverns. Lucas turned to Delvion, but looked to the ground.

Delvion lifted his chin so that they stared into one another's eyes. The Quag King spoke slowly—"Very good. You have proven your loyalty. Now then, you can hear the story of my people and understand why we must rule Allumbreve. You will learn of the people of 'Dephaer' and the seven clans who became *One*—'Quag'."

TRAINING AND FAREWELLS

In the morning, Catanya rose earlier than even Trax. She retrieved her bow and quiver of arrows from the end of her bed. It was the one part of her Ferustir attire she had not taken with her when she fled the Romghold a month ago to find Magnus.

She stood on the cobblestones of the common and cast her eyes toward the High Priest's prison cell. Brue stood to attention beside the cell's door. *There's no way Brue will let him escape.* The priest came to the door and stared at Catanya. She drew an arrow, loaded it into her bow and aimed it straight for the High Priest's head. The priest continued to stare at Catanya, as did Brue. She drew a deep breath, pulling back harder on the arrow, feeling the strain in her shoulder muscles—particularly the right shoulder where the other High Priest had stabbed her. Just two fingertips held the arrow from spearing toward the priest's forehead. She knew the priest would block the arrow somehow but did not care. The vision she had formed of the arrow flying toward the High Priest was more than satisfying enough.

Catanya released her breath and eased the arrow, sheathing it back in its quiver. She averted her gaze and walked toward the training field. Removing her boots, she strode barefooted across the perfect lawn. The sun was yet to rise and burn the morning dew from the grass stems and so the crisp, cool feeling soothed her feet and seemed to soak through her body and into her mind. Catanya had not dared step barefoot on the field since her 'cleansing' when she was forced to run around the field's perimeter, without footwear, for days until exhaustion—and the distinguished verity light—ended the cruel ritual. She had been through so much since then. Memories of it were less bothersome now.

"Catanya."

Catanya peered over her shoulder. It was Austagia. "Good morning," Catanya smiled.

Austagia stopped in front of her. A gentle smile came to his face. "Good morning to you."

Catanya was curious. Austagia seemed relaxed—perhaps even content—in her company. He had changed a lot from the estranged uncle who dragged her to the Romghold virtually kicking and screaming all those months ago. As always though, she had to remind herself that it was just as likely she had changed a lot too.

"Magnus will train with Simeon again today."

"Aye." Catanya knew this was Austagia's plan. After the High Priest told Magnus about Delvion's hidden army and the Rhydermere overthrowing the Authoritarium, they shared the news with Austagia and decided to remain in the Romghold another day. She was a little uneasy about Magnus learning from the Irucantí, but if it would serve to protect him later on, then she was all for it. *Just don't go swearing fealty to them,'* Catanya warned Magnus. Magnus assured her he would never and was keen to leave and help find Hannah as soon as he could. In the meantime, the issue of Delvion left something Austagia needed to clear up for her. "Austagia, the High Priests knew of Delvion's army amassing in the Caves of Cuvee. You only discovered it for yourself recently. Didn't they tell you this?"

"Apparently, we were not privy to such information."

"He told Magnus this is why it wasn't safe to defend the Fire Realm. Why then, did you think we should not defend our people?"

"It was not for us to dispute the decisions of the High Priests. That sounds ludicrous and I see now that it was. For my part, I made sure *you* were safe."

"Why me? Why not Hannah as well? Who was supposed to protect her?"

"The order would never have approved bringing someone so young into the Romghold. I did all I could do to bring you. If I thought as I do now, I would do many things differently."

It was a silly question—Catanya knew that. She had been drafted into the priesthood in a non-draft year and learned later it was her mother who asked Austagia to pull strings to organise it. Leaving Magnus was painful. Leaving Hannah was painful too but now she had Magnus back, Catanya needed to make sure Hannah was safe. She also needed to know if seeing Hannah in the temple chamber was real.

"Austagia, I need to get to Hannah. I need to make sure she's safe."

"I can see that." Austagia walked to the cliff edge of the field and gazed out over Froughton Forest. "The Quag may be monitoring movement through the skies to the south. We can fly at night." He pointed to the north. "To the Traas River then westward, above the clouds." Austagia moved his arm in an arc. "We will approach the Uydferlands from the quarry and enter Nuyan that way."

"You will come with me?"

"Aye. I need to assess the war myself and… speak with your father."

Catanya tried to hide the excitement bubbling inside of her. 'When? When can we leave?"

"All things squared away, this evening."

Catanya skipped her first steps back across the training field. She could not wait to tell Magnus they were heading home—if only for a short while. Austagia grabbed Catanya by the elbow, drawing her back.

"Catanya, Magnus needs to stay. He needs to train with the Irucantî, learn more of our ways if they are to invest in him. We need that for the protection of our people."

A shudder passed through Catanya at the thought of leaving Magnus again and even more so for leaving him in the Romghold. Catanya glanced back to the High Priest's prison cell. "Will he be safe?"

"I've just been thinking about that. Rubea will take us. Brue will remain, as will Liné. I will ask Färgd to stay until we return. Eamon is here and I will also ask Jael to remain. Simeon I trust to protect Magnus as well."

Catanya was satisfied there was a strong contingency supporting Magnus. "I guess then, we should leave it up to Magnus."

"Our new enemy…" the High Priest had said.

Even if I am to trust the High Priest's story about my mother, Magnus reasoned, *it doesn't make her an enemy to the rest of Allumbreve.* Magnus paced about the training field, twirling Lucas's sword in his hand. *Besides, I am sure the truth of the tale has become embellished… or the High Priest is deceiving me.* Not at all sure of the matter, Magnus did not mention his mother to Austagia when he relayed the High Priest's revelation about the Rhydermere destroying the Authoritarium.

Forgetting the High Priest's other revelations, Magnus went through a series of stretches Catanya showed him the previous day. He wished he were as flexible as her. Then again, she had been doing them daily for six months or more.

"I've been thinking, Semsdër." It was Simeon, walking onto the training field. "In relation to what Trax said over supper last night, you need to train not as an Irucantî would train, but as the Electus." He spread him arms wide for emphasis.

"How do you suppose we do that?"

"You need to use all your powers. Push the limits of what you know and work to evolve them. You are the greatest among us. You should use your skills."

Magnus liked Simeon. There was no nonsense to him. Magnus knew he was about twenty-five years old because he remembered when he was drafted into the order eight years ago. He was from farmlands north of the Uydferlands and was the middle of three brothers. His elder brother worked on the farmlands and the younger worked in the quarries. The younger brother was the same age as Magnus. They had sparred during the Authoritarium's Knighthood trials. Magnus had won, but Simeon's brother—Vinson—was a good swordsman.

"That all sounds good, Simeon, but I don't want to hurt you."

"That's my point, Semsdër. Yesterday you were trying to beat me at *my* game. You need to fight at *yours*."

"Please, can you call me 'Magnus'? These formalities give me the creeps." Magnus felt it was time to say something—at least to Simeon.

Simeon smiled. "Very well, Magnus. And no, I do not wish to be hurt. I think you should spar with the High Priest."

Magnus smiled at Simeon's jest, but the priest was not smiling back. "Are you serious?"

"Aye. Are you okay with this? We will all be here." Simeon came closer to Magnus and spoke quietly. "Austagia told me about Balgur's prophecy—that you will learn from the High Priest. I think now is the time. Never will you have such a secure environment in which to do it."

As Simeon spoke, other priests moved about the training field and took up positions at its perimeter. Dragons followed, positioning themselves between every second priest. They were organised like the hours of a clock, with a dragon at three, six, nine and twelve o'clock positions and Ferustirs at the other hours, giving a total of four dragons and eight priests. Simeon was flanking Magnus at the centre. Magnus turned about, looking at each of the priests and dragons in turn. He knew it was true—there was never going to be a more secure environment. It was also the first time the Irucantî had come together as one to support Magnus. *Unless they plan to support the High Priest...* Magnus shook the dark thought from his head.

"You won't let the High Priest kill me?"

"Certainly not. But if he does..." Simeon leant toward Magnus, now with a grin on his face. 'Rest assured we'll hang him by his entrails."

The High Priest walked to the centre of the training field with shackles about his wrists and legs. *Pointless... He could break free of those at any time.* Magnus watched as the disgraced head of the Irucanti order took the time to look at every priest and each dragon present, just as he had done. Magnus knew he was sizing them up, assessing his position, maybe even devising a plan of attack. The dragons shuffled about, making Magnus think the High Priest had closed his mind to their interrogations.

It was Trax who led the High Priest and so Trax released him of his shackles. The High Priest pulled his black robe from his body, revealing his Ferustir attire. It was similar to Eamon's armour that Marsala reshaped for Magnus, but as with all Ferustir armour, it was unique. Magnus looked over the familiar blend of fire-bronze and woven black armour, looking for weaknesses in the manufacture. He saw none, but noticed the vambraces had ominous looking spikes that revealed themselves when the priest bent his elbows. Trax handed The High Priest his Ferustir's lance, which he sheathed behind his back. *This is insanity...* Magnus released a nervous breath. *But it's what Balgur wanted...* Then he remembered his promise to Brue—he was not to trust the High Priest without Brue's consent. Magnus scanned the training field looking for the dragon. As if on queue, the clock-circle of priests and dragons formed a gap, allowing Brue to approach Magnus.

"I'll be by your side. Nothing will happen to you," Brue said.

"Thank you." Magnus chuckled at the irony that the very dragon he feared days ago now gave him the greatest peace of mind. In only served to make this training event even more bizarre than it was. He looked at the High Priest and imagined him hanging by his entrails as Simeon suggested.

"The entrails are the only part of him I will not eat," Brue said.

Brue is in my head... probably a good thing, Magnus thought. He walked toward the High Priest.

The High Priest came at Magnus. He moved so swiftly it was like a dream until Magnus felt the strike of an extended palm to his chest knock him off his feet. Magnus rolled back and sprung upright again. Heat seared momentarily through his chest, healing a cracked rib and bruised muscles. Several of the Ferustir's drew lances. Magnus raised a hand to suggest he was okay and took a deep breath.

My turn...

He squeezed his hands into fists and in a moment they ignited into flame. The High Priest whispered a spell, extending both hands at Magnus. A shimmering wall like a shield appeared midway between them. Magnus extended his hands. The flames danced about his forearms and thrust forward at the priest. The shield absorbed the flames entirely. A moment's silence passed. The flames shot out of the shield, back at Magnus. Magnus whispered a gypsy chant and his body displaced itself slightly to his right. The flames licked across his left shoulder. The pain passed momentarily and there was no trace of a burn.

The High Priest's lips moved—he was whispering another spell. His body displaced to the left as Magnus's had, but it did so three, four, five times. Each time the priest moved to a random location no more than a foot away from his last position until he was directly in front of Magnus. The Priest's lance was drawn, ignited and at Magnus's throat. The High Priest held his position. Magnus could not counter without the priest taking his head clean off. All the priests at the perimeter now had their lances ignited and Brue was inches from closing his jaws over the High Priest's head.

The High Priest extinguished his lance and took three steps back. Magnus replayed the scenario over in his head in slow motion, trying to comprehend what just happened. First the attack, then the priest's reaction time and Brue—*how did Brue counter attack so quickly?* A sinking feeling overcame Magnus. *I am useless against this High Priest.*

"Again." It was Eamon, pushing through the training field's guard.

"Steyne?" the High Priest said, recognising him.

Eamon rolled his eyes but ignored the question. "Again. You must spar again. Go!"

"But, Eamon—" Magnus started.

"No 'buts'," Eamon interrupted. "Again! And again, and again, and again… GO!"

The High Priest reignited his lance. Magnus sighed and yanked his sword from its scabbard. The next exchange was void of spells. It was lance against sword. Magnus maintained a defensive position. Taking Simeon's previous advice, he tried looking for patterns in the priest's technique. The priest separated Magnus from his sword within five strikes of the lance.

"Again," Eamon called.

The sparring continued. The High Priest's attack seemed to follow no pattern, but Magnus began to notice the smallest things. The priest would shift his grip ever so slightly, once in a while, for no apparent reason. He would over extend his arm when thrusting above shoulder height, rounding out with a seemingly unnecessary backhanded move after his overextension. He would also click his head to the right after such a manoeuvre.

"Again."

The High Priest's technique was flawless. Magnus dismissed his irregularities as style rather than weaknesses. But then it dawned on him. There was no 'style' to the Irucanti—not when it came to their fighting technique, anyway. They were all about efficiency and perfection. *And where efficiency and perfection lack, a weakness can be seen.*

"Again."

Magnus felt lightened by the realisation—*The High Priest has an ailment.* Magnus ran through the things he was noticing. The grip change, the overextension, the neck click. As the day wore on, these things became more apparent. The priest began cracking his knuckles then twirling his lance between moves to delay the next. Magnus had him figured—*He has a neck injury so he overextends to avoid jarring his neck, a weak left shoulder, and he has gout in his fingers.* They were simple weaknesses and Magnus doubted they could be taken advantage of in battle, for the priest was so deadly he would dispense with his enemies before they had made such observations. Then again, it was all a learning process. Magnus decided the next time he encountered a similar weakness he would exploit it immediately.

"Again."

It was time to go on the attack. Again, the priest came at Magnus first, working his way through a series of manoeuvres Magnus could not predict, before finally overextending and twirling his lance. Magnus seized the opportunity, thrusting his sword directly at the priest's chest armour. However, his sword never reached its target. The priest reacted with lightning reflexes, swinging one end of his lance directly to Magnus's exposed neck, while deflecting his sword with a spiked vambrace. His move was performed with absolute precision. It was then Magnus realised—he had looked for weaknesses and fallen for a trick. It was the very thing Simeon warned him *not* to do.

Simeon stepped forward to speak but Magnus held a hand to him. "I know, I know."

"Again," Eamon shouted for the millionth time.

Patterns... look for patterns...

"Two over, three under, four over, five." It was Brue. *"That is the pattern. He is a creature of habit."*

Magnus glanced at the big dragon to his left. The High Priest came at him again. From the first blow Magnus counted his moves. *One, two, three, shift of feet, spins lance overhead, four, five, six, seven, squats, lance sweep to feet, eight, nine, thrust to head, ten, eleven, twelve, thirteen…*

"Again."

Magnus recounted. The pattern changed. *What is Brue saying?*

"Add a single count from the start, two after the over, three after the under and so forth," said Brue.

"Again."

Brue seemed to be suggesting the pattern was evolving by following a mathematical system of progression. It was entirely unrecognisable without the math.

"When does the cycle repeat?" Magnus was careful to direct his question to Brue alone.

"It does not repeat. It is always progressing. Learn its rate of progression and plan your attack for the next cycle."

"That's enough," Simeon insisted. "We shall break and return later."

"No," Magnus insisted. "Keep going."

"Very well. Again!"

For three more bouts Magnus fought, observed and counted the High Priest's moves. It was finally evident. The pattern was not in the moves, but how the moves progressed. *Nothing* was random. *Nothing* was left to chance, for that was simply not in the Irucanti's nature.

"Again."

A fourth cycle came about and Magnus had done the math. He would strike when the priest swept for his feet, which would be precisely five moves after a backhanded thrust of his lance to Magnus's head. The head thrust came, then—

One move, two, three, four moves…

The low sweeping lance came and Magnus changed sword arms. He buried his left fist into the ground and his vambrace took the impact of the lance. His right arm thrust his sword to the High Priest's neck making contact at the throat.

The High Priest froze. The white tipped point of the fleu-steel sword had broken the priest's skin and a trickle of blood ran down his chest armour. His eyes stared hard at Magnus who rose to his feet and lowered his sword. He stepped closer to the High Priest so he could speak to him in confidence.

"Will you teach me?" Magnus said. The priest seemed unsure Magnus was serious. "Will you show me how you fight?"

"Will you swear fealty to the order?" The priest sheathed his lance and waited for Magnus's reply.

Magnus recalled Catanya's warning—*Just don't go swearing fealty to them.*' He promised her he would not. Magnus shook his head. "No. But I will swear fealty to our dragons."

Magnus could see the High Priest was thinking things over. Magnus had him—he knew he did. The priest could not deny Magnus's offer to swear allegiance to the fire dragons. If he did, it would suggest he placed his own interests above the dragons.

"Very well. I will teach you."

"What did he say?" Catanya stood with her arms crossed.

"He will teach me," Magnus said.

Catanya paced around her small room, behind Magnus and back in front of him again. "You best him just now. Are you sure you need him to train you?"

"I best him once in the day and only because Brue told me how to analyse his moves. There is a lot I need to know, Catanya." Magnus could see she was ill at ease with the idea, which only served to fuel his own self-doubts. However, it was what Balgur wanted.

Catanya stopped pacing and looked at Magnus. Her radiant brown eyes pierced through him. She brushed her fingers through her black hair and began to chew on her upper lip. He shared her discomfort, for it was not right. Magnus knew it was not right and not fair to have Catanya wait any longer to return to the Uydferlands to find Hannah.

"You know what—it can wait," Magnus conceded.

"What do you mean?"

"We should go. We should not wait any longer. We need to find Hannah."

"*I* need to find Hannah. *You* need to stay here."

"I don't want to leave your side, Catanya. Never again."

"That's exactly how I feel and you know it, but it had to happen at some stage, Magnus. And it will only be for a few days."

Magnus was shaking his head, trying to find a better way. "I can't watch you fly away again." He knew the words sounded weak, but he said them anyway.

"Austagia will travel with me and Rubea has agreed to take us there."

"Austagia and Rubea? Are you serious?"

"I know. I see the irony." Catanya raised an eyebrow. A thin smile came to her face. "It's different this time. They aren't forcing me to go. In fact, it was I who persuaded them. Austagia benefits from the trip too. He needs to assess the situation in the Uydferlands and when we return, we will know what we need to do. And Hannah… she'll be safer here than anywhere else."

"When you put it that way, it sounds like a good plan. But Catanya, I can just as well go with you and resume my training when we return."

"With time so precious, every day spent training could make all the difference." Catanya sat on her bed. "I think you are right about your training, Magnus. These days will prove invaluable."

Magnus considered things further—"How will you avoid Quag scouts?"

"Austagia has a workaround. We will travel toward the Traas River then over Froughton Forest, approaching the Uydferlands from the north. We'll return the same way in three days."

"Can Rubea carry all three of you?" Magnus knew he was needlessly looking for things to worry about.

Catanya stood again, came to Magnus and embraced him. "We'll be fine, Magnus. There's nothing to worry about. You just keep safe, *Electus*."

They both smiled.

"I'm glad Brue has my back. Who would have thought?"

"Nobody would have thought it. The dragon you feared most when we got here seems to have become your biggest supporter!" Catanya's face softened. "That's what's wonderful about you. You saw that side in Brue and brought him back."

"You brought *me* back."

They continued their embrace. Magnus wanted it to last forever, knowing he would be parted from her for the first time since leaving Ba'rrat. *A few days… It's only for a few days.* There was a knock at the open door. Magnus and Catanya were slow to pull away from one another. It was Trax.

"Ah! Sorry to interrupt. Supper is ready!"

"Thank you. There's something we need to do first," Catanya said.

After supper, there was a small gathering on the common at the foot of the temple stairs. Eamon, Jael, Simeon, Färgd, Brue and Liné were there to bid Austagia and Rubea good travels. Several other priests were waiting to also wish them well.

Magnus and Catanya were a short distance away, catching their last moments alone together. Catanya ran her fingers through his short hair. She had given Magnus his first haircut in close to a year and trimmed his beard short and neat. Magnus felt renewed because of it—as though he had shed the festering remnants of Ba'rrat from his body.

"You look more handsome than ever." Catanya was grinning, her white teeth shining in the moonlight. She was dressed in her Ferustir armour with a black priest's robe modified and shaped as a short dress. The dress raised more than a few eyebrows in the Romghold and Magnus was certain it was looked upon as desecration of the priestly attire. He was also certain it was the effect Catanya was after. She still wore her black boots although the burgundy lace of her right one had snapped and was retied with an additional black lace at the top. Over her dress was her sheathed lance and finally, she had her bow and quiver of arrows slung over her shoulder.

Magnus reflected on the travels they shared over the past weeks. In retrospect and mishaps aside, their time together had been wonderful. He held Catanya's hands.

"Travel safe and come right back with Hannah."

"I will. Train well and learn all you need to from the priests."

"I will."

Magnus held Catanya's face in his palms and stared into her eyes. *So far we have come… So much has changed.* He would have liked to witness Catanya and Hannah reuniting and seeing Hannah's smile for the first time.

"I cannot wait for us to return home together, when all this is over," Catanya said.

They walked to the common where they joined the others. They bid their farewells, Austagia taking the time to talk with Magnus. "Are you feeling well, Magnus?" It was the first time Austagia had addressed him in a casual manner. Magnus was glad he did.

"I am well and all the more so with you travelling together."

"See you in a few days."

Catanya and Austagia climbed into Rubea's saddle and fastened their legs into stirrups. Rubea walked to the training field. Simeon, meanwhile, was buckling into Braug's saddle, as it was decided they should run a clandestine patrol above the southern border of Froughton Forest to ensure wyverns were not scouting any further north.

Rubea and Braug took flight. Rubea banking northward toward the Traas River and Braug banked to the southwest over Froughton Forest. Magnus watched on until both dragons had flown beyond sight, then felt a hand on his back. It was Eamon.

"Magnus," Eamon said.

No more needed to be said between them. Magnus turned to his old friend, feeling blessed to have him there—in the Romghold of all places. But then, Eamon always was there when he needed him. Marsala believed it to be fate. Magnus was still sceptical of the certainty of fate, but if it meant Eamon would be by his side for years to come, he decided he was happy to go along with it. *For now...*

SOUTHERN PLAINS

Torchlights flickered across the still waters of the Plains Lake. Laughter filled the pine-scented evening and stars flecked the sky above the ancient trees of the southern border of Froughton Forest. Bonstaph breathed a sigh of bitter relief.

We made it...

The refugees successfully crossed the Southern Plains and arrived at the blue lake earlier that day. Of the three hundred ninety five travellers, over half were going to make their way westward to the Fire Realm. The remainder would take the Outer Rim through Froughton Forest to homes further afield, or follow the Red River to homes north of the Traas River, such as Kreeluck and the woodlands at the base of the Clouded Mountains. All were happy to make camp at the Plains Lake and rest for a couple of nights. It was only Sarah who did not make it.

Bonstaph knew full well Sarah was determined to find Lucas. There was nothing he could do to prevent it short of tie her up. Even if he could bring himself to restrain Sarah, he knew she would find a way of escaping. *Nothing's slipperier than a gypsy...* He hoped she would find her way free of the Caves of Cuvee. Her final words, though—*'Where I go there is no coming back,'* suggested this was never her intention.

Camp had been established, fires burned bright and the Plains Lake was rich with trout to feed hungry mouths. Bonstaph was seeing children play for the first time in too long. It seemed to be a utopian end to an arduous journey. Bonstaph, however, was ill at ease. Something was not right. Passage around the Corville Mountains was incident free. *Not a single patrolling wyvern all across the Southern Plains.* In the eyes of the former Knight Commander, this wreaked of warning more than luck. Accordingly, Bonstaph instructed the Perimetral guard to maintain a protective wall south of the camp. They were to have their eyes focused on the Corville Mountains at all times.

"Every second man is to be relieved every two hours," Bonstaph instructed Walt.

"Are we still in danger this far north?" Walt asked.

"This is how the Battle of Fire started." Bonstaph looked over the line of guards standing in the peaceful grass plains. "As calm before a storm."

"They came from the Corville Mountains?"

"They *bled* from the Corville Mountains." Bonstaph blanched at the dark memory. "Thousands of Quag warriors. The mountain wyverns were not a part of it in those days. Our dragons and the Irucantî made up for a lack of numbers. There were a few surprises from the other realms, as I recall." Bonstaph shook his head. "Sorry. It's a bad time for dark memories. Perhaps I am over cautious, Walt. But old habits die hard."

"I understand," Walt smiled.

Bonstaph looked at Walt. The young man had never faulted and never doubted Bonstaph in their weeks together. "Walt. Are you excited to be going home?"

Walt examined Bonstaph with a frown, then glanced across the lake and smiled. "I am. My mother is in Nuyan. She'll be glad to know I'm safe. If Kriser is still there, I will resume my training as a healer. That will be good."

To Bonstaph, Walt did not look so sure. "Is there a special lady waiting for you?"

Walt scanned Bonstaph's face again then lifted his eyebrows. "Not likely. Someday I may meet the right person."

"There's a special someone out there waiting for you, I'm sure."

"I'm regarded as… peculiar… back in Nuyan. Maybe there's another peculiar someone wandering about Allumbreve and we shall meet someday."

Bonstaph laughed. "That may not be necessary, Walt. They say opposites attract!"

"I'm not sure that applies in my case." Walt smiled awkwardly and Bonstaph looked at him, unsure what he meant.

The sound of gentle thunder began to peel through looming clouds to the south. "Hopefully that blows over. It could put a dampener on celebrations, don't you think?" Walt said in a light-hearted manner, changing the subject.

Bonstaph was not listening. He walked away from the light and noise of the camp into the deep grasses of the plains. In the dark silence he peered at the clouds. They were shifting eastward, yet the thunder rolled steadily closer, shaking the earth beneath his feet. He whistled loudly to the nearest of the fifty guards. They relayed the message down the east and westward lines of the Perimetral. Dread washed over Bonstaph and he felt his blood run cold. He glanced to the east. The first morning rays over the distant Romgnian

Mountains bloomed red against the inky sky. "A warning come too late," he lamented.

"What is it, Commander?"

"Get everyone up and armed. We're under attack!"

Within five minutes, all the refugees were in place. Everyone had a role to play. *Forty archers with flaming arrows, two hundred armed men and women...* The childish laughter had turned to high-pitched screams and parents tried their best to silence them. "Silence!" Bonstaph growled. "We need to hear... to *know* what is coming, how many and how fast."

Dawn's frugal light offered little vision. Bonstaph pushed through the grasses to a small rise giving vantage over the plains. He raked the windswept grasses with shrewd eyes and tried to make sense of a blotchy blackness that moved closer at an alarming rate. *What is that?*

"Three minutes!" Bonstaph shouted. His message was relayed again and again. Two minutes passed and the black blotches morphed into the most horrific sight Bonstaph had seen in two decades.

"WORGRIELS!"

But they were not normal worgriels. They were huge and... *They move as though possessed!*

"ARCHERS! VOLLEY!"

Forty flaming arrows disappeared into the tall grasses. Worgriel screams came shooting back.

"They bleed as any other wretched creature. ATTACK!"

War cries rose from the refugees. Bonstaph and the guard led the charge to meet the oncoming black menace. There were no Quagmen. *At least... not yet.* Bonstaph drew his sword as the first incoming pair of ghost-white eyes and open jaws closed in. The creature was a frenzy of frothing saliva and glistening fangs. Bonstaph drove his sword through its open maw and stabbed its throat until he was shoulder deep to the wyvern's mouth. The creature fell limp.

"Go for the throat!"

Two more came at Bonstaph. The second he dispensed the same way, the third he carved across its thick neck. A fourth came, knocking him to the ground leaving the worgriel's underbelly exposed. Bonstaph stabbed upward for a fourth kill. He leapt to his feet. Wails of pain came from the Perimetral guard, but the worgriels were yet to breach the barrier protecting the children and elderly.

Worgriel blood was smeared across Bonstaph's face and down his left arm. The blood turned black and wafted into the skies as a pungent black mist. *Their blood is cursed...* Bonstaph followed the mist's skyward trail and dropped his arms to his sides at a second ominous sight. It was an approaching storm of another kind. As before, it was not a storm of cloud, thunder and rain. This time, it was a storm of wyverns. Bonstaph shook his head slowly. "We were so close..."

Amidst the yelling of men and women, the screams of worgriels and the cries of scared children, a deafening roar peeled through Bonstaph's head. He dropped to his knees and covered his ears. The worgriels became distracted and paused their advance. A looming shadow dropped from the sky and a torrent of fire erupted across the glass plains.

"A dragon!" The call came from various directions. "Couldradt fire dragon!"

Bonstaph looked about. The roar repeated itself. It was a fire dragon with a Ferustir riding it.

"Thank the gods!" Bonstaph shouted. 'Everyone! ATTACK!"

A SINGLE CHANCE

It was early, yet all the Romghold was awake and teeming with activity. Magnus searched through the thirty Irucantî and more than twenty dragons for Simeon or Braug but could not find them. *Have they not returned from last night's patrol?*

"Semsdër-fatel, my name is Gianna," a priest said. A woman of about forty with the litheness of a twenty year old, Gianna stretched as she spoke. "Are you ready to train with the High Priest?" She stood tall and drew her Ferustir's lance, checking it over, which Magnus took as a sign that the priests would be protecting him again.

"Aye. Have you seen Simeon?" Magnus was keen to get started with the High Priest, but he needed to know that Simeon had returned. Even though he and Braug had flown a different direction to Catanya, Austagia and Rubea the previous evening, Magnus would see their safe return as a sign all was well and no Quag scouts had caused them grief.

"No, I haven't," Gianna looked about. "I will see if they have returned, Semsdër." She bowed formally and ran off toward one of the buildings.

Magnus rolled his eyes. *These formalities need to stop.* Still, every time a priest showed him respect it felt like a step in the right direction. He just did not think it necessary for respect to come with a ranking title.

Magnus fastened the buckles of his chest armour and unsheathed Lucas's sword, pausing to take in its detail. He had always thought of Ganister whenever he looked at it, but this morning he looked past that, beyond its tainted history, and admired the detail of the fleu-steel that bonded seamlessly with the bronze-steel pommel and cross guard. He thought of his own sword. It was the same, yet different—pure Icerealmish steel from pommel to tip. Both swords had dark red leather wrapping the grip and the same dark red leather scabbard. Magnus remembered the rocks west of Overpell at Realms End where he hid his sword in a crevice. *Simeon said I needed a second sword.* Marsala's instructions about his sword came to him—*'Reconcile them... sooner rather than later.'* He looked forward to doing so.

"Semsdër-fatel." It was Gianna again. "Simeon and Braug did not return. A second patrol left several hours ago to find them. We should know soon enough—"

A great roar from the west interrupted the priest. Everyone ran to the training field. Magnus followed. A dragon was approaching so fast Magnus thought it would never be able to stop. It bellowed its roar again.

"That's the second patrol now," Gianna said, startled.

The dragon drew to a halt a hundred feet beyond the training field with a Ferustir in its saddle, gripping fast to the saddle horn.

"BATTLE ON THE SOUTHERN PLAINS!" The dragon's thoughts ripped through Magnus's mind. *"SIMEON AND BRAUG FIGHT FOR THE LIVES OF HUNDREDS. WE MUST GO NOW!"*

A hand gripped Magnus's shoulder. It was Jael. "We ride with Brue. Come!"

"I'll ride with Färgd!" Eamon shouted as he ran by. Gianna sprinted toward the training field and leapt into a dragon's saddle with unnatural deftness.

The Romghold was action in fast motion. Priests armed themselves to the teeth. Those wearing black robes discarded them to reveal sculpted Ferustir armour while dragons formed rank across the training field and down the common. Within minutes, Jael had a saddle on Brue. Magnus seated himself at the front of the saddle with Jael behind him. He followed her orders.

"You've not flown before?"

"No!"

"Fasten your legs into the stirrups."

Magnus fumbled with the stirrup straps.

"Lace them up to the knees."

"Aye." Magnus watched Jael lacing her own straps then fasten the buckles. He did the same.

"Tighten the buckles some more."

Magnus did so.

"Tighter! They're all that's holding you in."

Magnus yanked at the leather straps, pulling them through the buckle frames an extra hole and fastening the prongs in place."

"Grip the horn like your life depends on it!"

Magnus's heart was racing.

"READY?" It was Brue.

"We're ready." Jael's thoughts swam through Magnus's head. He did not know that was possible. He turned and looked at her. She squinted at him. "Face forward, Magnus. Brace yourself. I'll be holding on to you."

Magnus faced forward. Jael's hands rested on his shoulders as Brue rose to his hind legs. Magnus felt the dragon's muscular haunches roll and flex beneath scales as he walked to the training field's precipice. Magnus swallowed hard—his mouth was parched. The sky was already filled with dragons and the beating drums of wings. To his left, Eamon sat in Färgd's saddle. He nodded to Magnus who nodded in return. He was sure Eamon could see he was wracked with nerves.

Jael pulled on Magnus's shoulders, bringing their heads closer together. "You'll be fine." Her tone was comforting.

"You never forget your first ride, Magnus!" Eamon shouted. Moments later, Färgd leapt up and dropped over the cliff. Magnus cursed to himself.

Brue stood with his claws overhanging the cliff edge. Jael's arms clenched tight about Magnus's torso. *This is it...* Magnus took deep breaths. Brue squatted, jumped into the air, and tilted forward. Magnus gripped the saddle horn with all his strength. He was staring straight at the clouds a mile below.

Brue dropped over the cliff edge, tucked his wings and plunged down, down, down and through the clouds. The wind pulled Magnus's hair, the clouds whipped his face and everything tried to prise his hands from the saddle horn. Brue punched through the base of the clouds into clear sky where he tilted up again, nearly driving Magnus's head into his own clenched fists. Their speed seemed to double with every thrust of Brue's wings. Magnus's vision blurred and his eyes stung from the wind and wet clouds. Jael was gripping his waist like a vice and began speaking quickly in Fireisgh.

"What did you say?" Magnus shouted. Suddenly his vision cleared and the wind no longer battered his eardrums.

"I'm placing enchantments to help you," Jael shared thoughts.

"How is it I can hear your thoughts?" Magnus did not understand.

"Through me," Brue said.

Jael gripped Magnus's waist harder still.

Brue tracked his way down the Red River, Froughton Forest's tall pines and oaks whizzing past below. A short way downstream, Brue banked to the right, away from the river and over the treetops. Magnus was dazzled by what he was experiencing. The world was so different all of a sudden. *Anything* and *everything* seemed possible. He was glad Jael was with him—her embrace was reassuring in this ludicrous world of dragon riding. He looked over

Froughton Forest to the west and back to the north. It seemed to go on forever and it was forever ago he was riding Breona through the Outer Rim, the Valley of Shadows, meeting Eamon, facing the Authoritarium, Thioci, Ba'rrat, Sarah, Delvion, Lucas, his father, Ganister... All his experiences came back to him, but this magical moment seemed beyond all of that. It was a dream. Catanya was out there somewhere with Rubea, riding as he was. He knew she was safe. How could she *not* be, riding a dragon as he was?

Magnificent.

As the sun showed itself above the Romanian Mountains, Brue flew beyond the southern border of Froughton Forest and was over a wide lake whose cerulean waters reflected the hulking formation of dragons. Just above the lake's surface, a hundred white cranes, fishing for breakfast, suddenly lost their appetites and dispersed. Magnus grinned at the spectacle. The sight beyond, however, was like a surreal incarnation of terror. The grasslands of the Southern Plains were ablaze with dragon fire, its oily residue wafting into a sky full of wyverns dog-fighting with dragons. The ground was peppered with black carcases and fighting bodies. By the banks of the lake, elderly people and frantic parents made a desperate attempt to protect children against manic worgriels and black-blade wielding Quag warriors.

Magnus felt a rumble begin to grow within the beast beneath his legs.

"Brace tight, Magnus," Jael said. She spoke another spell. It was one Magnus recognised. It was the spell Catanya used to protect against fire—*"Namon hama fara meo..."*

Brue dove toward the ground and banked hard to his left, releasing a vicious torrent of crimson fire along the lake's bank, narrowly missing the children but consuming a group of Quag warriors. Wind blew flames back across Magnus's face yet he felt no pain. Never slowing, Brue gained height again and came about for another offence. Some Quagmen fled but the worgriels were still focused on destruction.

"Let's go!" Jael shouted. She released her hold on Magnus and reached to her legs, releasing the stirrup buckles. Magnus did the same. Jael jumped to her feet on the back of the saddle as Brue fanned wings, breaking his speed near ground level. She then leapt from the dragon's back, rolled across the ground and flew into the chaos of fighting. Magnus hoisted onto Brue's saddle and jumped in the same manner, hitting the ground hard. A worgriel was on him in seconds.

Sword drawn, Magnus fought back, slashing at the worgriel's thick neck until it stopped its hysterical attack. A Quagman came next, but an arrow pierced his neck armour, bringing him down. Magnus didn't bother to look for the arrow's source. He ran for a group of four screaming children, putting himself in front of them and the elderly couple struggling to protect them against a worgriel with bloodstained fangs and a demonic disposition.

What is wrong with these creatures?

Magnus's sword severed the wyvern's front left leg, yet still it came, stumbling to one side. Magnus sunk his sword into its head, finally ending it. The elderly couple breathed a sign of relief.

"Magnus!"

It was Jael, pointing further down the bank. Magnus looked. Fifty yards away was his father, shielding more children at the water's edge as three Quagmen advanced on him. Magnus looked to the children next to him.

"All of you hold hands and come with me!" Magnus took the hand of the closest child then led them and the elderly couple toward his father. "Everyone stick together."

Jael came from behind and guarded the children. "I've got them... Go!"

Magnus threw himself toward the Quagmen. Sprinting, Magnus sheathed his sword and clenched his fists. Heat became fire and the usual eddies of flames that wrapped his arms took on a new level of intensity, spinning toward his hands like tempests of fury. One of the Quagmen turned, his terror filled eyes reflecting the flames. Magnus barrelled toward the three men throwing bulbs of fire, one after the other, until all three Quagmen writhed about in abject terror as tendrils of flame weaved about their bodies until they each lay, charred to black.

Magnus stood his ground, flames still leaping about his arms. Nearby Quagmen ran back up the embankment. "Electus!" one of them shouted.

Magnus calmed his breathing and the flames subsided. He looked about. All the children were staring at him, wide eyed and open mouthed. Someone grabbed him from behind and held him tight. It was his father.

"Magnus!" Bonstaph broke away and looked Magnus over then held his son's face between his palms. "It's as if the gods themselves blessed us with their presence, and now *you!*"

"Father!" Magnus embraced him. A thousand questions flooded his thoughts, but they could wait.

"Commander, is your son the *Electus?*" a child asked.

"Aye, child. He is!"

"'Commander'?" Magnus was most curious.

"A long story."

"We'd best get back into it."

'Aye.'

With no immediate threat to the children, Magnus, Bonstaph and Jael climbed the embankment. The Southern Plains were a patchwork of orange flames, dead worgriels, scorched wyverns and fallen warriors. The skies held another battle not dissimilar to Ba'rrat little more than a fortnight past. Fire dragons battled wyverns with the dragons outnumbered three to one. The dragons, though, had the monopoly with size, strength and Ferustirs.

Brue landed heavily in front of Magnus.

"I think you'd better come with me, Magnus."

"What is it, Brue?"

"An enemy that will take the both of us to bring down."

Magnus leapt onto Brue's back. He strapped one leg into its stirrup. Jael strapped in the other.

"The wards I placed will still protect you. Remember—hold tight," Jael said.

Magnus nodded in thanks and Brue took flight.

Half a mile through smoky skies, a large wyvern came into view.

"Is that it?" Magnus asked Brue.

"The rider is the problem."

The wyvern banked left, then right as if searching for something. On it's back was a tall figure of a man wearing a black, hooded cloak whose long sides flowed behind the wyvern's saddle.

"No! It can't be." Magnus stared at the hooded rider.

The rider pointed an arm to a man on the ground. A familiar, black substance leached from his splayed fingers and engulfed the swordsman. The black matter turned to coils that twisted and contorted about the swordsman's face and body. He collapsed, choking to death. Strangely, the rider withdrew his arm and doubled over as though in pain. He seemed to be suffering as he watched the swordsman suffer and recovering only once the man was dead.

"A sorcerer," Brue said.

The sorcerer spotted Magnus and sat tall again—apparently forgetting the pain. With long, bony fingers, the sorcerer drew back its hood revealing a pasty white face and sunken grey eyes.

"Lucas…" Magnus found the sight of him even more confronting than in Ba'rrat. His sunken eyes were ringed in shadows and his face was as thin as his reedy frame. Lucas looked thrice his age.

"MAGNUS..." Lucas's voice entered his mind like a sickening dream. Magnus tried to shake the repugnant feeling. Heat began to bathe at the temples and soaked inward, his dragon blood worked hard to fight the malevolence of Lucas's presence.

"Do not let him into your head," Brue warned.

Brue and the large wyvern circled around each other. Magnus knew things were about to get violent and when it did, he was pretty sure sitting in the saddle of a dragon was not the place to be. Lucas did not take his eyes of Magnus. The wyvern did not take its eyes of Brue. Everything about Lucas came flooding back to mind—

The wyvern attacking Lucas...

Kriser the healer drawing poison from Lucas's body...

Lucas's hostility toward Csilla's soldiers before fleeing the Uydferlands...

Lucas with Crugion in Delvion's chamber...

Then finally—*Ganister...*

"You killed your father!" Magnus shouted. "With the sword he made for you—our bond of brotherhood!"

Magnus drew Lucas's sword. Its white blade shone bright, reflecting the sun into the wyvern's yellow, crescent eyes. The black creature reacted. With a snap of leathery wings and a whip of its barbed tail, it catapulted toward Brue. Brue arched back, bracing for the impact. The wyvern slammed into Brue's underbelly, sending the four of them tumbling about one another in the sky. Magnus struggled with his one-handed grip of the saddle horn. Hurtling toward the ground, Brue wrapped his powerful hind legs around the wyvern and scratched at its face with his front claws. Flailing about, Magnus lost his grip on Lucas's sword and it flew away from him. He gripped the saddle horn with both hands. A hundred feet from the ground and still falling, Brue released fire from his open jaws, striking the wyvern's chest with cobalt flames that turned amber on impact. The wyvern, though, was unfazed.

Protected from the heat of the flames by Jael's spell, Magnus stared through the chaos and saw Lucas was mouthing words as though conjuring spells of his own. *He must be protecting the wyvern.*

Dangerously close to the ground, Magnus released his stirrup buckles. He knew he had to jump, or else risk getting crushed should Brue strike the ground. He opened his mind to Brue, letting him know his intentions. Thirty feet, twenty feet, fifteen... Magnus leapt from Brue's back and struck the ground, tumbling over himself. Brue twisted free of the wyvern just before impact and thrust into the sky, chasing it once again.

"MAGNUS!"

"I'm fine, Brue. Go get him!" Magnus stood and spat soot and grass from his mouth and dusted off. The whole experience left Magnus disorientated but as he blinked the dizziness away, he saw Lucas standing in front of him, still staring with his sunken, grey eyes.

"Do you have any idea what you've done, Lucas?" Lucas was completely expressionless. Unlike Magnus's dream, where Lucas sank back into the shadow of his hood, Lucas continued to stare. "How will your mother react when she learns you killed your father? Will she die from shame or sorrow?"

"She is dead. I killed her in the caves." Lucas's voice was raspy and strained. "She was in my head... always in my head, but now she is dead." He rubbed his temple with the heel of his right hand.

"You killed her?" shouted Bonstaph, stomping toward Lucas through the tall grass. "You poisonous, wretched monster!"

"Father, be careful!" Magnus jumped toward his father and grabbed his arm to keep him from approaching Lucas. There was no way he was willing to let him die the way Ganister did. "So what now, Lucas?" Magnus shouted.

"Everyone you've ever loved is dead—and by *your* hand," Bonstaph added.

"Delvion's sons are dead by *your* hand." Lucas pointed a bony finger at Bonstaph. "If I avenge their deaths, he may set me free."

Bonstaph clenched an angry fist. "You think that tyrant will ever free you? You're as much a fool as a monster!"

Magnus had to make a move to bring Lucas down. If his father did, he would likely be killed. Magnus at least had a chance of recovering from Lucas's dark sorcery. However, the more he looked at Lucas, the more he pitied him. Part of him felt a fool for feeling this way, but Lucas was yet to advance and his words seemed more provocative than threatening. Magnus considered a sad alternative—*Is Lucas's life so miserable that he wants us to kill him?* With that thought, Magnus risked an alterative.

"Father, I think we should leave him be."

"What?"

"If he attacks, we'll deal with it."

Bonstaph considered Magnus. The harsh scowl on his face softened. He scanned Lucas up and down. "We cannot turn our backs on him, Magnus. Like I always say, assume the worst—"

"Hope for the best," Magnus completed his father's words. They were wise words and their wisdom had saved him before. "I know."

"Be careful, Magnus. Please."

Magnus would have heeded his father's warning, but for Marsala's advice. What the mystic said had haunted him in the days since—'*A friend as a brother has fallen to darkness…*' Magnus knew Lucas was in a dark place, but if Lucas no longer had a heart of compassion somewhere within him, struggling to be found, then for how much longer would Magnus have his own? He had the blood of *two* dragons coursing through him, each vying for supremacy. He no more chose his fate than Lucas did. '*But a single chance to reconcile…*' Marsala had said. Magnus did not want to ruin that chance with violence that could result in one of their deaths.

"*Do you think it can be done?*" It was Lucas. Weak but true, the words drifted into Magnus's mind as though from a source so fragile, so weak, he could barely discern them. Magnus glanced at his father.

"Did you hear that?"

"Hear what?" Bonstaph asked.

"Give me a moment with him, father."

Bonstaph did not look at all convinced. He took a hesitant, single step back but reinforced the grip on his sword. Magnus turned his attention back to Lucas.

"*Can what be done, Lucas?*"

From behind his back, Lucas revealed his sword and examined it. He seemed lost in thought—thought that made him wince. The wince gave character to his lifeless face. For a moment, Magnus felt something. He felt his friend was right there with him and was certain Lucas felt it too.

Behind Lucas, a dragon made a pass, torching a long length of the Southern Plains with flame that effectively separated the Quagmen from the refugees who were fighting to defend their lives. Lucas remained still—a silhouette against the fiery background.

"*Can what be done, Lucas?*" Magnus repeated, trying to prompt a response.

Lucas looked from the sword to Magnus. The wince faded from his face and it was once again expressionless. Lucas turned and walked away toward the fire.

"Lucas!"

Lucas walked into the line of flames. A dark shadow appeared around him, protecting the sorcerer from fire. Soon, Lucas disappeared into the flames altogether. Magnus knew he could follow him. He knew he could walk through the flames unharmed and try to retrieve his friend, but he did not, even though this was the single chance Marsala spoke of. It was not for him to stop Lucas, nor convince him to stay, join him, or even kill him. Marsala's words were with him again—the haunting part of her words—*'but a single chance to reconcile, else fate be challenged.'*

"Else fate be challenged…" Somehow Magnus knew if he was going to make amends with Lucas it was not here, not now. He had seen the darkness return to his eyes. He was lost again—*for now…*

'Do you think it can be done?' That is what Lucas said. Magnus smiled to himself. There was hope, even if it came to him as a whisper.

"That was his chance, Magnus." He felt his father's hand on his shoulder.

Fate, then, will be challenged…

TWO TRUTHS

The sandstone of the Uydferlands quarry was a homecoming for Catanya. The straight-cut pits and teakwood-coloured stacks of stone were as familiar as the backs of her hands. More so, perhaps, for she had changed more than the quarry since she left. *Was it really only seven months ago?* There was, however, an air of sullenness to the quarry. The fine, cream—coloured dust from fresh excavation had given over to grey dust of neglect. Time had dulled the quarry's sharpness, dampened its spirit and robbed it of resolve. Catanya gathered its workers had exchanged shovels for swords and pickaxes for crossbows.

Rubea circled the quarry for a second time before landing a mile north of Nuyan. Catanya and Austagia alighted, ending a night and a morning of flight with only one stop in Froughton Forest to afford Rubea riverside replenishment. Catanya led Austagia and Rubea along the eastern quarry road through the sparse woodlands and tall grasses toward the township of Nuyan. The closer they got, the more attention they drew. By the time they reached the centre of Nuyan, everyone in the town was aware of their presence.

"A fire dragon has returned."

"The Ferustirs show themselves."

No one seemed to recognise Catanya. Then again, Catanya hardly recognised any of the Nuyan folk. There was no cheer, just the drone of necessary conversation between people worn to the bone from the war with the Quag. And the war was still happening. Catanya could hear all manner of commotion from the south.

Catanya strode along the side streets leading to her family home. She half expected Hannah to come sprinting down one of the alleyways squealing with excitement and yelling her name. Perhaps her mother would run to her with open arms and tears of joy or, perhaps, her father.

I have not given thought enough about what I will say to father...

Catanya removed the iris from inside her breast armour. She held it tentatively as she rounded a corner. Finally, after months of dreaming of it, her eyes fell on the sandstone walls, thatched roofing, white-framed windows and green gardens of home. The house looked as tired as the quarry, but nevertheless gave her comfort.

"Hannah! Mother!" The words came as a whimper. Hearing her, one onlooker did a double take—clearly not expecting a show of emotion from a priest. Catanya stepped up to the front door. "Mother?" she called. She turned the door's brass handle. It was unlocked. Opening the door, she peered into the living room.

'I'll take a look around," Austagia said. Catanya nodded without looking at him. She stepped into the common room. Sniffing the air, she expected the smell of her mother's cooking, or fresh-cut summer flowers sitting in the pitcher on the kitchen table, but there were neither of these things. Inside, the house looked as tired as outside. The floors and surfaces were dusty. The kitchen table a mess of dirty utensils, plates and bowls.

Catanya nervously felt the iris between her fingers. Then she remembered. She ran through to her bedroom and flung open the door. Four strides into her room, she opened the drawer to her dresser. There sat her diary. Too scared to touch it at first and knowing she was a moment from the truth about Hannah, Catanya stared at it. She felt its leather cover with her fingertips before lifting it from the drawer. She sat on the side of her bed, prising the book open to its centre pages. The iris was *gone*.

Catanya took a deep breath and blew through pursed lips. She looked at the iris found on the chamber floor beneath the Temple of Fire. She placed it on the centre pages of her diary and slid it into the indent made by the flower that had been there for so many years. It sunk perfectly into place. Each petal, stem and even an unopened bud fit into its respective pit in the paper.

It was the same flower...

The diary slipped from Catanya's fingers onto the wooden floor at her feet. She slid off her bed and fell to her knees and began to sob silently and uncontrollably. There was neither reason nor logic for Catanya to grasp. How Hannah found herself to be in the Romghold, let alone what she went through to get there, and even more so where she disappeared to afterwards, were questions too overwhelming to process.

Where is Hannah?

Catanya shook her head and lay on the floor of her bedroom, thoroughly exhausted. She closed her weary eyes and tried to will herself to sleep. She almost was when the sound of heavy boots reverberated through the floorboards of the house and into Catanya's head. Familiar voices followed.

One was quiet—the voice of reason. *Austagia…* The other voice was loud, aggressive and obnoxious. *Father…*

Catanya got to her feet reluctantly and replaced her diary into the dresser drawer. She rubbed tears from her cheeks with her palms and trudged back through the house to the living room just in time to see her father throw Austagia through the living room window with a violent shattering of glass. Catanya stared wide-eyed as her uncle landed in the overgrown vegetable garden. He got to his feet and calmly dusted off his black robe.

"Father! What in all the realms are you doing?"

Xavier turned and stared at Catanya. His face was red with anger.

"Ask him!" Xavier bellowed. Catanya had never seen her father lose control before. He drew his longsword and walked through the broken window making straight for Austagia.

"FATHER!"

Austagia held his arms up. "Xavier, we can talk about this civilly."

"*Talk* about it? After all the years of secrecy, you want to *talk* about it!" Xavier lifted his sword over his head, all the while cursing at his elder brother. Catanya threw herself through the window frame, drew her lance and igniting it before her feet landed. She shoved her father in the back, making him bring his large sword down off-angle. He swung back. Catanya caught his blade with her lance.

"WHAT is going on?" Catanya yelled. Rubea took steps toward the commotion, her thoughts as much awash with confusion as Catanya's. There was a crowd gathering. Half ogled at Rubea, the other half at Catanya's family dispute. Xavier stared at the interlocked weapons—his sword and Catanya's lance. His incredulous look found Catanya's eyes.

"You need to ask *him* what's going on." Xavier pointed to Austagia with his free hand.

Catanya looked from her father to her uncle and back again. Neither seemed keen to explain matters. "Well, someone needs to explain! And where is Hannah? Where is mother?"

An evasive look swept across Xavier's face. He looked away from Catanya.

"Catanya," a voice shouted. Csilla was rounding the back of the house, walking toward them. "Come with me." She pointed at Xavier—"So this is how you break news, Xavier?" Xavier lowered his sword and opened his mouth. "Spare me your nonsense," Csilla interjected. "Apparently, it's beyond a priest and a Knight Commander to speak truth. Then again," Csilla looked Catanya over, "you've probably figured that much by now."

Catanya considered her father and uncle one more time and retreated toward her aunt.

'Catanya," Austagia called after her. Catanya looked over her shoulder. "We will talk about this. When you are ready." He nodded apprehensively.

"What exactly do I need to be ready to talk about?" Catanya barked at her uncle. She swung back to Csilla. "What *exactly* is going on, Csilla?"

Csilla embraced Catanya. "Walk with me."

They walked to the back of the house and Catanya's eyes surveyed the overgrown gardens, the trees with fallen fruit and the unpruned flowerbeds. She knew her father took no interest in such things and could only deduce one thing—"My mother isn't here, is she?"

Csilla looked her in the eyes. "She isn't. Neither is Hannah."

"Where are they, Csilla?"

"They left a fortnight ago for the ӨhUidlands. An ӨhUidman I know and trust escorted them through Froughton Forest to safety, away from the war and—"

"And?"

"And the dispute between your mother and Xavier."

"You mean, between my parents?"

"That's what the dispute is about, Catanya."

Catanya was even more confused than when she opened her diary just minutes ago. "You of all people I trust to speak plainly, Csilla."

"You shouldn't be hearing this from me, but you need to hear it. Xavier is not your true father. Austagia is."

Catanya's lance struck the ground at her feet without her knowing she dropped it. Csilla's hands cupped Catanya's shoulders as though anticipating the giddiness she was feeling.

"This doesn't make any sense," Catanya mumbled.

"Come, sit with me and we'll talk."

Catanya sat right where she was, upon the grass of the garden, her legs straight out in front of her. She considered her boots with their odd laces. They made her laugh. She felt as if she was becoming entirely unhinged. *Nothing makes sense.* She scratched her head, feeling the priest markings over her left temple and tracing them back behind her ear.

"You've been through a lot. I can see that."

Catanya shifted her lazy gaze to Csilla, taking in her aunt's familiar scars and saw there were plenty of new ones. "How long have you known?"

"Your mother told your father... Xavier, I mean. It was after you left. I only found out recently."

"After all these years... why?" Catanya recalled her secret conversation with Austagia before she fled the Romghold at his insistence. Austagia said he had warned Catanya's mother about the Quag armies. *Why would you confide such a thing in my mother?* Catanya asked. Austagia had been slow to respond, but spoke then of family and told Catanya there was much to be learned.

"I think, with you gone, it all became too much for her," Csilla explained.

"But Austagia told me it was mother who wanted me gone."

"She wanted you protected." Csilla's eyes sharpened. "Austagia had gotten word to your mother that war was coming. She returned in kind, begging for him to take you into the priesthood as protection. Catanya, she thought your real father was better equipped to ensure your safety."

"She told you this?"

"Only after she told Xavier."

Catanya wondered at the long held secret. "Did Austagia know... all these years?"

"That's for him to answer."

Catanya winced. She had only come to respect Austagia as her uncle in recent times. She resented him for so long, wondering how a man could treat his niece so coldly. To treat his *daughter* that way—she was not at all sure what to make of that. The issue of Hannah made her stomach twist. "Who, then, is Hannah's father?"

"She is Xavier's child. Your mother swore it to be true."

"Hannah is my *sister*. Nothing less."

"Aye. And as much my niece as you are!" Csilla smiled affectionately. Catanya did not bother to feign a smile in return.

"I need to find her, Csilla."

Csilla nodded. She glanced eastward, as though toward Froughton Forest. Her smile faded to a frown and she cracked her knuckles—a habit Catanya had always seen her do when she was troubled.

"What is it?"

"Nothing, I'm sure." Uncharacteristically, Csilla hesitated—"I was to receive word from the ꝊhUid folk once Alessandra and Hannah reached Mount Earthwood. It is yet to come."

"When would you have expected such word?"

Csilla shook her head. "Who knows the logic of Earth Realmers?" She locked eyes with Catanya who was all of a sudden worried. Csilla knew it and confessed—"I should have had word before now."

With war ever present south of the Nuyan River, together with dwindling resources, mealtimes had become a communal affair. Rather than gatherings around large bonfires with music and merriment, they were limited to small fires reserved for cooking. Once cooking was done, quiet discussions would ensue around the dwindling embers. Spells gave the embers an occasional nudge to keep them glowing and the Nuyan folk warm. Everything about life in Nuyan had dwindled down to nothing more than was necessary. Catanya's people were *surviving*—nothing more.

In the evening, Catanya found Austagia seated cross-legged beside one of the fires. There were other townsfolk around the fire, but they were leaving one by one to retire for the night or join Xavier for the war council meeting. Catanya watched Austagia from behind as he stared into the flames as though lost in thought. Catanya wondered if he was thinking of her, or perhaps her mother. *Is he still in love with her? Did he wish things could have been different?* Catanya approached and sat beside him. "Good evening."

"Good evening," Austagia replied.

The fire gave Catanya an excuse to avoid awkward eye contact. Austagia, who had been feeling the warmth of the fire with long, outstretched hands, drew them in and held them in his lap. Catanya did the same.

"Catanya. I need to apologise." Austagia paused, perhaps to gather words or find a way through the uncomfortableness. Catanya waited. "I wanted you to hear it first from your father... from Xavier, I mean or," Austagia was quick to add, "or your mother." He sighed softly. "I am sorry. Things have been so difficult for you."

Catanya wanted to tell him off, or tell him it was okay. Anything would have done, but she did not know what to say. Tears began to brim her eyes, which was ridiculous, because her thoughts were conflicted and she was unsure how to feel about them. She sniffed them back then winced at the sobbing sound it made. She quietly cursed to herself. There was no right thing to say. She closed her eyes and squeezed them—the salty sting of tears felt deserved. When she opened them again, she was surprised to see Austagia extending a hand to her. She drew a breath and softly rested her hand in his. They watched the fire together in silence and Catanya yearned to sit just a little closer and lean her head against his shoulder.

Two of Xavier's knights stood either side of the large canvas marquee. They stepped aside, pulling the two flaps back, letting Catanya and Austagia walk through the entrance. Over a hundred men and women stood and listened as Xavier spoke. His commands were both precise and finite. Catanya felt sorry for him. For all the months of battle, each day for Xavier would have been the same with war meetings at dawn and dusk. Battle plans forged, resources allocated, defences reinforced and, most importantly, the collective morale sustained. As Knight Commander, Xavier was responsible for all of this. It made Catanya all the more frustrated that the Irucantî had not intervened.

Austagia told Catanya he had sent word via an Ahrona swallow to Simeon. He gave instructions that they should find their way to Nuyan via Froughton Forest as they had done, with ten dragons and their riders. "It will be discrete and destructive." Austagia had whispered to Catanya before they entered the marquee. "They can retreat to the Romghold afterward before Delvion can form an ambush from the Caves of Cuvee."

"Stelvak, your men need to keep the catapults at the Nuyan River bifurcation facing east and southeast," Xavier shouted. "It's up to you to stop the bastards crossing."

Catanya smiled. At least time had not waned Xavier's manner.

"Pallo, for the love of all the gods... *two* sets of volleys in *tight* formation, progress through to *three* after the counter offence."

"What if the wyverns—" Pallo started.

"If the wyverns approach from overhead," Xavier sighed, "by all means, unleash everything in their direction. Remember though, all airborne arrows are to be tar dipped and ignited. The black mongrels seem to have an aversion to them. Can't possibly see why..."

The gathered warriors laughed at Xavier's dry humour. It was then that Xavier spotted Catanya and Austagia at the back of the marquee. Xavier crossed his muscular arms over his chest. His jaw muscles flexed. "Daughter... Brother... Have you anything to offer the war meeting?"

Catanya looked at Austagia. "Go ahead," he whispered.

"I do," Catanya announced to the room. Xavier raised eyebrows and the room divided, making a path for Catanya to the raised platform where Xavier stood. She stood beside him. "Thank you."

Xavier bowed respectfully, but without condescension, which Catanya appreciated. He stepped back and Catanya turned to address the gathering.

"After months of fighting, you've likely gathered that the Quag are not here to completely annihilate us."

"What are they here for, priest?" A voice called out.

"They are here as 'bait'."

"What?" the crowd repeated, confusion written on every face.

"Delvion made this attack, with the support and alliance of the Authoritarium, to lure the Irucanti and our dragons from the Romgnian Mountains."

"Well, that didn't work, did it?" a bearded man yelled out.

"It was supposed to be a trap. Delvion has a far greater army hidden within the Caves of Cuvee. They were to attack us when we were most vulnerable—defending the Fire Realm. The Irucanti learned of this plan and so devised a different approach."

"What approach?"

"We have destroyed Ba'rrat and freed its prisoners, hundreds of whom are our people." Catanya knew she spoke half-truths, but it served a purpose. She was hardly keen to say the Irucanti followed the order of the High Priests who sought to kill the Electus and that Ba'rrat's destruction was a convenient coincidence.

The room was filled with surprised faces, including Xavier's. Voices rose in volume as the warriors spoke among themselves.

"What you hear next should not leave this company," Austagia called in a commanding voice. The room fell to immediate silence. All eyes turned back to Catanya.

"There will be a clandestine attack on the Quag, here, within twenty four hours. But we will need your full support."

"What kind of attack?" the bearded man asked.

"Take a look at her," Xavier shouted back. "She's a Ferustir, by gods. What kind of attack do you think?" Xavier winked at Catanya. Excitement rose in the room. "Silence, please," Xavier continued. "Let my daughter finish. This is clearly important."

Catanya looked at Austagia at the back of the room, standing tall over all but a few of the warriors present. He looked pleased that his brother had set aside his animosity. Catanya continued—"When the attack comes, we need all warriors ready to support us. Hold nothing in reserve. This attack is about *complete* annihilation. No stone unturned, no Quagmen or wyvern left to flee home and tell tale of it. When all is done, all that shall remain is ash, dust and silence. By the time Delvion learns of the attack, it will be over."

Cheers rose in the marquee. Xavier hushed them to silence.

"It's been a long time coming," said the bearded man. "But when you Irucantî go to war, you don't muck about, do you?"

'They're of the Fire Realm. We expect no less," Xavier said.

"One more question, if I may." It was a clean-cut elderly man with a quiet voice.

"Of course," Catanya said.

"There are rumours the Fire Realm Electus has been chosen. Are they true?"

Catanya stared at the man for a long moment. She felt a buzz of excitement in her chest and recalled her repeated dream of Magnus riding Balgur through the setting sun.

"It is true, yes."

The marquee was elevated with chatter. Questions fired at Catanya from everywhere.

"Who is it?"

"Is it a priest?"

"Will they show themselves?"

"When will we meet the Electus?"

Xavier raised a hand, bringing the room to silence once again. Catanya knew for certain that when the dragons and riders arrived at the battlefield, Magnus would be among them. He would not be riding with Balgur as she had dreamed, but would most certainly be riding with Brue. She spoke once again to the war council—"You will meet our Electus on the battlefield tomorrow."

JAEL'S TALE

It had been a long day on the Southern Plains. The green sheets of grass were charred black with burnt grass, stained red with blood, and for many, plagued with haunting memories of a much larger battle waged east of here twenty one years ago.

The fight was over by mid-afternoon. Bonstaph had seen to the capture of two Quagmen and Magnus watched on as he interrogated them. Once he learned all he could, Bonstaph set them free and presented his findings to a collective of Ferustirs, the Perimetral guard as well as Magnus and Eamon.

"The Quag knew of our migration from Brindle but only after leaving Thwax. Delvion also knew that I was involved. It would appear this strike was, to some extent, aimed at me as revenge for killing Delvion's sons. I believe it was also a test, if you will, to see if the Romghold would react to a threat closer to home, after not reacting to the six month ordeal in the Uydferlands." The bitterness in Bonstaph's words was obvious, though Magnus sensed he was trying to move past his old resentments. "A much larger army spawns within the Caves of Cuvee. With Ba'rrat fallen, the Authoritarium's rule ended and Crugion dead, Delvion may be somewhat disorientated. He waits for reinforcements from beyond the Neverseas. This is when the real war will begin."

With Austagia absent, Simeon spoke for the Irucantî—"We believe it is time," he surmised. "The alleged 'trap' that is the war in the Fire Realm shall draw its catch tomorrow."

"With Delvion at an impasse, it would indeed be wise to end it now," Bonstaph said.

It was decided. At dawn, the refugees would leave for their homes as planned. Those returning to the Fire Realm would hopefully meet with a war at its end, for most of the fire dragons and Ferustirs in attendance would fly for the Uydferlands to achieve that end.

As darkness fell, the refugees settled once again around the warmth of fires along the southern bank of the Plains Lake. They were fifty-nine less than they were the night before. The Perimetral guard would keep watch all night, only this time supported by thirteen fire dragons whose collective fiery eyes overlooked the Corville Mountains from the ground. Three more patrolled the skies.

Magnus warmed his hands at one of the fires. A young girl, three years old, sat on his knee. Her long, curly blonde hair traced down to the waist of her tattered lavender dress. Her gypsy parents were taken prisoner four years before and used for labour in Ba'rrat. The young girl was born soon after they arrived and had never known the warmth of a fire, a glistening lake or laughter. The girl's mother survived, but her father had died here on the Southern Plains, protecting his family. A funeral for those who died was taking place, but the mother did not want her daughter present. Magnus had taken care of the girl in the afternoon and she had refused to leave his side.

The little girl stretched her arms toward the fire, trying to reach as far as Magnus could. He took a hold of her little arms and pretended to stretch them without success. "You will have to wait until you grow and then you can reach for the stars!" The girl giggled and reached up to the stars above. "That's it."

Magnus looked to the stars then returned his gaze to the warm fire. He thought of Catanya and hoped she had found Hannah and was enjoying her company. It was then that he saw Jael standing on the far side of the fire. She was looking through it, studying Magnus. She smiled and walked over to him.

"May I?" Jael gestured to the log Magnus sat on.

"Please." Magnus shifted slightly to make more room. Jael sat beside him.

The little girl looked wide-eyed at Jael as if waiting for her acknowledgment.

"Hello," Jael said. The girl smiled then buried her face in Magnus's side. "It suits you," Jael added. Magnus looked at her, unsure of what she meant. Jael nodded at the girl. "You'll have a family of your own someday."

'Oh." Magnus smiled, realising what Jael was saying.

"I have something I think belongs to you." Jael lifted a sword and handed it to Magnus. It was Lucas's sword. "I found it on the plains. Did you drop it?"

Magnus took the sword, remembering Lucas standing on the plains. "He was holding it," Magnus whispered to himself.

"The sorcerer?"

Magnus looked at Jael. Her fine, dark eyes sparkled the fire's reflection and Magnus thought of Lucas, walking through the flames. Jael blinked and looked at Magnus who looked away, aware he had been staring.

"I want to thank you," Magnus said, changing the subject.

"For what?"

"For today. For helping me with Brue, telling me what to do when we rode him, protecting me with spells."

"It's something you never forget." Magnus looked at her again. "Your first ride on a dragon." Jael's eyes seemed to sharpen at the thought.

"I can't imagine I'll ever forget. Tell me about your first time riding a dragon." Magnus was curious about Jael, but his question unsettled her. Her eyes hardened into a frown. She crossed her arms and stood.

"Are you okay, Jael?"

Jael sucked her lips inwards and turned away, took a few steps and stopped. "Some other time, Magnus."

Magnus opened his mouth to respond, but was interrupted. It was the little girls mother.

"I'll take her, Magnus. Thank you." She gently picked up her daughter who was drifting off to sleep.

Magnus smiled, feeling a deep pang of sympathy for their loss. "If you need me to take care of her later, let me know."

The mother smiled weakly. Deep sorrow was carved across her tired, gypsy face. She walked off to her camping spot a little distance away—the first lonely night of sleep without her husband. Magnus knew it was not for him to do any more and so turned back toward Jael, but she had moved on.

As the night progressed, Magnus talked more with his father and learned of Sarah's fate in the Caves of Cuvee. Magnus recalled Lucas saying— *'She is dead. I killed her in the caves.'* With agonising sorrow, he tried to fathom what Lucas had done.

Magnus needed to know if his father knew about his mother. *Does he know she is a grandchild of the Ice Realm Electus?* He kept the question in his mouth, knowing the time would come.

Midnight approached. One of the refugees kindly donated Magnus a blanket that he wrapped himself in. He laid down, staring into the fire once again. An hour or so passed and Magnus heard approaching footsteps.

"Magnus."

"Walt!" Magnus sat up on his elbows. He could hardly believe his eyes. "I can't believe it!"

"It's so good to see you again," Walt said.

Magnus recalled them saying their farewells back in Ba'rrat when they were both being sold into slavery. At the time it seemed Walt was destined for a life beyond the shores of Allumbreve. "You never left Ba'rrat?"

"Nay. Just as well." Walt seemed a little agitated.

Magnus got to his feet. "Everything ok?"

"I think so. Your father asked me to fetch you. Can you come?"

"Of course."

Magnus followed Walt a short way along the river's edge past dozens of sleeping bodies, then up the embankment again to where the wounded were being treated. His father was there, holding the hand of a woman on a crudely made stretcher. Magnus stepped closer. He recognised the woman. It was Sarah.

"Magnus," Bonstaph spoke softly. "One of the priests found her stumbling across the plains."

"She just appeared out of nowhere." It was Gianna, standing nearby with a dragon right behind her. "We combed the Southern Plains twice over and were returning when she appeared out of nowhere, less than a mile from the Plains Lake."

Magnus went to Sarah, kneeling beside her. He was taken aback by her condition—she looked an inch from death. "What happened to her?"

"She's been through a living nightmare, I'd say," Bonstaph said. Magnus could see relief in his father's eyes. He felt the same way. They were both present when Lucas said he had killed his mother. Had she survived his attempt on her life?

"She'll recover. She just needs rest." It was Walt. He was grinding powder in a stone mortar—just as he did when he treated Lucas long ago.

"Has she been beaten? Poisoned?" Magnus studies his father's face.

"Walt thinks otherwise," Bonstaph said.

"I believe this is self-inflicted." Walt poured liquid from a small clear bottle into his mortar and continued stirring. "I'm no sorcerer, but I'd say she's suffering the after effects of some powerful magic. She's not altogether there, if you know what I mean."

"I don't know what you mean, Walt." Magnus was confused.

Walt sampled his mortar mixture with a spoon and licked his lips, then added more fluid. "The spell cloaked her somehow. It's wearing off, but look—she has no shadow."

Magnus, Bonstaph and even Gianna looked closer as Walt removed a torch from its picket and held it over Sarah. Sure enough, her body cast no shadow.

"It will return as the spell fades. This mixture should help with that." Walt looked at Gianna. "That's why you didn't see her crossing the Southern Plains until she was a mile from the lake. I'm guessing she was invisible before then."

"That's powerful magic," Gianna said.

"Aye. But as the magic fades, her strength should return."

Bonstaph took the mortar from Walt and spooned some of the mixture, pouring it over Sarah's parted lips. To Magnus, she looked like a corpse, for her skin was grey and her hair even greyer.

"What was she trying to do?" Magnus whispered to himself.

"She was trying to find her son," Bonstaph answered.

After two hours, Sarah's shadow began to return and her chest started lifting with strengthening breaths. Bonstaph insisted on attending to her and so Magnus retired to his place near the fire on the other side of the camp. When he arrived, Jael was seated once again on the log. She was alone, staring into the fire.

"Is your friend recovering?" Jael asked. The fire reflected off her Ferustir armour. Magnus walked around the fire and sat next to her.

"Slowly. She's been through a lot."

"Aye—a Tenebris spell. It'll do that to you. She must have a lot of willpower to push that far with it."

Magnus looked at Jael, wondering at her knowledge of such things. "What's a Tenebris spell?"

"Dark magic. Some gypsy's claim it as Paragon magic, but it's not."

"How would Sarah know of it?"

"I'm not sure." Jael studied Magnus then looked away. "Magnus... I want to tell you about the first time I rode a dragon." There was reluctance in her voice. She struggled to look at Magnus again.

"I apologise if I was abrasive before."

'You weren't abrasive. You asked a question. And I'd like to answer it." Magnus nodded and kept his silence. "I was thirteen. Austagia found me by the Traas River. I don't know..." Jael closed her eyes like she was trying to remember. "I can't explain what happened or what led to me being there, but I was injured—*badly* injured. It was years later Austagia told me the nature of my injuries." Jael glanced briefly at Magnus then lowered her head again. "He said I had been beaten—perhaps tortured." Jael shook her head slowly.

Magnus stood and removed his blanket, wrapping it around Jael's shoulders. He sat beside her again.

"And so, Liné carried me." She smiled wryly. "Austagia held me tight. Liné climbed and climbed, up through the clouds, above the mountain peaks and away from whatever darkness I had come from. It was wonderful. I was given another chance at life in the Romghold."

Magnus studied Jael as he listened to her tale. Her pale skin was radiant and in stark contrast to her black hair. She had a small scar over her left eyebrow that he had not noticed before. Her features looked familiar in a way, but he could not place them. She reminded him of someone, but he was not sure whom.

"I gave my life to the order," Jael continued. "I healed, worked, learned and trained among the priests. For three years I never once left the Romghold. At sixteen, I began my formal training. I became Joffren's Semsarian. I was later inaugurated into the order."

"That must have felt—" Magnus stopped, not wanting to put words in her mouth.

"It was enlightening," Jael said. "With the inauguration came a blessing." Jael pointed to her markings on the left side of her head. "I'm sure Catanya told you about that."

"Aye," Magnus contributed.

A gentle smile came to Jael's face. "The measure of dragon blood I was given triggered something in me. It seemed to allow memories of the past to come back. At first it was fleeting memories of a brother, sisters, a mother and a father."

"Was that a good thing?"

"It should have been, shouldn't it?" She looked again at Magnus—her face once again a contemplative frown.

"Did you tell Austagia about your memories?"

"Joffren was my Semsdi. My place and loyalty was with him for three years. I was never meant to be a priest. I was not selected by my merit. I had spent my years watching other priests train. For me, every test and every challenge was twice as hard. I was expected to be twice the Irucantî they were to prove I was their equal. Joffren was focused. He was determined. I took on those traits as an Irucantî. They held me in good stead and I put my past behind me."

Magnus was intrigued. Catanya had also trained under Joffren and was also selected outside of the usual system of merit. Magnus thought about this for a moment, then dared to ask—"Did Joffren train Catanya as he trained you?"

Jael's eyes flashed sultrily at Magnus. "I was absent for most of her training," she said dismissively. Jael drew a breath and ran her fingers slowly through her hair, revealing a large scar across her scalp that made Magnus wince. Magnus remembered Catanya saying that Jael had gone missing for most of the six months of her training. When Jael finally returned, she had been beaten once again just short of death. "From the little I saw and from what Austagia has told me, Joffren trained Catanya harder than he trained me."

Jael's words seemed to come as a confession she did not want to admit to, but Magnus admired her for doing so. He had so many questions but had to remind himself to keep quiet and let Jael speak. He was sure she had come to him for a reason beyond sharing her story.

"Magnus," Jael looked him over. "Your mother is not of the Fire Realm, is she?"

"No." Magnus wondered if Jael knew his mother was from the Ice Realm.

"Neither were mine. But I guess you knew that." Jael's eyes sharpened. Her pupils, usually hidden within her dark eyes, shone with the flames of the fire. "Perhaps we have more in common than either of us know." Jael leant forward until her forehead touched Magnus's. Cupping his cheeks in her hands, she tilted her head up, bringing her lips toward his. Just short of touching, Magnus gently brushed his hand between them, covering her lips with his fingers. Jael lent back, studying him. After a moment's reflection, she nodded, stood and reached for Magnus's hair, stroking it.

"She doesn't deserve you," Jael said.

Magnus could hear the bite in her words—the jealousy in her tone.

"I don't deserve *her*," Magnus said, holding her wrist and drawing her arm away.

CALM BEFORE THE STORM

Magnus confessed to himself he was curious about Jael kissing him. He could not get the thought of it out of his mind. The smell of her hair and skin was etched in his memory. He felt heat in his chest just thinking about it. Magnus imagined over and over being in the moment again and letting Jael kiss him. He dreaded to think how he would feel afterward, so it was just the kiss he played over in his mind, curious as to what it would be like. He robbed himself of sleep because of it. He knew though, if he relived that moment, he would stop her once again.

Magnus was still keen to learn more about Jael. She admitted her parents were not from the Fire Realm. He had guessed that much—*for one, she is right-handed.* What more had she remembered from her past? Even more so, he wanted to know what happened in the six months she went missing, only to return to the Romghold as beaten and traumatised as when she first arrived at thirteen. Were the two connected? Magnus knew he would likely never know after refusing her kiss. Was that the price for getting to know her? *If she is playing games,* Magnus decided, *it isn't worth it.* He decided Jael would have to remain an enigma.

An hour before sunrise, an Ahrona swallow arrived with a message for Simeon. It was from Austagia.

"Austagia commands a clandestine attack on the Quag approaching from the north. He says ten dragons will suffice," Simeon announced before a gathering of every priest, half the dragons, Magnus and Eamon.

"We can approach from whatever way is most effective," Bonstaph interjected. "Austagia doesn't know we're positioned on the Southern Plains and we've the measure of Delvion's army."

"Austagia's orders reinforce our decision," Simeon said. "We are thirteen dragons strong. Three more wish to maintain patrol over the Southern Plains—as it was before the days of the Authoritarium."

Magnus watched in awe as his father worked with the priests to form a deadly assault strategy designed to bring an end to the battle of Nuyan. They would approach the battlegrounds from the south near Overpell. It would convert the Quag's northerly offensive to a southerly defensive. Conversely,

Xavier's legions would logically convert their six month defensive from the north at the Nuyan River into an all out attack with Austagia, Catanya and Rubea's support. This would force the Quag to defend from both sides—a perilous position for them.

"Färgd suggests we lay interlacing runs of dragon fire," Simeon said.

"Lay them east to west," Bonstaph said. "The summer southerly winds will kick up by midday and push the fire tracks, burning the voids between runs and completing the job for you. By evening, a northerly change will keep the fires south of the river to protect the Nuyan township."

"There's no need to overexpose ourselves," Brue contributed. *"We will each do a return run then climb away. There's enough of us to keep the interlace continuous."*

Bonstaph looked to the dragons—"That would be wise. And with a good count of dragons scouting from high, escaping wyverns can be effectively dealt with."

"It is imperative that no Quag and no wyvern escape to tell Delvion of this attack," Simeon warned. "Another reason to approach from the south."

The attack was planned down to every detail. Magnus's astonishment for his father's knowledge of such things was only abated when Eamon leant in and discretely explained Bonstaph's position. "Remember, your father was Knight Commander when the knights fought alongside the Irucantî and dragons. He's the most qualified here to get this job done."

Magnus continued to watch proceedings. The priests were drawn to silence whenever Bonstaph spoke. "The priests show him respect."

"And so they should," Eamon agreed. "The Battle of Fire may not have been won without him."

Magnus considered Eamon then looked back to his father. "He never wanted to be a part of this again." Even as the words spilled from his mouth, Magnus realised—"Actually, it was the Authoritarium's regime he never wanted to be a part of."

By sunrise, the refugees had bid their farewells and gone their separate ways. Those headed for the Fire Realm would transport the wounded. Sarah was among them. She was recovering under Walt's diligent care, yet was still unconscious. The Fire Realm folk would follow the Outer Rim of Froughton Forest until they were north of the Nuyan River sections. By the time they reached Nuyan in three days time, the war would hopefully be over. If not, they would hide in the forest until notice reached them that it was safe to come home. Two thirds of the Perimetral guard were travelling in their company.

There was little to organise, as the priests left the Romghold in a hurry with few supplies other than weapons. The previous night, several dragons had hunted for deer in Froughton Forest to ensure their brethren were well fed after the previous day's battle. Word was sent to the Romghold of the situation and more dragons would soon join the three-dragon patrol of the Southern Plains in case Delvion mounted a surprise attack. The rest of the fire dragons were ready to fight.

Thirteen dragons formed a five hundred foot line of sparkling bronze brilliance. Magnus found the spectacle dazzling. Ferustirs made final adjustments to their armour—tightening buckles and saddles, sheathing lances and grooming fletches of arrows. The dragons started making guttural grunting sounds Magnus had never heard before.

"They're getting the juices flowing, so to speak," Simeon explained.

"The dragons? What do you mean?"

Simeon stared blankly at Magnus. He then coughed up a mouthful of phlegm and spat on the ground. "A little like that, only dragons make fire where we spit."

Magnus could not help but laugh at seeing a priest do something so unrefined as spit and soon they were both laughing. Simeon regained his composure first.

"When we're in the throes of battle today, Magnus, don't try to fight like us. Fight like only our Electus can fight—the way you did here, yesterday."

"You saw that?" Magnus recalled his fire display by the riverside.

"Aye. When our people in the Fire Realm see that, it will do as much for morale as seeing our dragons return."

Magnus and Simeon gripped forearms and wished one another well for the battle. Simeon was growing on Magnus more and more and he realised how much he had missed Lucas's close friendship. *Perhaps Simeon will be a good friend some day...*

Magnus knelt to check the two daggers sheathed at the sides of his greaves. Holding Lucas's sword, he jogged down the line of dragons, looking at each in turn and searching for Brue.

"It looks almost as good on you as it once did on me."

Magnus stopped and doubled back. It was Eamon, readying himself beside Färgd.

'Eamon!" Magnus embraced his old friend. "This armour is magnificent."

"It's magnificent on *you*, my dear friend."

"I wish I could have seen you wearing it. You're joining us?"

"Aye. There's sure to be celebrations after the battle and I intend to join you then as well."

"Very good," Magnus smiled. He knew he should feel nervous before the battle, but with everyone in attendance, he felt charged with energy and anticipation.

"Keep safe, Magnus. Promise me that." Concern washed over Eamon's face.

"I will." Holding Lucas's sword, Magnus punched his own chest armour.

"You managed to get Lucas's sword back," Eamon frowned. "It seems destined to be yours."

"Jael found it on the burnt plains."

"Indeed." Eamon stepped toward Magnus and whispered—"Between us, I believe Jael has a sweet spot for the Electus."

"You think so, Eamon?" Magnus tried to look surprised.

Eamon tapped the side of his nose. "See you on the battlefield."

Magnus smiled and jogged further down the line of dragons until he found Brue. In the line up, Brue was the largest dragon present—with the exception of Färgd—and clearly had the longest tail by far. His large muscles flexed and his scales glistened as he shifted about, eager to get going. Magnus slipped into Brue's thoughts.

"May I join you today, Brue?"

"Certainly. Will Jael be joining us?"

"I will." It was Jael, walking through the tall grasses toward them. Magnus was glad, but felt a little awkward after the previous night.

"Jael…"

Jael lifted a hand to Magnus. "Let's pretend it never happened." She raised eyebrows at Magnus then leapt onto Brue's saddle, keeping the front free for Magnus.

Magnus smiled back. "I'm still eager to learn more about you."

"I'm sure you are."

Magnus was glad there was no discomfort between them. *Flo Ena… 'Move on…'* He sheathed Lucas's sword, swinging the scabbard over his back as he had always done. Back to his right, Eamon was climbing onto Färgd with another Ferustir. Two dragons to his left, his father was strapping his legs into the saddle of another dragon.

"Have you done this before?" Magnus shouted to his father.

Bonstaph looked up at Magnus. "Once or twice."

Magnus was sure his father was not at all keen to be riding a dragon. *A Wardemeer suits him far better...* Magnus wondered what ever happened to 'Staeda'—his father's Wardemeer horse.

"Magnus." Bonstaph's voice softened. "Be careful today."

"I will," Magnus assured.

"Once the Quag see your powers... Once they know you're the Electus, you'll become a target."

"I know." Magnus tried to hide the anxiety that was beginning to crawl through his stomach.

"Eyes in the back of your head—you'll need them today," Bonstaph said as though trying to lighten the mood, or perhaps appease his concern for his son going into battle for the first time.

"I'll be those eyes, Magnus," Jael said, channelling her thoughts through Brue.

"Thank you." Magnus genuinely appreciated it.

Moments later, the thirteen dragons and a total of twenty Ferustirs were ready to leave the Plains Lake for the battlefields south of Nuyan.

BATTLE AT NUYAN

All thirteen dragons took flight and fell into formation heading west. Braug was at the lead, Färgd behind Braug and Brue third in line. The rest fell into pairs or threes, falling into one another's slipstream to conserve strength. The flight seemed calm and effortless to Magnus, unlike the furious pace the day before when they charged to support Braug on the Southern Plains.

"No point wasting energy before battle," Brue explained to Magnus. *"When we are closer, our formation will change and our pace with quicken."*

By the time they reached the western end of the Plains Lake, Braug fell back from his lead position to the rear of the formation and Färgd took the lead. Jael explained that by rotating through like this, all dragons had the opportunity to rest. By the time Brue was the lead dragon, Magnus could see the western border of Froughton Forest and a hint of the lands beyond.

"The Fire Realm…" Magnus strained to see more of home, but Brue went into a gradual dive until they flew no higher than the tallest of Froughton's ancient pines. The other dragons followed.

"We're using the forest as cover," Jael explained. *"The closer we get before wyverns spot us, the greater our advantage."*

Once beyond the western border of the forest, they rose again. Higher and higher they rose until they disappeared into a layer of cloud and broke out into the clear sky above. They kept their westerly direction for some time, always remaining above the cloud.

"We got lucky." Jael said.

"With the cloud?"

"Aye. We'll soon go higher so that when we dive, we can build a lot of speed for our attack north of the Cliffs of Overpell."

Overpell… Magnus remembered his father saying this was where the Quag seized him and his mother. He glanced over his shoulder at his father who raised a hand, signalling back. Magnus took an anxious breath. *This is it!*

The dragons fell into single file and formed a ring of dragons, circling around and around until Braug broke formation and ascended. The other dragons followed to form a spectacular, ascending spiral of dragons. The higher they went, the thinner the air seemed to become until Magnus started to struggle for breath. His lungs started heaving and his head began to spin. Jael squeezed Magnus's waist from behind.

"Are you okay?"

"A little light headed." Magnus was glad he could communicate with thoughts rather than talk through struggled breath.

Jael mumbled a spell in a dialect Magnus did not recognise. The words were sharp and succinct and were definitely not Fireisgh. In response, his breathing relaxed and the air seemed to become pleasantly thicker.

"Better?"

"Better. Thanks."

The Dragons reached their peak and hovered, miles above the clouds. Jael reinforced her grip around Magnus's torso.

"Hold tight to the horn. This is going to be fast."

Magnus formed a white knuckled grip about the saddle horn. To his right, he noticed Eamon wrapping a leather strap about one hand, binding it about the horn, then holding fast with the other. Magnus took it as a bad sign of what was to come.

In one synchronised movement, all the dragons dove into perpendicular falls. They picked up speed at a ferocious rate. Magnus's heart felt as if it would leap out of his throat, for they were not just falling, they were driven faster and faster with each sweep of dragon wings.

The clouds below rushed toward them, folding around Magnus's face as they passed through thanks to Jael's wards. Moments later they were beneath the clouds. The scene below made Magnus gasp in terror.

The Quag offensive was the embodiment of every nightmare Magnus had ever suffered, brought together to be worse than the sum of its parts. It was an endless collage of Quag legions, wyverns, catapults, warhorses and discarded bodies of dead warriors piled ten feet high—most with the flesh torn from their corpses, leaving Magnus with only one conclusion—

"The wyvern feed on the dead?"

"Don't think about it, Magnus," Jael instructed.

"How have the Fire Realm survived this long?" Magnus thought.

"The same way you did in Ba'rrat."

Magnus knew what Jael meant—*Because I didn't have a choice. Sarah's life depended on it. And here in the Fire Realm, people fight to protect those they love.*

Magnus gritted his teeth and mustered a surge of heat through his body. *"Let's end this for our people, Brue. And for Thioci, Liné and for your soon-to-be-hatched son."*

"A Zenith dragon!" Jael said.

"*AYE…*" A tremor tore through Brue's body. It rose up to his throat. Then came a united roar from all thirteen dragons. It was the most blood curdling, ferocious display of power Magnus had ever experienced. Magnus thought back to the day Brue attacked him in the enclosed room in Ba'rrat—the roar that tore through him. This was *thirteen* times more ferocious. Magnus knew too well what came next. He just hoped Jael's fire-protection spell would still hold.

South of the Nuyan township, Catanya sat on her haunches behind a barrier. A Quag legion had started their morning raids from south of the river.

"It's the same every morning," Csilla explained. "In the beginning, wyverns flew over the river to form a breach. They soon learned that was a mistake."

"What do you use to fight them off?" Catanya asked.

Csilla looked at her with weary eyes. "We throw everything we have at them—from the quarry."

"Stones?"

"Aye. Ten years worth of the finest building stone from the quarry has been thrown over that river with catapults—dozens of them—made from Froughton's hardwoods. Both resources are in endless supply, so it's been quite effective."

"The quarry looked unused when I arrived yesterday."

"It's been unused for two months. The quarry workers were exhausted and we needed them to fight. It was faster to break down homes and use the stonework. We can always rebuild when this is over. If what you say is true and the dragons come, we'll celebrate tomorrow and start rebuilding the day after that!"

Csilla and Catanya both laughed. Catanya hoped her promise of a dragon assault proved true.

"CATANYA!" Csilla pointed to the southern sky.

Catanya looked and saw dragons. They were diving through the clouds directly over the Quag legions north of Overpell. As sure as sound follows sight, the air was torn open with the guttural roar of nine, ten, eleven…

"There are *thirteen* of them!" Csilla shouted. "What a sight!"

"Catanya!" Rubea was stomping eagerly, breathing across Catanya's neck. Catanya leapt to her feet.

"Where's Austagia?"

"He's with Xavier," Rubea explained. *"Come—we must get into the fight."*

Catanya scrambled into Rubea's saddle.

"Are you coming, Csilla?"

"I very much want to ride a dragon. But… into battle?" Csilla paced about anxiously.

"Up to you, Csilla." Catanya shouted above the roaring boom of dragon flames. She wrapped and strapped her legs in place. Csilla looked over the Nuyan River as flames engulfed a legion of Quag troops. Wyverns screamed as their leathery hides charred to ash. Catanya was keen to get into the fight. "This time tomorrow when the battle is over, do you want to say you were brave enough to get on the dragon?" Catanya said, tying to goad her aunt into action.

"By all the gods—YES!" Csilla climbed into the saddle behind Catanya.

Once Csilla was strapped in to the second set of stirrups, Catanya cast the usual protective spells over her—fire and wind protection. Rubea squatted, flexed her muscles and thrust upward. Three, four, five beats of dragon wings saw the young dragon three hundred feet above Nuyan River. A crossbow bolt shot out from the smoky confusion toward Rubea. Catanya ignited her lance and was quick to deflect the bolt. Rubea banked, turned over herself, and thrust toward the chaos releasing a fiery torrent at the bolt's origin.

Catanya felt Csilla's arms grip her waist. "YES!" she screamed.

Catanya smiled. Rubea unfurled her wings, levelled out, then tucked them in again, thrusting her at breakneck speed over the Quag legions just above the tracks of dragon fire. Her draught made the flames lap over her sides like rolling waves of a sunset ocean. Catanya's spells protected both her and Csilla's fragile human flesh from the searing heat. Several miles south, Rubea circled around and fell into a flight pattern with the other dragons, laying another track of fire from east to west.

Rubea weaved as she went to avoid the other dragons. Catanya realised the dragons were passing through one another's trajectories. *"This is called 'interlacing',"* she explained to Csilla with thought through Rubea. The tracks of fire interweaved like bright threads of woven cloth. The dragons were like shuttles in this giant, fiery loom. Csilla continued to grip Catanya's waist. As the dragons narrowly missed one another with their attacking passes, Catanya looked for familiar faces. She saw Färgd with Eamon, Braug with Simeon, and Brue with Magnus and Jael. Jael was gripping Magnus firmly about the waist. Most surprising of all, Catanya saw Magnus's father riding a dragon.

Magnus spotted Rubea from a distance as Brue weaved his fiery attack on the Quag. As they came closer, he saw she was carrying Catanya and another. Just as they passed, Magnus risked a wave. Catanya held her lance high in return and Magnus recognised her companion—"Csilla!" Knowing Csilla had survived the long war delighted him. He only hoped Catanya had equally good news about the rest of her family.

Brue banked and twisted into a sharp turn for another pass. Magnus was able to look directly down at the damage the dragons had dealt. Beneath the continuous blanket of smoky haze burned a vermilion blaze. Then, through the chaos and flames, came dozens of wyverns. They streamed vertically through the smoke like long, black spears launched by giant catapults.

"Now the battle begins," Jael said.

Five dragons, including Brue, broke out of formation and climbed to face the airborne attack. The Ferustirs ignited lances and braced for impact. Wyverns began slamming and slashing the dragons that clawed and bit back while the priests wielded lances. Three more dragons joined the fray, charging at the wyverns, torching them as they approached. Wyverns soon outnumbered dragons four to one. To his left, Magnus saw Färgd with a wyvern gripped fast between his jaws, another between his powerful hind claws. A third wyvern had Eamon madly swinging a sword at its head while his long, grey hair and beard danced in the wind. Magnus wondered how the old man and older dragon would fair, but Eamon was quick to end his wyvern and Färgd's feet dexterously tore one wyvern in half while his jaws crushed the neck of the other.

"Brace yourself, Magnus!" Jael shouted.

Magnus gripped the saddle horn. A wyvern slammed into Brue's underbelly. Magnus's torso jerked to one side but his strapped legs held him in place. Jael let go of Magnus's waist and arched over to one side, slicing at the wyvern with her lance's unforgiving blades. Realising he was not going to fall, Magnus drew his sword. Two more wyverns hurtled toward them. Brue showered one in flames, the other got by and Magnus swung his sword, missing it. It came back for another pass and Jael thrust her lance into its underbelly leaving the creature to tumble to the ground, dark blood spraying over the smoky sky.

"Next one is mine," Magnus said, keen to make an effective contribution.

"We should get to the ground and help the townsfolk in their attack from the north," Jael answered.

Brue circled around toward Nuyan. *"A quick pass to ensure the Quag have not breached the river,"* he explained.

As they approached the Nuyan River, Magnus could see men and women of the Fire Realm taking advantage of the battle as they had hoped. They were crossing the river in the hundreds, attacking the Quag. Even without any battle experience, Magnus immediately saw a pattern to his peoples' attack. They were crossing to the southern bank with preformed bridges thrown across the river at one hundred foot intervals. They crossed in groups of twenty or more, led by the strongest fighters—knights on Wardemeers. Other swordsman and anyone else keen to wield something sharp followed the horsemen. Back at the northern bank, archers sent volleys of arrows southward to cull any immediate threat, paving the way for their people. Behind the archers, to Magnus's alarm, were children—one to each archer. Each child held stacks of arrows, handing them one at a time to their archer to allow them as little time as possible before unleashing the next. Behind the children were a line of catapults, each serviced by a team of four. Piles of sandstone—most of it cut all too well for this purpose—sat in great piles at the rear of the catapults, doubling as a final wall of defence, behind which rows of armoury stood waiting for any available hands to procure and charge into battle. Steady streams of rocks were flung into the Quag legions over the river, beyond the march of the Nuyan folk. It was effective. The Nuyan folk were making it clear across the Nuyan River to face the hefty Quag defence.

Two miles on, the township of Nuyan had not been breached, so Brue doubled back to the south bank of the river. Magnus watched as more of his people made contact with the Quag warriors. He quickly realised he had grossly underestimated the savagery of Quag retaliation now that they were cornered.

A memory forced its way into the forefront of Magnus's mind. It was a shocking, revelatory memory that seemed to return at moments like this. It had plagued him greatly months ago when he travelled alone through Froughton Forest. It returned when he faced Briet in Ba'rrat's arena. The memory always came uninvited and with the same, shocking intensity. He was outside his burning home in the J'esmagdlands. In the dark of night, the flames shone across a terrifying figure of a man who was lumbering toward him. Wrapped in burnished armour, a spiked helm and black cloth, the huge warrior attacked him and Ganister. *Ganister...* He was greatest warrior he had ever known yet was matched for strength by the Quagman. Their swords clashed and grated violently over one another. Ganister used speed unnatural for such a big man. Perhaps it was born of desperate necessity. Perhaps this was how normal people fought when they fought for their lives. Whatever it was, Ganister slayed the Quagman just as he was about to kill Magnus. At the time, Magnus felt like a helpless, powerless child. He was exposed and vulnerable. All his years of sword training meant nothing next to the brutality of the Quagman's attack and Ganister's retaliation.

Looking down on his people, the Quag were brutal once again. They were more than a match for most of the tired, war-ravaged people of Nuyan, yet the Nuyan folk fought as Ganister did—out of desperate necessity and fighting for their lives.

"They're going to be killed," Jael said, shaking Magnus from his surreal thoughts. "We have to get in there."

Brue let out a bellowing roar and targeted his landing at the frontline of Quagmen, squashing several. Brue's jaws found another and shook him about like a rag doll then discarded his broken body. Nearby Quag warriors rose black blades to attack only to be scorched by Braug making a low, flame-throwing pass. On Braug's back, Simeon raised his lance at Magnus.

Magnus and Jael alighted and threw themselves into the northern assault. Magnus wielded Lucas's sword to great effect and he soon found a second sword on the battlefield. His body, though, began to exhibit strange feelings. He suffered surges of hot and cold, as though he were suffering from a sickening fever. The heat was welcome but the cold made him shudder and he willed it to pass.

The fight raged on and Magnus was injured twice. The first was a gash to his right calf. A flush of searing heat quickly mended it. The second injury came when a Quag blade lacerated the back of his right hand. The cut was deep, making it hard for Magnus to grip his second sword. He tried to squeeze it into a ball to generate heat but it would not comply. Instead, the gaping red wound morphed into an iridescent slash of blue across his hand. The pain became a cold ache, as though he had held the wound to a sheet of ice. Magnus knew the blood of Iisilée was working its magic within him. Catanya had seen it—*felt* it—first hand while he slept in the crevice on the Romgnian Mountainside. It was foreign to him. It lacked the soothing reassurance Thioci's blood gave him.

Distracted by the wound, a burly Quagman took advantage and struck Magnus in the chest with his baulk sending them both sprawling to the ground. Recovering first, the Quagman grabbed Magnus by the wrists, pinning him to the ground. Magnus writhed beneath the huge warrior, using his knees to strike the Quagman in the stomach. It had little effect for he was too strong and his black armour too thick. The Quagman's deep-set eyes glared at Magnus. Even behind the dark kerchief covering most of his face Magnus could see the scowl across his brow. It was the dreaded dream all over again. But his face changed. The scowl became surprise and then terror. He began to bellow in pain. The Quagman looked at his left hand, wrapped like a great iron shackle about Magnus's right wrist. Magnus followed his gaze. Half the big man's arm was frozen blue.

The creeping ice worked its way up to the Quagman's elbow. Cracks formed in the metalwork of his bulky vambrace, which then shattered like glass, falling from his arm, revealing the creeping ice over his muscular flesh. He tried to yank the arm free with his other hand without success. Magnus swept his now-free left arm and found the pommel of Lucas's sword. He gripped it fast. A bronze flamed danced about its white blade. Magnus thrust it into the distracted Quagman's thick neck muscles. As the Quagman fell, Magnus pulled his right hand free, stood, and looked it over. His veins pulsed with surges of liquid ice. The wound to his right hand was now a fine, sapphire blue scar.

The mark of Iisilée...

FIRST WYVERN

Catanya found Magnus on the battlefield. She forewarned of her approach with a shout and Magnus was glad, for he had worked himself into a fiery fury. He was consumed with a continuous surge of hot rage that he dared not let wane. It fuelled his rampaging attack on the Quag, protected his mind from wyvern attack and healed wounds. There was another, deeper reason for sustaining the hot rage. He was sure that the countermeasure in him—*Iisilée*—was waiting her turn to release an equal measure of strength. Magnus would not allow this to happen. The unfamiliar nature of Iisilée's power could cost him his life. He tried to reason with the unknown power within him—*"When the battle is over you may come as you wish, but here, now... I need to stick to what I know."* Part of Magnus wanted to curse his mother for not teaching him to harness his Ice Realmic powers. He knew why, but in the throes of bloody battle, all reason had become skewed.

"Catanya..." He looked to her, having heard her shout. Bloodied and bruised but well, she was still with Csilla, who stared wide-eyed at Magnus until a Quagmen crossed her path. Magnus went to help but a shriek from behind tore his attention from her. It was a wyvern, but no ordinary wyvern. It looked somehow familiar. Magnus peered into its jaundiced eyes as it sidestepped, edging closer. He could not place it, but *knew* this creature.

"That scar on its left leg..." It was Csilla. She and Catanya were standing either side of him—the Quagman now dead. "Only a fleu-steel blade scars like that."

Magnus saw the scar. It ran the full width of the wyvern's thick leg. The wound seemed to run deep and had raised track marks running perpendicular to the main scar. "Ice burns," Magnus deduced and then realised—it was the wyvern that attacked and poisoned Lucas. It was his own fleu-steel blade that had scarred the beast when he slashed its leg trying to keep it from killing Lucas. *Now it seeks revenge.* Magnus was delighted to have the chance at his own vengeance for the curse placed on his dear friend, but there was something he needed from the wyvern first.

Catanya and Csilla stepped forward to meet the wyvern.

285

"Wait. I need it alive." Magnus took Catanya's arm, holding her back. He eyed Csilla. "Give me a moment, please." Csilla looked apprehensive but nevertheless, stepped aside.

The wyvern immediately attacked Magnus's mind. He should have been equipped to deal with it, but the wyvern had been there before and traced its own mental footsteps, finding footholds where a new invader would not be able. With a gritty mental battle, the wyvern's mind gradually pushed its way further into Magnus's thoughts.

"Magnus…" It was Csilla. Magnus caught the warning in her tone.

Magnus hesitated to push back on the wyvern's mental assault. He wanted to garner information from it, so needed to find a way in without giving it cause to flee. He took a breath and eased the protective heat from his mind, preventing his dragon blood from burning the wyvern's presence away. With the wyvern right there in his mind, there had to be a way to infiltrate its own mind and find out what it knew about Lucas.

"Magnus!"

A shudder passed through Magnus making his whole body shake. Someone grabbed him. A voice warned him. It may have been Catanya, but her words were muffled… cloaked… like a surreal dream. Another shudder passed through him only more violent this time. *I can beat this… I can infiltrate the wyvern's mind…* The obstinate wyvern had a firm grip on something. Magnus tried to fight back but could not get traction. There was nothing in the beasts mind to hold on to. The arms holding him tightened. They were keeping him from falling, but he fell to his knees anyway. A third shudder rippled through him. Magnus kept his focus on the wyvern's eyes. They were beginning to glaze over with hoarfrost, extinguishing their yellow glow, replacing it with frozen, ice blue orbs. The wyvern released itself from Magnus's mind, opening its own to interrogation. An icy chill creaked through Magnus. Glimpses of the black creatures memories came to him in jarring flashes, most of them irrational but some of them recognisable. He saw Lucas screaming as the wyvern's fangs sunk into his body. He saw Breona defending Lucas, stomping at the wyvern. Just as quickly, the memories were warped with anger then vanished. The more he encountered, the quicker they vanished until the icy chill in the wyvern's mind was too much to bear. Magnus was so close. The wyvern's thoughts were laid bare but hoarfrost was freezing them over faster than Magnus could witness them.

"Damn it!"

Magnus wrenched his mind free of the wyvern and leapt to his feet, pulling from Csilla and Catanya's protective embrace. Magnus jumped at the wyvern—the cursed creature who cursed Lucas—with Lucas's own sword, but there was nothing for him to do. The wyvern lay dead on the battlefield. Its open eyes filmed with frost. Blue mist rose from its nostrils and open mouth.

"What just happened?" It was Csilla.

Catanya placed an arm on Magnus's shoulder and spoke softly to him. "It was Iisilée working in you, wasn't it?"

"Aye," Magnus mumbled. He knew what had happened. By keeping Thioci's blood at bay, he had inadvertently given his other Electus blood an opportunity to exert its strength. It was effective—even if Magnus had neither control over the power nor any idea how it worked. It was also powerful. *Somehow, I killed the wyvern with my mind...*

"Are you okay?" Catanya asked.

Magnus gritted his teeth. "I just wanted to learn more about Lucas before we killed it."

"What just happened?" Csilla demanded.

"Magnus killed it."

"I gathered that much." Csilla pulled Magnus and Catanya closer, out of earshot of a gathering crowd of battle weary Nuyan folk who witnessed the spectacle. "It was not fire magic that killed the beast—look at it!"

Magnus realised—if Csilla knew, many of the other folk nearby knew it as well. It would not be a secret for long that their Electus was in fact a *double* Electus.

ELECTUS REVEALED

The 'False Battle' of the Uydferlands ended late in the afternoon.

"The name will stick," Magnus said. "Everyone is calling it that."

"The name does nothing to honour our people, does it?" Catanya said. "Certainly not my father, who worked tirelessly to defend our lands all these months."

"It certainly doesn't honour your father. Are you still comfortable calling him your father, now you've learned the truth?" Magnus could hardly believe she was confronted with such a truth just as she arrived back in Nuyan, only to then learn Hannah and her mother were gone.

"I'm not comfortable calling him 'Xavier'. Despite our disagreements over the years, he was always my father. Besides, calling Austagia my father is way too strange. That, I can never see myself getting used to."

"I wonder…" Magnus thought, as he looked at Austagia who was about to address his fellow Irucantî and the Couldradt Fire dragons. 'I wonder if Austagia, in his heart, has always considered you his daughter. Perhaps being called 'father' some day may be his greatest wish."

An awkward smile came to Catanya's face. She looked at Austagia as well.

Even if the False Battle was a ruse, the seven-month ordeal came at a huge cost and no more so than on the final day of battle. Among the fallen was a dragon named Meggän.

"The lost lives of our people will be honoured," Austagia began his address. "But we must acknowledge Meggän's passing before the sun sets this day. She will join Balgur, Thioci and others of her fallen kin in the Couldradt constellation—home of the Fire god."

The dragon's funeral was to be at the Cliffs of Overpell at sunset, which gave Magnus an hour of summer sun to do something he had been keen to do ever since leaving Thwax. Brue flew Magnus and Catanya to Realms End at the southwest border of Froughton Forest. They landed and Magnus found what he was looking for—the small group of boulders beside a hill. It was here he hid his own fleu-steel sword before turning himself in to the Quag prison train heading for Ba'rrat.

Magnus searched about the boulders and found two with a narrow opening between them. He peered into the opening. His heart skipped with joy—the sword was just as he left it.

"Is it there?"

"Aye, Catanya. It is!"

Magnus reached through. Just inches from retrieving it, his arm stuck. He laughed.

"What's so funny?"

"I think I was a lot skinnier when I hid it."

"Here, let me get it." Catanya shook her head in amusement and reached through the opening, stretching through until she was shoulder deep. "I've got it."

Catanya pulled the scabbard free, looked it over and handed it to Magnus. Brue came closer and sniffed at the reclaimed treasure. With Lucas's sword still slung across his back, Magnus held the pommel of his own sword in his left hand and dusted it off. He paused.

"What is it?" Catanya asked.

They are different, yet the same...' Magnus remembered the day Sarah gave the swords to Lucas and him. He remembered her emotional story behind the blades once again. Both were forged by Ganister with skills learned from his swordsmith father—*Gilfieüg.* Both were forged of fleu-steel gifted by his mother's people.

"I think," Magnus deduced. "I am meant to wield this with my *right* hand."

"But you're left-handed. We all are," Catanya said.

"Twice now, Lucas has left his sword for me. His is fire, mine is ice. Simeon said I need a second sword. I shall wield Lucas's with my left hand. My right hand..." Magnus showed Catanya the iridescent blue scar across that hand. She examined it closely. "My right hand shall wield my reclaimed sword." Magnus turned the scabbard about, gripped the pommel with his right hand and unsheathed it.

The moment the sword was freed, the scar over Magnus's hand shone bright, creating a sapphire-blue shimmer that eddied about his arm, down the white blade of the sword. The pure-white blade changed before his eyes. Intricate Icerealmic glyphs began to form on either side of the blade from the cross guard to the tip, shining as bright as a frozen cobalt lake. Magnus dropped the scabbard and drew Lucas's sword with his left arm. Exactly the same thing happened, only this time familiar amber flames eddied about his left arm, coursed down the blade forming orange flamed engravings of Fireisgh glyphs, never before seen on Lucas's sword.

Magnus took three steps back from a wide-eyed Catanya and equally alarmed Brue. *It's as though the swords come to life in one another's presence, now that I have access to both Thioci's and Iisilée's strengths.* He allowed the swords to dance about one another, spinning them this way and that in a dance of fire and ice. Magnus could feel the swords talking to him—*through* him. He felt the fire of Thioci and the ice of Iisilée, *Couldradt and Ertwe,* finally working together, affording him greater strength.

Magnus stilled himself and drew a steady breath, holding the swords to his sides. All was calm and a silence seemed to permeate through him. His body felt at peace for the first time since he became the Fire Realm Electus. His swords at rest and his mind at peace, each blade paled into its pure white form. Magnus sheathed them one at a time and belted their scabbards together over his left shoulder.

"Perhaps you should name your swords," Brue said. *"That is what they do in the Ice Realm."*

Catanya came forward and held Magnus's right hand, looking at it. The blue scar on the back of his hand was still there. She turned his hand over and rubbed the scar on his wrist—the scar given by Thioci. Magnus squeezed Catanya's hands and she looked into his eyes. "I think you have finally made peace with yourself."

"Aye. And I think I have names for my swords," Magnus said. Brue stepped closer and stood beside Catanya. The name 'Balgur' had served him well in Ba'rrat's arena for a long time. It seemed appropriate that he continue the honour of dragon names. He shared the names as thoughts, using Brue so Catanya could hear, too.

"'Thioci' for the fire-sword, 'Iisilée' for the ice-sword."

The Irucantî and dragons congregated on a field near the Cliffs of Overpell and formed a circle around Meggän. Magnus stood with Catanya. She held his hand, tracing his blue scar with her thumb. Austagia spoke to the gathering, wishing Meggän best of travels as she joined her kin in the stars. As proceedings concluded, the sun set in the west and the sky turned from blue to black. To Magnus's mind, the Couldradt constellation shone a little brighter than usual. *So it should,* thought Magnus. *There is one extra star in the sky tonight.*

When all was done, a mound was built of quarry stone over Meggän's body and a stonemason began carving a dedicated inscription upon a slab of granite from the Western Margins.

Back in Nuyan, a final war council meeting was taking place. Csilla led Magnus, Catanya, Austagia, Jael and Eamon into the marquee. Xavier, who was bloody and bruised, spoke with a weary voice, giving praise to the men and women gathered before him. He stopped when he saw Catanya.

"Catanya. The attack went exactly as you said."

"Aye. It did," Catanya agreed.

"Some say they saw the Electus on the battlefield today, other's disagree. What do the order of the Irucantî have to say—do we have our Electus, or not?"

Magnus looked at Catanya who flashed a furtive glance at him. She walked to Xavier's platform and turned to the gathering.

"Not so long ago, I asked my teacher—my 'Semsdi'—'how will we recognise the Electus?' He said that we would recognise the Electus when they present themselves at the right time. He said that they would not be able to hide from who they are. And so, people of the Fire Realm, it is time to meet your 'Electus'."

Catanya looked at Magnus. The room turned about, following her gaze. Soon, everyone was looking at Magnus, including Xavier. The remaining Ferustirs entered the Marquee and, together with Austagia and Jael, stood behind Magnus and bowed their heads to him. Magnus could see the collective were waiting for some sign—something to show he was indeed the Electus—and so he reached over his left shoulder and unsheathed 'Thioci' and 'Iisilée', reproducing the show of Electus power he had united earlier.

"A 'double' Electus?" Eamon chugged another pewter of ale, spilling half the contents down his long, grey beard. "By all the gods, this is beyond the dreams of mortal men. Indeed—it is beyond the dreams of dragons!"

Eamon's jovial speech ignited cheers through the gathering of exhausted, yet happy people of Nuyan. There would be a time for grieving but the township would celebrate the end of the war throughout this night. Hundreds sat at hastily made trestle tables and hundreds more, including children of all ages, danced the night away. Musicians plucked strings and chefs prepared feasts of roasts and stews, ale and wine.

Magnus sat next to Eamon, for there was none whose company he wanted to celebrate with more. But having eaten his fill of honey-roast venison and savoured every dish presented to him, he excused himself to join Catanya.

Csilla had procured maps of Froughton Forest and spread them across one of the tables. She and Catanya poured over them, devising a way to navigate through the Valley of Shadows to find Hannah and Alessandra.

"These maps are old. Did your ӨhUid friend not show you his route to their lands?" Catanya asked.

"No. ӨhUid folk never carry maps. Discretion is everything to them. Creighton knows the ins and outs of Froughton Forest but that knowledge is guarded up here," Csilla pointed to her head. "With wards to protect from prying minds."

Magnus remembered Eamon telling him of the ӨhUid people when they travelled through the Valley of Shadows long ago. Eamon said one had to travel far deeper in the forest than the Valley to find them— *To The Core you must go.'* Though the thought unsettled Magnus, he knew Catanya and Csilla would leave no stone unturned seeking out Hannah and Alessandra.

"Joffren told me of the ӨhUid folk," Catanya said. "He said discretion ensured their survival."

"Indeed." It was Eamon, walking to join them. His jovial demeanour had mellowed. Csilla looked at him warily. "Catanya informed me of your predicament. I know of ӨhUid ways and routines that may be of help. The key is to find a course between checkpoints."

"Checkpoints?" Catanya asked.

"The problem with ӨhUid checkpoints is they change. What you find is usually abandoned," Csilla said.

"Precisely. You will only find one if it has been abandoned. That's what they *want* you to find. Distraction is a fabulous ally."

Magnus was intrigued. Eamon's riddles always proffered wisdom— particularly where Froughton Forest was concerned. "But you didn't say to find a checkpoint, Eamon," Magnus said.

"That's right—you said to find a course 'between' checkpoints," Catanya completed Magnus's sentence.

"Precisely!" Eamon repeated, pointing a finger for emphasis.

Csilla, who had been leaning over one of the maps, stood tall. She crossed her arms and stared blankly at Eamon. Magnus gathered riddles were not Csilla's style.

"The relocation of ΘhUid checkpoints follows an evolving pattern," Eamon explained. "The tricky part is working out how far the pattern has evolved. Once you know precisely where you are in the pattern's evolution, you can plot a probable course."

The notion of 'evolving patterns' reminded Magnus of the High Priest's fighting technique. He was keen to learn more.

"And you know how to do this?" Csilla asked.

"Aye. But it is a pain in the backside trying to work it out alone."

"I won't be travelling alone," Catanya said.

"Good. So, let's assume you've found an abandoned checkpoint. Remind me again how you've done this in the past, Csilla?"

Csilla looked hard at Eamon for a moment, then explained. "There's always a checkpoint to the west, on the fringes of the Valley of Shadows." Csilla pointed to her map. "In my time, I've found three. I've *smelt* them before I've seen them."

"Smelt them?" Magnus asked.

Eamon lit his pipe—a knowing glean shone in his eyes.

"Lavender oil," Csilla said. "They use it in the torches they travel with. Creighton always smells of lavender."

"It's a good insect deterrent, so it serves two purposes," Eamon added.

"The scent always leads to a small clearing with a dirt mound from an extinguished fire and there will be a tree nearby with a sconce hanging from it."

"And the torch mounted in the sconce is the source of the lavender smell," Magnus guessed.

"Aye," Csilla said.

"Right." Eamon placed his pipe beside the map. "From here you need one of two things. A Jasper stone, which is nigh impossible to procure, or a Juniper stone. Magnus or I can help you with that. We always carry a Juniper stone." Eamon winked at Magnus.

"It's true. We do," Magnus said.

Eamon shifted closer and spread his arms. "Come in, come in," he whispered. Everyone came closer. "This next part is not for prying ears. It's something I've devised during my years of travels through Froughton Forest. It could compromise the discretion we all agree is essential for ΘhUid survival. So listen carefully and keep your knowledge of what I'm about to say hidden."

"Aye," Magnus, Catanya and Csilla said together.

PIECE OF MY MIND

Eamon devised an eclectic way for Catanya and Csilla to navigate through the Valley of Shadows and into The Core where they hoped to find the ϴhUid stronghold. He then excused himself and re-joined the celebrations. Csilla agreed to meet Magnus and Catanya at dawn to begin their search for Hannah and Alessandra. Finally, Magnus and Catanya retired for the evening to Catanya's family home, where they sat on chairs in the common room, drinking in the warmth of the fire.

"You don't have to come with Csilla and I, Magnus. I know you need to find your mother," Catanya said.

Conflicted, Magnus ignored the question for a moment and stood to place another log on the fire. He gazed at the warm flames and was reminded of Hannah showing him the spell she had learned, right here at this very spot. It was her first spell and she was only six. "I wonder if Hannah has learned any more spells since we left?" Magnus sat in the chair again.

"She's seven now. I never want to miss another of her birthdays."

"I want to help you find Hannah. And I want to remain by your side."

Catanya leant across and kissed Magnus softly.

The front door swung inward and Xavier stepped in, followed by Austagia.

"Well, isn't this a lovely sight," Xavier proclaimed.

"And a familiar one." Catanya stood and looked at Austagia, then Xavier. "Will you be interrogating us separately or together this time?" She crossed her arms.

"There's no need for that," Xavier grumbled. "At least I don't have to accuse you of stealing Trillium, what with you arriving on a dragon and all."

"I *left* on a dragon and all, if you recall." Catanya moved her hands to her hips. Magnus turned back to the fire, hiding his amusement.

"All jokes aside, Magnus—may I speak with you? In confidence?"

Magnus got to his feet. He was surprised that Xavier would want a private audience with him after the way things ended last time. Nevertheless, he was intrigued. "Of course," Magnus said. "After you."

Xavier led Magnus to the familiar door at the back of the room. They stepped inside the den and Xavier shut the door behind him. Magnus had gone back to this room so many times in his thoughts, rewording what he said on that fateful evening long ago when he asked Xavier's permission to marry his daughter. So much had changed since then. Not least of all, the fact that Catanya was not even Xavier's daughter.

Predictably, Xavier went to the tall cabinet against the wall, removed a flask and poured two glasses of red wine. He handed one to Magnus. "Congratulations," Xavier said, extending a glass.

"This *is* a familiar sight." Magnus clinked his glass against Xavier's.

"Indeed, *Electus*." He shook his head and smiled. "I can only imagine what events led to that, let alone what you've been through since I last saw you." Xavier looked Magnus up and down. "You've certainly filled out."

Magnus frowned, though not intentionally. "Catanya and I have both changed since we last saw you."

"Indeed," Xavier said again. "Six months a slave-fighter in Ba'rrat," he sighed. Magnus wondered how he found out. "I've spoken at length to your father. He's been through as much as you, by the sound of it."

"Aye. It seems you have too—fending off the Quag for seven months without pause. I can't imagine there was a single good night's sleep in that time," Magnus pushed back. He wanted to hold a mirror to Xavier's callous demeanour and yet he could not help feeling compassion for the man. After months of leading the defence as Knight Commander, Xavier was sure to be at the end of his tether. Finding out Catanya was not his daughter would not have helped matters.

Xavier refilled his glass, offering the same to Magnus, who had not touched his drink. Xavier then sank into one of the two leather-bound chairs.

"Tough times for us all, Magnus. It seems that it continues. Please." Xavier gestured to the second chair. "There is a pressing matter I need to discuss and have not done so with anyone. Your father seemed the logical choice, but learning you were the Electus—of both the Fire and Ice Realms—brings greater relevance the issue. I think, therefore, it is a matter better discussed with you."

Magnus took a sip of his wine. Xavier stood again and walked to the long desk at the centre of the room, opened a draw and pulled out two scrolls. He returned to his seat and handed one of them to Magnus. "Read it, please." Xavier's face twisted as though with fear. He rubbed the back of his neck.

Magnus lingered on the man for a moment, wondering what could have him so frazzled. He looked at the scroll and rolled it between fingers. His heart leapt when he saw the broken blue wax seal with the Ice Realm symbol of two icicles imprinted on it. He unfurled the scroll and read it aloud—

'To the Authoritarium's Knight Commander of the Fire Realm,

The order of the Authoritarium has been officially disbanded. Its elders have been executed. Guame is now under martial law by order of the Rhydermere of the Ice Realm.

All knights who served under this regime are given until winter's first moon to swear allegiance to the new Ruling State of the Ice Realm.

All Knight Commanders are to be replaced with a Rhydermaël—our most senior and accomplished Rhyders. As a former Knight Commander, you have the opportunity to swear allegiance alongside your fellow knights and, if one's mettle is proven, advance through the ranks under the Ruling State.

Complete and sign this charter nominating both your former position, and whether you intend to retire or swear allegiance under the conditions described above.

Alavia of the Rhydermere,

Imperial Rhydermaël.

Ruling State of the Ice Realm."

Magnus let the scroll drop to the floor. Dumbfounded, he stared at Xavier.

"This is the charter your mother would have me sign," Xavier said through gnashed teeth, red wine bubbling from his anxious lips. He wiped his mouth clean with the back of his hand and handed Magnus the second, larger scroll.

Magnus turned from Xavier to the charter, but his mind was fixed on a memory. It was the High Priest staring through the bars of his prison cell in the Romghold—*'The Electus of our realm carries the blood of our new enemy,'* he had said. *He spoke the truth...*

"This isn't going to happen," Magnus said. He handed the charter back to Xavier without bothering to read it.

"Don't you want to look at it?"

"No. It isn't going to happen."

"Oh, come now," Xavier scoffed. "I'm sure Alavia's got a special spot in the new regime for her son!"

"Is *that* what this is about?" Magnus was on his feet, shouting. "*Your* position? *Your* personal aspirations?" Xavier was silenced. Catanya came bursting through the door. Magnus kept staring at Xavier. After all these months of battle to save his people, he could not believe Xavier was letting a threatening letter have this effect on him. He was disgusted at the idea. He was disgusted at the sight of him. "No wonder your wife left you."

"Magnus!" Catanya touched him on the shoulder. He brushed her away.

"I get it—I do," Magnus continued. "You couldn't wait to get rid of your oldest daughter. The windfall for you is she's not even yours to worry about. And your wife and youngest have gone!"

"Keep going," Xavier spoke calmly, watching Magnus.

Magnus felt his ears burning with rage. He knew he would stop himself if he paused for thought, but quite simply did not want to stop until he was done. "When last we spoke in this room, you told me our people need warriors who are prepared to fight for what is right. Yet now, after everything we've been through, you are left with nothing but your position, which you're bemoaning, and why? Because someone writes you a damn charter saying you should sign off!"

"MAGNUS!"

Magnus took a step back and raised his hands. "I'm done... I'm done."

"You're done? Are you sure?" Xavier asked. He was still in his chair, calm and composed. "It seems there's a lot on your chest you need to vent, Magnus."

Magnus nodded. He was half a step away from apologising, but was afraid more anger would pour from his mouth if he opened it again.

Catanya stood between Magnus and Xavier—apparently anticipating a backlash.

"You are right, Magnus," Xavier said, looking directly at him. Catanya turned slowly to look at him. "Everything you say is right and there's plenty more you could say as well."

"Sorry?" Catanya looked dumbfounded. Magnus waited for the catch.

"And I'd deserve it. All of it."

"What do you mean?" Catanya asked.

"Bonstaph told me far more than I admitted before. I also spoke at length to my brother and to Eamon," Xavier chuckled. "What you two have done for one another is something I have never done for my family. You put each other *first*. You risked everything to be together and... I am humbled."

Catanya's wide eyes looked at Magnus. He dared not budge an inch.

"Furthermore, you opened my eyes just now, Magnus. I felt threatened that someone should try to take my position away from me. You were shocked that I'd consider letting someone do that—with a *charter* no less!"

"It's just a piece of paper," Magnus said.

"That's right. It's just a piece of paper. And the next piece of paper I intend to sign, as Knight Commander, is your marriage agreement."

"What?" Magnus and Catanya both said.

"I know it's not for me to give you permission. Not now. Not after all you've been through. But I would be honoured to do you this one good deed as a father, if Austagia doesn't mind."

"I don't mind at all." Austagia was standing in the doorway looking as puzzled as Magnus felt.

"And Magnus, in my ten years as Knight Commander, you're the first person to ever give me a proper piece of their mind and damn, it feels good to hear it." Xavier stood and took two long strides toward Magnus and shook his hand enthusiastically.

"Well, thank you," Magnus said, giddy with shock and yet Xavier's firm grip was testament to how real it all was. He was sure he would remember this conversation in Xavier's den as much as the first.

Magnus tried to sleep as best he could in Catanya's bed that night, but the conversation with Xavier ran over and over in his mind. His mother's actions did the same. *What exactly were her intentions?* In the end he gave up on sleep, stepped out of the room and peered into Hannah's room. Catanya was lying on her sister's bed with hands behind her head, peering out the window. The moon's rays penetrated the lace curtains, casting pale blue patterns over her body and face.

"Hello," Catanya said softly.

"You're thinking of Hannah?"

"Aye." Catanya sat up, inviting Magnus to sit next to her. She was clutching a leather bound book in her hands.

"Is that...?"

"My diary, yes." Catanya opened it. The flower was resting in its centre page. The flat petals were purple in the moonlight. The second petal had the black inclusion Catanya mentioned. Each petal sat in its perfect depression in the page.

"You will find her, Catanya."

"I hope she's okay."

"What does your heart tell you?"

"That she's alive… lost… scared."

"You'd best find her, then," Magnus concluded.

Catanya smiled. "You sound like me." She punched Magnus lightly on the shoulder. "You'd best sort out your mother." Magnus knew what she meant. They had to go their separate ways. "We'll both be safe. Anywhere I go, Rubea will come. Anywhere you go, Brue will follow. The two of you are kindred."

Magnus had not paid thought to it, but Brue did seem to be kindred to him.

"Catanya…" Magnus wanted to ask her the question once again, more so as an affirmation than anything else.

"Yes?"

"We're different people now. A lot has changed and we need to go separate ways again. But before we do, I want to ask again, just for the record. Will you marry me?"

Catanya closed her diary and stared at Magnus. She traced his cheekbones with her fingertips—her touch so beautifully familiar.

"Aye."

HUNTERS

Catanya admitted to herself she was glad to be going into Froughton Forest. She would finally be looking for Hannah and her mother, but it was more than that—it was a chance to get away from the priesthood. Not for the first time, Catanya reflected on how every relationship she had formed since leaving Nuyan had evolved. Some had done so for good, some not so good.

Jael...

Catanya was unashamedly happy to say goodbye to Jael. She saw no chance of warming to her again until she knew the truth of what happened to her all those months she went missing. Was she mentally scarred as well as physically, or was there something more going on that not even Austagia understood?

Austagia...

As for Austagia, she needed time to sort through her emotions and what it meant now that her once-estranged uncle whom she hated, then learned to respect, turned out to be her father.

Father...

Or Xavier—whatever he would be to her in the future—had shown a true change in himself the previous night. Catanya took it as a good turn of fate that they were parting on good terms. She hoped they would see eye to eye next time they met.

Eamon...

Other than Magnus, the only difficult farewell was Eamon. How could someone she'd only known for a measure of days be so endearing to her? His strategy for finding the OhUid folk was eccentric and typically Eamon. She loved him for it. The sight of him leaving the fire-sword at Balgur's feet in the Temple of Fire had moved her so, and the thought of it now still did. She hoped he found peace knowing Balgur's death was not at all in vain.

The last kiss goodbye would be the sweetest. Catanya looked to her left wrist. Her brown bracelet, which has seen its own journey across Allumbreve, was now stowed away in her dresser drawer. In its place, Catanya wore one of a pair of cream-coloured leather bracelets. They were pousse-plaited and enchanted, just like the brown one. Magnus was wearing the other—a mark of betrothal in the Fire Realm. It was always given by the woman to the man she was going to marry. Catanya would meet Magnus back here, in Nuyan, as soon as they were able. Part of her wanted to be first back, another part did not want to be the one waiting.

Catanya had sorted through her things and found very little she needed to pack. She did find Hannah's wardrobe was missing her favourite pomegranate dress. Catanya's brown suede jacket was also missing. These were the two items of clothing she remembered Hannah wearing in the chamber beneath the temple. Catanya had no doubts what she saw was true.

She considered changing out of her Ferustir suit and wearing some of her own clothes, but knew she was kidding herself—they were designed for a slimmer, curvier version of herself. Besides, in the dark depths of Froughton Forest, her Ferustir armour could save her life again. And so, Catanya checked over her weapons one more time before squatting to retie her mismatched bootlaces.

Csilla looked every bit the warrior she always had to Catanya. She had her dragon-hardened bronze-silver longsword sheathed over her back, a myriad of knives of various lengths stashed all over her copper and patina-blue body armour—some hidden, some easily accessible. Her crimson, hooded robe covered all but the sword.

"Shall we?" Csilla said, handing a second crimson robe to Catanya.

"What's this?"

"Can't have you dressing like a Ferustir whilst wearing a betrothal bracelet. Besides, I'm sure you can make this work better than that black robe you've butchered."

"Absolutely," Catanya replied, removing her rolled up priest robe from Rubea's saddle and replacing it with the new one.

Catanya turned to Magnus who was waiting with Brue to see them off. She hugged him with all her strength and kissed him one last time. "I love you, Magnus."

"I love you too, Catanya."

Catanya and Csilla climbed into Rubea's saddle with Catanya to the front, gripping the saddle horn. Rubea pushed off from the hard-packed ground. Catanya looked down to Magnus and waved goodbye. The dragon unfurled her huge wings and ascended, banked to the east and made for Froughton Forest.

HOME

Magnus watched Rubea climb into the morning sky. He waved a final farewell to Catanya, still able to taste the sweetness of her lips. When she was gone from sight, he turned to Brue and rested his forehead on the dragon's nose.

"To the Western Margins, Magnus?"

"Aye, Brue. To the Western Margins."

Magnus turned to those gathered to wish him well. He first addressed Xavier. "I will speak with my mother. This *will* be resolved amicably."

"Let's hope so, Magnus," Xavier shook his hand again. "For all our sakes." Xavier handed a large folded robe to Magnus. "I want you to have this. It is something I think your father will appreciate as well." Bonstaph approached to see what it was. "It is my knight's robe from the old regime—the Knights of the Realms."

Magnus let the robe unravel. It was a magnificent, suede robe of smoke-grey finished with silver, embroidered lining. The back of the robe continued the embroidered theme with the four realms of Allumbreve represented as four symbols in four distinct colours. The *Jaat*, Air Realm wind symbol in white, the *Spindlefax*, Earth Realm leaf in green, *Ertwe*, Ice Realm icicles in pale blue and the *Couldradt*, Fire Realm flame in bronze. Magnus removed the scabbards of his twin swords—*Thioci* and *Iisilée*—and fitted the robe. It was form fitting and had a satisfying weight to it.

"Well, I'll be damned!" Bonstaph remarked.

"You never had the chance to be the knight you and your father would have been proud of—under the *true* regime of knighthood," Xavier explained. "Now you carry our hopes and dreams and represent everything we were and more. I would be honoured if you would wear it."

Magnus looked to the sky. "If only Catanya could see me now!" Xavier and Bonstaph laughed. "Thank you, Xavier. When I travel to the Ice Realm, I will wear it as a symbol of unity of the realms."

"Brilliant," Xavier said. He and Bonstaph broke off for a conversation together and Magnus turned to Jael.

"Are you going to be okay?" she asked.

"I am. This has to be done." Magnus knew he was the only one who could reason with his mother.

"I haven't given up on you," Jael whispered.

"Given up on me?"

"You know what I mean. See you back in the Romghold—to continue your training." She gave Magnus a soft kiss on the cheek.

Magnus smiled sheepishly and turned to Austagia. The priest embraced Magnus's forearm and looked him in the eyes. "It has been quite a journey, Semsdër," Austagia said. Magnus was sure he was using the formal name in subtle jest. He appreciated that. "I dare say the journey has much to come. But know this, Magnus—we are with you. As friends and as family, you can always count on us."

"Thank you, Austagia." It meant a lot to Magnus. Austagia did not mince words and it gave him confidence knowing no matter what he faced in the Ice Realm and beyond, he had the support of this group before him.

Finally, Magnus turned to his old friend. "Eamon…" Magnus embraced him, for a handshake simply would not do. His other companions walked away, giving them space to talk. "Eamon, I wanted you to know, Marsala told me the origin of your name."

A smile crawled across Eamon's face. "She did, did she?"

"Aye."

"Then you know I was named for you."

"I do. And I thank you once again. Eamon…" Magnus struggled for words. "I also want you to know… I consider you to be the best of friends."

Eamon embraced Magnus again. "And I you, Magnus. And I you." The old man blinked away tears through a smile. "Such adventure… Such a story! And to think as little as a year ago we didn't even know each other."

"And yet, as Marsala would say, we were destined to."

"A wise woman. She and Catanya are the greatest women I have ever known!" Eamon's grin widened. "Aren't we a lucky pair?"

Magnus frowned as he smiled, not for the first time wondering at Eamon and Marsala's relationship.

"Travel well, Magnus!" Eamon blew him a kiss and waved.

Bonstaph came to Magnus. "Are you ready?"

"Let's go home, father."

With all the farewells done, Magnus slung Thioci and Iisilée's scabbards over his new robe and climbed into Brue's saddle with Bonstaph seated behind him.

"You've earned yourself an impressive collection of friends, Magnus," Bonstaph said as Brue leapt into the sky.

"I think I have, haven't I?"

"And if it were up to Jael…" Bonstaph paused.

"What are you saying, father?"

"Well, if she pushes any harder, Catanya will have her guts for garters!"

They both laughed as Brue set course for their homestead in the J'esmagdlands.

Brue touched down in the gravelled courtyard beside the stone well. Magnus and Bonstaph walked about the black ruins of their home in silence—their high spirits diminished. Bonstaph kicked aside the roof beams, perhaps hoping to find something to salvage. Magnus did the same to the broken glass over what was once his bedroom, recalling his close escape with Ganister.

"We all survived, that's the most important thing," Bonstaph said. His voice was muffled by the westerly ocean winds.

Magnus nodded and walked back to the courtyard. He looked at the horse trough and then the stone well. Magnus sat on the wall of the well. There was a folded towel beside him and several suede wraps tangled with fine, silver rope, lying over the wall.

"What do you make of this, father?" Magnus held the rope, running it between his fingers. It was spun from a fine fabric he did not recognise.

Bonstaph walked across the courtyard to the well and pondered over the wraps. "Your mother has been here." He took the towel and smelt it, then stood in thought for a moment. "Come."

Magnus followed his father back over the house ruins. They stood where the living room used to be and Bonstaph kicked away a mound of burnt thatching. There was a stone missing from the floor.

"Alavia has most certainly reclaimed her old life," Bonstaph said. "It was hidden beneath this floor."

"As were the fleu-steel swords at Sarah's home."

"Aye. The difference being, your mother tried to forget her past. Sarah celebrated hers."

"So you knew then, of mother's history."

"Aye. I knew her father and her grandfather before that."

"Hasledom and Hasdereq." Magnus pictured Marsala reading from the 'Iceralem', revealing to him his family history leading back to Hasdereq's bond with Iisilée.

"Indeed." Bonstaph looked at Magnus. "I knew the truth, Magnus. I knew of my wife's pain, her need to forget, and the need for a new life with her son and husband. And I gave her that life." Bonstaph sighed. "The Quag took it away."

"Father, we had a wonderful life."

Bonstaph paced about. "Do you think so?" He flashed a hesitant look at Magnus.

Fond memories came flooding back to Magnus. "We had good friends and a loving family. You built all this for us. I'll be eternally grateful for that."

Bonstaph looked to the ground, his back to Magnus. Magnus walked to his father and put an arm around his shoulders. His father began to cry in silence. Time passed and Bonstaph took a few deep breaths, wiped his face with his hands and looking red-eyed at Magnus. He chuckled. "You look damn good in that robe, my son."

"Thanks," Magnus smiled. "You know, we can rebuild this place when we return. Make it better than ever."

Bonstaph looked about and sighed. "That's exactly what I will do. But you, Magnus, need to find your mother."

"You're not coming to the Ice Realm?" Magnus was not planning at all to make the trip alone.

"No. I am home now. For the second time, I will retire from my role as Knight Commander. I will rebuild our home and who knows... in time, perhaps your mother will wish to return. If not, I look forward to your frequent visits. Perhaps even those of my grandchildren."

Magnus liked the thought, but all the same did not want to leave his father. "Perhaps I could stay and get things started—help you clear things away."

Bonstaph looked blankly at Magnus. He knew what his father was going to say. "Your mother needs you and time is of the essence. You have Brue. There is no better company for certain. Isn't that right, Brue?"

The long-tailed dragon was sniffing about the stables. *That is correct. I am with you, Magnus.*

A neighing sound came from the stables and out of the doors came a stomping warhorse, clearly alarmed at the sight of a dragon. Brue reeled back.

"Staeda?" Magnus and Bonstaph shouted together. The brown Wardemeer came to them. Bonstaph rubbed his neck and chest.

"Where have you been?" Bonstaph looked the horse over, checking his hooves. "He's been well taken care of... well fed." He loosened and lifted the saddle. "The saddle has been oiled—he's not been wearing it all these months, that's for sure." Bonstaph looked bemused at Magnus.

Magnus knew there was only one explanation—"Mother must have found him when she returned. Perhaps she has seen to his care and returned him for you."

A horse whinnying from afar drew their attention to the northern rise. Two Rhyders were seated upon Astermeers, looking directly at them. Their blue robes and long, blonde hair flowed in the wind. A moment passed in silence, then the Rhyders turned and rode away. Magnus and Bonstaph looked at one another.

"She knows we are alive." A glimmer came to Bonstaph's eyes. It was something Magnus had never seen before in his father. "Perhaps this is a sign, Magnus. Perhaps it's a sign there is hope for our family. Go to your mother. Tell her I am here and will wait for her."

Magnus and Brue took to the skies. They flew north over the two Rhyders on charging Astermeers, over the Crescent Woods, over the charred remains of the Bowthwait homestead and on toward the Ice Realm. They shared thoughts of their hopes for the future.

"Perhaps we will find an ice dragon north of the Ice Breach, Magnus," Brue said.

"An Ertwe dragon? That seems unlikely," Magnus laughed.

"No more so than my Electus bearing the mark of Iisilée..."

EPILOGUE

Simeon sat up on his elbows. Jael placed a hand on his naked chest, pushing him back to the ground.

"Again." Jael's voice was demanding, her demeanour firm. She started moving her hips over him once again. When finally done with Simeon, Jael dressed and left the tent without a word.

"Could we speak in private?" The softly spoken voice came from shadows away from the Nuyan campfires and away from the post-battle celebrations. Jael ignored it and continued to walk back to the priests' camp.

"*Jaelerisé...*" The voice said. "We must speak in private."

Jael turned, squinted and stared at the shadows. A man stepped from the darkness toward her. He wore an Uydferman's crimson robe. Jael knew it was a disguise. The man's fine features, dark eyes and calm demeanour gave him away—he was not a man of the Fire Realm.

"What do you want of me?"

"Someone needs to speak with you."

"I told you, I'd be in touch when I had results."

"Someone needs to speak with you *now*."

Jael stepped tentatively past the tent she left Simeon in so as not to raise his attention and followed the imposter through a grove of trees to a clearing. Here, five kinsmen were waiting, like pale blue phantoms in the patchy moonlight—each of them dressed in white. Jael froze. A flash of terror crossed her mind that revealed itself in a nervous squint.

The man who stood at the centre of the five men—the elder among them—stepped forward. Like his kinsmen, he had fine features and a neatly cut head of black hair. His silk white robe was sewn with the finest fabric embroidered with cream-coloured patterns depicting the winds of the Clouded Mountains. Of all the people in Allumbreve, he was the one Jael most wanted out of her life. He was the one she most wanted to kill. In the best of her dreams, she almost could. In the worst of her recurring nightmares, she remembered the torture. The most torturous part of all was that Jael thought he was dead—killed by Alavia and her Rhydermere when they overran Guame.

307

"Jaelerisé… The prodigal stepdaughter of Aefordale…"

"I am no relation to your Electi."

"*Your* Electi! You may be the 'Nilnova' daughter in a blessed Airisth bloodline, but you still have a duty to your people." He pointed an accusing finger. "You were perfectly positioned to become the Fire Realm Electus, yet failed."

Jael said nothing more. *He called me 'Nilnova'*… The word seared her heart like a red-hot knife. It always had, even as a child. *Nilnova*… *'No Star'*. The name hurt and there was nothing she could do about it—nothing that could make her special like her Electus-born siblings. Especially now that Magnus was the last chosen Electus—not her.

The elder came to Jael and placed a hand on her shoulder. "Your courtship with the chosen one is your recompense. You know this. It is your last chance to claim your place among your people. Bring the Fire Realm Electus into our fold and give us the progeny of his blood.

"Things have changed," Jael stammered. "Magnus… their Electus… is that of *two* realms. His mother is a grandchild of Hasdereq."

The elder withdrew his hand from Jael's shoulder and tilted her chin up. He stared into her eyes, examining them for truth. He seemed to find it. "Iisilée's bloodline survives. All the better." The elder squinted. "But there is something else?"

Jael hesitated. "He is betrothed to a Nuyan woman."

"They are not yet wed?"

"Not as yet, but—"

"Where is this Nuyan woman?"

"In Froughton Forest, seeking her lost family members."

"Her name?"

"Catanya."

"We shall deal with her."

"She will not be easy to kill. She is an Irucantî, as is another who tried to assassinate her but died in the attempt."

"Our means and ways will be more effective. You concentrate on fulfilling your obligations."

"And what if Magnus refuses me?"

"You have trained for this your whole life. You lost your way and we spent six months reconfirming your allegiance." The elder traced the scar over Jael's left eyebrow with his thumb. "Make it happen, Jaelerisé." His stare lingered a long, nauseating moment, then he turned and disappeared into the darkness with his kinsmen.

In the shadows, Simeon watched in silence. His eyes were fixed on Jael.
Jael is a traitor…

THE END

www.ingramcontent.com/pod-product-compliance
Lightning Source LLC
Chambersburg PA
CBHW021950010726
47494CB00003B/665